PARIS
RANSOM

Also by Charles Rosenberg

Death on a High Floor
Long Knives

CHARLES ROSENBERG

PARIS RANSOM

A LEGAL THRILLER

 THOMAS & MERCER

Published by Thomas & Mercer, Seattle

www.apub.com

Amazon, the Amazon logo, and Thomas & Mercer are trademarks of Amazon.com, Inc., or its affiliates.

ISBN-13: 9781477827710
ISBN-10: 1477827714

Cover design by Paul Barrett

Library of Congress Control Number: 2014958151

Printed in the United States of America

This book is dedicated to my family and all those friends, new and old, who lent me their expertise, their time in reading and critiquing drafts, and their overall support, thus making this novel possible.

CHAPTER 1

Robert Tarza

It was Christmas Eve, and it was growing dark and snowing heavily. I had gone out several hours earlier, when the sun was still warm on my shoulders, without a coat. Now, on my way back home, I was cold and shivering. It had happened before. My more than thirty years in balmy Los Angeles always seemed to prevent me from acknowledging that Paris, the city I now called home, had a real winter.

Earlier that afternoon, Tess Devrais, the lovely *française* with whom I had been living, had proposed—out of the blue as far as I was concerned—that we get married. When I had not immediately responded with an enthusiastic *"Oui!"* she had gotten upset.

She had gotten even more upset when, in foolish candor, I had explained the reasons—too great a gap in our ages (I was almost twenty years older, sixty-five to her forty-six) and too large a disparity in our wealth. I was very well-off myself, but I didn't hold a one-half share in a twelve-passenger Citation X or own a high-floor four-bedroom apartment across from Notre Dame. She had replied, with some asperity, that I had seemed happy enough living across from Notre Dame with her for the last five years and had not appeared unduly bothered by flying around Europe in her plane. All of which she had said in French because her English isn't up to slicing and dicing with so fine an edge. She had ended by calling me *un crétin*, which you can translate as "jerk" or "dumbass" or a lot of things in between.

I told her I needed to think it through some more, so I left and went for a walk. I had not gone three blocks when a figure emerged out of nowhere directly in front of me, causing me to come to an abrupt halt. He was young, short and, like me, coatless. He shot out his hand and held up a gold-colored wedding band, almost touching my nose with it.

"Sir, you dropped this, I believe," he said in perfect English.

I knew instantly what was about to go down. I was being hit with a common tourist scam. The guy's goal was either to wheedle me into paying him for the stupid ring—it was probably lead, painted gold—or, better yet, get close enough to lift my wallet or my cell phone. Then, if I wanted to bother, I could spend Christmas Eve sitting in a Paris police station, waiting to report the theft.

I snatched the ring from between his fingers, uttered the crudest insult I could muster in French—no doubt way over the top for the situation, but it's hard to learn to curse at just the right level in a foreign language—and heaved it across the street. I watched it roll into a culvert.

The guy looked taken aback. He'd clearly mistaken me for a foreign naïf and had probably expected, at the very worst, a polite rebuff. Without saying a further word, he turned on his heels and walked quickly away in the opposite direction. He didn't cross the street to retrieve the ring.

I walked on, trying to shake the event, which bothered me more than it should have. Petty street crime was rampant in Paris, and I don't know why I had come to think of myself as immune. I finally realized that what really bothered me was that the guy had mistaken me for a tourist. Despite living in France, speaking French and buying most of my clothes in Paris—everything except for my shoes—I still apparently stood out as an American.

Eventually, I ended up at my favorite Left Bank café and sat there for almost three hours, watching the snow start to fall and drinking Ricard. And I don't even like Ricard. I decided Tess was right; I was being a jerk. I loved her and would enjoy being married to her. I'd return and say yes—assuming it was still a welcome response.

On the way back home, I turned my thoughts to the evening ahead. We had invited two guests for a nine o'clock Christmas Eve dinner—Jenna James, my former law partner, who had gone on to become a respected law professor at UCLA, and Oscar Quesana, an eccentric, brilliant old criminal defense lawyer, also from Los Angeles. Both were spending the Christmas holidays in Paris. While the three of us had had quite a few raucous legal adventures together in the not-too-distant past, I was looking forward to an uncomplicated, convivial evening with old friends. Which would now be made joyous by, I hoped, Tess and I announcing our engagement.

It didn't exactly work out that way. And although I don't believe in such things, I now look back on the ring incident as a portent of what was coming my way.

CHAPTER 2

Upon my return to our apartment building, I discovered that during my absence, Tess had replaced the brass name plate beneath the lobby buzzer for her apartment so that it showed both our names. It now read:

> "Tess Devrais
> Robert Tarza"

I assumed that she'd had the new plaque prepared days before, in anticipation of my saying yes to her proposal. And now, even though I'd not yet said yes, she apparently believed that I'd return and agree. It was so very logical, and so very French.

I wondered if the addition of my name would mean that Pierre Martin, the concierge—that fixture of French apartment buildings, part snotty doorman, part guardian of the gate, part busybody—would, snuggled inside his little glass booth in the outer lobby, deign to look up from his newspaper and actually greet me before I greeted him. And whether he'd let me into the elevator lobby without first checking to see if my name was on the guest access list, despite the fact that I had a key to the apartment and had been coming and going for five years. But any reassessment of my relationship with the concierge would have to wait, because at that very moment there was a loud pounding on the outside door, and someone started to scream, "Help!" More faintly, I heard a second voice.

My immediate thought was that it was the ring scammer—that he had somehow followed me to the café, waited, followed me back to my building with a friend in tow, and was trying to lure me out, intent on revenge. I looked over at the concierge for help, but he was calmly reading a newspaper. Whatever was happening was outside, and he concerned himself only with goings-on inside.

But then I realized it was ridiculous to think it was the scammer. If he was after me, he would have attacked on my way to or from the café. I yanked the door open. To my astonishment, Oscar was standing there, struggling to hold on to a large box as a tall, thin, very young-looking guy dressed almost entirely in black from hoodie to toe tried to wrest it from him. Oscar tried to keep the box, failed and fell.

Without thinking—had I thought about it I surely wouldn't have done it—I ripped the box from the tall guy's hands, gripped it to my chest and heaved myself on top of it. The man glared at me, seeming to assess the situation. I tried to get a good look at him, but it was already deep into twilight and between that and the snow I couldn't see him very well. Instead of trying to take the box back, he fled up the street.

I doubt the thief thought I was too much for him. More likely he thought it was just going to take too long to extract the box from under me. I also noticed a black car, which had been idling beside us in the street, accelerate and disappear into the traffic, its tires slipping on the snow.

Oscar struggled up and held out his hand to help me up. "You okay, Robert?"

"I think so, although my chest is probably bruised."

We both stood there, trying to brush the wet snow off. I looked around to see if there were any witnesses. I saw no one. Either no one had been around, or whoever had been there wanted to avoid spending Christmas Eve talking to the police. The concierge was nowhere to be seen, despite the fact that he must have seen the whole thing via the camera above the door that displayed its image on a little screen in his cubicle.

I handed the box back to Oscar, and we walked into the building. The concierge looked at me, said, "Police!" and pointed to his cell.

Oscar said, loudly, "No police! If you've already called them, please call them back and tell them not to come. That they mistook me for someone else, and they are long gone."

To my astonishment, Oscar had addressed every word to the concierge in, if not flawless French, perfectly understandable, grammatical French.

"I didn't know you spoke French, Oscar. Where did you learn it?"

"During the war."

"Very funny. Assuming you mean World War II, you weren't even born when that war ended."

"You're right," he said, smiling. "That was a joke. The true story is that my parents sent me to a French lycée in Los Angeles from preschool through high school. They thought it was more cultured or something."

"Oh," I said. "I never knew."

By then we were in the elevator, heading up to Tess's apartment on the sixth floor.

"Thanks for rescuing the box," Oscar said. "That was heroic. I owe you a debt of gratitude, but I'm so sorry you had to be subjected to this."

"What's it all about?" I asked. "And who do you think they mistook you for?"

He pointed to the small camera in the corner of the elevator cab and put his finger to his lips in the universal sign for "shh." We rode the rest of the way in silence.

I unlocked the door to the apartment and said, "Why don't you set the box on the dining room table?"

As Oscar plunked it down, Tess walked into the room. As usual, she looked quite *soignée*. Her freshly cut hair, done in a bob, showed off her high cheekbones to advantage, and she was immaculately dressed in an ecru blouse and a black wool skirt that hugged her slim thighs to just above the knee. She was wearing her usual Louboutin shoes, this time in suede.

"Oscar, this is so great to again see you!" She gave him a hug and then a kiss on both cheeks. "What is this big box?"

He leaned his head back and scanned the ceiling. "Are there any microphones turned on in here? Or hidden video cameras?"

"No, of course not," I said, although I noticed that Tess had not actually responded to his query.

He looked around some more, as if expecting to find someone hiding behind the curtains, then said, "Alright, I will show you, and I assume you will keep this strictly to yourselves."

"Oh, of course," I said. Tess nodded, in what I supposed was a yes. Oscar took out a small knife from his pocket, cut the string that was wrapped around the package and pulled away the butcher paper that enclosed it. That revealed a red cardboard box with a satiny finish, topped by a slightly crushed, paste-on white bow. It was the kind of box in which fancy shops often package their wares, so that the lid can be taken off without being unfastened. After Oscar lifted it off, I peered inside and saw five large cloth-bound books. They looked to be in pretty good condition, but they were clearly old, and each was protected by a clear plastic cover, like the kind I used in law school to protect casebooks I wanted to resell when I was done with them.

"My friends, I have begun to collect antiquarian books," he said. "And not just to collect them, but to sell them to others. To be a dealer. On a small scale for now, of course."

As a collector of ancient coins myself, it didn't really surprise me that Oscar had acquired a collecting bug of some sort. He was fussy enough that it fit.

"Now let me show you the jewel of my collection," he said. "It's a first edition in English of Victor Hugo's novel *Les Misérables*. All five volumes." He hefted the books out of the box and lowered them to the table.

"What's so special about that?" I asked. "Is it rare?"

"Not so rare in general, Robert, but please pick up the first volume and open it to the title page."

I did, and read aloud the inscription. "'*Pour Charles Dickens, le plus grand écrivain en langue anglaise depuis Shakespeare.*' Wow. This looks like a British first edition of *Les Misérables* in English, inscribed by Victor Hugo to Charles Dickens, saying he's the greatest writer in English since Shakespeare. Really? That's incredible."

Tess took it from me, looked at it and said, "*Incroyable.*"

Oscar beamed. "Yes, incredible is exactly what it is. But this edition was printed in America, not England. The Americans translated *Les Misérables* into English first."

"What is the little drawing after the signature?" I asked.

"That's what makes this piece so truly special," Oscar said. "It's a small self-portrait of Victor Hugo that he added after his signature. It may be the only known example of his having done such a thing."

"He was an artist, too?" I asked.

"Yes, a great one. The man was a true polymath—artist, poet, novelist, playwright, politician. The list goes on."

"That must make this incredibly valuable," I said.

"It is."

"What is the folded piece of paper that's sticking out of the last volume?"

"It's just a bill of sale," Oscar said. "It's of little importance, because I have an offer from a buyer to pay me a very substantial sum for it, vastly more than I paid for it."

"Why so much more than you paid?" I asked.

"It's a long story. I'll tell you more when the sale is close to being finalized."

"Oscar, how do you know that this is real?" Tess asked.

Oscar smiled, as if it was not the first time he'd heard the question posed. "We can get into that, too, a little later, Tess. Let's just say for now that after a lot of research, I found what I call an authenticator. Something that sweeps away all doubt."

"Do you have that with you?" I asked.

"No."

"Well, why was someone trying to grab this from you out on the street?" I asked.

"I'm not sure. There was another bidder for the book who dropped out. Maybe it was someone he sent, although I thought he was happy in the end. Perhaps it was just an attempted street theft. A random kind of thing."

Tess gave me a sharp look, and I could tell she was about to ask the details.

"I will explain later," I said.

Tess didn't challenge me on that, but just said to Oscar, "You must rest here until the dinner. It will be more safe."

"Thank you, Tess. I appreciate it," he responded, and made a slight bow in her direction. "You see, I was nearby when it suddenly occurred to me that if you and Robert were home I might leave the box here for safekeeping while I continued to run some errands."

"Eh, I see," Tess said.

"May I, then, leave the box here?" Oscar asked. "If I'm being followed—and I don't know that I am—but *if*, it will be safer. I ask only that you not tell anyone it's here."

"But of course. We are able to put it in my study," she said. Without waiting for him to agree, she picked up the box and headed in that direction. To my surprise, Oscar didn't follow her.

While we waited for her to return, I said, "Oscar, seriously, don't you think we should call the police? I'm guessing that was not a random act out there. Someone must be following you."

"Look, my friend, I stand to make a profit of close to half a million dollars on this. I don't want the police anywhere near it. If I involve them, there will be too many questions about the book."

"What kind of questions?"

"Just questions."

We waited a few minutes, but Tess did not return.

"I guess she's not coming back right away," I said. "Sometimes she does that."

"That's odd," he said. "But sometimes wives can be odd."

"Well, you would know," I said, laughing. "How many have you had?"

"Six, I think, including the current one. But only three of them were truly odd. In any case, I must go. I will be back for dinner at nine, and I am looking forward to it. *Au revoir.*"

* * *

When ten more minutes had gone by and Tess had still not returned, I concluded that she wasn't going to, or at least not right away. She was probably just puttering away in her study, doing whatever she did in there.

Although I had been invited into the study a few times over our five years together, she had made it clear the first night we ever spent together that she preferred to leave it as her private place. And, obviously, there were things in there she considered off-limits. All the cabinets and drawers had locks, and one filing cabinet had a glowing green light on it, suggesting some kind of alarm. We soon turned the fourth bedroom into my study, so it really didn't matter much, and I gave it little thought.

Maybe after we were married, I would ask what was locked up in her study. Which reminded me that amidst Oscar's unexpected arrival, I hadn't yet had the opportunity to tell Tess yes.

CHAPTER 3

While I waited for Tess to emerge, I went out on the balcony to smoke a cigar and admire the floodlit Notre Dame, which was visible through the bare branches of the trees.

After the cigar, which I'd started the day before, burned itself down to a nub, I came back in, sank into my favorite chair and scanned *Le Monde,* more or less the *New York Times* of France. It was filled with the usual French fare—a sinking economy, restless immigrants and the latest exploits of Roland de Fournis, an investigating judge who had been looking into alleged financial scandals of former cabinet members. Such judges in France are super-powerful and, assisted by their very own judicial police, can jail people for up to forty-eight hours while they question them. Which is exactly what de Fournis had been doing for weeks. Photos of the formerly powerful being hauled off to jail, one by one, had made it onto even the staid pages of *Le Monde.* I loved it, and so did all of France.

Next I inspected Tess's elegant table setting and then opened the red wine to let it breathe. We were serving two *grand cru* wines—a white 1989 Bâtard-Montrachet and a red Château

Margaux of the same vintage. Nineteen eighty-nine was the 200th anniversary of the French Revolution, so if I brought that up at dinner, perhaps it would generate some good table talk.

I was surprised to see that the table was set for six. While I was reading *Le Monde*, I had heard Tess leave her study and make her way into the kitchen. "Tess," I yelled through the swinging door that led from the dining room to the kitchen—"I thought there were only going to be four of us. Who are the extra plates for?"

She came out of the kitchen sporting a white apron and a chef's hat and wiping her hands on a napkin. "*Eh bien*, while you were on the balcony an old friend, Jean Follet, telephoned. His wife is dead this last year and I find myself to have sorrow for him. *Donc*, I invited him at, how do you say, the final second?"

"Oh, okay. But there are six place settings."

"Yes. He will bring a guest, he says."

"I hope he won't be a drag on the party."

"What does this mean, 'a drag on the party'?"

"I hope he will not be depressed and depress us all."

"Oh no. He is very *animé*. He is a retired army general and has many stories to tell."

Tess turned as if to head back to the kitchen. I reached out and touched her on the shoulder, and she turned back toward me.

"Tess, I want to say yes. And I want to apologize that I didn't say it immediately. I love you and I want to marry you."

She beamed and gave me a giant hug and then a kiss on the lips. "Ah, this is great. Did you see that I added your name to the plaque?"

"Yes."

"We will be very happy I think. Do you not think so?"

"Yes, I do. And I thought we could announce the engagement tonight during dinner. I would love to raise a toast to you."

She seemed to stiffen slightly and said, "Eh, maybe not at this dinner. The general, he is an old friend, but we are not close, and I do not know at all this person he will bring. Let us instead have a special dinner with good friends to announce this."

"Okay," I said. "That works me for me."

She started to head back to the kitchen. "Tess, I want to tell you the details of what happened to Oscar in front of our building," I said.

"Yes?"

I told her about the tall young man who tried to grab the box, about my falling on it to save it from being stolen and about the car that had been idling nearby.

"*Mon Dieu!* Why did Oscar not to tell me all of this?" she asked.

"I think he just wants to minimize it."

"We should call the police, do you not think?"

"He doesn't want to do that."

She paused for a moment, then said, "It is his head, I suppose."

"We would say it is his neck."

"Eh, whatever part it is, it is his."

Not long after that conversation, Jenna arrived for dinner, wearing an ankle-length alpaca coat, black boots and a jaunty red beret. When she doffed her coat, I could see that she was wearing a swanky designer dress and five-hundred-dollar shoes.

"Hey, how come you never dressed like that when we were trying cases together back in Los Angeles?" I asked.

"I didn't want the jury—or you—to think I was a rich bitch," she said, and gave me a kiss on both cheeks and proceeded to do the same with Tess.

I pointed to her beret. "And I see that you've also adopted French habits even though you've only been here a few days," I said.

"Oui."

"And now you speak French, too?"

"Oh no! *Oui* is pretty much my only word."

"Fortunately, my French is much better."

"*Pas du tout!* Not at all!" Tess said. "Robert's French, it needs work. Much work."

I was about to respond by saying that my French was at least as good as her English, probably better, when Oscar arrived, looking Christmas-dapper in a dark-gray windowpane-plaid suit, white shirt and red-and-green bow tie—a far cry from his appearance earlier, when he'd been wearing an old raincoat and a floppy hat. He was clutching a bouquet of fresh flowers, which he handed to Tess as they, too, exchanged the mandatory two-cheek buss.

I was on the edge of asking him some more about the book in the red box, still in Tess's study, when the general arrived. Tess introduced him as General Jean Follet. He was tall, thin and fit, and looked to be in his late fifties. He had graying hair, still in abundance, and a full, jet-black mustache. I had half expected him to show up wearing his dress uniform and the traditional high hat with the small visor and the round top—the kepi—that French army officers are always seen wearing in old war movies. He was dressed instead in an ordinary blue suit and was hatless. Considering his advertised status as recently widowed, I was surprised to see that he had on his arm a young Russian woman at least thirty years his junior. Not of course that I had standing to object since Tess was twenty years younger than I.

The woman was rail thin and an inch or so taller than the general, who was himself at least six feet tall. A skintight red dress hugged her figure from neck to knee. She was introduced as Olga something or other. I couldn't quite make out the last name. I assumed she was a model of some sort.

I made drinks for all and poured a vodka martini for myself. We stood and chatted awhile—almost entirely in English—until Tess announced that dinner was ready. Olga, however, had said nothing.

We all sat down at the table and dined on roast beef and quail, although Oscar, who is a vegan, had *boeuf à la tofu*, or so Tess named it. Many toasts were drunk to the chef and to Franco-American friendship. During the dinner, the general regaled us with amusing stories about how he had tracked down thieves and con artists while he rose through the ranks in the military. He had apparently spent his career in supply and logistics, where theft and fraud were endemic. His English was impeccable, and eventually I inquired about it.

"General, your English is perfect. Which is, if I may be frank, unusual for the French." I cast a glance at Tess and got a glare in return.

"Please do not call me 'General,' Robert. I am retired from all of that. To answer your question, my father was a French diplomat posted for many years to English-speaking countries, so I went to American, British or Australian schools from grade school through high school."

After that, the conversation rolled on, spurred by the six bottles of wine we were in the process of consuming. Eventually, I tried to draw out Olga, who had sat almost entirely silent throughout, but I got only yes and no answers from her to the simplest questions.

Finally, the general broke in. "My niece is from Russia. She has only recently arrived here, fleeing persecution there. She speaks very little English and very little French, and it makes her very nervous to speak either language with people she does not know." He looked over at her and she smiled shyly.

At the mention of persecution, Oscar, who had spent his life as a criminal defense lawyer, sometimes in defense of people prosecuted for doing the unpopular, perked up. "What kind of persecution?"

"Her father, Igor Bukov, is a wealthy businessman who has fallen into disfavor with the Kremlin, and he is trying to get his family relocated outside of Russia. I agreed to take Olga in until he can find more permanent lodgings for the whole family."

At the mention of Bukov's name, Oscar had gone pale. "Is Igor here in Paris?"

"I don't know where he is, Oscar. All I know is that he is coming here soon. He first had business in the South of France. Do you know him?"

"I only know of him. But it's of no import."

Dessert was a wondrous apple tart. After dinner, more toasts were drunk, including toasts of appreciation to Tess for the wonderful meal. Only I knew that most of it had been delivered by a caterer via the back stairway, which opened into the kitchen.

By the end of the dinner, almost every guest had gotten up at one point or another to use the guest bathroom, which was across the hall from Tess's study. When Olga went, she was gone a very long time, and I noticed that Oscar kept glancing toward the back of the apartment, pretty clearly wondering what she was up to.

After fifteen minutes had gone by, I got up, explaining that I had drunk too much wine and urgently needed to use the other bathroom. When I reached the back of the apartment, a light shone under the door of the guest bathroom. I knocked and asked if she was okay, but got no response. Suddenly, the door flew open, and Olga emerged. She said nothing, but I could have sworn that she gave me the finger as she brushed by me. But then, maybe she didn't. It might have been my imagination.

After she had disappeared down the hall on her way back to the dining room, I turned around, turned the knob on the study door and found it unlocked. I flicked on the light switch and observed the red box sitting on Tess's desk, lid still on and apparently undisturbed. I went in and lifted the lid. The books were still there. I shrugged and returned to the dinner table. There was no way to tell if Olga had been in the study.

* * *

Not long after that, as midnight approached, the general and Olga said their good nights and left. We had all clearly been waiting for them to go so we could speak more candidly.

"Oscar," I said, "you looked—I don't know, shocked maybe?—when you heard Olga's father's name."

"It was just a surprise. Her father is sometimes a business competitor of mine."

"What kind of business?" Jenna asked. "I thought you were a lawyer, Oscar. Or were you faking it when we defended Robert on that ridiculous murder charge?"

"Ah right, you were not here this afternoon when we discussed this," Oscar said. "I now *also* collect and sell antiquarian books. Robert can catch you up on the details. I need to go now. And Robert, I will call you tomorrow and tell you some more of this affair."

Tess walked back to her study, returned with the red box and handed it to Oscar. Then Jenna said that she, too, needed to get going, although I could tell that she was curious about the contents of the box. Maybe Oscar, despite his sensitivity about the book, would choose to show it to her.

As we all bussed each other's cheeks in the French manner and headed for the door, we made plans to get together again for New Year's Eve. Tess agreed to pick a restaurant and let everyone know when and where.

After the door closed behind our guests, Tess said, "I am afraid for your friend. Afraid that he is in this, how do you say, above his head?"

"Something like that."

"Are you hurt from the fight today?"

"A little."

"You did not say anything."

"I didn't want to spoil the dinner or upset you."

"Come to bed, and I will make you forget this hurt."

Later, after we had lain there, I said to her, "Tess, why do you love me?"

"Eh, it is perhaps that you are handsome." She reached out and brushed my thinning gray hair off my forehead.

"I don't think I'm that handsome—maybe once upon a time I was, but this is now. And, anyway, looks can't be the basis for love."

"They can. Or at least the love that comes first."

"There must be some other reason."

There was a silence, and just the darkness around us, until, finally, she said, "It is because you are a wonderful person. But also because you treat me just as an ordinary person. You do not care that I am very, very rich or how I became this. Or you care, maybe, only that I am too rich, like you said today about the airplane."

"I don't care that you are rich, this is true. In fact, I don't even know how rich you are."

"Do not ask. The amount is almost to me embarrassing."

"I won't."

"It took me many years to find you, Roberto. So many men, they care so very much about my money. You do not. But we must turn this conversation around. Why do you love me?"

"For your airplane."

She turned in bed and punched me on the shoulder. Hard.

"Ouch."

"You merited this."

"Maybe I did."

"Robert, does your friend Oscar have love in his life?"

"He's married."

"This does not mean he has love in his life."

"True."

"How many wives does Oscar have?"

"Pandy is number six. He doesn't have the others anymore."

"He did not bring Pandy on this trip."

"Apparently not."

She was silent for a moment. "*Alors*, he must pay money to the other wives? I do not know what is the word in English."

"'Alimony.' In California we call it 'spousal support.'"

"Eh, we call this '*une pension alimentaire.*'"

"I don't know, Tess, if Oscar has to pay alimony to any of his former wives. Why are you asking?"

"This is perhaps why he has started this new business with books. He has need for money. If he has five wives who need this money, this could be much."

I had never thought about it, but I realized that she might have been right. In truth, I knew nothing about Oscar's finances or his former wives. He could be poor as a church mouse or as rich as Croesus. He could be paying no alimony at all or be on the hook for tens of thousands of dollars a month. And if it were the latter, it might explain his new business, because if a lawyer who has reached his sixties isn't yet rich, he never will be.

CHAPTER 4

I slept late on Christmas morning. When I woke up, Tess was no longer in the bedroom. I didn't immediately remember the episode on the street until I tried to stretch and felt my whole body screaming at me to stop moving. When I pulled up my pajama top, there was a large purple mark on my chest in the general shape of a square box.

When I moved slowly into the dining room, Tess was sitting at the table, sipping an espresso.

She saw me and said, "I will make you one also."

"Thank you. I have been thinking about our conversation of last night."

"About love?"

"No, about airplanes."

"This is now not funny."

"I'm sorry. Yes, about love. I don't know what it is, Tess, but our life together these last five years has been almost perfect."

"But it will be still better if you speak my language more. For five years we speak mostly in English to one another."

"That's true, but when we have your friends over who don't speak English, I speak French with them."

"Yes, but you are held back in French. You are not in French the charming man I know."

"Flattery will get you everywhere."

"I am serious, Robert. If we are to marry I wish you to be a bigger part of my world. It is a world where people speak French *couramment*—fluently."

She had a point. "What do you want me to do about it?"

"Look under the Christmas tree, you will see there my big present to you."

The present was in a large box. When I opened it, there were several smaller boxes inside until I finally got to a bright-red envelope. And inside that was a certificate for fifty "French and French Culture" lessons with a Madame Riboud.

"Fifty?"

"Oui! One each week for fifty weeks with two weeks off."

"Who is Madame Riboud?"

"She is an older woman who lives in the 16th arrondissement. She is *formidable* to help people learn French. Especially the Americans. She can fix your *accent terrible*."

"You think I have a terrible accent?"

"I exaggerate. It is not so terrible, but so . . . American. You know?"

"I have had people tell me my accent is good."

"They tried to be kind, I think."

"Alright, I will do this, but on one condition."

"Which condition?"

"You will take lessons in 'the English.'"

"Okay. I will."

I decided to change the topic. "Where do you think Oscar got the very rare inscribed copy of *Les Misérables* that he showed us?"

"I do not know. Perhaps you should ask this of him."

"I want to. When he is willing to talk about it. Something bad is going on."

"Why do you say this?"

"Think about it. Oscar needed to hide that box here for a few hours and asked us not tell anyone it was here. And when that girl's father was mentioned he blanched. Not to mention that someone tried to snatch the box from him in the street."

"Did he not promise to call you this morning to explain?"

"Yes, he did, but it's already ten o'clock and I haven't heard from him."

"Why do you not worry only after today has reached its end and he has not called? He enjoys his Christmas Day, maybe with the other friends, and perhaps this thing that happened yesterday is only a simple robbery. Even in this part of Paris this thing happens."

Oscar did not call me back on Christmas Day. Nor, despite multiple calls, emails and texts, did he call me back on the following six days. It was enormously frustrating, and I began to fear that Oscar was dead—that maybe the people who had attacked him in front of our building had tried again to grab the book and killed him in the process.

On December 30, I told Tess, "I'm going to call the police and see if they can help me find Oscar."

"It is useless to call the police because they will not help you," she said.

"Why not?"

"This is Paris. At this moment the police interest themselves only in terrorists and hoodlums."

On the morning of the thirty-first, Tess left to run errands. As soon as she was out the door I called and texted and emailed Oscar once again, but still got no response. I picked up Tess's landline phone and called the *Commissariat*—the police station—in the 5th arrondissement and explained my problem to them, but avoided the mention of the attempted theft of the box on Christmas Eve.

After extracting from me the admission that Oscar wasn't a relative, wasn't my law partner, wasn't the other kind of partner either, and had a wife in New York, the officer told me that I was being a *mouche du coche*—which even I knew meant 'busybody'—and that, in France, privacy, even that of foreigners, was highly valued. He closed by saying *"occupe-toi de tes fesses,"* which, even though I'd never heard the phrase before, I understood had to mean "mind your own business." He had also used the informal *tu* form of address, which was insulting since he didn't know me and I wasn't a child. When I looked up the idiom for *occupe-toi de tes fesses* later, I found it literally means "mind your own buttocks."

I sulked for an hour, berating myself for not having mentioned the attempted theft. Surely had I told them, they would have helped me. I tried to shove the police putdown out of my mind by reading a book. Just as I concluded that I wasn't going to get any reading done, Tess returned and said, "I have now chosen a place for dinner tonight. It is the restaurant Aux 2 Oliviers near the Jardin du Luxembourg." As I watched, she texted Oscar and Jenna with the suggestion that we meet there at nine.

"Good choice, Tess," I said. "I like that place. But you know, I've always wondered whether it's named for Laurence Oliver and his brother or for two olive trees."

She rolled her eyes. "Two olive trees, *sans doute*. Why would they wish to name their restaurant for this English actor and his brother?"

Two beeps sounded on my cell phone only seconds apart. They were texts back from Jenna and then—to my astonishment and annoyance—from Oscar, both saying they would see us there at nine that evening. I immediately texted Oscar: *Where the hell have you been? Trying to reach you for a week.* The formerly techno-phobic Oscar, who until two years ago had had neither computer, nor cell phone, nor fax machine, responded instantly: *Telu@din.*

By the time nine o'clock rolled around, and we were all seated at a small table at Aux 2 Oliviers, I was brim full of questions for Oscar. But every time I tried to bring the conversation around to the book and where he'd been and why he hadn't responded to me for a week, Oscar put me off, at one point looking around and saying in a low voice, "This place is too small and too full of listening ears. We will talk of it later."

Finally, as the dinner wound to a close—we had lingered over our espressos and shared a wonderful tarte aux poires—I couldn't stand it any longer. "Oscar, if you won't talk about it here, let's go back to Tess's apartment and talk about it there. I am very worried about you."

"Robert, we do need to talk, but I would rather take a walk and talk about it then. That way we will be sure not to be overheard. Who knows who might have bugged Tess's place?"

"My place is not been bugged, merci," Tess said.

Oscar's mouth turned down into a frown. "There's no way to be certain of that."

Jenna finally chimed in. "Why don't we all go for a walk, then?"

"You walk, but I will leave you to walk without me," Tess said. "I will return to my apartment and its bug. You can pay the bill, Robert."

With that, she got up abruptly and left. That didn't surprise me much. When Tess was miffed at something, she sometimes just departed. I watched her at the front, talking to the maître d', clearly asking him to call her a cab, which arrived only minutes later as I arranged to pay the tab.

It was almost midnight as Jenna, Oscar and I headed for the front door. We were clearly shutting the place down, as most of the other diners had long ago departed, heading home or to their celebrations. The owner was standing by the door, ready to wish us a *bonne année*. The three of us stepped out into a steady drizzle. Oscar was the only one of the three of us who had had the good sense to bring an umbrella, which he popped open, then offered to Jenna.

"No thanks. I've got this beret on and this fur coat, so I'll be okay unless it turns into a downpour."

I kind of expected he'd offer it to me next, but he didn't.

The restaurant was across from the French Senate building, a stark white, hulking edifice on the edge of the Jardin. We turned left out of the restaurant and then quickly left again, heading down into the narrow streets near the Odéon theater.

"Well, Oscar, is this obscure enough a place that you're confident there are no bugs?" I asked.

He paused and looked around. "Yes."

"Okay then, what is going on with you?"

"I have had the feeling the last few weeks that I am being followed, but I've never been able to catch anyone doing it. It's just that every once in a while I'll be out walking and the hair on the back of my neck will stand up."

"Are these worries why you didn't return my messages, Oscar?"

"Yes. I think my phone may be bugged. I think someone is after my inscribed copy of *Les Misérables*."

"Have you carried it with you the whole time?" I asked. "Why not put it in a safe place, like a vault?"

"I do at night. But I have to carry it with me. I'm trying to get an even better price for the book than I've already been offered, and I have to show it to the collectors and dealers so they can see it for themselves. And have their doubts about its authenticity put to rest."

"Have you been in Paris the whole time since we last saw you?"

"No, I've been traveling. Paris is not the only place with antiquarian book dealers and collectors. And I've been to places where wealthy foreign collectors vacation in the winter. The Côte d'Azur and the ski resorts."

"Where did you get the book?"

"At a place in the South of France that had a large collection of old books, some dating back almost two hundred years. I bought *Les Misérables* and a couple of other books."

Jenna, who had been silent, broke in. "Did the seller know about the Hugo inscription on *Les Misérables*?"

"Oh yes. He is very open about the fact that many people think the inscription and the drawing are forgeries."

"But you bought it anyway."

"Yes. This book is not unknown to people who collect forgeries, and there are such people. But I have done the research and found the authenticator for this book. And so I paid the man a slightly higher price than he thinks it's worth, but not so high a price as to indicate its true value or make anyone think it has the huge value I believe it does."

"So, do you think it was ethical to buy it 'for a slightly higher price' without telling him about the authentication you found?" Jenna asked.

"He could have done the same research I did. In my view, having information someone else doesn't have doesn't mean the purchase is fraudulent unless they lacked the same opportunity you had to find out the truth. And anyway . . ."

The rest of Oscar's answer was drowned out by the bang of private firecrackers being set off just down the block from us. Then, suddenly, a bright white fire-cracker dropped directly in front of us with a loud pop, and I heard teenage laughter from one of the windows above. It was starting to rain more heavily, and I suggested we look for an open café, if there was one open this late on New Year's Eve, where we could get out of the rain and away from the firecrackers.

Just then another one, red this time, exploded in front of us.

"Shit," I said. "We're gonna get hurt if we don't get out of here."

A few seconds later, I heard the sound of car tires rolling on wet pavement, and a large black Mercedes pulled up alongside us and stopped. Both back doors flew open and two men, not tall but big, and wearing masks, grabbed Oscar and pushed him into the back seat. It was over in a few seconds.

The car accelerated away. Jenna grabbed her cell phone and snapped two quick pictures of the departing car. The flash from the camera illuminated the night, competing with the flare of a third firecracker, this one blue, that fell in the middle of the street.

CHAPTER 5

Jenna managed to snap one more picture as the car careened around the corner and sped out of sight. She lowered the phone and we both stood there for a second or two, stunned.

"I'll call the police," I said.

"Maybe there's a cop near here."

We both swiveled our heads, looking. There was no one—no cops, no other pedestrians—and it was eerily quiet. The firecrackers had, at least for the moment, stopped raining down on us. I looked up and saw no lights in the windows above us on either side of the street.

"Do you know the number, Robert?"

"I do." I punched in 112, which is the pan-European all-purpose emergency number. It rang for at least two minutes before it was finally picked up.

"*Allo,*" the voice said, "*s'il vous plaît dites-moi votre nom et votre problème.*"

I knew that 112 operators are trained to speak several languages or to pass you off to someone who spoke your language. But since the matter was urgent, I thought it would be fastest to answer in French so I'd be sure to be understood. First, as requested, I stated my name. After that I said clearly and simply that my friend had just been *kidnappé* off the street and shoved into a car. The operator said she was so sorry, but she could understand neither my name nor what I had just said, and could I please repeat. I said it all again, slowly.

Then she said, "You are an American, *n'est-ce pas*?"

"Yes."

"It is okay, I speak English. What is your name and what is the problem?"

"I'm Robert Tarza, and my friend Oscar Quesana has just been kidnapped while walking down the street—shoved into the back of a car by two men."

She asked where I was and then for more details—a description of the car, of Oscar and of the men who grabbed him. She also asked whether anyone was with me. When I had finished, she said, "Stay where you are, and if there are any witnesses, please ask them to stay also. I will send the police to you soon. But it is Saint-Sylvestre. I am sorry, I do not know this phrase in English."

"New Year's Eve."

"Yes, and so the police, they are very busy with the *voyous* everywhere. They will be with you as soon as possible, but this may not be so soon. Again, do not leave, and please leave your phone not in use. I may have need to telephone you."

Jenna had been leaning against me—I could feel her shivering—straining to hear. "I couldn't make all of that out. What'd she say?"

"She said the police will be here soon, but because it's New Year's Eve, they are busy with the hoodlums. I assume she meant the revelers are busy burning cars, which is a New Year's Eve French tradition."

"Around here?"

"No, mostly in the poorer areas in the suburbs, but I guess a lot of police are tied up out there."

"Jeez."

"Jenna, call Tess and tell her what's happened. The 112 operator asked me to keep my phone open."

After a moment, she said, "There's no answer on her cell. It rang into voice mail. I left a message."

"Try the home phone."

I could hear the number ringing on Jenna's phone.

"No answer there, either, and no voice mail pickup." Jenna glanced at her watch. "Did you note the time it happened?"

"Not exactly. I'd guess we've been here two or three minutes."

"We need to do something, Robert. We can't just stand here doing nothing."

"What do you suggest?"

"Let's try to call him."

I watched her dial, tap the button for speakerphone, and we listened together. It rang five times and then went to voice mail, where Oscar's abrupt message said, as it always did, "Leave a message."

We looked at one another, and we both clearly had the same thought: what message do you leave for someone who's been kidnapped?

I spoke first, "Oscar, it's Robert and Jenna. Call us and tell us what's going on. Please." Then she ended the call.

"I know it sounds crazy," I said, "but why don't you email him, too?"

"Will do."

I watched her tap in a message.

"What did you say?"

"I just asked him to please get in touch."

"Any response?"

"It's weird."

"What?"

"It bounced back. It says 'Temporarily Out of Office.'"

"Do you think he did that, or the kidnappers?"

"I have no idea."

After Jenna put her phone back in her pocket, she looked at me and said, "What if they come back?"

"Why would they come back?"

"To kill us?"

"I don't think kidnappers come back."

"Based on what, your experience with kidnappings?"

"No. But I'm staying. You can do whatever you want."

She chose to stay, so we just stood there in the drizzle, the water running down our noses, waiting for the police. As is typical of many Paris streets, there was nowhere nearby to shelter ourselves—no indented doorways or overhangs, just blank walls, gates and shops closed tight with metal shutters. We could have moved down the block where there was an indented nook of sorts, but without speaking we clearly both knew we shouldn't abandon the exact place where the car had pulled to the curb.

CHAPTER 6

It took the police almost fifteen minutes to get there. When they finally did come, we heard them before we saw them—the distinctive *whoop, whoop* of a Parisian police siren, followed seconds later by a white Peugeot, the word POLICE emblazoned within a blue side-stripe, a blue light bar flashing on top. It screeched to a stop in front of us, and two officers jumped out. A second car followed close behind and seemed almost to exhale two more cops.

Suddenly, the almost pitch black of the late night was replaced by four police officers standing amidst blinding blue lights, three with their guns drawn.

The officer who seemed in charge—and was gunless—approached us, while the other three stood back.

"What is going on?" he asked in French.

I told him, and he, at least, seemed to understand my French. When I'd finished telling him what had happened, I asked him if he had any *parapluies*—umbrellas—and he produced two from somewhere. By then, a paddy wagon, what the French call colloquially, for some reason unknown to me, a *panier à salade* (literally, a salad shaker), had also arrived.

The cops then spoke briefly among themselves, and the leader turned back to me and asked, "Do you have any idea why this man was picked up?"

"He wasn't picked up, he was kidnapped."

"Yes, yes. I understand your interpretation of what happened. But I ask again if you know why."

"All I know is that he had recently purchased a very rare antiquarian book and he feared that someone was after him for it."

"Rare books, Monsieur, are sometimes used to launder money. Was your friend involved in that?"

It took me a second to understand what he had asked me, because the French phrase for money laundering—*le blanchiment d'argent*—literally the cleaning of money, wasn't in my daily vocabulary, so I needed to translate it.

"Ah, no, officer, he is simply a lawyer from America on vacation here."

"Ah, so he is an American?"

"Yes."

"Why did you not say so immediately?"

"I don't know."

"This is an important fact."

I was about to ask him why it was important, but I decided to suppress the urge to play lawyer.

At that point, Jenna broke in. "Excuse me, do any of you speak English?" she asked, addressing the cops. "I don't speak French, and I don't understand what's going on here."

"I'm sorry, Jenna," I said. "I forgot that you can't understand. They are asking if we know why he was kidnapped—I told them about the book—and they are wondering if he was involved in money laundering."

"What?"

One of the other officers, who had not yet spoken, stepped forward and said, in pretty good English, "I speak English. I was an exchange student in Omaha when I was in the *lycée*—high school. I will translate for you, Madame, when it's needed."

I thought, although I might have been mistaken, that he was looking at Jenna with an interest that was not entirely *policier*.

The first officer then continued with me, in French. "Do you have a photo of this person, this Oscar Quesana?"

"My friend here, Jenna, has a couple on her cell phone, I'm sure. She also has pictures of the car that took him."

"We need her phone, then."

"Jenna, they want your phone for any pictures you have of Oscar and pictures of the car."

The first cop held out his hand, and Jenna burrowed in the pocket of her coat and handed over her phone. Her hand was shaking from the cold and her teeth were chattering.

"Will I get it back?"

The officer who spoke English whispered something in the ear of the lead officer, listened for a second and said, "You will get it back."

"When?"

"Soon. But it's evidence, if you get me. Right now you need to chill."

Despite the seriousness of the situation, I almost laughed out loud. The guy's Omaha experience had clearly taken place sometime in the '90s.

Jenna didn't seem at all amused, and I feared she was about to hit him with a typical Jenna outburst—blunt and acerbic— when I put my hand up. "Let it go, Jenna. I'm sure you'll get it back. Right now it's more important to get Oscar back. And we need to get dry."

I addressed the lead cop. "Officer, can we go somewhere where we can dry off? We're both cold, and my friend here is on the edge of hypothermia."

There was again a quiet conversation among the four of them that I couldn't overhear. Finally, the officer in charge said, "You are both too wet to get in our cars. That would be very messy. Please get in the *fourgon*"—the official name for the *panier à salade*—"and we will take you where we are going."

"Which is where?"

"To 36 quai des Orfèvres."

"Which is central police headquarters, right?"

"How do you know that?"

I knew it, actually, because I was a fan of the potboiler French movie of the same name, starring Gérard Depardieu, in which two cops compete to replace the retiring chief of the Paris police, but somehow I thought it was best not to mention it right then. "I don't know," I said, "it's just something I know."

"I hope it's not because you have watched that dreadful movie."

"What movie? I only watch American movies."

He gave me an odd look and waved toward the back of the van. "Please get in."

We climbed into the van and sat on the padded benches, facing one another. Shortly thereafter, someone closed the doors and the van began to move.

"Are we suspects or what?" Jenna asked.

"I don't really know."

"Where are we going?"

"To police headquarters."

Just then my cell phone rang. It was Tess. "I got the message of Jenna. Where are you?"

"In the back of a police van, heading for police headquarters."

"To 36 quai des Orfèvres?"

"Yes."

"I will meet you there."

"I think that place is like a fortress, especially at night. How will you get in?"

"I am Tess Devrais. This will not be a problem."

I knew of course that Tess hobnobbed at times with the wealthy and powerful in France. I'd even met some of them. But the police? That was a new wrinkle.

CHAPTER 7

We arrived at our destination within minutes, sirens whooping. We were ushered out of the van, through the inevitable giant metal gate, down a marble corridor, and into a small, sparsely furnished office. The cops who had transported us disappeared. Inside the office a uniformed woman police officer with gray hair sat at a desk piled high with papers. She was neither small nor large, but well-muscled, and looked like she could beat the shit out of me.

After introducing herself as *Capitaine Bonpere*—using the French pronunciation—and inviting us to take a seat in two of the metal chairs scattered around the office, she looked closely at Jenna and asked, in French, if she was cold. I answered for her and said yes. The captain came around her desk, helped Jenna shed her soaking wet alpaca coat and left with it. She came back a few minutes later with a police jacket and draped it over Jenna with a motherly air. Then she left again and returned with two steaming cups of coffee and a big towel that Jenna used to try to dry her hair, face and arms.

Captain Bonpere went back behind her desk and said in French, "Monsieur Tarza, do I understand correctly that your friend does not speak French?"

"Correct."

"Okay, since we need to interview both of you, we will need a translator. The police officer who helped bring you here, Lieutenant Joly, speaks good English. I will see if he is still in the building."

"That won't be necessary," a voice behind me said in English. "I can translate." It was Tess.

Captain Bonpere jumped to her feet. "Bonsoir, Madame Devrais. I did not know you were involved in this. Had I known, I would have called."

"I'm involved here only on a personal basis. Monsieur Tarza and I are engaged to be married."

Jenna looked at me and asked, "What's going on?"

"Tess and I are going to get married."

"What?"

"I'll explain later."

Meanwhile, Captain Bonpere was finalizing with Tess that Tess would join us and translate.

Once that was all taken care of, Captain Bonpere got started. Looking back and forth between the two of us, she said, "I assume you know that antiquarian books can easily be used to launder money."

I not only didn't know that, but I found it highly unlikely and said so. Once Tess understood, she seconded my thoughts.

"Madame et Monsieur," Bonpere said, "let me assure you that you are utterly wrong."

"How can one possibly use an old book to launder money?" I asked.

"It is simple, Monsieur, a person with cash he has made from, for example, smuggling drugs into Marseille from the Middle East, will use that money to buy a rare book. Let us say he pays one hundred thousand euros for it."

"Almost a hundred and forty thousand dollars."

She smiled. "Yes, but in real money, one hundred thousand euros. And so the bookstore owner, who is in the business of selling books, deposits that money in his bank along with his normal monthly receipts, and no one thinks anything of it. Or, if that is an extra-large deposit for him, he deposits about five thousand euros each month for ten months, varying the amount somewhat each month."

We waited a moment for Tess to catch up with the translation.

Jenna listened and said, "Yes, I know how this works. What happens next is that the drug dealer, let's call him Bob, puts the book on his own bookshelf, waits awhile and then sells it back to the same book dealer from whom he bought it in the first place. If Bob is later asked where he got the money, he says, 'Oh we had a rare book in our family and I sold it.' Of course, the book dealer gets a percentage for helping him out. Just as a bank takes a fee to change money."

Bonpere did not wait for Tess to translate. "That's right," she said. "And there are much more sophisticated versions of the same thing, using third parties."

Obviously Bonpere spoke at least some English.

"What makes you think that Oscar was involved in this?" I asked.

"Monsieur, was Oscar someone who collected these books all his life?"

"No."

"Was he a man who was a trader in goods?"

"No."

"Why then, Monsieur Tarza, do you think he became suddenly interested in rare books?"

"If he was doing this for criminal reasons, as you seem to think, why did he let us in on it?" Jenna asked. "After all, he showed us the book and seemed very proud of it."

This time Bonpere waited for the translation. I realized, as she did so, that although she probably understood what Jenna had said, waiting for the translation gave her time to think about what she wanted to say in response.

"I think," Bonpere said, "that he had become afraid for some reason, and he allowed you to know about the book because he thought you could help protect him."

She had a point. The whole thing about leaving it at our place in a gift box and asking me to keep it safe, plus his startle when he heard Bukov's name, fit with her theory.

"Wait," Jenna said. "This makes no sense at all. We know Oscar well. We've known him for many years. We've practiced law with him. He is not a criminal and this is simply not the kind of thing he would do."

Bonpere again waited for the translation, then said, "Sometimes those we think we know best we know least."

"Is that an old French saying?" I asked.

"No, it is an old Bonpere saying."

At that moment, the cop whom I'd come to think of as "Officer Omaha" stuck his head in the door. "We can look at the film now," he said in English. He took out an iPad with a bright green cover and handed it to Bonpere.

Bonpere pointed to him and said, "I have asked Lieutenant Joly here to access the imagery that we have from a security camera not far from where the alleged kidnapping took place. We can all watch it on this iPad." She set the iPad on a small easel on her desk, swiveled it to face us and walked around so she could see it herself.

I noted with some trepidation that she had called it an "alleged" kidnapping. If it wasn't a kidnapping, what was it?

The film rolled, without sound. The image was fairly dark, but I could make things out. As we watched, I saw the three of us walking down the street, Oscar in the middle. Suddenly, there were flashes of light from the firecrackers all around us. I saw the black car glide to a stop beside us—I had remembered it as stopping more abruptly. The two rear doors sprang open, and the two big guys jumped out and shoved Oscar into the back seat, just as I remembered it. Then the car sped away. The image continued, showing Jenna and me standing there as Jenna snapped the three pictures of the car.

Bonpere let it run for a few more seconds, then touched the screen and froze the image. "We will turn this over to our technical analysts for what they can see that perhaps we cannot see. But I note that the car has no license plate, and it is a recent model Mercedes D, of which there are thousands in Paris."

"Why did you call it an alleged kidnapping?" I asked.

"Because there are certain things about it that look not like a kidnapping. Let me show you." She touched the screen again, ran the film back to the beginning, and started it forward again, but on a slower speed.

She froze it when it reached the frame where Oscar began to be pushed into the car. "First," she said, "he ducked his own head when he got into the car. Usually, when someone shoves someone into a car against their will, they shield the victim's head." She ran the film for a second or two, and I could see that Oscar had indeed lowered his own head. "That is unusual. Even more important, though, is this." She started it forward again on an even slower speed. "What do you see, Monsieur Tarza?"

What I saw was dumbfounding. "He folded his umbrella before he got in. I don't remember seeing that, though."

"People who are in shock are not the best observers."

I could tell that Tess had been struggling to keep up with the translation. "Give me a minute to catch up," she said.

Bonpere paused while she did that.

After listening, Jenna said in English, "You have to know him. He is just very fastidious."

Bonpere looked to Tess. "What does this word *fastidious* mean?"

Tess clearly didn't know, so I added, "It means careful."

"I see," Bonpere said. "Well, I have been in this police business a long time, and I have never heard of or seen someone who was under attack being careful enough to fold an umbrella in the middle of it."

Tess then said something to Bonpere in French so rapid, so intentionally slurred and so filled with words I didn't know that I had no idea what she had said.

Bonpere looked thoughtful and responded, "Non."

Tess continued, this time in French I could comprehend. "Capitaine, what is the next step?"

"We have put out an alert for this car, although that is probably hopeless given how many of that model there are. Through other cameras, we have seen the driver turn onto a street where there is not a camera, and from that street, if he knows what he is doing, he can drive at least a kilometer without being watched by a camera again. And there are many other streets into which he can turn, also without cameras."

"But they have to emerge somewhere," I said.

"If they are smart, they took the car into a garage or parked it on the street. We are looking for it now, but even if we find it, they will not be in it. They will have transferred your friend to another car. And this car, if we find it, was probably stolen and so will not trace to them."

"Now you have to look for a car with three people in it."

"Monsieur, if he was truly kidnapped, he will now be in the trunk. And if he was not truly kidnapped, he is perhaps in the trunk anyway, with one other person in the car only—the driver. We cannot stop every car in Paris being driven by one person with no passenger. Or even with one passenger."

"Are you telling us that there's nothing you can do?"

"No, there is much we can do, but unless we are very lucky, it will not be by finding the car."

Tess stood up. "What do you want Monsieur Tarza and Madame James to do now?"

"Lieutenant Joly will take them to another room and gather detailed personal information about the alleged victim and learn where we can contact them."

Lieutenant Omaha leaned over and whispered in Bonpere's ear.

"Ah," Bonpere said, "it seems we cannot find where your friend Monsieur Quesana is living. We have checked, and no hotel in Paris has reported anyone named Oscar Quesana as a guest. You must know that all hotels are to report the names of their guests. Is he staying with any one of you?"

There was silence.

"We have also asked of hospitals and other places where a missing person might be. There is no clue of him in these places."

"Will you be the police officer leading the investigation?" Tess asked.

"No, it will be given to the *Brigade Criminelle de Paris*. As I'm sure you know, they investigate certain types of major crimes, like kidnapping."

"And like money-laundering," Tess said. It was more a statement than a question.

"Yes."

"Which one will be the focus here?" I asked.

"Perhaps both."

"Is there anything else?" Tess asked.

"Only if you learn where he was staying, please let us know immediately."

"Maybe his wife knows," I said.

"Where is she?"

"In New York City."

"Are they having marital difficulties?"

"Not that I know of," I said.

"It was just a thought."

"Captain, perhaps she knows where Oscar is staying. I'd call her and ask, but I've only met her once. Perhaps it would be better if you called."

"No. In my experience, it's better if you, someone she's at least met, calls her. She will also be more inclined to believe that her husband has been taken away if it comes from you. She will not think it is a bad joke. If that does not work, we will either contact her directly or have our friends in the NYPD call upon her."

"Alright, we will call her," I said.

By "we" I knew we were talking about me. But oddly enough I didn't feel I had the kind of close personal relationship with Oscar that I needed to be comfortable making that call. That was true even though Oscar had brilliantly created the winning strategy in my murder trial in Los Angeles. Without him as my defense lawyer, I would have lost. But despite the hundreds of hours we'd spent together during that trial, it was a professional kind of closeness we'd developed, not a deep personal connection. Calling his wife—whom I'd met only once—to tell her that her husband had been kidnapped in Paris was going to be hard.

I saw a solution, though. "Jenna, why don't you call her?"

"You're closer to Oscar, Robert. He and Pandy even visited you in Paris last year."

"Well, true." I was about to add that Oscar had represented Jenna the prior year in that nonsense at UCLA about the dead student in her office, and that she'd therefore had the most dealings with him lately. Fortunately, at the last second, I realized that that was not the kind of dirty linen I wanted to wash in front of the Paris police.

I realized Jenna was staring at me. "Bottom line, Robert, I'm not doing it. And by the way, weren't you the managing partner of a thousand-lawyer law firm? Doing that for all those years must've given you *some* backbone. Just suck it up and do it."

"Okay, okay. I'll do it."

Captain Bonpere had been listening to our exchange with interest. "As long as one of you does it," she said. "Tell us if you reach her."

CHAPTER 8

Captain Bonpere called a cab for us. I guess when the police call, even at three in the morning on New Year's Day, the cabs come. At first, the cab driver didn't want to let us get in, because our clothes were still soaking wet. But the policeman at the gate told him that he *would* take us, and he did. Tess got in front, and Jenna and I squished our way into the back.

"You need to call her," Jenna said.

"Maybe this isn't the best place." I motioned toward the cab driver. "Even the walls have ears."

"This wall speaks English," the cab driver said. "But this cab is equipped with a privacy shield. Do you want me to raise it?"

"Tess, you won't be able to hear if we do that," I said. "Do you mind?"

"No, go ahead."

"Wait," I said. "Before we do that, what did you say, Tess, to Captain Bonpere in super-rapid French? I assume so I wouldn't be able to follow it."

"Eh, I explained that if she looks the two of you up on the Internet she will find that you were accused of murder, Robert.

Of a partner. And Jenna was suspected of murder at UCLA. Of a student."

"Did you have to tell her that?" I asked.

"Yes. Or she will find it herself. In this way I get to tell her it is nonsense."

"Still . . ."

"Leave it, Robert," Jenna said. "She's right."

"I suppose. But it is so irritating to have that junk follow us all over the world."

"Get over it," Jenna said.

"Wow," the driver said. "If you didn't need to be private about that, I wonder what you're going to talk about next that you consider *really* private."

I ignored him and said, "Please raise the partition."

It slid up in front of us.

I found Pandy's number in my contacts and dialed her. The call dropped into voice mail after only two rings. All it said was, "This is Pandy. Leave a message."

Oddly, I hadn't considered that I might need to leave a message, or what it should say if I did. Did it make sense to tell her the blunt truth? *Hi, it's Robert Tarza. Just thought I'd let you know that your husband's been kidnapped, and the police think he might be involved in money laundering.* I chose instead something that I thought more nuanced. "Hi, it's Robert Tarza. Serious problems here in Paris. Oscar's not hurt or anything, but I need to talk to you as soon as possible. Please call me." I left my cell number.

"Don't you think, Robert, that being kidnapped is a form of being hurt?"

"You're over-lawyering it, Jenna. I didn't want to upset her too much."

I rapped on the glass, and the cab driver lowered it.

"How did that go?" Tess asked.

"It went into voice mail. I left a message."

We reached Tess's place in only a few minutes. "Jenna, do you want to stay here tonight or go back to your hotel?" I asked. "I'm not even sure where you're staying, come to think of it."

"I'd like to stay here."

"Great."

I was glad the concierge was not on duty. I'm sure he would never have permitted me to come in wearing soaking-wet clothes. Once we got inside the apartment, I went to our bedroom to change, and Tess directed Jenna to the guest room and went to find some dry clothes for her to wear.

After a while, we all gathered in the living room. Tess had found dry clothes for Jenna that seemed to fit.

"I think the question of the hour is what we are going to do now," Jenna said. "Do we just sit here and wait for the police to find him, or do we look for him ourselves?"

"I think we should look ourselves," I said.

"Agreed, but since we don't even know where he was staying, how do you suggest we go about that?"

"No clue."

At that point, we both looked over at Tess, who had been sitting across the room, somewhat removed from us, saying nothing.

"Why are you regarding me?"

"Well, for one thing, you seem to have some kind of connection with the cops," I said. "You got into that police fortress in the middle of the night, and Bonpere not only seemed to know you, but stood up when you came into the room."

"I do know her."

"How?"

"You do know, do you not, that I became rich in the tech business in the '90s?"

"Yes."

"Well my business had certain duties in the security of the nation. And during these times, I came to know many police."

"High-up police or regular police?"

"Both."

"Do you still work for them?"

"Sometimes."

"Can I ask exactly what you do?"

"If we are married, I can tell you some things. But I am not permitted to tell her"—she nodded at Jenna—"even then."

I wasn't sure whether that was intended as a put-down of Jenna or just a statement of fact. In any case, Jenna ignored it and turned herself into classic Jenna—organized and focused. "I think," she said, "that we can break the problem down into two parts."

"Which are?"

"Part one: If we can find out where Oscar was staying, we can get a good lead on who took him."

"Why?" Tess asked.

"Because, wherever he was, he was probably there for over a week. And when you stay in a hotel for a week you leave clues. Hotels are filled with spies—doormen, valets, desk clerks, maids, you name it."

"You must first find the hotel," Tess said. "And you assume him to stay in a hotel and not with a friend."

"Tess," I said, "do you remember when Oscar and Pandy visited us here in Paris last year?"

"Yes."

"Do you recall his mentioning any other friends in Paris, or wanting to see them?"

"No."

I looked at Jenna. "When he was here for dinner, do you remember his saying anything about that?"

"No."

"I just remembered," I said. "When he got in a cab right after he was mugged, I heard him tell the cab driver to take him back to his hotel, but the cab pulled away as he was saying it, so I never heard the name of the hotel."

"Okay, he is therefore in a hotel, but we do not know how to find it," Tess said.

"Right. Thus, we must use the second approach, which is to find out where he got the book. If we learn that, it might help lead us to the kidnappers, which will lead us to him."

"I can help with this," Tess said. "I have a good friend here in Paris who is a dealer in rare books. We can talk to him to start. He will know where one might buy such a book."

"Excellent, Tess. Let's call him."

"Robert, it is the middle of the night. We must all go to bed and wake up in the morning and begin the search then for the hotel and the book."

"What if they are going to kill him?"

"If the plan is for him to be dead, he is already dead. If he is not dead, he will be alive in the morning."

She was right. Jenna headed to the guest room, and we retreated to our bedroom. Once the light was turned out and we were in bed, I turned to her and said, "Are you a cop?"

"No."

"In the military?"

"No."

I tried to think what else there might be. "A spy?"

There was a long pause. She turned on her side in the bed so that she faced me, although it was so dark I could hardly see her. "*Pas exactement.* I help my country when it asks my help. Which is not so often."

"I think I need to know more about this."

"Marry me and I can tell you much more."

"Is this why you want to get married?"

"*C'est parce que je t'aime, Robert.*"

I was struck by the fact that she had switched to French to say "I love you." It seemed so much more intimate in her own language.

"I love you, too, Tess." I paused. I knew where I was about to go was not very romantic. "But is being able to tell me these things the primary reason you want to marry me?"

She actually laughed out loud. "You are always the lawyer. I admit that it has bothered me, to always be hiding this thing from you for much time. *Donc*, yes, if we marry each other, I can talk to you of this. But it is not any part of the reason I wish to marry you. If I had not so much love for you, I am able to hide this from you for more days and years."

"Will your position, whatever it is, help us find Oscar?"

"I hope this."

Tess fell asleep almost immediately after that. I did not. Instead I tossed and turned thinking about the fact that Tess's secret life had been revealed accidentally, not because she decided on her own to tell me. And wondering, if she had hidden so important a thing from me all these years, what else had she not told me?

CHAPTER 9

An hour later, I was still awake, thinking, not anymore about Tess, but about my friend Oscar—thinking if he was not already dead, he was being held somewhere against his will, and God knew under what conditions. I felt guilty just for being safe in a warm bed. Eventually, I realized that I was not going to go to sleep. I got up, went into my study and began to surf the Net again, looking for information on first editions in English of *Les Misérables*. A floorboard creaked behind me, and I whirled around. It was Jenna, wrapped in one of Tess's bathrobes.

"Hi, Robert. I'm sorry for startling you. I couldn't sleep, thinking about Oscar and what he must be going through."

"Me neither. Do you think they're torturing him to get information?"

"I don't know," she said. "They could be. And he's getting old, you know, so he probably can't take much of that. But what are you doing, Robert?"

"Like we talked about earlier, I'm trying to learn more about the rare book Oscar bought. So maybe we can figure out what's going on and have a better chance of finding him."

Jenna went over and snuggled into my big leather easy chair. "I know we said that. But maybe that's not the right approach. Maybe we should just let the police take the lead."

"I don't trust the police to make finding Oscar a priority. They seem like they have other fish to fry."

She said nothing for a moment, then said, "As I think about it, you're probably right, Robert. And I want to help."

"Good. But we don't have much to go on."

"I know," she said. "Hey, can I put my feet up on the coffee table?"

"Sure, even though your feet are bare. But how are we going to start our search?"

"I'm not sure," she said. "But I guess I'm going to try to go back to sleep."

After she left the room, I puttered on the computer for another half hour. The only things I learned of interest were that old books were called *anciens livres* in French, that first editions were called "firsts" and that there were, unfortunately, at least a hundred antiquarian bookstores in Paris and at least that many in other parts of France. It would be a long search if we had to talk to each and every one. Then I went back to bed myself and finally managed to fall asleep.

When I woke up, at about nine, Tess was no longer in our bed.

After noting her absence, I stretched, admired the dazzling sunshine pouring through the windows—the rain had clearly ended—and started to get out of bed. Then the temporary amnesia that had been forced on me by sleep lifted, and I remembered with a start what had happened.

If I was right that finding Oscar was not a high priority for the police, I needed to get a move on with our own investigation. I showered, dressed hurriedly and went out into the apartment.

Jenna was sitting at the kitchen table, staring into a cup of tea. Tess was nowhere to be seen.

"Good morning, Jenna. Have you seen Tess?"

"She went out."

"Have you heard anything from the police?"

"Not a thing."

"Want me to make you some eggs?"

"No thanks. I'm just trying to think how to find Oscar. Food will get in the way of thought."

"In my case, I think it will help."

I busied myself scrambling some eggs. When I sat down to eat them, Jenna looked over at me. "Can I have some, too?"

I got up, grabbed another fork and a second plate and shoveled half of my eggs onto it. "There you go. But I thought eating was going to get in the way of your thinking."

"It would, except I just came up with an idea. Now I need to feed the idea."

"What's the idea?"

"Find the cab that brought him here."

"When he arrived for Christmas Eve dinner?"

"Yes."

"There are thousands of cabs in Paris."

"I bet the police can find it if they want to," she said. "Cab companies in the US keep logs of where passengers are picked up and dropped off, and the police can access them. I bet that in a country as snoopy as this one, they do that here, too."

"You might get some argument about which country is snoopier."

"I suppose. But why don't you call your new friend Captain whatever-her-name-is and make sure she's looking for it."

"Captain Bonpere, you mean. It's a good suggestion. But it's New Year's Day."

"She gave you a card. See if it has her cell number on it. Maybe she'll pick up despite the holiday. After all, she was there last night."

I started searching my pockets for her card, with no luck.

"Try the breast pocket of the shirt you were wearing yesterday. You always stuff things in that pocket."

Back in the day, before I retired, when I was still a big-time civil litigator at my old law firm in Los Angeles, Jenna had been my best-ever associate. We'd tried seven long cases together, and by the end of the first one she knew my work habits almost as well as I did. Thus it wasn't surprising that when I went back to the bedroom to dig the dirty shirt out of the laundry basket, Bonpere's card was right there in the pocket.

I didn't feel like being overheard when I made the call—maybe I'd become sensitive about my French, which was stupid since Jenna didn't speak French. I went back to the bedroom to try to reach Bonpere.

"So what did she say?" Jenna asked when I returned.

"She said, '*Je ne suis pas née de la dernière pluie.*'"

"Which means what?"

"I wasn't born in the last rain."

"Oh. The French version of 'I didn't just fall off the turnip truck'?"

"Yes. They're already looking for the cab number."

The turnip truck idiom was one of our favorite expressions. Jenna and I used it often over the years to respond to people who urged the obvious upon us. Now the cart or the rain or whatever had been turned back on us.

"What else did she say?"

"That they started looking at the cab records last night, but that it's a long task because it's not automated, and there are a lot of cab companies. Plus Oscar might have taken a limo or used Uber, whose records are harder to search, or he could have been dropped off by a friend. She also said that some cab drivers skim fares from the company by not recording every fare and not every company has functioning GPS on their cabs."

"Anything else?"

"Uh-huh. I asked her if they were looking for the bookstore at which Oscar had bought the book. She said no, that even if they identified the store—and it could be anywhere in southern France from what Oscar had said—the owners would probably just deny any knowledge of anything. They'd say Oscar was just a customer like any other who wanted to buy a book. She said the police would instead concentrate on where the money came from to buy the book, since Oscar wasn't rich."

"Did she say anything else?"

"Yes. She said that they are working hard at this, and that if we learn or remember any new facts at all, we should call her, but that we should absolutely not try to investigate this ourselves."

"So are we going to follow her advice?" Jenna asked. Based on our late-night conversation, we both knew the answer without having to speak it out loud.

We got started by trying to catalog what we already knew. We rounded up several pieces of paper. Then Jenna put them on the dining room table and labeled them "Where is Oscar's Hotel?" "Where Did He Get the Book?" and "What Do We Know about Oscar?"

"We don't," she said, "have any information about the hotel or how to find it, so we'll leave that one blank for the moment. We can fill in a little information on the Where Did He Get the Book page, though. He told us he got it in the South of France from a store that had a large collection of old books and was run by a very old guy." She wrote that all down.

"We know a lot more about Oscar," I said.

But in the end, after we'd filled in Oscar's sheet, it turned out all we knew about him was that he'd gone to Southwestern Law School in LA, had briefly been an assistant District Attorney in LA, had practiced criminal law there for more than forty years, and was on wife number six, Pandy. It was not a lot. We didn't even know Pandy's last name and address or the names of any of his earlier wives. All we had was Pandy's cell number.

"So," Jenna said, "Oscar is almost as blank a slate as the location of the hotel and the place where he bought the book."

"Despite the fact that we've known him for quite a few years."

"Yeah. Hey, this is awkward," Jenna continued, "but don't we need to add a sheet for Tess? I mean, she is apparently some kind of cop."

"I asked her about that. She's not a cop, just a once-in-a-while analyst when the government needs her."

"I still think she needs a sheet."

"No, Jenna. I'm not going to put the name of the woman I love on a suspect sheet."

"Okie dokie."

Just then I heard the *snick* of the electronic lock on the front door, and Tess walked in.

"Hi," she said. "I brought some things you will like, I think." She was carrying one of those little white cardboard boxes that you get from neighborhood French bakeries when you buy more than one item. "I found a patisserie open today, even though it is New Year's Day, and I have brought some things to eat." She opened the box and revealed four beautiful fruit tarts. To the side of the box she placed a baguette. We devoured all of it in short order.

"Alors," she said, "have you two solved the mystery while I was out?"

"No," I said. "But we have put together three sheets of paper so that we can organize what we know." I pulled out our three labeled sheets and showed them to her.

"You two are very much lawyers," she said.

"Guilty. But it is a method that works. Gather the facts first."

"Let me see what you have put down."

She looked over the three sheets. "You do not know very much."

"No, Tess, we don't," Jenna said. "Can you add anything to any of them?"

"Like I said last night, I know someone who is a seller of antiquarian books."

"What's his name?" I asked.

"He is Karl Deutsch."

"He's German?"

"I think no. His ancestors, they were perhaps German. He is very French. I know him since we are at the lycée together."

"Okay. I will go see him."

"I've already made an appointment for you to do that. Even though it is New Year's Day, he has agreed to meet with you at eleven this morning."

"Great. Thank you."

"A suggestion, Robert," Tess said.

"Which is?"

"You should buy a book from him while you are there. He will help you more if he thinks you will buy from him again one day. This thing you buy does not need to cost many euros."

I called Captain Bonpere twice more before I left to see Deutsch. On the first call, she again reported that they were "working on it" but had made no big breakthrough. I had expected her to be irritated that I was calling again, but if she was, she hid it well.

On my second call, she asked if I had heard from Pandy, and I told her that despite having phoned her a couple of times after my first call, I had still only gotten her voice mail, and that I'd been unable to find her address on the Internet or learn what last name she was using. Bonpere said I should stop trying to reach her, that they would have the NYPD go find her, but to let Bonpere know immediately if Pandy finally called back. At the very end of that second call, I asked Bonpere the question that should have occurred to me earlier: "Do you think Pandy herself is at risk?"

"This is a distinct possibility, Monsieur."

With that sobering thought in mind, I went off to see Monsieur Deutsch.

CHAPTER 10

Monsieur Deutsch's store was located on a small street near the Odéon Theater. I decided to walk there, which took me through the student quarter, past the old stone edifices of France's great medieval university. I still call it the *Sorbonne*, even though much of it is now called the University of Paris, accompanied by a numbering system so complicated I have been unable to master it. No one seems to mind that I still just call the whole thing the Sorbonne. Or perhaps they are just forgiving of an ignorant American.

After about fifteen minutes, I came to Monsieur Deutsch's shop, which was not a retail storefront, but a small office on the third floor of a nineteenth-century building. It was reached through a gate, which gave way to a shabby courtyard. On the other side, there was an elevator.

I took the elevator to the third floor and rapped on the door using a wooden door knocker carved into the shape of a pointing human hand. It was clearly intended to be a three-dimensional copy of Michelangelo's pointing hand of God on the Sistine Chapel ceiling. The door was opened after a few seconds by a tall, gangly gentleman with a thin face, whose straggly gray hair hung down to the middle of his back, even though he had no hair at all growing from the middle of his freckled scalp forward. He looked to be fifty or so and wore a gray suit, which hung loosely on him, almost as if he had once been much heavier but hadn't found time to have his clothes altered to fit his reduced frame. Beneath, he had on a collared white shirt, but no tie. I could see the initials KD written in cursive script on the cuffs of the shirt.

The office had no windows, just four walls of floor-to-ceiling oak bookcases, each shelf crammed end-to-end with books, most old looking, with beige or white sewn-on cloth covers, plus a few in tooled red or black leather. The only un-booked space in the room was the doorway in which I was standing. Being from Los Angeles, my immediate thought was not to admire the display, but to think that in an earthquake he'd be killed in an avalanche of falling books.

"Bonjour, Monsieur Tarza," he said, apparently oblivious to the danger. *"Bienvenu. Parlez-vous Français?"*

"Oui," I said and then added that although my French was passable, it was not as good as it might be, and I hoped we might switch to English if needed.

He smiled, continuing in French, and said, "For an American, your French is quite good."

I wasn't sure what to make of this damning by faint praise, but I decided to take it as a compliment and barged on in my "quite good" French.

He moved behind his desk, an elaborate piece of furniture that, like Tess's dining room table, had lion's feet, while gesturing to me to sit in one of the two red velour chairs that faced the desk.

"Well," I said, after lowering myself into the chair and noticing that a puff of dust sprang up as I sat down, "my, uh, fiancée, Tess Devrais, suggested you might be able to help me with a problem I have concerning a rare book."

"Yes. She called to ask that I try to be of help, and I would be delighted to do so if I can. What is the name of the book?"

"*Les Misérables.*"

"A first?"

"Yes."

"Those are not so rare. I have several. Are you looking for one in fine condition? I happen to have one on the shelf." He turned, reached up and pulled a volume off the shelf directly behind him.

"Yes, a first in fine condition. But I am focused on a first in English, specifically the one printed in the United States in 1862. And I am not looking for one to buy, I am inquiring on behalf of a friend, who is not so much looking for one, but already has one."

"And wishes to sell it."

"Not exactly but close enough."

He riffled through the pages of the book he had been about to show me, looking at it rather than at me. Eventually, just as his prolonged silence began to be awkward, he stood up, replaced the book on the shelf, turned back toward me and said, "Monsieur, perhaps you should tell me the full story." He sighed. "Whatever it is."

"What makes you think there is a story?"

"In this business there is always a story."

"I would like to do that, but I would need your pledge of total confidentiality."

"I cannot promise you total confidentiality if I am truly to help you. I can only pledge to be cautious with what you tell me, taking into due account the value to you and your friend of the information you entrust to me, while balancing your desire to keep it secret against your need to know things you do not currently know."

In a broad way, he was speaking truth. As a lawyer, I had sometimes taken liberties with confidential information entrusted to me, but in a way that I thought honored the spirit of the original commitment even if it might betray the letter of it.

"Alright," I said. "Here's the story. My friend recently purchased, for a lot of money, a first American edition of *Les Misérables*. It was inscribed by Hugo to Charles Dickens."

"What did this inscription say?"

"Pour Charles Dickens, le plus grand écrivain en langue anglaise depuis Shakespeare."

He raised his eyebrows and said, in English, his voice dripping incredulity, "To the greatest writer in the English language since Shakespeare?"

"Yes. But there's more. There's also a self-portrait of Hugo after his signature."

He steepled his hands in front of his face, pressed them to the tip of his nose and said, returning to French, "A self-portrait? Really? Do you actually believe *cette histoire à dormir debout*?"

Translated literally, he had just asked me if I believed "this story of sleeping while standing up," and it took me a second to grasp that what he'd said must be the French metaphorical equivalent of "a cock-and-bull story."

"I don't know," I muttered.

He slammed his hand down on the desk. "This has gotten out of hand!"

"What has?"

"These forgeries of famous authors' inscriptions. And now the outrage of a supposed self-portrait."

"I don't understand."

"In the last ten years, we have had a plague of forged inscriptions supposedly from famous authors, with gullible people paying tens of thousands of dollars for them. And when that is revealed, it is not good for our business."

"Why has this happened?"

"Because, you see, they are so easy to fake."

"Why so easy?"

"Because the handwriting of these authors is easily available. Before the twentieth century, authors wrote their manuscripts in longhand. Thus a forger can just take a manuscript from the right time period—there are copies in many libraries and even high-quality copies on the Internet—look for each word he wants to put in the forged inscription, carefully copy that word or even trace it, and create something that, at least to a non-expert—or even sometimes to experts—will look real."

"Is it just as easy to fake the self-portrait?"

"Probably easier, especially if it is just a few sketched lines. Is it?"

"Yes."

"There you go," he said. "The fraudsters have been driven to even greater outrages."

"Surely," I said, "there must be a way to test the ink or the paper or something."

"The paper will be real enough." He reached up, removed the first of *Les Misérables* that he had shown me earlier and handed it to me. "Please open it to the title page."

I did as instructed.

"Do you see an inscription?"

"No."

"Well, suppose there is a forger, Monsieur Tarza. All he has to do is buy this first from me—it is only three thousand euros—and then add the fake inscription and sell an inscribed copy of a French-language first of *Les Misérables* for five times that amount, depending on to whom it was supposedly inscribed. The book and the paper will be very genuine. Only the inscription will be fake."

"Are un-inscribed firsts hard to come by?"

"I would guess that there are hundreds of them in France alone."

"Suppose I want to test the ink before I buy it?"

"The seller will object that taking your ink sample will damage the book."

"What about lasers?" I asked.

"What about them?"

"Couldn't I use one in some fashion to test the ink without taking an actual sample of it?"

"Possibly, but a chemist can also use a laser to analyze old ink and figure out how to duplicate it and age it. Plus, it's not hard to find nineteenth-century pens and quills to apply it. Indeed, a laser may have been used to create the very ink you are testing."

"What is a buyer to do then?"

"There are two solutions, Monsieur. The first is to buy only books where the provenance of the inscription is known, and that means a book whose inscription was laid down during the author's lifetime and mentioned at the time in reliable historical sources."

"For example?"

"Mentioned by the author in letters—people back then wrote a lot of letters—or by the recipient."

"What are the other historical sources I could consult?"

"Catalogs of the time. And you are in luck because I just acquired something like that." He got up from behind his desk, walked over to a filing cabinet and pulled out a slim brochure that looked like a magazine. "This is a catalog of anciens livres, put out by a dealer here in Paris in 1890." He opened it to a page in the middle and handed it to me. "Read the third item down."

I picked it out and read it. "It says that the dealer has for sale an 1831 first edition of *Notre-Dame de Paris,* inscribed from Victor Hugo to Sophie Bergeret, a maid in his household." (The catalog listed the novel that is usually translated into English as *The Hunchback of Notre-Dame*).

"Yes," he said. "And here we have a book being sold today that will interest you. Look at the page I have marked with a piece of paper." He opened a side drawer in his desk and handed to me a glossy catalog that was dated only a few months earlier.

I looked. "Someone is selling the same book that was sold in 1890. Or at least it looks that way, since it has the same inscription."

"And so do you see?"

"Not exactly. What are you getting at?"

"The very age of the inscribed book's first sale tends to lend credence to its authenticity. It's a pretty good authenticator."

"Why? It could have been a fraud back then, too."

"Yes, it could have been, but not likely. Because in 1890, Hugo had been dead only five or six years, and the maid herself might still have still been alive—or one of her children. Or if not the maid and her family, a member of Hugo's family, or Hugo household help. So someone at the time could probably have authenticated the inscription. The fact that the book is still around today and is on sale without apparent challenge, more than one hundred years later, says that it's likely real. And that's especially true if the dealer can show us the name of each owner between 1890 and now."

"What if it was real and remains real, but today someone fakes *that* inscription and puts out a new book with that inscription which *is* fake?"

He smiled. "You are clearly a clever man, Monsieur Tarza. Someone could do that, and if the forgery were well done, there might be no way to tell."

Then it occurred to me. "How do you just happen to have on hand a copy of a Hugo inscription in an old book when I pop into your office to ask about a Hugo inscription?"

"When Madame Devrais called to arrange your appointment, she told me you were coming to try to authenticate a Hugo-inscribed book a friend had purchased."

"She did?"

"Yes. And I did a little research before you got here and found I had something relevant in my files."

"I suppose she operates under the same flexible standards of confidentiality that you do."

"I should have mentioned that she had told me some of the details of your visit, but it seemed superior to me to hear the details directly from you since intermediaries sometimes get facts wrong or leave important things out."

Had Tess also told him about the kidnapping? It seemed unlikely that she had gone that far, but I needed to find out.

"Did she say anything else?"

"Only that your French was limited. Although I think from talking with you that it is much less limited than she believes."

He took the catalog back from me, replaced it in the file drawer, and looked at his watch. "Is there more you would like to ask me? I have another appointment only a little time from now."

I did have one broad question, and I asked it. "Do you think it even plausible that Victor Hugo inscribed a copy of *Les Misérables* to Charles Dickens?"

"I would like to tell you that it is. Imagine it!" He put his hands up in the classic French fashion. "The greatest modern French author complimenting the greatest modern English author and even adding a little sketch of himself to make it even more intimate. And whoever owns the book can know that both men held the book and feel somehow associated with each of them when he holds it."

"Is there a 'but' coming?"

"Yes. The rational part of me tells me this is almost certain to be complete and utter nonsense."

"Why?"

"Two reasons. First, I am not an expert on Hugo—I specialize in eighteenth-century French authors, not nineteenth. But I know a little, and I have never read or heard that Hugo spoke English well or at all, so how could he begin to say that Dickens was the greatest writer in English since Shakespeare? Victor Hugo was a serious man. I do not think he would have said such a thing unless he *knew* it to be true."

"And second?"

"Do you know if Dickens and Hugo ever met or corresponded?"

"I have no idea."

"That is the first thing I would try to find out. Because one does not write an inscription such as this one—not to mention the little drawing—to a stranger. And I have never heard that they were intimates. This kind of fact would be well-known."

"I can do the research you suggest, I suppose, and try to learn the answers to those questions. But I prefer to start by talking to people who are experts. Do you know an expert on Hugo and another one on Dickens?"

"Yes." He scribbled a name on a piece of paper and handed it to me. "Here is the man to talk to about Hugo. Henri Moreau. You may tell him I sent you."

"And Dickens?"

"The experts on Dickens are in London and America, not in France, and I am not able to recommend someone." He looked at his watch again.

It was clear I was wearing out my welcome. But I did not want to fail to buy something from him, as Tess had suggested.

"Before I go, I must say that I have become interested in this whole area of collection—I am myself a collector of ancient coins—and I would like to buy something from you to start a collection of my own. It will be my first ancien livre."

"Ah, Monsieur, you are very kind to suggest this. But do not feel compelled to purchase something. And if you are truly interested, I would suggest that we make another appointment and we can discuss what might interest you most to collect. Perhaps, if you will forgive me, you might be interested in collecting English-language books."

I ignored what I took to be a very polite brush-off and another insult to my French language skills, thanked him for his time and his advice and got up to leave. We stood at the door and exchanged the usual French departure pleasantries (*merci, au revoir, à bientôt*—goodbye, thank you, see you soon). Just as I started to walk through the doorway, he put his hand on my shoulder and said, "Oh, there is, come to think of it, something else I did want to ask you."

"What?"

"Do you know from whom your friend purchased the book?"

"No, sorry, I don't. He never mentioned it. Why?"

"Perhaps he would have some things your friend did not buy that I would be interested in."

"Why would you want to buy from someone who has just sold my friend a forged inscription?"

"I am an expert. I could tell the difference between a fake one and genuine one."

That made no sense to me, but I decided not to challenge it.

I was soon back out on the street and realized I had failed to ask him what the book might be worth on the off chance the inscription and the drawing were real.

CHAPTER 11

Just as I was considering whether it would be too rude to go and knock on Monsieur Deutsch's door again in order to query him about the possible value of the book, my cell rang with Jenna's special ring. I had chosen the overture to the opera *William Tell* for her. I thumbed "answer."

"Hey, listen, Robert, I need to check out of the George V before one o'clock or I will get charged for a late checkout or an extra day. I've booked a smaller, cheaper hotel in the Marais. Do you want to meet me near there for lunch? I can give you the address."

The Marais was the old Jewish quarter of Paris, now among the hottest of hot places to live, especially for the young and trendy. Jenna would fit right in.

"Jenna, I'd actually like to see you sooner. This thing is getting ever-more complicated. Why don't I just meet you in the lobby of the George V, and we can go over to your new hotel together and get started on the conversation without any delay?"

"Okay. I'm on my way there now."

"See you shortly."

I grabbed a cab, and told the cabbie to take me to the George V. I could tell that he was impressed. Or maybe I just felt like he ought to be impressed. The George V, which dates from 1928, is one of Paris's swankiest and most expensive hotels. At Christmastime its rack rate is more than a thousand dollars a night for a starter room. Located in the 8th arrondissement, the hotel is only a few blocks from the glittering Champs-Élysées, close to the Arc de Triomphe and within a short walk of the elegant presidential residence, the Élysée Palace, the interior of which makes the White House look like someone's country home.

When I got to the hotel, Jenna was already in the marbled lobby, sitting in a posh red velour chair, right next to a bouquet of bright-red flowers set in a three-foot-tall black onyx vase that looked like it had come directly from Versailles. She was wearing a bright green dress, a black beret, and three-inch patent-leather heels.

"Well," I said, "don't you look *soignée*?"

"I know that's an English word, too, but I can't recall exactly what it means."

"It's kind of a combination of neat, cool and well-dressed. It's a compliment."

"Well thanks, then. Do you want to see my room before I check out?"

"I'd love to. They've redone it since the last time I stayed here, so I'd be curious."

As we passed the reception desk, the man behind the counter said, in English, "Ah, Madame James, there is a delivery for you. One moment, please."

"Are you expecting anything?" I asked.

"No."

The desk clerk handed her a package about the size and shape of a large Kleenex box, wrapped in Christmassy paper and tied with a red ribbon. A white card was stuck under it. On the elevator, I began to brief her on what Deutsch had told me. Once inside the room, I looked around while Jenna worked the gift card open. The decor was all understated elegance: arm chairs upholstered in subtle floral fabric, an armoire, bureau and desk in inlaid rosewood, and a waist-height round glass table with a spray of flowers in a glass vase in the middle. Jenna had clearly not chosen the hotel's most modest room.

"The card's not signed," she said.

"Well, what does it say?"

"It says, 'Hope you enjoy this Christmas present, honey. Sorry it's a bit late.'"

"Do you know anyone who calls you honey?"

"My boyfriend back in the States."

"Dr. Nightingale?"

"The very one, although I usually call him Bill."

"Are you going to open it?"

"Sure, although it's kind of odd, since he gave me a Christmas present before I left." She unwrapped it, revealing a small wooden box in dark wood with a hinged lid, much like a cigar box. She opened it, looked inside and screamed.

I had never heard Jenna scream before. I rushed over, pulled her aside and looked in myself. It was, quite clearly, a human finger, severed at the base with two knuckles showing. The bottom was still bloody, although the blood was old enough that it was brown, not red. Most sickening, the finger was torn, with pieces of skin, blood vessels and bone poking out, as if it had been ripped off rather than cleanly cut away. There was dry ice underneath the whole thing, giving off a spray of cold fog.

"Oh my God," Jenna said. "I think I'm going to throw up."

"There's a note taped to the inside bottom of the lid."

"What does it say? I'm not looking in there again."

"It says: 'We know you have book. If do not want more pieces Oscar to arrive in bigger box, text us at this number and tell you will give us book. We will send instructions how deliver.'"

There was a phone number scrawled at the end of the note.

"Could be someone who speaks Russian as their native language," I said. Then added, "Or like someone trying to sound like someone who speaks Russian. But then again, could be some other language where they drop the article before the noun." My analytical comment was, of course, an attempt to distract myself from what I'd just seen and my revulsion and fear—revulsion at the sight of it and growing fear for Oscar's safety. I felt almost as if I were trembling inside.

Jenna wasn't listening anymore, though, and she was visibly trembling. I went over and put my arm around her shoulder. "It's okay, Jenna. We'll get the police. Calm down."

"They think I have the book, Robert. Why the hell do they think that? I don't have the damn book!"

"I know, I know. And I don't know why they think so. Do you have any idea?"

"No."

"I'm calling hotel security. That's a better bet than the police, I think."

The phone was answered on the third ring, by a male who identified himself as "Bruno."

"Hi," I said in French. "I'm in Madame James's room with Madame James. A mysterious package just arrived for her and it appears to contain a human finger." I listened for a moment. "A joke? I don't think so. Please send security up here right away."

Not two minutes later, two men, both beefy beneath elegant suits, entered the room and scanned it. One was tall, the other short.

The tall one pulled out his wallet, flashed a George V ID card at us, and said, in English, "I'm Bruno Bourdal, hotel security. My colleague is Monsieur Fronert. Are you the only two people here?"

"Yes."

"Please show us the finger."

As he spoke he continued to scan the room. I wondered if he thought there might be someone under the bed. It was the only place in the room someone could possibly hide, and even then, they'd need to be thinner than a runway model.

I pointed to the table. "It's in that box over there."

Both of them went over and peered inside. "Could be a prosthetic," Bruno said. "Like in the movies."

His partner bent over, put his nose inside the box, sniffed and said. *Pas d'odeur de pourriture.*

"What did he say?" Jenna asked.

"He said 'No smell of decay,'" I answered. Then I addressed Bruno. "Madame does not speak French. Can you and your partner speak in English?"

"I can, but my partner, not so well. Like you speak French, if you will pardon me. But I think what he is trying to say is that, normally, for something like this, if it is real, there would be a smell, even from something so small. So my guess is that it is a clever prosthetic and this is some kind of sick joke."

"I see," I said.

"What does this note about the book mean, Monsieur?"

In a millisecond, I decided to lie. "I don't know," I said.

"If you do not think this is a joke, you should take this to the police."

Jenna spoke up. "Shouldn't the police come here? This is the crime scene."

Bruno looked horror struck. "Oh, no, no, no, Madame. The hotel, it does not wish the police to come here when no crime has been committed here."

"Well, the box was delivered to me here."

"It was left at the front desk?"

"Yes."

"So really, it has nothing to do with our hotel except that you had the misfortune to receive this joke here and to open it here."

"That's not the way crime scenes work."

"Ah, in America, perhaps. But here in France, this is not a crime scene. I was a police officer for many years and I know."

Jenna's mouth twisted in a way that I knew, from our many years of practice together, meant that she thought what he had told her was bullshit.

"If you say so, Bruno," she said.

"Madame, we will take you directly to the police if you wish. And I will carry the box."

I saw by her body language that Jenna was about to reject the offer, and I intervened. "We will be delighted to do that."

Jenna gave me a dirty look.

I ignored her because it had occurred to me that if the police came to the hotel, the whole thing was much more likely to become a matter of interest to the press. And we were trying to avoid that.

"Please wait here," Bruno said. "I will call for a car." He withdrew a pair of blue plastic surgical gloves from his suit coat pocket, skinned them on, picked up the box and exited the room. Fronert remained, standing discreetly in a corner.

"How do we know that we are not about to be kidnapped ourselves by these guys?" Jenna asked in a low voice.

"We don't, but we're going to risk it."

Ten minutes later, we were in the back seat of a black Mercedes, with Bruno and the box in the front seat. Fronert was driving.

"Which police station are you taking us to?" I asked.

"The one in the 8th arrondissement, on the rue Clémenceau."

"We insist on being taken instead to 36 quai des Orfèvres."

"Ah, non, Monsieur. This is not the right place to go. It is the headquarters. We need to go to the local police station."

"Please raise the privacy shield and give me a minute."

I watched as the glass slid up and dialed Captain Bonpere. Luckily, she answered. I described the situation to her for a moment, then rapped on the glass partition. It was lowered immediately, and I handed the phone to Bruno.

"Someone would like to have a word with you."

He listened for a moment, said something about a box that I could not make out, handed the phone back to me and said to Fronert, *"Emmenez-nous au 36 quai des Orfèvres."*

As the car moved slowly down the hotel driveway, he turned around, handed the phone back to me, stared at us for a moment and said, "Who *are* you people?"

I saw Jenna flip her right hand over, one step away from serving up her finger. I put a restraining hand on hers, and we sped off down the street.

CHAPTER 12

The car sped through the streets at break-neck speed, and we pulled up in front of 36 quai des Orfèvres in what seemed like no time, coming to such an abrupt halt that I was thrown forward against my seat belt. If I hadn't known that Jenna was an honored guest of their hotel, I would have thought that these guys were anxious to be rid of us.

The last time we'd been to the quai, it had been in a paddy wagon, which had taken us down a ramp into a garage. This time we were being delivered to the main entrance, which featured a set of tall, wooden double doors recessed into an arched stone doorway, a cop posted on each side. To the right was a glassed-in guard shack not much bigger than a phone booth. A small French flag fluttered overhead.

I tried to open my door, but it wouldn't budge. "It's stuck."

"Child lock," Bruno said. "Fronert will unlock it."

I wondered if they had been worried we might escape, return to the George V and bring the police to their treasured hotel that knew no crime.

Jenna was already rounding the back of the car, heading for the entrance, when Captain Bonpere emerged from the stone doorway. She, too, was wearing blue vinyl gloves. She took the box from Bruno, looked briefly inside, wrinkled her nose and handed it off to the plainclothes officer who had accompanied her. Just then the cop from the night before, whom I'd come to think of as Officer Omaha, emerged from the same doorway and led Bruno and Fronert away. We then followed Bonpere to a conference room on the second floor.

The conference room had a polished wood table and six swivel chairs. There was nice art on the walls and fruit juices and coffee on a sideboard. It was a cut well above the office in which Bonpere had met us on New Year's Eve.

"I will speak English today," Bonpere said. "I hope you will pardon mistakes I make."

"Of course," I said. "And in any case, your English seems quite good."

"I want to interview both of you about what happened today. Please do not leave something out. I have arranged for our conversation to be recorded. In the ceiling, there is a microphone." She pointed up.

Jenna did most of the talking. I interrupted occasionally with a correction or an addition. When we were done, Bonpere asked a few questions, and I assumed we were finished. Instead, she turned to me and said, "Have you learned anything else in these last two days about this whole *histoire*—sorry, I mean this whole story—that you will wish to share with me?"

I noticed that she hadn't said we *had* to tell her. She had asked me what I wished to share. On one level, I didn't really wish to share anything, but decided that if we were to save Oscar, we needed to share what we'd learned in our own investigation with the police. They had so many more resources than we did. I knew I kept flip-flopping about how I felt about them.

So I told her about my visit to the bookshop. She nodded from time to time but otherwise seemed uninterested. Finally, when I was done, she said, "We know Monsieur Deutsch."

"You do?"

"Yes, he consults with us on special projects."

"I see." And I did see. Deutsch was a police spy, apparently, and his whole elegant speech that morning about confidentiality had been a cover for the simple fact that he intended to report our entire conversation to the cops. I was about to ask Bonpere if Deutsch had already related it to her when, after a perfunctory knock, the door opened, and a woman's head peeked around the edge.

"Capitaine, puis-je vous parler en privé?"

"Please speak English, Claudette. One of our friends does not speak French, and there is no need for privacy before them. And please come in."

The woman, who was middle-aged with graying black hair, stepped fully into the room. She was wearing a white lab coat and carrying a small briefcase.

"What did you find out?" Bonpere asked.

"It is a real human finger."

Jenna jerked back in surprise. "How do you know?" she asked.

"When I picked it up I squeezed it to sense its—I'm sorry, I do not know the word in English . . ."

"Consistency," I suggested.

"Yes. Its consistency. And a very little blood dripped out. Fake fingers do not have some blood in them."

"Blood?" Jenna asked. "Hadn't it dried?"

"Well, okay, not really blood, but a red ooze."

"That's disgusting," Jenna said. "It almost makes me sick."

It wasn't "almost" for me. I jumped up, raced over to a metal wastebasket in the corner, leaned into it and vomited. After about a minute, I stood back up. "I'm sorry. The image of you squeezing ooze out of it just got to me somehow."

"It happens to every person at some point," Claudette said. She picked up a glass, filled it with juice and handed to me. "Try this. It will take away the bad taste."

"Thank you," I said, and sipped at the juice. I noticed Jenna staring at me, no doubt remembering the time I threw up on the cops when they were threatening me with the death penalty. Finally, I recovered my aplomb and managed to ask, "Madame, did you find out anything else?"

"Yes. Following this I took a little of the tissue—skin and of blood—and studied them beneath a microscope. They have some cells." She looked first at me and then at Jenna. "Even the movies with the grand budgets do not have these prosthetics with cells. There is no reason to do this." I guess someone had told her we were from Los Angeles and thus experts on special effects or something.

"Are you going to do more?" Bonpere asked.

"Yes, we have sent the finger to a special lab, and they will say if I am right. And they will also say, if they can, when this happened. And here at our lab we will now match this finger to an international fingerprint database." She paused. "Now I must ask a question." She looked back and forth between me and Jenna. "Did either of you touch the box?"

"Yes, we both did," I said.

"I did, too," Bonpere said. "And so did the gentleman from the hotel, Bruno Bourdal. But I wore gloves, and Monsieur Bourdal informed me that he did, too."

"I will need to fingerprint Monsieur Tarza and Madame James so we can rule them out when we dust the box for prints. We already have your prints, Capitaine, and I have already taken prints from Monsieur Bourdal." She smiled. "Just in case either you or the monsieur somehow touched the box without gloves on."

She opened her briefcase and rummaged in it. I expected her to take out an ink pad. Instead, she removed a small metal box with a glass top. She wiped each of our hands with what smelled like hand lotion, asked me to put my hand on the glass plate and clicked a button that made the box light up for a few seconds. She proceeded to take a whole-hand print, left and right, from each of us.

"Why did you put lotion on our hands?" I asked.

"This machine works better if your skin is not dried out."

"Oh."

Finished with printing us, Claudette headed for the door.

"Thank you, Claudette," Bonpere said, and we saw no more of Claudette.

I assumed we were done and started to push my chair back, when the door opened again and in walked General Follet.

What the hell is he doing here? I wondered. Jenna must have had the same thought, because I heard her suck in her breath.

"Good evening, Capitaine," the general said. "And good evening to you, Madame James and Monsieur Tarza. It is a pleasure to see you again."

I stood up and offered him my hand. "Good evening, General, it's nice to see you again, too. But I thought you had retired."

"Yes, I am retired from the army, but I still do special assignments for the Brigade Criminelle de Paris."

"You were a general, but now you work with the police?"

"Ah, Monsieur, in this country, the police are part of the military, just with special duties. That is why people like Captain Bonpere have military ranks. Why she is no longer called by the old title of *Inspecteur*. And the group I work with is not just the police, it is an elite unit of the police."

"Still, this is very unusual, a retired general working with the police." My mind was at work trying putting it all together. Finally, I said, "So, General, if it is not secret, what kind of special assignments do you do?"

"I cannot reveal all of that to you, but many involve terrorism and, in particular, its frequent funding source—money laundering."

"Does that mean you guys are still pursuing the crazy theory that Oscar was involved in money laundering?"

"Yes. And it is not a crazy theory. I can explain it to you if you like."

Captain Bonpere, who had been sitting quietly through the entire exchange, spoke up. "I have already explained this to them, mon général."

"Yes," I said. "You did, and we get it. But if this kidnapping is all about money laundering, how do you explain that the kidnappers just cut off Oscar's finger and sent it to Jenna with a note demanding she give them the book?"

General Follet looked momentarily perplexed. "I did not know this."

"Excuse me, Madame et Messieurs," Bonpere said, "we do not yet know if it is truly Oscar's finger that was cut. And if I must guess, it is not."

"You know," Jenna said, "this is all very informative, but I need to go and check out of my hotel. I am already past the deadline, and they're soon going to charge me for an extra day."

The general looked startled. "You are not going back to America, I hope?"

"No, just moving to a cheaper place. I was originally going to go home to Los Angeles this evening, but now it's clear I need to stick around."

"Good, good. I was worried that you might leave in the middle of our investigation. But you do not need to seek out a hotel. My late wife owned a lovely furnished apartment that I rent out. And as it happens, now that the Christmas season is over, it is empty for the next month. You could stay there without paying. And it will be easier to, uh, protect you there."

"Why do I need to be protected?"

"The kidnappers think you have the book, obviously."

"Alright, thank you for the offer. I accept."

"Good. My driver can take us there in my car, and on the way we will stop at your hotel and I will make sure they do not charge you extra. We will also cancel your reservation at your new hotel, and we will be sure they do not charge you."

It was clear the meeting was over. We all stood up, and except for Jenna, participated in the usual post-meeting French goodbye pleasantries. But we dropped the expected à bientôt. No one says "see you soon" to the police, and especially not me. Jenna just said, "Later." No one attempted to give anyone a kiss on the cheek.

Not long after, we found ourselves ensconced in the back seat of the general's black Citroën, complete with uniformed driver. Between the siren and the three-star flag waving on the bumper, the traffic seemed to melt away. When we arrived at the George V, we were met not only by Bruno and the hotel's general manager, but by the hotel's chief of protocol. Who knew hotels even had such things?

The bill proved not to be a problem—there were no extra charges for the late checkout—and we were soon on our way to the general's wife's apartment, which was not far from the

Panthéon, the domed, neo-classical monument on a hill in which France buries many of its cultural and political heroes and, on occasion, military ones as well. Victor Hugo is buried there.

On arrival at the general's wife's building, I was pleased to see that there was no concierge. The apartment itself, which was on a high floor, was large and beautiful. It was furnished in a comfortable contemporary style—no lions' feet on anything—with a gorgeous view over the rooftops of a major science campus of the Sorbonne. The apartment even had a small balcony with a table and chairs. The kitchen, too, was well done, spacious and modern, with every appliance you could ever want, including an espresso machine.

After we had toured the place, and the general was preparing to leave, Jenna turned to him, and said, "Thank you so much for this place, General. It's gorgeous. So much better than a hotel. I can't thank you enough."

"You are most welcome," he said. "And should you wish to reach me, there is a landline phone on the table in the kitchen. If you dial '72,' it will reach me. We used to live here, and the phone still knows me. Also, I will give each of you a card. It has my cell number on it and a code word. If someone else answers, they will know, if you have the code, that you are an authorized caller."

"Thank you," Jenna said. "Can I ask a favor of you?"

"Of course. What is it?"

"Will you take the espresso machine with you? I'm a coffee addict and I'm trying hard to break the habit. That devil machine will be too much of a temptation."

"Of course. I will have someone take it away."

After the general's driver had collected the machine, the usual polite French goodbyes were said, this time with full-bore cheek kissing. When I pressed my face close to the general's, I said, "I will walk out with you."

Which I did, saying to Jenna that I'd be right back.

Once we were in the building's lobby, I said, "Why will Jenna be safer here? There's no guard, not even a concierge, and although a mugger would need the keypad number to get in the front door, I don't imagine it's hard to get in without it." And as I said it, I thought to myself how surprising it was for me to *want* a concierge.

"You are right to be concerned, Robert. However, I have assigned a team of agents to keep watch over the building and Jenna while she is here. They will be discreet—you should not be able to detect them—but they will be here if needed. Trust me."

"I do, General. But let me ask one more thing."

"Yes?"

"What are you doing to find Oscar?"

"We are doing a lot. Why don't you and Jenna meet me for breakfast tomorrow, and I will brief you? There is a café around the corner called Le Café Grand Pain. I will see you there at eight o'clock. You may bring Tess if you wish."

"Sounds good. But wouldn't it be better to meet somewhere more private?"

"No. In fact, if someone ends up observing us, my security people will be able to follow them and it will be a plus."

"What if instead of observing us, General, they kill us?"

"This is not that kind of matter."

I sighed and said, "Okay, if you say so."

"Robert, now that you have asked me your one more thing— two things, actually—I have something else to ask of you."

"What?"

"Please stop trying to find Oscar yourself. It is dangerous."

"Shouldn't we at least respond to the message in the box? We can just text back."

"The message was addressed to Jenna, so under French law she can respond if she wishes. But we strongly advise you not to respond at all."

"Why?" I asked.

"We have dealt with many kidnappings, and although there are those in which you might wish to negotiate, this is one where we feel to negotiate is to assure the death of the victim."

"Why?"

"Because everything about this seems amateurish. And amateurs get nervous and kill."

Something seemed wrong with that logic, and I said so. "General, not too long ago, you were telling us this looked like a staged kidnapping by professional money-launderers. Now you say it's amateurish. Which is it?"

"With the arrival of the ransom notes and the severed finger—whether it belongs to Oscar or not—we have changed our views."

"You think it's a real kidnapping done by amateurs?"

"No, we think it may be a staged kidnapping by amateurs that is now somehow spinning out of control, and one in which Oscar is no longer fully in on it and is suddenly at risk."

I decided to let the contradictions in that go for the moment and said, "And if Jenna doesn't respond to the note, what will you do instead?"

"We will find him and rescue him."

Or, I thought to myself, you will kill him in the effort.

I went back into the apartment, made sure that Jenna was okay, and then headed home.

CHAPTER 13

The next morning, Jenna and I were at Le Café Grand Pain early. I had invited Tess to join us, but she had declined, saying she had other things to do. The café was typical—there was a rather cavernous and somewhat gloomy interior with a bar at which no one was sitting and tables at which there were no patrons. With the weather considerably warmed up, the place to be was out front.

Lined up on the sidewalk on bentwood chairs facing outward, dozens of people sat at small marble-topped tables, sipping their morning espresso in white demitasse cups and munching on buttery croissants while brushing the inevitable crumbs off their laps. In my five years in Paris, I had yet to meet anyone who could emerge crumb-less from an encounter with a croissant.

The appointed time, eight o'clock, came and went, with no sign of the general. After a while we decided not to wait for him. I ordered an espresso; Jenna ordered an herbal tea (causing the waiter to give her an odd look since the French don't much like tea, and especially not in the morning).

While we waited, we watched the parade of people walking by, which is, after all, the great joy of a Parisian café—university students on their way to class, rucksacks on their backs, dressed-to-the-nines; twenty- and thirtysomethings heading off to work; and mothers escorting their small children to school. The only difference between those kids and little kids back home was that the backpacks slung over their tiny French shoulders sported French corporate logos. But America is everywhere, so we also saw several branded with Minnie, Mickey and other assorted Disney mice, plus at least one Angry Birds lunch box.

The general finally arrived, pulled up a chair and joined us at our table.

"Bonjour, Jenna, bonjour, Robert," he said. "Sorry to be late." It was the most perfunctory apology I'd heard in a long time.

"Well," he continued, "I assume no one has bothered you since we last met." He looked directly at Jenna.

"I've been fine," she said.

"Me too," I added. "I went back to Tess's last night and all seemed as before."

A waiter came up, and the general ordered an almond croissant and a café Americano, the latter being an espresso with enough hot water added to it to fill up an American-style coffee cup. Americanos, though, bear little resemblance to a real American cup of coffee. I had long ago concluded that if you want a good, plain cup of American coffee in Paris, you should go directly to McDonald's. There are more than fifty of them in Paris.

Jenna and I were anxious, of course, to hear what the police had found out. Had we been in America, I would have cut right to the chase and asked. But the French have a different ethic about food. I had come to think of it as the "half-croissant rule." You don't bring up business until half the croissant is gone. Unfortunately, the general was a slow eater. Finally, half his croissant was gone, and it seemed to me okay to talk business.

"General, Jenna and I are most eager to hear what's happening with the search for Oscar. You said last night that you'd made a good deal of progress and would give us a report."

"Yes, I did."

"And so?"

He looked around to see if anyone was close enough to overhear. Apparently satisfied with the security of our location, he said, very quietly, "The first thing we have discovered, working with our American colleagues at the Federal Reserve Bank of New York, is that Oscar withdrew a hundred thousand US dollars in cash from his bank account in New York several days before he came to France."

"If he brought that to France," I said, "wouldn't he have had to declare on the customs form that he was carrying such as large amount of cash?"

"Yes, and he did declare it."

Jenna spoke up. "Didn't French customs interview him as to what he was going to do with it?"

"Yes, Madame, they did."

"Well, what did he say?"

"He said that he was intending to buy some antiques and that he tended to get a better price if he paid in cash."

"But it was in dollars."

"Yes, but some people here are happy to get dollars, particularly those in the business of money laundering. Dollars are still more widely used there than euros. Drug dealers in particular savor dollars."

"You're not suggesting he was a drug dealer?"

"It's one possibility, among others, that we've been exploring." He stopped talking, looked around, including behind him, and said, "Perhaps this would be a good time to return to the apartment to continue our discussion."

"What's wrong with here?"

"If you look at the café directly across the street, you will see a gentleman in a tweed jacket. He has been staring directly at our table since I got here. I'm going to have a man from my security detail check him out and follow him if he leaves, but I'd prefer to be elsewhere when that occurs."

It occurred to me that the guy might have been staring at our table because his table was directly opposite ours. But I let it go. We paid the bill and left. As we walked back to the apartment, I looked to see if I could detect the general's security detail. Unless they were secreted among the backpack-toting grade-schoolers, they were invisible.

Once in the apartment, we continued discussing the police investigation. Jenna was anxious to find out more about the finger.

"General, have you been able to match the finger?"

"No. The preliminary genetic test tells us it's a finger from a man. And an anatomist has told us it is a right-hand ring finger. We also had a dermatologist inspect it, and she confirmed that the skin is consistent with the skin of a man in his fifties or sixties who hasn't had a lot of sun exposure. So what we've got is that the finger came from a male of about Oscar's age. And it's a ring finger from the right hand. That's it."

"Maybe," Jenna said, "we could try again to find Pandy. She might have pictures of Oscar's hands or be able to identify his finger from a photo."

"Oh, we already located her and interviewed her. I'm sorry. I should have told you. The NYPD is amazing when you want to find someone."

I felt my face getting red. "Shit!" I said. "Don't you think you could have let us know as soon as you found her?" They'd let me go on desperately calling her. It was embarrassing.

"There's no need to use profanity, Robert."

"That word's not actually profane, General. It's scatological, but profanity wouldn't be uncalled for."

"Well whatever, I *am* sorry. It was an oversight. My apologies."

"Apologies don't really help all that much. But let's move on. Did Pandy say why she hasn't returned my many phone messages? I've been calling her twice a day. It kind of pisses me off that she was happy to talk to the NYPD and you but not to me."

"She said her mother has been very ill, and she's been visiting her in Alabama, so she hasn't been checking messages. She just got back to New York last night."

"Well, what did she say about the finger?" I asked.

"We sent her several photos of it, but she wasn't sure it was his. She said if it had been a left ring finger, she would have been able to tell because it would have a white mark where his wedding ring is. She looked but couldn't find any photos that showed his hands."

"What about DNA?"

"She doesn't seem to have anything likely to have DNA on it. She said Oscar took his toothbrush and his comb and hairbrush with him, and she washed all his dirty clothes and all of their sheets after he left."

"Why don't you send an expert to their apartment in New York to look for his DNA?" Jenna asked. "It's got to be on *something* there."

For the first time, the general looked uncomfortable. "We do not have an unlimited budget. We have instead asked the NYPD to have one of their people swab the apartment for DNA, but they are backlogged with very important things, so it will take a while."

I could tell that there was a head of steam building beneath Jenna's skull, and it was only a question of when it might blow through. "Isn't *this* important, General? After all, a man has been kidnapped off the street!"

"Frankly, Jenna, it's only of medium importance. There are kidnappings in France every year, to be sure, but there are also other major crimes that must be investigated. This kidnapping would be of higher importance if we could link it to a large money laundering operation or terrorism."

"But you can't."

"We're trying. One hundred thousand dollars in cash doesn't disappear without a trace. We are looking for that money."

"But you're not looking so hard for Oscar."

"We believe that when we find where that money went, we will quickly be able to find Oscar."

There was a small silence in the room as Jenna and I came to understand that what we regarded as top priority, the general and his team regarded as something lesser.

I broke the silence and said, "Don't you even care that a man's finger has been cut off? Even if he weren't my friend, I'd think it ought to be a matter of a lot higher priority. I'm worried he's going to be killed while you guys screw around with this."

"It is a high priority, and of course we care. But whoever it was whose finger was cut off, it's already off. It is the fact that they sent a finger that's important, not finding out if this finger is really Oscar's. But I agree that either way, it is a tactic of barbarians. Who are probably not French."

"Is there anything else you can tell us?" I asked.

"Not very much. We have still not found the car in which he was driven away."

"You still refuse to use the word 'kidnapped,' don't you?"

"Yes, based on what we know, whatever it is now, this was not likely a kidnapping when it started."

"Then why did whoever *drove him away* send the finger and the note?"

"It is no doubt some falling out among thieves. But in a long career, I have never heard of a kidnapper asking for a book to pay a ransom. Money can be spent anywhere. The book will be useless to them because we will eventually publicize this."

"Maybe someone just really wants the book," Jenna said. "A collector, for example."

"Maybe."

I could tell that we were starting to waste our time. I stood up and said, "Thank you, General, for coming by to brief us."

"You are welcome."

But Jenna wasn't ready to let it drop. "There's gotta be some way, General, for us to find him without figuring out first where the money went," she said.

"Jenna, I will tell you what I told Robert. Do not try to find him yourself. It is very dangerous."

Jenna said nothing in response.

Finally, we all said *au revoir* and the general left. I noticed that he didn't use any form of "see you later." All he said was *"bonne journée."* Have a good day. Maybe he had just blown us off.

I looked at Jenna. "He's probably right that what we're doing is dangerous."

"So what? Wouldn't Oscar come look for us, danger or no danger? Can you imagine him giving up? I can't."

"No, I can't, and I'm not backing out. But Oscar would be the first one to say that if we get killed in the process, it won't do him a bit of good."

"Robert, the longer he's missing, the more likely it is that he's going to be found dead. We need to continue looking for him, just like we've been doing."

"I want to find him as badly as you do. But we need a better plan, so let's get to making one instead of arguing about who cares the most, okay?"

I thought to myself, as I said it, that Jenna and I had had this problem during all the years we practiced law together back in LA. She was always the jackrabbit, racing ahead, and I was usually the tortoise, equally committed but slower and more cautious. Usually, the combination worked out well. I hoped it would here, too.

CHAPTER 14

After an hour's intense discussion, we had failed to come up with a plan that was much more developed than our original plan to find either Oscar's hotel or where he bought the book. We simply added to it a third idea: find the book itself, which we assumed must be somewhere in Paris. The only problem was that, despite the urgency and our growing anxiety about Oscar's fate, we had no idea how to do any of it.

"You know, we are ignoring the most obvious strategy," Jenna said.

"Which is?"

"We should respond to the note in the box by texting that number and telling them that we don't have the book, but if they give us some hints about where to look we'll help them find it."

"That makes no sense at all, Jenna. If we do that they'll just pressure Oscar more to give them those hints."

"They're already pressuring him. They cut off his finger."

"If it is really his finger."

"Listen, I'm not pulling this strategy out of my butt. I went on the Net last night and read up on how to negotiate with kidnappers. And it said that the most important thing to do is to start talking to them, even if you can't give them what they want, or at least can't give it to them right away."

"What do you mean by 'it said'?"

"I mean that most of the articles I found say that that's the thing to do."

"But there are other articles that say it's the wrong thing to do, isn't that correct?"

"Yeah."

"What do those other articles think the right approach is?"

"They say not responding is the best strategy because most kidnappers have decided in advance whether to kill the person or let him go. And that it has nothing to do with what you say or whether they get the ransom."

"Well, if you don't speak to them, don't you just speed up the killing of their victim?"

"The theory goes that if the kidnappers were going to let their victim go, they let them go sooner when they see that they're not going to get the ransom they want. And if the kidnappers were going to kill the victim no matter what, they'll just do it sooner, so it'll all be gotten over with, with minimum bother to the victim and to you."

"Jenna, candidly, that seems to me like the kind of heartless, logical approach the old Jenna would've preferred."

"In a way it still is, but there are other considerations."

"Such as?"

"If you don't talk to the kidnappers, and they end up killing the victim, you'll never know if they wouldn't have done it if you *had* talked to them. And the result is you will never forgive yourself."

"So you want to talk to them."

"Yes."

I thought about it for a few seconds. The whole thing about not talking to the kidnappers seemed like the kind of high-flown strategy that a government would employ. If the strategy killed someone, there was always a next time to try to make it work. We were just two people with one close friend we wanted to save. There wouldn't be a next time. Back in the day, when I had to deal all the time with people on the other side of my litigations—some of whom were impossible jerks or worse—it almost always made things better to just call them up.

"Let's do it," I said.

We then spent half an hour trying to come up with the perfect text to send the kidnappers. In the end, we crafted something on the theory, as the old Shaker hymn puts it, "tis the gift to be simple":

We don't have the book.

We don't know where it is.

Help us find it for you.

As I drafted it, I wondered why Oscar just didn't tell them himself where the book was so he could be released. In a sense, he held his own ransom in his hands. Now the answer to that question was a puzzle. Was the book and its sale his retirement? Even if it were, would that be worth his life? I didn't really know anything about his finances or his psychological state, so it was at least possible. Another explanation was that Oscar himself didn't know where the book was.

We sent it off and waited. Perhaps an hour went by. I read a book. Jenna folded sheets of paper into smaller and smaller halves, as small as she could manage, and tossed each one into the wastepaper basket. Jenna is a poster child for OCD.

The phone rang with a large jangle. We both jumped.

"It's them!" Jenna said, and ran to grab it. She picked it up, listened for a second and said, "It's the general. He wants me to put him on the speakerphone."

She did, and the general's voice came through loud and clear. "I see you're not going to follow my advice."

"What are you talking about?" I said.

"I'm talking about your sending a text message to the people who drove Oscar away. I thought I told you not to do that."

"No, you *advised* us not to do it. But since you guys are apparently putting this on the back burner, we're going to find him ourselves."

"We are not putting it on a burner in the back. Our burner is very hot. It is just on a different part of the stove."

I decided I wasn't going to get into the geography of burners. "How did you even find out we sent a message?"

"We've been monitoring that cell number ever since you gave us that note."

"So you read what we wrote in our text?"

"In a word, yes."

"An invasion of our privacy."

"Permitted in this circumstance, without question. If you don't want us to read your texts to the kidnappers, stop sending them."

"We won't."

"Well then, do keep us posted," he said, in a rather clipped tone.

"So you're not angry at us?"

"Angry? Why should I be angry? He is your friend, and if you want to do something stupid in order to try to find him, I can only hope you will not find him dead. Or get yourselves killed, too."

I started to say something but realized he was no longer there.

"So, I guess they're not very happy with us," Jenna said.

"Apparently not. But what he said doesn't make sense. If the general's strategy is to avoid contact with the kidnappers because they've already decided what they're going to do anyway—kill Oscar or let him go—and we can't change their minds, why would communicating with them make any difference?"

"All I said, Robert, was that that was one theory discussed on the Internet. We really don't know why these French cops don't want us to communicate. They never said. But I've got a feeling that something else is going on here besides a disagreement over negotiating theory."

"You could be right, Jenna. If you are, we need to think about next steps."

"Any ideas? I mean, we haven't thought of any way to find either his hotel or the book."

I actually slapped my forehead with the palm of my hand. "God, there's something we haven't thought about and it's so obvious."

"What?"

"Oscar is a US citizen. We can ask the US embassy to help us find him. And they probably have access to great technology to trace text messages and where they're coming from. And unlike the French, they'll actually care about him."

No sooner had I said it than Jenna was on her laptop searching the US embassy site. After a few minutes she said, "There's good news and there's bad news."

"Do you want to tell me even though this place may be bugged, Jenna?"

"I don't think I care if they hear this."

"Okay, hit me with the good news first."

"There's an entire page on their website called 'US Citizens Missing Abroad.' And it says that they can check places like hospitals and prisons and will also check with local authorities."

"What's the bad news?"

"There's something called the Privacy Act. Because of that, they may not be able to share what they learn with us. But there's a loophole. It goes on to say that exceptions can be made for the health and safety of the individual."

"Well, if this isn't a health and safety issue for Oscar, I don't know what is," I said. "Let's go see them."

"Should we call first?"

"No. If the general and his friends can read our texts, they probably have enough sophistication to eavesdrop on our ordinary phone calls, too. Let's just go there."

We did, but on the way we stopped at a self-serve kiosk and bought two throw-away phones, one for me and one for Jenna. After that, we took the metro, which is almost always the fastest way to get around Paris. On the way, huddled in a corner of the subway car where we hoped we wouldn't be overhead, we talked about how much we should tell the embassy about the investigation already under way by the French. We decided to tell them about it, but to disparage it as ineffective. We were going to be talking to Americans, right? They'd be inclined, we hoped, to believe it about the French.

Thirty minutes later we emerged onto the east side of the place de la Concorde, the twenty-acre plaza in the heart of Paris, with its soaring, gold-tipped Egyptian obelisk smack in the middle. From there, it was only a two-minute walk to the US embassy, which is at an angle across from the Tuileries Garden, set behind tall trees.

In my many visits to the consular section of the embassy, back in the seventies, when I had first been in Paris and was trying to get a lost passport replaced, I had been able to walk past the marine guards and into the consulate to state my business and be directed to the right person. The guards had seemed almost ceremonial.

The events of 9/11 had changed all of that. The entire complex was now set behind large concrete bollards, and we didn't even get as far as the marines. Instead, we walked up to a uniformed policeman standing under a square green tent set on tall aluminum poles. We told him we were there to report a missing US citizen, and he politely told us, in grammatically perfect but heavily accented English, that we could not get into the consular waiting room unless our names were on the daily access list. He started to look at the list, and I told him that he needn't bother because our names were not there.

"Well, then, sir, I'm afraid you won't be able to get in today."

In saying it, he looked almost as pleased with himself as I imagined Tess's concierge, Pierre, would be to deny me total access to her building.

"But it's important. A man is missing—kidnapped—and every minute counts."

"Did this happen today?"

"No. Several days ago."

"Well, if every minute counts . . . eh, never mind, I am just a policeman, and my job is not to comment, but to not let you in unless you're on the list."

"What should we do to get on the list?"

"I suggest you call the consulate and make an appointment. And you should also call the police." He handed me a card with the number on it and waved us away so that the next people in line could approach. We headed into the Tuileries Garden and found a café. Once seated, and using the first of my throw-away phones, I called the consulate and was immediately greeted by a phone tree. After climbing through the tree, I finally found a twig on which I could leave an "emergency" message. I decided to be direct and say that I was calling about the kidnapping of an American citizen, and left my cell number.

Then we ordered coffee and waited. To my surprise, my cell rang no more than ten minutes later. The caller identified herself as "Helen Klarner" from the consular section of the embassy. At first, when I told her that we had witnessed the kidnapping, she seemed sympathetic and anxious to help.

She first asked for Oscar's full name and his birthdate. Fortunately, I had attended his 65th birthday party not long before, and I was able to remember the day and month and work backward to the year. It seemed to be going well.

As the conversation went on, however, and I admitted that the event had taken place a couple of days ago, that we were already working with the French police—but unhappy with their progress—and that we were not related to Oscar, who had a wife in New York, her enthusiasm to help seemed to cool.

Finally, she said, "Look, I doubt I'm going to be able to help you very much with this. I will make some inquiries of my contacts at the French police and perhaps at the Foreign Ministry, but I doubt I will learn very much that you don't already know."

"Can you at least check the hospitals and so forth?"

"Sure, but you said the police have already done that."

"Yes, but I don't know if they're telling us the truth."

I realized as I said it that saying so had not been smart. I was probably on the edge of sounding like a crackpot.

There was a long pause.

"I see. Well, you know the French police are really quite efficient. They work in somewhat different ways than we do, and it sometimes seems odd to us, but they take this terrorism and money laundering stuff very seriously and they have lots of experience with it. They are usually *very* effective."

Which wasn't exactly what I had hoped to hear.

"Well, this isn't about terrorism or money laundering," I said.

"I thought you just said, sir, that was what they are investigating."

"They are, but they're on the wrong track."

"Why do you think that?"

"We know the guy very well and we know he wouldn't do that kind of thing."

There was another long pause—I could almost hear her brain searching for a way to end the call—and I thought I knew what was coming.

"I see," she said. "Well, one more thing I should tell you—maybe you already saw this on our website—is that due to the Privacy Act, even if I learn something, I may not be able to share it with you."

"Could you share it with the police if it's something new?"

"I suppose so. In any case, I'll get back to you."

"Thank you."

"Is this the best number at which to reach you, Mr. Tarza?"

"Yes."

"You will hear from me, but it may take a few days."

Jenna had not said much during our embassy efforts. She had just sat there, watching and listening.

"Well," she said, "it looks like we're on our own."

I didn't immediately respond.

"Earth to Robert."

"Yeah, I guess you're right, Jenna, in the sense that now the police, if they managed to listen in even though I used a throw-away phone, know we don't trust them. Which is perhaps unfortunate."

"Why is it unfortunate?"

"Because we need them."

"I think it's not so much trust, Robert. It's that they just have a different agenda. But let's go back to the apartment—which, come to think of it, *is* probably bugged—eat something, and then go walk in the park and talk there, where it will be safer."

So we went back to the apartment and cobbled together a meal. We were sitting there, dejected, when Jenna's cell phone beeped.

"It's a text," she said. "It says just, '*We want book!*' There's a sound file attached to it."

"Open it."

What we heard was a very distinct thwack, like an axe biting into a board, and then a loud, piercing scream. Followed by silence.

I looked at Jenna and she looked at me, and I wondered if my face was as white as hers.

"Do you think that was Oscar's voice?" I asked.

"I don't know. I've never heard him scream, or even yell."

"We need to forward this to the general right away. I'm going to call him and give him a heads-up that it's coming."

"Okay."

Just as I picked up my cell to call the general, it rang. It was Helen Klarner from the embassy.

She started to talk without preamble. "I don't know if I should be telling you this, Mr. Tarza, but your friend Oscar Quesana is not a US citizen, at least so far as I can determine."

"What?"

Jenna had crowded closer. "What's she saying?"

I put the phone against my hand and whispered, "Saying that Oscar isn't a US citizen."

I put the speakerphone on so Jenna could hear, as Helen was continuing. "Or at least there is no record of a US passport having been issued to him. We only work with our own nationals, so we can't help you. But due to the Privacy Act, I can't tell you anything else."

"Can you tell us what country he's originally from?"

"Well, I can tell you he has a green card. But beyond that, I'm sorry, I can't tell you anything else."

"Can't you help find people who have a US green card?"

"Unfortunately not. You'd have to go to the diplomatic authorities of the country of which he's a national."

"But you won't tell us what country that is."

"It's a catch-22, I know. And I'd like to help, but I'm stuck."

"It would be really helpful to us if you could tell us more," I said. "We're desperate and worried he's going to be killed."

"I'm really, really sorry, but I just can't. But the French police are good. Work with them."

"Well, thank you, I guess."

"You're welcome."

Jenna and I looked at one another. "Another dead end," Jenna said.

"You know, there have been a number of surprises about Oscar lately," I said. "In fact, we already agreed we don't know very much about him. And I know I just told the woman at the embassy that Oscar couldn't possibly be involved in money laundering, but maybe we should start taking a more neutral position on that."

"Wait. Are you saying he might be guilty of arranging the kidnapping as part of a money laundering scheme? Are you really saying that?"

"No. I'm just saying Oscar's always been mysterious about his life, and he's always seemed to have more money than one would expect with his low-key law practice. And . . . I don't know."

"Maybe he inherited it."

"Maybe. But whatever, I'm thinking this thing is getting ever-more complicated—and maybe more dangerous—and maybe we should just leave it to the police after all."

"What, you, big bad super-lawyer Robert, are afraid? Weren't you on that list of the fifty best lawyers in LA a few years ago?"

"That was a list of civil lawyers. And I'm not afraid. Just thinking we're in over our heads and we're going to make it worse for Oscar than if we let the police handle it."

"You mean we should butt out entirely?"

"No, Jenna, of course not. We can pass the messages we get on to the police, and let them suggest how to respond. Or not respond. Because I don't know anything about kidnapping or how to handle it, and neither do you, despite all your Internet research."

I felt like a total wuss for saying what I'd just said. Because on one level, Jenna was right. I was retreating from my take-charge personality of old, and it was particularly painful to have that pointed out by someone I'd raised up professionally and taught how to be a lawyer. On another level, with age I'd come—more than I wanted to admit—face-to-face with my own limitations, which included not wanting to plunge into things I didn't know anything about. Jenna was young and didn't have those hang-ups. Hell, maybe she never would.

While I was thinking all of that, Jenna was just looking at me with that Jenna stare of old. Finally, she said, "You remember my college nickname, right?"

"'Steel Boots.' As you've told me many times."

"Well, I'm not giving in—like you are—I'm putting on my boots, and I'm going to go kick butt until we get Oscar back from the assholes who took him."

"As I long-ago learned, there's nothing I can do to stop you."

"There isn't. And the only question is, are you going to help me or just limp off to be with your rich girlfriend?"

"I'll help where I can. But you will have to let me know what you want, and I'll decide if I want to do it."

"Fine."

"But, Jenna . . ."

"Yes?"

"Be careful what you kick with your boots."

CHAPTER 15

Jenna James

Robert is a great lawyer. But he's sometimes too cautious. His retirement seems to have made him even more so. Back when he was the managing partner of our old mega law firm Marbury Marfan—and my mentor in the litigation game—he seemed made of sterner stuff. Sure, he had the occasional soft spot even back then, but it was just a spot. Now it seemed as if the spot had grown to cover his entire body.

Maybe it had to do with my being thirty-five and his being sixty-five. Or maybe the stern stuff had always been a front for him. But either way, it was clear to me that the police weren't really making a serious effort to look for Oscar, and I was going to have to do it myself. With or without Robert. Somehow. Or maybe the somehow included using my boots on Robert, too, so that he would help.

Job one was to learn which country Oscar really came from. He'd hidden that from us, and people hide things for a reason.

If I could learn the reason, I might start to unravel the mystery and find him. I had an idea how to find out. But I was reluctant to do anything about it in the general's wife's apartment on the off chance it was bugged—even though I seemed like too minor a player to bother with, especially if I was right that they weren't really trying to find Oscar. Maybe I was just plain paranoid.

Robert went back to Tess's, and I walked down to the Jardin du Luxembourg, about ten minutes away, and found a chair by the central fountain, with its sculpture of naked men and women holding up the world. I got out my iPad, put "Helen Klarner" into Google and discovered that, before joining the US Foreign Service, she had gone to law school at UCLA. The woman was an alum. Perfect! I moved my chair as close as I could get to one of the jets of the fountain. They were just noisy enough to keep any busybodies from overhearing. I dialed the American embassy and asked for Helen Klarner. When queried, I said it was personal.

She came on the line quickly.

"Hi," I said. "This is Professor Jenna James. I'm at UCLA, and I'm putting together a course on the law of diplomacy. I looked in our alumni directory and saw that you're a fairly recent grad who's chosen a career in diplomacy. I'd love to interview you about your experiences. I'd hope to get some personal anecdotes to liven up my classes. And if you get to LA you could be a guest speaker." I loved to dangle the guest speaker hook. People bit every time.

"Well, I'm not sure how my personal experiences would really fit into an academic class, but I'd be glad to chat about them. Right now isn't the best time, though. Maybe we could set something up that would work for us both, given the nine-hour time difference."

"Oh, I'm in Paris on Christmas vacation right now. We could meet in person. I've got a small grant to do the research for the course, so I can take you to lunch or dinner if that isn't somehow forbidden by the embassy's rules."

"Oh, not at all."

"Great. Let's pick a date, then, in the next few days if you can do it. I'm going back to LA soon."

"I could do it tonight if I can bring my boyfriend."

"Is he in the foreign service, too?"

"Yep."

"Great. Do you guys have some favorite place?"

"Let me talk to Lars and get back to you, okay?"

"Sure, let's say eight o'clock, and you just text me later and tell me where."

"Sounds good."

I gave her my throw-away cell number, and clicked off. After that, I spent about an hour on the Net doing a once-over-lightly on the law of diplomacy, including diplomatic immunity. I needed to create an actual course project just in case Helen had maintained her contacts at UCLA and made an inquiry. I sketched out a proposal and sent Dean Blender an email outlining the course I'd like to teach. The law school would probably think it too narrow a topic for a full course, but the dean owed me one—or maybe three or four—for the events of last year. To remind him that he owed me, I tossed in a request for a small planning grant.

I spent the rest of the day wandering around Paris and avoiding the apartment. I needed to move somewhere I felt less watched. At around four, Helen called and suggested we meet at a small restaurant on the Right Bank called Maison Bonne Cuisine and confirmed eight o'clock. She promised to make a reservation. I googled a translation of the restaurant's name and saw that it was the French equivalent of Good Home Cooking.

Given the name, I expected, if not a flashing "EAT" sign out front, at least a down-home look—red and white checked table-cloths, the French equivalent of hooked rugs, funky wooden chairs and maybe an old clock on the wall. Instead, when I got there I was greeted by stark French contemporary—everything white and black, done in chrome, onyx and glass. The maître d' seated me, and I ordered a glass of house red. I sipped at it and waited for my guests, who showed up only a couple of minutes later.

Helen, tall and skinny, was wearing three-inch heels and a subtly patterned blue suit, with a skirt that ended well above the knee. Not what I had imagined as the diplomatic look. Lars, who was introduced with no last name, was even taller, attired in blue pinstripes and looking every inch the ambassador, even though he couldn't have been a day over thirty.

My goal was to get them both drunk.

I told them my grant was way larger than it needed to be, and we ended up consuming, between us, two bottles of a very good French red, a 2010 Pavillon Rouge du Château Margaux. I had looked up wine vintages before I got there. This one, at one hundred fifty euros per bottle, was quite good, but I still felt Oscar could afford it, and I was planning in the end to send him the bill. There was another that tempted me—it was a vintage that one reviewer had called an "Oh my God wine," but it was a thousand euros a bottle.

Along with the wine, we ate really scrumptious *bœuf bour-guignon*, *petits pois* and *pommes au gratin*, which my guests explained was what Mama might have served fifty years ago in a little village somewhere in the French heartland. The wine loosened their tongues—I drank sparingly myself—and I heard great stories, some about real topics like diplomatic immunity, and some just fascinating tales about life in an embassy. As the evening dwindled down, Lars was going on about still another story.

"The best one recently was when a wife who was here with her husband on vacation called," he said. "She was frantic because he had been gone for a day and a half without contacting her."

"Where was he?" I asked.

"Well, one of our duties in the consular section, which is where Helen and I work, is to visit Americans who are arrested and are in jail. When the wife called, I had just visited her husband, who had been detained by the police the night before up in Montmartre, the red light district of Paris."

"I assume that he had just wandered up there by accident," I said.

"No," Lars said, smiling at my little joke, "I don't think he was exactly lost. He had been feeling frisky and wanted to check out the French girls who were selling themselves up there. Unfortunately, he'd been making a dead-drunk spectacle of himself out on the street and got arrested. The French police were letting him sleep off his inebriation and were planning to release him without charge an hour after I saw him."

"So what did you do?"

He smiled. "Well, I decided to apply the Privacy Act strictly, and concluded his wife had no need to invade his privacy because he was about to be released."

"You should have told her," Helen said.

"Why?"

"Because the guy was a schmuck and she had a right to know."

"Well, Helen, sometimes different consular officers interpret the Privacy Act differently," he said.

I saw my opening. Finally. "Do you get a lot of reports of missing Americans?"

Helen rolled her eyes. "Enough. But most are like the one Lars just described. I can't think of anyone who ended up being missing for more than a day or two."

"Hey, there was that funny one the other day," Lars said.

"It was only funny because of the name."

"What was the name?" I asked, wondering why the name 'Oscar Quesana' would be funny, if, in a long shot, that's who she was talking about.

"I don't know, Lars. The guy who called about it seemed pretty upset."

"Come on, Helen, don't be such a stiff ass. It's funny."

"Okay, I don't suppose it's giving away the embassy security codes."

I waited, saying nothing, trying not to look too anxious. I poured more wine into Helen's glass.

"It went down like this," she said. "This guy called, looking for a friend who's been supposedly kidnapped. Although I have my doubts about that. Anyway, it turned out he's not a US citizen."

"The guy who called?" I asked, hoping to seem not too focused on the whole thing.

"No, the supposed kidnap victim."

"Oh."

"He was actually from France. So we couldn't help. We only do our own nationals."

"Why is that funny?"

"In the process of researching the whole thing, I not only learned the guy isn't a US citizen, but also that he has a green card and, years ago, changed his name. It was in his green card application. His original last name was *Brioche*! Oscar Brioche."

Lars laughed.

"I still don't get it," I said.

"Well, I guess you need a little bit of French history," Lars said.

"Hit me with it."

"Do you remember the story that Marie Antoinette, when she was told the people had no bread, said 'Let them eat cake'?"

"Sure."

"There's a lot of debate about whether she actually said anything at all along those lines, but if she did say something, she didn't say cake, which would be *gâteau* in French. She said, '*Qu'ils mangent de la brioche.*'"

"What's '*brioche*'?"

"You really don't know?" she asked.

"No, should I?"

"I would have thought that, given your education . . . well, never mind. It's a little sweet bun, made with eggs and butter. Kind of like a dry, sweet muffin, although there's not anything truly like it in the US. Next time you're in a patisserie here, ask for one."

"Okay, I will. And now I see why you think it's funny. It would be like someone in America having the last name Pie."

"Exactly."

"But it gets better," Lars said, smiling broadly.

"I don't think it's all that funny, Lars."

"I do. Tell her! Come on."

"Okay, he is originally from *Camembert*."

Lars had doubled over with laughter and managed to wheeze out, "*Brioche* from *Camembert*! Can you imagine any worse combination?"

He was laughing so hard that other people in the restaurant were staring at us. I didn't think it was all that funny, but I tried to laugh, too. I guess it was all the wine he had drunk.

"I suppose," I said, "it would be like having the last name Pie and being from Apple Valley, which is a town near LA."

Eventually, in order to avoid seeming too interested in the brioche story, I turned the talk back to diplomatic immunity and similar topics. At about ten o'clock, I thanked them. We exchanged business cards—I was careful to give them only my UCLA email address—and promised to meet again sometime, somewhere. They staggered out, and I watched them go.

I had gotten what I wanted. Oscar's real name and where he was from.

CHAPTER 16

I got up very early in the morning, went to a patisserie around the corner and ordered a brioche. I sat on a nearby park bench and ate it. I didn't like it much. Unlike Robert, who enjoys foreign cuisine, I'm more of a down-home girl when it comes to food.

While I ate, I tried to figure out whether Oscar's real name could help me find the hotel where he had been staying. Since the police hadn't been able to find him at any hotel under the name Oscar Quesana, was it possible he had reserved a room under his original name, Oscar Brioche?

I went to an Internet café—my searches on the Net would be harder for the general to spy on there than if I used the Wi-Fi in the apartment. After a little work, I rejected my first hypothesis: that Oscar had changed his name legally in the United States but not bothered to tell the French government, just kept his old name on his passport and used it to register at a hotel. That wouldn't work because the name on his US green card had to match the name on his French passport. Nor could he have used his old French identity card to register, because, according to what I read, those had to be updated regularly and the format had been revised.

Then it hit me: Perhaps he had simply taken his old French passport—from before he changed his name—and hired a forger to update the picture, issue date and expiration date. The original name and other pieces of information on the passport would already have been correct. How hard would that have been for Oscar to accomplish? And how useful—he would have been able to stay in a French hotel without using the name Oscar Quesana.

My first Internet search on the issue turned up three ads from people offering to sell me entirely new fake French passports. If those were available, it couldn't have taken much for some forger to update the issue date on a real French passport instead.

And here was the clincher: I discovered that a French person who registers at a hotel needs to show either a current French identity card or a current passport. Oscar wouldn't have had a *current* French identity card with his original last name on it. But if he got a forger to update his old passport by adding a current issue date to it, he could have registered at a hotel as Oscar Brioche. That way, anyone looking for him as Oscar Quesana would fail to find him.

I was immediately suspicious of my own conclusion, though. Couldn't the police, even assuming they didn't know about Oscar's name change, have found him just by looking for anyone registered at a Paris hotel who used the first name Oscar? It wasn't that common a name in France. Could Oscar have updated the passport with a new first name, too? It seemed logical.

Next I looked at the genealogical records for Orne, the *department*—much like a county in the United States—in which the town of Camembert is located. After not too much work, I found that a Georges Brioche had lived in Orne, born there in 1920 and died there in 2005, age eighty-five. His wife, Marie Dupont Brioche, had been born there in 1922 and died in 2007 in Paris, also age eighty-five. In a different database, I found that they had had one child, born in 1950, but I couldn't immediately find a name or gender. If that child was Oscar, it fit because Oscar was, according to Robert, now sixty-five.

But, brilliant as my detective work and suppositions were, they didn't really help me much, because I couldn't go around and ask every hotel in Paris if they had a Monsieur Brioche registered. The police could, of course, but I wanted to get there first.

I decided to go and kick the problem around with Robert. He might be becoming too cautious in his old age, but he still had a first-rate mind. I decided not to call, but just to show up.

When I got to Tess and Robert's place, the concierge did not appear to speak English—he indicated by sign language that he needed to call up for permission to let me in. Just then, however, a black town car pulled up in front—he appeared to spot it on a little video screen he had in his glass cubicle—and he went to welcome some people and usher them through the double glass doors into the elevator lobby. He finally turned back to me, called up to the apartment and let me go up.

Robert gave me a hug, and said, "Welcome. But why didn't you just call me on your cell and let me know that you were coming?"

"I'm trying to avoid using either of my cell phones, including the throw-away one, as much as possible. I'm paranoid that the general not only reads my texts, but may listen in, too."

"I guess I must share your view, Jenna, or I wouldn't have bought that throw-away to call the embassy. Anyway, what can I do for you?"

"I wanted to let you know that I learned Oscar's real name."

"Tell me. I'm all ears."

"First you have to promise me you won't tell the police."

"Why shouldn't we? It's a clue they can use to find Oscar."

"I'm not persuaded that they're really trying to find him," I said. "But even if they are, if they get the name they'll find his hotel and get there before me."

"Okay, I promise, Jenna. Now tell me."

"His name is Oscar Brioche."

"*Brioche*? Really?"

"Yes."

"That name will seem funny here in France. A lot of people will end up laughing at it."

"It's even funnier than that," I said. "His family is from Camembert."

"Oh my God. That will cause people to double over with laughter."

Just then Tess walked in from somewhere in the back of the apartment.

"Bonjour, Jenna. *Ça va?*"

After almost ten days in France, I had finally learned that that meant, "How's it going?" I responded, as best I could, that it was going well, *"Ça va bien."*

"You will learn French well one day," she said, smiling. "I will now change to English for you." She looked at Robert and added, "and for him," and laughed.

Robert, I noticed, did not laugh.

"Well, Jenna has just come to tell us that she has figured out that Oscar is French by origin," Robert said.

"*Vraiment*? Truly? This hits me like a thunderbolt."

"Not only that, but his real name is Oscar Brioche, and he is originally from Camembert."

Tess began to laugh uncontrollably. After her laughter had subsided, she looked at me and asked, "How did you learn this?"

"I got some people from the US embassy drunk on great wine."

"That is very clever."

"Yes, but I am really no closer to knowing which hotel he was staying at."

"Why do you not tell the police and let them use that name to check?"

"Because arriving at his hotel before the police get there will permit me to look things over before they mess up the scene. And I hope you will not tell them."

"I will keep your secret. Would you like a piece of baguette? I have just bought some fresh ones this morning and I think they remain good."

"Yes, thank you."

We all sat down at the kitchen table, and I was soon biting into bread and jam, and sipping tea. After a while, I hit Robert and Tess with the idea I'd had while waiting for the concierge to greet the guests who had arrived by cab. "I noticed that the concierge has a camera with which he can watch the outside of the building."

"Yes," Tess said. "We have installed it maybe two years now."

"Does it record on tape or disk?"

"I do not know. Why?"

"Christmas Eve was not much more than a week ago. If it records and it has not been erased, there may be a recording of Oscar arriving. If so, maybe we can identify by number the cab that brought him here and ask the cab driver where he picked him up. I think they keep a log of that. Maybe the pickup was at his hotel."

"This is a brilliant idea, Jenna," Tess said. "Robert, why do you not go down and demand of Monsieur Martin if this exists?"

Robert didn't look very happy at the idea. "Tess, Pierre and I are not on the best of terms. I think you should ask him."

"I will do so, but if we are to be married you must treat him with more of respect so he will do the same thing for you. And to show that respect, you should call him by his last name, Martin. You always call him Pierre."

"What? You must be kidding about my not treating him with respect. And he is welcome to call *me* by *my* first name. I get tired of all this French formality shit."

"It is not shit! And he will not call you by your first name even if you ask him to. But this does not matter now. I will go." And she was out the door, not even bothering to close it behind her.

She was back only a few minutes later. "*Hélas*, Jenna, Monsieur Martin says it does register the image, but he does not turn on the feature that does this."

"Why not?"

"He says that if someone arrives, he knows they are arrived, and he does not need to look at it later to see that they did."

"That's ridiculous."

"Jenna, he is not Parisian. He is from Ariège. So he is not so sophisticated."

I looked at Robert. "Ariège?"

"It's like saying he's from Fresno."

"Oh."

Tess was continuing with the excuses. "And he has been sick with *crise de foie*."

Robert was smirking. "He's an idiot and you should fire Monsieur Martin," he said. "And, by the way, *crise de foie* means 'liver problem,' and it means nothing at all except that the French are obsessed with their livers."

I decided that we needed to move on. The idea had been a bust and I had no time to get involved in a dispute between the two of them. I wanted to talk to Robert some more, but not in Tess's apartment. I didn't think it was likely bugged, but I couldn't be sure.

"Would you guys like to go for a walk in the park?" I asked. "I need the exercise."

"I would," Robert said.

"I do not wish to do this," Tess said. "But before you go, there is something I must discuss with you both."

"What?" I asked.

"Please come into my study."

CHAPTER 17

We walked back to Tess's study, and she gestured for us to sit in the two comfortable chairs. After we were seated, she took a tiny key from a desk drawer, crouched down and opened a small half-height closet. It was lined with bookshelves. She reached in and pulled out a large book with the same kind of transparent plastic cover that Oscar had used to protect his books.

"Here," she said, rising and handing it to me. "This is the first volume of *Les Misérables*, like the one Oscar showed you on Christmas Eve, except it has no inscription. It is plain."

Robert opened it to the title page. "It appears to be a first edition in English, also the American printing."

"Yes, it is."

Robert handed it to me and asked, "Do you have the other four volumes, too?"

"Yes, but that is not all that I have." She crouched down again and extracted another volume and handed it to Robert, who opened it to the title page.

"Ah, this is a copy in English of *The Hunchback of Notre-Dame*. Is it also a first edition?"

"Yes. And I also have two more famous Victor Hugo novels, all first editions in English. You can look if you wish."

Robert was still paging through *The Hunchback of Notre-Dame*. Finally, he passed it to me, and asked of Tess, "Why does this matter?"

"It matters because I know you want to find Oscar's book. I think that I can help this by the people I know in these special stores who know editions in English of Monsieur Hugo."

"You already connected me up to that antiquarian book dealer, Monsieur Deutsch."

"Yes, but as you have learned, he does not know much the English Hugo editions. I can give you the names of people who do."

"Why will that help?" he asked.

"A book like this one Oscar showed to us does not appear by magic. Someone else knows about it."

Robert got up and began to pace the room. "Tess, let me just say that I do not like it when you keep things from me. Like you also kept from me that you are a spy."

"I am not a spy."

"And now you have kept the fact that you own a first edition of *Les Mis*érables from me, too. Is there anything else?"

"No." She paused. "Eh bien, yes."

"What?"

"The general, he is also a collector of ancient books."

I broke into the conversation. "Why is that important, Tess?"

"Because, Jenna, I have fear that if this book of Oscar's is found by the general, he will find a way to guard it for himself."

"Are you also a collector?" I asked. "Or do you just have these four novels?"

"I have just these four."

"Then why do you know all these book dealers?" I asked.

"Once upon a time I thought of selling these books. When I was young and poor. But at the final I was not able to do it."

"What I don't understand is why you didn't simply tell me, when this whole thing came up, that you also owned a first edition of *Les Misérables* in English," Robert said. "I mean, what is the big deal?"

"You would ask me where I got it, *n'est-ce pas*?"

"Yes, I would. So let me ask. Where did you get it?"

"There is a story with these, you see. And it is a story that embarrasses me."

"You stole them?"

"Ah, non. Certainly not. Do you wish me to tell you the story?"

Robert and I both said yes at the same time. My yes, though, was primarily to stop Robert and Tess from bickering about something that didn't seem all that important. So she had a copy of *Les Misérables* and had not told him about it? So what?

"Okay, I will tell you," Tess said. "But to begin, Robert, please take the first volume of *Les Misérables* and read the first line aloud."

Robert took the book back from me, opened it and read, "An hour before sunset, on the evening of a day in the beginning of October 1815, a man traveling afoot entered the little town of D———."

"*Exactement*," she said.

"Huh? Exactly what?"

"Do you not know what 'D' is for?"

"No, I don't. Should I?"

"Everyone in France knows, but I forget, you are not French. Victor Hugo meant it to be the city of Digne. It is a small town in the mountains, about three hours north from Nice if you drive your car. Now it is named Digne-les-Bains because it has hot pools. And it has many tourists."

"Tess, just tell us the effing story," Robert said.

"I will if you will please be quiet. During the Great War, in 1914, when the *Boches*—I am sorry, that is what my grandmother called them—I mean the Germans, were only forty kilometers from Paris and you could almost hear the great guns, the family of my great-grandmother became worried, and they sent their only daughter, Dauphine, to Digne, where they had friends. They thought it was very far from trouble. My great-grandmother, she had only seventeen years then."

"So she became Dauphine from Digne," Robert said, laughing.

"This rhyme is not funny, Robert."

"Ok," he continued, "but I'm guessing Dauphine in Digne ran into some kind of trouble that didn't involve the Germans."

"This is true. She had a liaison with a priest in Digne."

"An affair?"

"Yes. And he was not just a village priest, but a *monseigneur*, a man sophisticated and who traveled the world. And who was a collector."

There was suddenly a silence in the room. Robert was looking at his hands and saying nothing, and Tess appeared to be waiting for someone else to pick up the questioning.

"What did the priest collect?" I asked.

"He collected first editions of Victor Hugo's novels. In many languages. They were not so rare one hundred years ago as today."

"And why did the priest collect them?"

"Because he was from Digne, and *Les Misérables,* like I just showed, commences in Digne."

"Did your grandmother stay there?" I asked.

"No, no," she said. "Certainly not. This liaison was discovered in Digne. It was a *grand scandale*. She was sent back to Paris on the next train. But before she left, she took first editions of four Victor Hugo novels and put them in her trunk."

"The editions in English?"

"Yes. The history goes that they were the only books my great-grandmother could grab quickly in the wine cellar where the priest kept all his books, even though, at that time, my great-grandmother, she could not speak English."

I did not know Tess at all well, and I did not know how sensitive she was about the family history she was telling us. I hesitated to say what I was about to say, but I went ahead and said it anyway. "So she stole them?"

"In the family, we say she borrowed them. But, Jenna, that was not the only thing she took away from Digne."

"What was the other thing?"

"My grandmother."

"She was pregnant?"

"Yes. And that is the story of how I got the books. I inherited them."

Finally, I said, "Is there more to the story?"

"I wish you would not call it a story, Jenna, because it is true."

"Tess, in English stories can be true."

"Yes, but you have two words in English, history and story. We have only one word, *histoire,* for both. When you and Robert use 'story' I think it means you do not believe what I say. It is only when you use 'history,' that you think it is fact."

Robert, who had been silent for some time, spoke up again. "Jenna, since I speak both languages, and we are talking about this whole thing about *story* versus *histoire*, let me ask some questions.

"Tess, what happened to Dauphine when she got back to Paris?" he asked. "Her parents must not have been happy."

"When she returned to Paris from Digne, they learned in not too long that she was *enceinte*—pregnant. That was an even bigger *scandale* than the affair, and you are right that they were not so happy."

"Did she have the baby?"

"Yes. But before she could show, they sent her to live with a friend in London. They made up a story—that she was a young widow of the war. That her husband had been killed by the *Boches*. After that my grandmother, Marie-Claire, was born in London, and when she grew up she married an Englishman."

"Wow," Robert said. "You never told me. Is that why you're named Tess? It is not a common French name."

Tess laughed. "Yes, my grandmother, she loved Thomas Hardy. I am named for *Tess of the D'Urbervilles*. She made my mother name me this."

Robert was smiling. "I don't know why I never asked you before how you came to have that very English name. But anyway, what happened next?"

"My grandmother's English husband died in 1945, in the last year of the second Great War. Marie-Claire and my great-grandmother, Dauphine, returned to Paris after the liberation. Marie-Claire married again, a Frenchman this time, who was my grandfather."

"Do you have pictures of these people?"

"Yes. There is an album." She climbed up on a small library ladder and pulled down an old red leather photo album. She spread it open to a page in the middle and pointed to the first picture. "This is Dauphine when she was seventeen. Before she went to Digne."

"Are there any pictures of her while she was in Digne?" I asked.

"No, and there is not even a single one when Dauphine was in England, pregnant with Marie-Claire. The next picture of Dauphine is from when Marie-Claire is five." Tess turned the page and pointed to another picture, which showed a woman in her early twenties in very conservative dress—long wool skirt and high-collared gray blouse—standing beside a little girl, who wore a heavy, dark-colored sweater and a dark skirt.

"May I take the picture out of the album and look on the back?" Robert asked.

"Certainly, but why?"

"Sometimes people write things on the back of photos that are interesting to know." He lifted the photo out of its tabs and turned it over.

"Alors, is there something there of interest?"

"No, afraid not. It just has their names, which we already know."

"This does not surprise me."

"But," Robert said, "there is something that puzzles me, Tess. I thought it was okay for French people to have affairs. Your last three presidents have had them. Openly."

"It is okay for *men*, Robert. It is not so okay for *women*, and in 1914 it was not okay at all. *Pas du tout.* Even today, it would still be a scandal if it became known. You will both keep this histoire of my family to yourself even now, eh?" She looked from me to Robert and back again.

"I will," I said.

"Thank you, Jenna. And you, Robert, will you also keep this secret?"

"Yes, I will, too. But may I ask you another question?"

"Yes."

"How do you know this histoire is true?"

"What do you mean?"

"Well, did you know your great-grandmother Dauphine?"

"No. She died before I was born."

"So you did not hear this histoire from her."

"No. I heard it from my grandmother Marie-Claire, and also from my mother."

"How do you know that Dauphine didn't make a lot of it up to make her histoire sound more romantic?" Robert asked. "And that she didn't just buy all of the novels in an English antiquarian bookshop after she got there? I mean, maybe she just had an affair with the local bookseller in Digne, and not with this world-traveling monsignor. Maybe she learned about books from him, but didn't take anything with her at all."

"Why do you think this, Robert?"

"Because it is a much simpler story—I mean, histoire. Otherwise, I have to believe there was a priest in Digne who not only seduced seventeen-year-old girls, but also collected first editions of Victor Hugo novels in, among other languages, English."

"That is not so complicated an histoire," Tess said.

"It is, Tess, when you have to add to it that your great-grandmother managed to stuff four novels—which would equate to about twenty big volumes—into a trunk without the priest or anyone else noticing that they were missing. Or coming after her to get them back."

"I think Dauphine's parents, they would have killed him if he had followed her to Paris."

"Maybe," Robert said.

I was beginning to feel a bit uncomfortable. Robert had dropped into his life-long role as an adversary—a skeptical listener, an asker of questions, a pusher of boundaries. And yet he was doing it to his own fiancée.

Tess felt it, too, clearly. "Robert," she said, "I feel like you are a lawyer asking me questions before a judge."

"I can't help being a lawyer."

"Well, *Monsieur l'Avocat*—Mr. Lawyer—is there anything else you want to know?"

"Yes. After you got the novels, did you want to collect more antiquarian books?"

"Non."

"So you didn't catch the collecting bug?"

"Non."

"But you have figured out the value of these books you own, right?"

"*Sûrement*. I have not become rich in ignoring of the value of things."

I looked at Robert and then at Tess, who had their eyes locked on one another. I was starting to feel uncomfortable about the tone of the conversation. It reminded me too much of the way my father used to question my mother about how much she had spent at Marshall Field's on her frequent trips to Chicago. But it was continuing . . .

"You know, then, at least a little bit about the world in which these rare books are bought and sold," Robert said to Tess.

"Oui."

There was silence all around.

"Robert," Tess asked, "are you now *terminé* with this inquisition?"

"Yes, I think so."

"Good. Go for your walk in the park with Jenna, then. While you are not here, I will put the copies of my books on the open bookshelf. I am proud of them. I do not need to hide them away like this."

At which point, with Tess pulling books out of the closet and re-shelving them on the open shelves, we left.

CHAPTER 18

As we closed the apartment door behind us and waited for the elevator, Robert was unusually quiet.

"Hey, are you upset with Tess?" I asked.

"Wouldn't you be?"

"I don't know. I think she genuinely thought the fact that she owned a first edition of *Les Misérables* in English wasn't important. At least when it all first came up."

"I've lived with Tess for over five years. I thought we shared pretty much everything."

The elevator doors opened and we got in.

"Plus," Robert said, "I am generally not welcome in her study. She calls it her private space."

"So?"

"Well, the fact that this book was in there makes me wonder what else is in there."

"Haven't you wondered that before?"

"Not with such intensity."

"What about the whole spy thing?"

"She's not a spy."

"Okay, what about whatever it is that she is?"

He didn't answer, and a few seconds later we reached the ground floor. We were in one of those old-fashioned elevators where the door doesn't open automatically. As Robert reached for the handle to open it, I put my hand on his arm to stop him, so that we remained in a private space.

"What is it, Jenna?"

"Robert, I think that what you're upset about isn't that Tess kept the book thing from you, or that you don't know exactly what's in her study or that she might be a spy or any of that."

"What is it then?"

"You're upset that your whole relationship with her is shifting. Once upon a time you could afford to ignore certain things or not know certain other things because, however long you'd been together, nothing was permanent. And you had made no commitment. Now she wants to get married, and you feel you need to know everything."

"Maybe you're right."

"So you want some advice?"

"Sure."

"When this whole thing with Oscar is over, the two of you should go away somewhere for a long weekend and agree that you're going to tell each other your complete stories, no holds barred, no secrets, no embarrassments."

"God, then I'd have to tell her about my first wife."

"Can I be there for that part?"

"No." He reached for the door and pulled it open. I noticed the concierge sitting there, looking toward the elevator, no doubt wondering why we hadn't emerged right away and probably imagining all the wrong reasons.

"One other thing, Robert. Don't forget to be nicer to the concierge. He could be of use at some point."

We exited the elevator and Robert practically shouted to the concierge, "Bonjour Monsieur Martin! Comment ça va?"

Monsieur Martin looked surprised at the greeting—apparently Robert often didn't greet him at all—and said, "Ça va bien, merci. Et vous?"

The two of them then proceeded to have a voluble conversation in French, in which, toward the end, Pierre pointed toward his head a lot. As in most situations in which people are speaking a language in front of me that I don't understand a word of, I just stood there feeling slightly uncomfortable.

Finally, after they finished talking, Pierre gave us both a rather friendly seeming version of the standard quasi-distant French goodbye, complete with hand-wave and "au revoir, bonne journée!" and we walked out the front door and headed for the Jardin.

"What did he say?"

"He apologized for not having had the recording feature on. He tried to explain why he had not found it important—none of which made sense to me—but said the building has just given him a brand new camera that is even better because it records automatically, and although it's still in its box, he will install it right away. But then he said something really interesting."

"What?"

"He said that he did recall that when Oscar's taxi arrived, the driver came around and opened the passenger door for him. And he recalled it because it's unheard of for a Parisian cabbie to do that unless the passenger is old or infirm or something."

"Maybe Oscar offered him a big tip."

"Maybe. But here's the really interesting part. He remembered that the cabbie was wearing a blue turban."

We stopped walking and just stood and looked at each other.

"So are we thinking the same thing?" I said.

"I'm thinking, Jenna, there can't be too many taxi drivers in Paris who wear blue turbans. If we can find him, maybe we can find out where Oscar's hotel is, if that's where the cabbie picked him up."

"My thoughts exactly. But I thought you were withdrawing from this whole thing and were inclined to let the police handle it." I put on my best sardonic smile.

"Yeah, I know I said that. But finding a cab driver with a blue turban sounds like fun—like a puzzle—and I don't see how it can be dangerous. If we find him, and he can identify the hotel, you can follow up on that part."

"Okay. I'll do that. But the big question is, how are we going to find him?"

"I don't know, but I'm going to text Tess about it and see if she has any ideas. After all, she lives here and understands how you find things out in Paris."

After that, we walked in the Jardin for almost an hour, mulling over various strategies for finding the blue-turbaned driver. We even detoured a few blocks out of the park to use an Internet café, thinking maybe we'd luck out and just by chance we could quickly find something about the taxi driver on the Net. But we couldn't.

Finally, I said, "You know, Robert, we could crowdsource it."

"How would that work?"

"I'd put up on my social media pages—Facebook and Twitter and maybe some others—that I'm looking to connect with a blue-turban-wearing taxi driver in Paris. And ask my friends to ask their friends, and so forth."

"Sounds promising. Do you have any friends in France to ask?"

"Just Tess, but her friends will ask their friends and it will multiply. But maybe that's the answer. We ask Tess to crowd-source the problem among her French friends."

"Will that improve the odds?"

"Sure, because if Tess does it, it skips one degree of separation from me to people in France, and it's people here who are most likely to know the answer. Let's go ask her."

"We can ask her later. Right now I want to continue my online research for the blue-turbaned cab driver."

CHAPTER 19

I decided to change Internet cafés again, just in case. I left the Left Bank and took the metro to the glitzier side of town, down by the Place de la Concorde, even though that particular plaza tended to give me the creeps. Every time I went there, I couldn't get it out of my head that I was standing where over one thousand people had been guillotined during the part of the French Revolution known as the Terror. The last time I had been there, with Robert, when we had tried to get into the American consulate, I hadn't mentioned it to him. It was the kind of fear he tended to make fun of.

I started my search for the blue-turban guy by doing another, even more extensive online search, using all of the search engines I knew about. Nothing turned up. Before I moved to trying to crowdsource it on social media, I decided that I needed some plausible story as to why I wanted to know. After a little bit of thought, I decided to say I was involved in a scavenger hunt. Then I put up a request on Facebook, tweeted the question out on Twitter, posted it on Reddit, and put up a query on LinkedIn. I even used the largely impenetrable Google+.

I didn't expect any instant responses, so I went off to have a late morning snack in a café near a big cab stand. Maybe through some lucky twist of fate, blue-turban man would show up there. But an hour later, after an apple tart and three cups of tea, all strung out to maximum eating and drinking time—no one ever asks you to leave a French café, no matter how long you linger—I had seen cabbies wearing caps and fedoras, colorful scarves and assorted kaffiyehs, but nary a turban.

I kept checking my various social media accounts to see if anyone had responded. As usual, quite a few people had, but the responses were all jokes of one kind or another. Seems as if the similarity between *turban* and *turbine* inspires all kinds of punsters. The worst one began "a turban and a turbine walk into a bar . . ." By mid-afternoon, I was discouraged, even though I knew crowdsourcing could take days and my lack of contacts in France was likely to make it an even a longer process.

I paid my bill and left. On my way to the metro, my phone rang. It was Robert.

"I have something exciting to tell you," he said.

"What?"

"I found a picture of the cabbie with the blue turban and his name."

"How?"

"On Pinterest. There's a picture of him standing beside his cab. The number's visible and it's labelled with his name."

"I'm shocked you even know about Pinterest."

"I'm very Internet savvy, Jenna."

"No you're not. You can hardly boot up your own computer. Who suggested you try Pinterest?"

"Tess. Just a few minutes ago, when I told her what the concierge had said and how we were trying to look for the guy using the Net. She instantly said, 'Try Pinterest,' and suggested

I search under 'blue turban taxi Paris.' Apparently Tess is a big pinner herself."

"Strange. But anyway, what's his name?"

"Colin O'Connor."

"Why would someone named Colin O'Connor wear a turban?"

"I don't know. Why don't you ask him? He's listed. I'll text you his phone number."

My phone beeped almost immediately with the number.

"Got it, and I will, as soon as we hang up. I hope he speaks English."

"Let me know what you find out, Jenna."

I figured there was no time like the present, so I found a park bench and dialed his number. He answered almost immediately.

"Allo?"

"I'm sorry, I don't speak French," I said.

"Ah, well, as happens, I also speak English. This is Colin O'Connor. How might I be of service to you?"

As soon as he began to speak in English, the beautiful Irish lilt that emerged left no doubt where he had been raised, and it wasn't France.

I decided to be direct. "Hello, Mr. O'Connor, this is Jenna James. I'm a law professor at UCLA currently on vacation in Paris. I know this will sound strange, but I'm investigating the disappearance of a colleague, and I think you might have some information that would be useful to me. Would you be willing to meet me somewhere?"

"For sure I can. Assuming you have ID that confirms you are who you say you are, come on over to my apartment, and we'll have some fine Irish tea. Where might you be now?"

I told him.

"Ah, you are but a few blocks away. You can walk or hail a taxi. Do you know where rue du Faubourg Saint-Honoré is?"

"Not exactly."

"You are close. I'm near the corner of that street and rue des Saussaies. You can walk here in twenty. Give me your cell and I will text you the address and a map link."

I chose to walk, and it was soon apparent that I was walking through one of the wealthiest areas of Paris. I actually passed the Élysée Palace at one point and smiled at the uniformed guards at the gate. When I reached the address he had texted me, his apartment turned out to be in what otherwise looked like a commercial building, with ultra-swank shops on the ground floor and a marbled elevator lobby. On my way up the elevator to the sixth floor, I realized I had failed to ask the guy if he was a cab driver. Maybe Robert had found the wrong person named Colin O'Connor.

The guy let me in without hesitation—which was a bit surprising considering I was a total stranger, but maybe five-foot-six women are somehow not threatening—and motioned me to a seat by the window. Between his lilt and his looks, there was no mistaking he was an Irishman. He was about five foot ten, with jet black hair and green eyes, a look I sometimes heard people call "black Irish" when I was in law school.

"Would you like some tea?" he asked.

The apartment was ultra-modern, in the style of the restaurant in which I'd dined with the embassy folks, with a huge window that looked out on the Eiffel Tower off in the distance, the Arc de Triomphe to the right and the gold-topped obelisk in the Place de la Concorde to the left. It was breathtaking.

We introduced ourselves and, on his request, I showed him my UCLA ID card. He seemed satisfied, and busied himself getting the tea as I talked.

He served it in beautiful cups and asked, "What might this all be about?"

"I have to start by asking, are you a cab driver or do I have the wrong Colin O'Connor?" I raised my eyebrows and gestured at the sweeping view.

He laughed, clearly getting my not-so-subtle question: *How can a cab driver afford to live here?*

"My father made a fortune in Ireland and died young. I moved here to write a graphic novel set in contemporary Paris."

"What's it about?"

"It's a new take on Victor Hugo's *L'Homme Qui Rit—The Man Who Laughs.*"

"I'm sorry, I've never heard of it."

"It's the original inspiration, by way of some other works, for the Joker character in Batman."

"So how is yours different?"

"Laughs more at himself than others."

"And driving a cab helps that how?" I asked.

"Driving a cab helps me see the city and its people. And the tourists, of course."

"Do you work at it full time?"

"No, I work two or three days a week, and I'm known to the company as someone who's willing to work nights and holidays, and when it's raining or snowing. The best stories are out there then."

"Do you wear a turban?"

"I do." He went into another room and came back with it on his head. It was indeed blue.

"You like?" he asked.

"Yes. Why do you do it?"

"It encourages conversation with my fares. They can't resist asking about it, and that always breaks the ice and I can find out about them."

"You speak French?"

"I do. And German and Russian, so I can chat up a lot of tourists."

"Why blue?"

"It has to be some color, so why not?"

"Do you have other colors?"

"I do not. But tell me why you are here. Surely 'tis not to find out about turbans."

I asked him if he would agree to keep what I told him to himself. He agreed to do that, and I then explained it all.

He listened patiently, pursed his lips and said, "I suppose it invades a customer's privacy, but if he's truly been kidnapped, there ought to be an exception to that."

"Yes, I would assume so."

"Alright, I recall your man, actually, even without looking at my log book. I picked him up at a small hotel over in the Marais. Do you know that area?"

"Yes. Do you remember the name of the hotel?"

"Yes. It's called Hôtel des Antiquaires. I can give you the address."

"What kind of place is it?"

"It's a two-star hotel, I think, which means it will be clean and without obvious bugs, and it has a working elevator, but nothing fancy."

I thanked him for his time and we promised to stay in touch. He said if I needed more help to feel free to call on him. As he put it, "I always enjoy being part of a good story."

After I left, I called Robert and told him what I had learned.

"What are you going to do?"

"Well, I need a place to stay other than the general's apartment. I don't really have any hard basis for thinking I'm being bugged there, and I know you thought it would be good for me to be watched over, for my own protection. Somehow, though, I feel like I'm under surveillance, which is different."

"Why do you feel that way?"

"I can't put my finger on the exact reasons, but I'm suspicious of the whole setup. And back when I was a lawyer, paying attention to my suspicion-o-meter, as I used to call it, often proved the right thing to do. So I want out. If this hotel has a room free, I think I just found a new place."

CHAPTER 20

I stopped at an Internet café and made a reservation via the hotel's website. The rate was reasonable, and I reserved the room for a week. The Google map estimated it was only twenty minutes by car from the apartment, so I could just take a cab. I went back to the apartment and packed.

Once packed, I considered my problem: I had to get out of the general's apartment without being detected. I was sure I would be if I just walked out the front door with my suitcase. I had noticed two large men loitering outside the building who looked nothing like bums and every inch—or, since it was France, every centimeter—like cops. They look alike everywhere, and I was sure they belonged to the general, who had, after all, said I would be "protected."

I had explored earlier and found a door at the back of the lobby, locked from the inside with a dead bolt. It led to the building's trash cans, which were stored in an outdoor enclosure surrounded by a concrete block wall. Fortunately, I had traveled light and had only one small, wheeled suitcase. I packed, put on my blue jeans, took the steps to the lobby so as to avoid running into someone in the elevator, undid the bolt lock on the back door, and walked out into sunshine. I tossed the suitcase up on top of the wall. Next, I hoisted myself up to the top, too—working on my upper body strength at the gym had paid off—and lowered myself down on the other side. I grabbed the suitcase off the wall and looked around. I was on a small side street. No one seemed to have seen me, and there were no goons in sight.

I walked several blocks, hailed a taxi and was at the Hôtel des Antiquaires within twenty minutes. I noticed after exiting the cab that there was an antiquarian bookstore next to the hotel called À la Recherche des Livres Perdus. I wondered if it was under the same ownership. I would also need to ask the hotel owner what the name meant. Assuming, of course, that he spoke English.

A bellman emerged from the hotel, which was six stories high, with a pastel front, red shutters on the windows, and geraniums growing in planter boxes set on tiny balconies. He took my bags to the front desk where a kindly looking, rather old gentleman with half-glasses on a chain around his neck looked up my reservation and asked, in English, to see my passport.

He took it and said, "Do you speak French?"

"No, I'm sorry, I don't."

"Well, we will press forward, then, in English. I learned it during the Vietnam War—yours, not ours—when I was attached to the French embassy in Saigon. The city was full of Americans, so there was little choice but to learn English if I was going to have any friends beyond my own embassy."

"You learned it well," I said.

"Thank you."

He had been examining my passport as we spoke. "Do you want us to keep your passport for you? It would save you the risk of having it pickpocketed on our wonderful subways, which are filled with them. We would store it here, and you could retrieve it when needed." He pointed to a row of numbered wooden cubbyholes behind him, some of which had passports resting in them, along with envelopes that were presumably arriving mail.

"No, thanks. I think I'll keep mine."

"Your choice, of course. May I also have your credit card? And will you please sign here and initial here and here."

As I completed the paperwork, I tried, surreptitiously, to see if there were any American passports in the slots, then stopped myself, realizing that in Oscar's case it would have to be either a French passport or a French identity card. I decided to hazard getting some information.

"Monsieur, I'm curious, do you offer the same passport protection services to your French guests?"

He gave me an odd look and shrugged. "Yes, of course, but most of them use their French national identity card for verification of who they are. And most French would not wish to be separated from that card. If the police stop them and they do not have it with them they may go directly to jail." He smiled. "Isn't that the Monopoly game card, 'go directly to jail'? We used to play that with our American friends in Saigon."

"What would happen if *I* did not have my passport?"

"Eh, if they thought you were a tourist, they would take you back to your hotel to find it."

"And if they thought I was not a tourist?"

"Go directly to jail!" He laughed uproariously at his own joke.

"I see," I said.

Once the formalities were completed, the bellman took my bag up to my room on the *4e étage* (what we'd call the fifth floor in the United States, because the first floor in France has a name instead of a number and isn't counted).

The elevator was old and positively creaked upward, but it was better than walking up four flights. The room itself was plain but serviceable. The bathroom was clean and the toilet didn't run, even though it had one of those old tanks hung on the wall above the toilet bowl. I tipped the bellman, and as I handed him a two-euro coin. I asked, as casually as I could, "Are there other guests here who speak English?"

"I do not speak *anglais*," he said. "*Désolé.*" I was coming to understand that word meant "sorry." I was embarrassed at having assumed that because the hotel owner spoke English, so did the help. In any case, my task now, without being too obvious about it, was to find out which room Oscar had been staying in and then get into it. That proved a little time-consuming, but not too difficult.

I went to a stationery store and bought a big manila envelope and some copy paper. I filled the envelope with paper until it was bulky, then took the metro across town to a bicycle messenger service I'd found that advertised that they spoke English. I paid them cash to deliver my envelope *livraison urgente* (rush) to Oscar Brioche, care of the hotel. Obviously, if he hadn't used that name to register—I suspected, of course, that he had used it—the delivery would fail, so I'd learn something that way, too.

For a return name and address, which they required, I channeled my college art history course for a name and chose *Charlotte Corday*. For the address I used the address of the restaurant at which I'd dined with the diplomats. I was worried they would ask for ID, and was prepared to say I'd left my passport in my hotel room, but they didn't ask.

I took the metro back to the hotel. On the way, I bought a copy of the European edition of the *Wall Street Journal* and sat reading it in the hotel lobby, waiting for the envelope to be delivered. Less than forty minutes later, the messenger arrived, and I watched as the desk clerk signed for it and placed it in a cubbyhole behind the desk labeled "406." So Oscar's room number had to be 406, which was, by delightful happenstance, only two doors down from my own.

Just then my throw-away cell rang. It was Robert. "Hi, where are you?" he asked.

I insisted on walking out of the hotel before responding—my suspicion-o-meter was still showing a high reading—then briefed him on the name and address of the hotel, my room number, and the fact that Oscar had stayed at the same hotel, on the same floor, just two rooms down from mine. We agreed to meet at the hotel at 11 p.m.

I waited about fifteen minutes, returned to the hotel and went back up to my room to consider my options. One option was to make up some excuse that would gain me access via the hotel's master key, but I couldn't think of a good excuse. Another was to steal a master key, but I couldn't think of a safe way to do that, either. The third was to pick the lock. I had learned how to do that during my gap year after high school, which I had spent in Hawaii with my somewhat disreputable private detective uncle, Freddy. In recent years, though, I had restricted my activities to parties where I demonstrated to the hosts that I, a law professor, could pick the lock on their front door. Or at least most locks. I had even joined a local chapter of TOOOL (The Open Organization of Lockpickers), which ran contests like who could—legally—pick a lock the fastest. I was, at best, in the middle of the pack.

But I was good enough, I thought, to take the lock on Oscar's hotel room door without any trouble. The only problem was that I hadn't thought to bring a lock-pick kit with me across an international border, since in some countries it's illegal to possess lock-pick tools. That left me with what I had with me or could buy without suspicion. I checked my suitcase. I had packed a metal nail file, which would help. But I also needed a thin probe of some kind to hold the tumblers while I used the nail file to turn the lock cylinder.

I dumped the contents of my purse out on a table to see what I had that might work. Amidst the debris there was a flat-sided bobby pin. With the rubber tip removed, it would probably do. I was going to have to wait, though, until very late evening, when the maids were gone, most guests had already checked in and the hallways were otherwise deserted. So I had some time to kill.

I started by calling the general and reached him almost immediately.

"Hi," I said. "I wanted to let you know that while I appreciated the loan of the apartment, I've moved to a hotel."

"Why?"

I had thought carefully about how to answer that question with something that was at least mildly plausible.

"I just had the sense that the kidnappers knew where I was staying, and although I appreciated the security you provided, I just feel safer being somewhere anonymous."

"You can tell me, certainly, where you are."

I had thought about how to respond to that, too.

"I think my phone is being tapped. I keep hearing strange clicks. I'll keep in touch, and let you know after I get a new phone."

"Well, I am glad you called."

"Why?"

"The kidnappers have delivered an ultimatum."

"To you?"

"It was addressed to you, care of us."

"But you opened it."

"Yes. Désolé. But it was necessary."

"Why?"

"To protect you."

"Will I be unhappy with what it says?"

"Probably, but I think you had better come here right away."

"To 36 quai des Orfèvres?"

"Yes."

I had developed something of an aversion to the place, so I declined. "I'd rather go somewhere else. How about you buy me a late lunch?"

"Okay. Where?"

"I'll find a place and text you the address in a couple of minutes."

"Alright."

I went on the Net and located a small restaurant about a thirty-minute walk from the hotel. I figured that would be far enough away that he wouldn't be able to figure out where I had come from, and it was only a block from a metro station, so he'd probably think I'd taken the metro from some place much farther away.

I texted him the time and place and made it a point to get there a little early.

CHAPTER 21

The restaurant was small—only about ten tables—and clearly a mom-and-pop kind of place. Mom was the waitress and Pop was the cook, and they kept yelling at each other. I couldn't understand a word of it, but from gestures and context, Pop was saying, "Hurry up," and Mom was shouting back, "No, *you* hurry up."

I watched the show for a while. Finally, the general arrived—about fifteen minutes late.

"Désolé," he said. "I was held up by many phone calls."

"Doesn't matter, General. I don't have a lot of pressing things to do. In fact, I'm thinking of going back to Los Angeles, where my behavior will no doubt be more to your liking."

I said it because I thought threatening to leave might gain me some leverage.

"Why?" he asked.

"Well, there doesn't really seem to be much I can do here. I'm just sitting around, you know. Mostly, I just talk to you on the phone. I can do that from home, and I have things to do at the law school."

"I looked you up on the UCLA website, Professor, and I see you are on sabbatical this semester."

"Sabbatical isn't a vacation. I have two law review articles I'm researching and writing, and it's easiest to do that there, where I have access to a law library where most of the books are actually in English."

"I really can't permit you to leave."

"Do you have the power to stop me?"

"Yes, I do."

"How?"

"I will ask a judge to detain you as what you call in your legal system a 'material witness.'"

"Well, I guess I have to stay, then. But I hope you can speed up the search."

"We are working hard on it."

"With no results."

"Let's order," he said.

He ordered a croque madame, and I ordered a croque monsieur, sort of a sandwich gender switch.

The food was taking forever to come, as Mom and Pop continued to hector one another. While we waited, I finally asked the general about the message from the kidnappers.

He reached into his jacket pocket and produced a single sheet of paper, which he handed to me, saying, "This was texted to my cell phone—which is itself very concerning since my number is private—but it is addressed to you." He handed it to me and I read it:

Jenna James, we lose two days with you and are tired wait. We give you four days find and deliver book. Today is the Day 1. Place book in box and leave front desk of your hotel.

If not there by sunset Day 4 you never see this friend Oscar again. Tomorrow and every day we send you text message and you respond to number we give you in and confirm you receive message. If we no receive text back in three hours, we assume worst and dispose Oscar without wait more. NO MONEY. WE WANT BOOK.

P.S. We can send additional souvenirs Oscar. We hope you enjoy finger.

When I had finished reading, he asked, "What do you make of that, Jenna?"

"It's scary."

"And beyond that?"

I took the note and read it again. "Well, for one thing, the person speaks English, but not well."

"Yes. We have had a linguist analyze the language pattern."

"And?"

The general smiled a broad smile. "Likely written by a Russian."

"Like your niece, General," I said.

"Yes, but her English hardly rises to the level of 'Where is the toilet?' so I don't know how she could possibly write that."

"General, how do they know where I'm staying? And anyway, if someone tries to pick the book up at my hotel, won't we see him?"

"I do not know how they know where you're staying. But I can only protect you if you tell *me* where it is. That way I can post someone at your hotel to watch over you. He can both protect you and keep on the lookout for the pickup person—assuming, of course, that you ever find the book."

"Won't you just find out by running my name through whatever database you have of who's staying at each hotel?"

"It's a myth that we have an instant database like that. We have to go through the hotel reports by hand, and since you only checked in today, we won't even have those until late tonight or tomorrow morning. And you could simply move every day, and we'd have a problem tracking you. We don't have endless manpower to follow you around Paris."

"Oh."

"It would be so much easier if you just told me. Frankly, you are being childish. Again."

"The problem is, General, that I don't trust you."

"You have no basis for distrust."

Just then the waitress appeared and put our respective croques in front of us, along with a very small green salad for each of us.

"My basis for distrust, General, is, among other things, the fact that you also collect antiquarian books, and I think you should have told us that. For all I know, you are the kidnapper."

He actually drew back, startled, or at least he put on a good show of being startled. "This is insane. It is true I collect rare books, but only from 18th-century French authors, and only in French. I have no interest in a 19th-century book in English, even if it is by a French author and even if it is inscribed."

"You could be hoping to start a collection of that kind."

He took a huge bite of his croque madame, chewed for a while and said, "Madame, you do not understand collectors."

"What do I not understand?"

"Collectors are obsessives. Once they begin to collect something, they rarely change the focus of their obsessive love. And that is especially so as we grow older."

"So if someone gave you that book, you wouldn't want it?"

"Oh, I would want it. But only so that I could sell it and buy more of what I really want. And then only if I could obtain the book legally."

"I will think about what you have said, General, but I still don't trust you."

"Then you had better change hotels tomorrow morning or we will find you, and this time you will not slip away by climbing over the garbage cans."

"That will be a drag. But let me change the topic."

"Change if you wish, Jenna."

"Have you made any progress in finding Oscar or the kidnappers?" I asked.

"No."

It was my turn to chew on my food for a while. And to wonder why technology couldn't solve the problem of where they were, like it could on TV.

"General, if they send me a text, can't you track where it came from?"

"Yes, but it takes some time and is not very precise. We can narrow it to within a few kilometers in a rural area and within a couple of blocks in an urban area, but not to an individual building or room within a building. It is not like you see on TV. And by the time we trace it, they will be long gone from that area."

"I thought you could find someone as soon as the signal leaves his phone."

"Your NSA can do that, but only if it has a drone or plane overhead nearby. The police, with whom I am working, have very good technology, but it is not quite that sophisticated. And, in any case, the kidnappers will change phones every day and use each phone only once."

"Can't the police trace where the phones were bought?"

"Yes. But the kidnappers probably planned this a while ago and were smart enough to buy each one in a different place and look for places to buy them that don't have security cameras."

"If you haven't made any progress in finding Oscar and the kidnappers, have you at least made some progress in finding the book?"

"No."

"So, General, you have done nothing."

"Working with the police, I have done much. We are close to finding the complete money trail, and that will lead us to both Oscar and the book. But if we join forces, we will get to both goals more quickly."

"I will think about it."

"I hope you will," he said. "Now a question: How are you going to respond to the text message?"

"Do I actually have a choice in that, since it was sent to your cell phone?"

"Under French law, you do."

"Which reminds me, since we're on the topic of your cell phone, why did they send the text to you instead of to me?"

"To show that they know a lot about what's going on on our side—that they know, for example, that we are working together. Their knowledge of that is supposed to make you afraid."

"I see. Well, since we're working together, do you have any advice on how I should respond?"

"As you know, I would not respond at all."

"And as *you* know, I don't agree with that approach."

"Yes, I understand. Will you at least let me know what you do say?"

"Can't you just read it when I send it?"

"Yes, but if you call me, it will be a better way of keeping in touch. And one more thing, Jenna."

"What?"

"Be very careful. You can get yourself *and* Oscar killed. Whoever these people are, they are not amateurs."

"I thought you said, not long ago, that they were amateurs. Which is it?"

"We are changing our minds as we watch how they operate."

That made little sense to me, and the needle in my suspicion-o-meter was pushing against the far side of the dial. But there seemed little point in pressing it, since I was just going to be on the receiving end of more BS.

We finished eating, skipped dessert and parted. I was concerned enough about being followed that I took the metro to the Opéra, bought a ticket, spent some hours wandering in the nearby giant department store Galeries Lafayette, with its neo-Byzantine glass dome, treated myself to a pastry in its dome-top café, returned to the Opéra and merged myself with the crowd going into the 8:00 p.m. performance. Then I slipped out a side door and took a cab back to the Hôtel des Antiquaires.

I got back around nine, and walked slowly to my room. As I passed by Oscar's room, I looked at the lock on his door as carefully as I could without stopping, trying to imagine, by looking at the shape of the keyhole, what type of tumblers and lock cylinder lay behind that keyhole. I did the same thing when I reached my own door, feeling the way the key slid into my lock, which looked to be the same as Oscar's lock. I also tried to get the feel of the tumblers as I turned the key. After that, I waited until it seemed very quiet in the hotel. It was ten thirty, but Robert wasn't coming until eleven. If I could do it at all, it wouldn't take long to pop the lock, and I'd be back in my room before Robert got there. Then we could go out to a midnight dinner. I suspected that in Paris you could do that.

CHAPTER 22

I took the nail file and the bobby pin in hand, dropped my travel flashlight into one pocket, stuffed a small washcloth from the bathroom into the other, and slowly opened my door. I peeked outside, saw no one, and moved quickly and quietly to Oscar's door. For a second, I thought I saw motion at the end of the hall, but concluded it was only headlights reflecting off a window.

The lock proved a lot more difficult than I had hoped—the tumblers kept slipping away from the bobby pin—and it took me almost two minutes to pop it. By the time I was done, sweat was dripping from my forehead onto my hands. I let myself in and swiped the washcloth over the doorknob to wipe off my damp fingerprints. Not wanting to turn on the lights, I began to look around by the narrow beam of my tiny flashlight.

The room looked pretty much like my own, except reversed in plan. The bed was made up, and all the surfaces were bare. No books, no paper, no nothing. I put the sleeve of my blouse over the handle to the closet, opened it and looked inside. There was a single suit hanging there. I ran my hand around the inside of each of the outside pockets. There was nothing in them. I had just started on the inside pockets when I heard a slight noise behind me. As I turned my head, the room lights came on, illuminating three uniformed cops—a tall man, a short man and a muscular woman who looked like she could pound me through the floor—plus the elderly hotel owner.

"Arrêtez! Mettez vos mains dans l'air!" the tall cop said.

I didn't understand the exact words, but I got the gist of it from the tone, turned fully around and put my hands in the air. I was on the edge of tears, whether from the shock of being caught or regret at being caught I couldn't tell. But I was damned if I was going to cry, particularly in front of the hotel owner. Somehow I willed the tears not to come, although if someone had touched my lower eyelids, they probably would have found them wet.

The old hotel owner pointed at me. "I could tell that you were up to no good here," he said.

The muscular policewoman stepped forward and patted me down from head to toe. When she was done, she looked at the others and said, *"Rien."*

The tall policeman said some other things I didn't understand, put his hand on my shoulder and pushed me toward the door. I was marched like that down the elevator and through the lobby—thank God no one else was there—and then into a paddy wagon that was waiting outside. I was pushed down onto a bench in the back, whereupon the short policeman got in with me, the back doors were slammed shut, and the wagon began to move, picking up speed.

"Where are we going?" I asked.

"No *anglais,*" the short cop said.

I noted that they hadn't handcuffed me, but, whether the cop was an English speaker or not, I decided it wasn't prudent to inquire about the cuffs lest he somehow penetrate the language barrier and change his mind.

We rode the rest of the way in silence. After about twenty minutes, I felt the van tilt, as if we were going down a hill. Shortly after that, we came to a halt, the rear doors were thrown open and I was pushed down a long corridor, the tall cop's hand gripping my shoulder. Along the corridor, we passed other men and women looking out at me with curiosity—the cell doors were some kind of glass or Lucite framed in metal. Finally, we got to an empty cell, and I was unceremoniously shoved inside. The door clicked shut, and the tall cop turned and said, "Translator soon." Everyone left. I sat down on a bench and waited. And cursed myself out for being an out-of-my-depth moron.

I was left in the cell for what seemed like an eternity. I didn't even have my cell phone with me. I had left it in my room when I went to pick the lock. Finally, I dozed off, then woke up with a start when I heard a noise outside the cell. When I looked up, there stood Officer Omaha.

"Well, if this isn't the cat's pajamas," he said.

"That's from the 1920s," I said. "And you've used it out of context."

"I was in a Jazz Age play in Omaha."

"Were you the lead?"

"Hey, I was. I was!"

"So to what do I owe the pleasure of your company?"

"I'm your translator."

I wanted to groan, but decided against it.

"What do I need translated, exactly?"

"Well, to start I'm going to tell you your rights. But I need another policeman present to do that. He will be here in a moment."

Sure enough, the tall cop showed up and Officer Omaha began to speak.

"You are in *garde à vue*," he said, "which means you have been arrested and are being held for investigation. You have the right to an attorney if you want one. You also have the right to remain silent if you wish."

"That's it?"

"Yes."

"What am I accused of?"

"Not accused, suspected."

"But suspected of what?"

"*Vol*," he said.

"What is that?"

"Theft."

"But I didn't steal anything."

"That remains to be seen, and I'm sure other things will be added later for investigation."

"When can I get bailed out?"

"For the first forty-eight hours there is no bail."

"That's outrageous."

"That is how we do it here in France. The forty-eight hours is for an investigation, and while we are doing it, you cannot flee and by doing so interrupt the investigation."

"And I get out after forty-eight hours?"

"Usually. Unless you are charged with terrorism or something like that, in which case you might be held in preventive detention."

"Am I entitled to call someone?"

"Yes, a relative or your lawyer."

"I don't have any relatives here and I don't know any French lawyers." I thought to myself that I could call Robert, who could ask Tess, who could call somebody, who could . . . but I never got to finish the thought because, suddenly, I heard footsteps coming down the hallway, and, after a few seconds, the general appeared.

"You pick locks?" he said. "Like a common street criminal?"

"I am choosing to remain silent."

"Do you pick pockets, too?"

"Like I said, I'm not talking."

"Well, there will be time to talk later." He turned to the cops and said something in rapid French. They listened in silence. Then he handed them a piece of paper, which they scanned.

"*Ouvrez la cellule, s'il vous plaît.*"

The only word I caught in that was "cell," but he must have asked them to let me out, because a few seconds later, the tall one produced a large ring of keys and unlocked the door.

"Follow me," the general said.

We ended up in his car. "I'm going to take you back to your hotel, now that I know where it is. And when we get there, we are going to have a talk. You need to keep in mind that this is not your country, this is not a game, and you are not doing yourself or Oscar any good."

"How did you get me out?"

"I talked to the public prosecutor and explained that this was all a giant mistake. I hinted that you were helping us with a major investigation."

"Thank you."

The thank-you was heartfelt because I was relieved to be out of jail. But I also knew that on some level I was now in debt to the general. I hated being in debt to anyone.

"Well, don't thank me too much, Jenna, because that was a one-time get-out-of-jail-free card."

"You too?"

"What?"

"Never mind."

He put the car in gear, burning rubber as we pulled away, which is really something for a French car.

After a couple of blocks, he said, "Why are you staying at the Hotel des Antiquaires?"

"It was cheap and they had a room available."

"It had nothing to do with the fact that Oscar was staying there before he was kidnapped?"

I just looked at him.

"I read the police report. It names the guest who was staying in the room where you picked the lock."

"Oh."

I felt stupid. Of course he had read the report. And of course the report said that.

"Do you think, Jenna, you'll be welcome back there after what you did?"

"We'll find out. But I paid for tonight, so I think they have to keep me. And as for the long talk, can we do it another night? I'm exhausted."

"No. We have to do it now."

So we had the long talk, which consisted, entirely, of him telling me, in rather strong terms, that I was being childish, that I was in over my head, that I was making his task more diffi-cult, that I might get myself, not to mention Oscar, killed, that I might end up doing hard time in a French prison, and a vari-ety of other ghosts and goblins that might come in the night to haunt poor little me. It reminded me, in tone, of my crazy mother, on a day she wasn't talking to the house plants, telling me not to go to law school, that it would do all kinds of bad things to my already too-harsh personality, and in any case, I probably wouldn't do very well there.

I think you're usually expected to say "thank you" after the kind of adult-to-errant-but-well-intentioned-child advice the general had just delivered, but instead I said nothing at all, which seemed to discomfit him. Which was exactly what I intended. When he was done, he dropped me off at the Antiquaires, but didn't offer to escort me in. When I walked into the lobby, Robert was sitting in one of the chairs reading the *Financial Times*.

"Robert! What are you doing here?"

"We had an appointment at eleven o'clock, remember? I've been waiting for you for a very long time."

"I was in jail instead."

"I know."

"How do you know?"

"Let's go for a walk," he said.

We walked for two or three blocks in silence and finally sat down on a park bench.

"I saw it all," he said.

"You did?"

"Yes. I got here maybe fifteen minutes early for our meeting. There was no one at the front desk, which kind of surprised me, but since I knew your room number, I just took the elevator up."

"And?"

"I got off the elevator just as three cops and an old guy were rushing into a room a couple doors down from yours. I ducked into a broom closet and waited. I left the door cracked so I could see."

"What did you see?"

"After a while, I saw you being led away."

"Must have been a thrill."

"No, but after you were all gone, I noticed that in the excitement they had left the door to 406 open. So I went in. And I found something of great interest."

I found myself trembling with relief. "You found the book!"

"Sorry, no. But I found these." He reached in his pocket and handed me a small map, torn in half, and three other pieces of paper. I looked at them carefully, although the dim light made them hard to see.

I held the two pieces of the map together. "This looks like the map of a cemetery."

"Yes, it's a map of the Père Lachaise Cemetery."

"Why would Oscar want that?"

"I don't know, Jenna, but one of the other pieces of paper you're holding is a metro ticket, which can also be used on the bus. On the back of it someone has written the number 69. I looked it up, and the number 69 bus goes to that cemetery."

"Does your cell phone have a flashlight app?"

"Yes. Here."

I took it from him and turned on the app so that I could see better. "It's hard to tell with just a number, but I'd bet that that's Oscar's handwriting. What are the other pieces of paper?"

"One is a round-trip train ticket for one person to Digne-les-Bain, dated several days after Christmas. The other is a receipt from a cab driver in Digne-les-Bain, undated."

"Where were they?"

"In the wastebasket in the bathroom, mixed in with lots of used paper towels, crumpled tissues, a few receipts for fruit from a nearby market, and a couple of colorful wrappers for something called *Friandise Végétalien*, which I think translates roughly as 'vegan tidbit.' Did you get to search the bathroom before you were, uh, interrupted?"

"No, I didn't search the bathroom—or much else for that matter. The police may not have searched the room at all since their main focus seemed to be on arresting me."

"That makes sense."

"Did you find anything else?"

"No, and I looked around quite carefully."

"How did you manage not to be seen after you left Oscar's room?"

"I *was* seen. I followed the rule of 'in order not to be noticed, pretend you belong.' I took the elevator down, walked boldly through the lobby, said, 'Bonsoir, Monsieur,' to the desk clerk, sat down in a chair and began to read a newspaper."

"What should we do now, Robert?"

"I think we're going to Digne."

"What about the cemetery?"

"I don't know what we'd do if we went there. We have no idea what to look for, and it's over a hundred acres."

"How do you know that?"

"I took a tour once, not long after I moved in with Tess. In fact, I think she went with me."

"Why would anyone tour a cemetery?"

"Because there are a lot of famous people buried there. Chopin, Molière, Marcel Marceau and, of all people, Jim Morrison of the Doors."

"Does Jim sing at night?"

"Very funny."

"I'm going to go out there."

"What for? What can you possibly find out?"

"I don't know, but I'm going."

"Jenna, that's impulsive. Why don't we wait until we know what we're looking for at the cemetery?"

"Okay, I guess, although sometimes impulsiveness works, you know?"

"Other times it gets people killed."

"So what do you suggest we do now, Mr. Cautious? We can't go to Digne, if we're really going there, until tomorrow."

"It's very late, Jenna. I, for one, am going to go home and go to sleep."

"I'm wired and don't want to go to sleep right now," I said.

"Alright, why don't we take a moment to visit the bookstore next to the hotel? It's a logical place for Oscar to have gone with his book if he was looking for a buyer."

"But, like you just said, Robert, it's late at night."

"Well, I noticed a light on there when I arrived. Someone may still be up."

CHAPTER 23

As we approached the bookstore, I saw that there was indeed a light on inside, just as Robert had observed, although it seemed to be coming through the plate glass windows from somewhere in the very back of the shop. I had my hand raised to knock, when it suddenly occurred to me that I didn't know why we were so focused on this bookstore. "Robert, what made you say this was a logical bookstore for Oscar to have visited?"

"Because of its name. The title of Proust's most famous novel is *À la Recherche du Temps Perdu,* often translated into English as *In Search of Lost Time.* The sign on the bookstore says 'À la Recherche des Livres Perdus,' which I'd translate as 'In Search of Lost Books.' So it must be a place that sells rare books."

"That's seriously lame."

"Yes, it is. But at least it gets the message across."

I knocked, loudly. No one came. After a few minutes, I knocked again, even harder. Finally, I heard footsteps coming toward the door, and a few seconds later it was opened by a young man, maybe twenty years old, who said, *"Alors, qu'est ce qui se passe? Il est tard et le magasin est fermé!"*

As usual, I didn't know exactly what he had just said, although the scowl on his face made it pretty clear that he didn't like being disturbed at such a late hour, and I knew from signs I'd seen in store windows that *fermé* meant "closed." Robert then engaged him in French, and the guy opened the door wider and waved us in, although his body language said that the welcome was grudging. I knew it was irrational, but the inability of most people in France to speak English was starting to annoy me big time.

After we got inside, the guy offered us seats at a small wooden table. As he and Robert began to converse in French again, I got up and started to examine the store's books, which were shelved from floor to ceiling on all four walls. The owner raised no objections to my wanderings, even when I went farther back into a second, smaller room. I noticed that one shelf in that room held four or five copies of *Les Misérables*. I pulled the first volume of each set off the shelf and opened it to the title page, looking for inscriptions. There were none. One set, however, was a copy of the same 1862 American first edition that Oscar had shown us. All the rest were second editions or later, although all had nineteenth-century publication dates.

Just as I was putting a volume back on the shelf, I noticed a door in the very back that was slightly ajar. I could see from moving shadows that there was someone inside. I moved closer, to see if I could catch a glimpse of whoever was there. I finally got so close that I could see someone on the other side of the door peering out. Suddenly, the door was flung open. There stood the general's niece, Olga, in all her tall thinness.

"Что ты хочешь?"

I had studied Russian in college. She had just said, "What do you want?"

Without missing a beat, I answered: "Что ты тут делаешь?"

I could tell from the look on her face that she was not only shocked that I spoke Russian, but that I had had the temerity to ask what she was doing there without any of the myriad polite introductions, circumlocutions and endless toasts of which Russians are so fond before getting down to business.

She responded in the same blunt fashion: "Я живу здесь. А теперь иди отсюда!" *I live here. Now get out of here!* She slammed the door in my face.

The noise roused Robert from his quiet conversation with the owner. They both came rushing to the back.

"What's going on, Jenna?" Robert asked.

"Olga, the general's niece, is in there," I said, pointing at the door.

Robert turned to the owner, and they spoke rapidly back and forth.

"What did he say?"

"He said she is a friend of the owner of the hotel, who is also a part-owner of this bookstore. And that he requested that she be able to stay here. He says that she's a pain in the ass, and he wants her gone."

"Did he say how long she's been here?"

"Since New Year's Day."

"Did he say what she's doing here?"

"He says she just talks on the phone all day in Russian."

While we spoke, the owner had opened the front door of his shop and was gesturing toward it.

"Bonsoir, Madame et Monsieur," he said, as we walked through the door, "Bonne nuit." He closed the door firmly behind us, and I heard the lock snap closed.

"What else did you learn?" I asked.

"He said he specializes in nineteenth-century French novels and that about two weeks ago, Oscar had tried to interest him in helping him market his inscribed first edition of *Les Misérables*. He says he passed on it because he thinks both the inscription and the self-portrait are obvious forgeries."

"Did he say why?"

"Yes. He said that Victor Hugo had a huge ego. And if he was going to say that anyone was as great a writer as Shakespeare—in any language—he would have said it about himself."

"Was that it?"

"No, he also said that Oscar, not knowing enough about France or Victor Hugo, was probably overly impressed by the surface plausibility of the story."

"Why is it plausible?"

"Because one of Victor Hugo's sons, Victor Charles Hugo, was *the* major translator of Shakespeare into French at the time. And because Victor Hugo not only wrote an introduction to that translation, but also wrote a book about Shakespeare."

"That makes it sound very plausible," I said.

"Yes, but he argues that, because Hugo didn't speak English well and so far as anyone knows, the two men met only once and briefly, there was no personal relationship."

"When was that meeting?" I asked.

"He said it was in 1843, almost twenty years before *Les Misérables* was published. Some kind of salon Dickens attended at Hugo's house here in Paris, back when Dickens was a young writer."

"So his bottom line is what?"

"That there was no opportunity for Hugo to meet Dickens long enough to strike up the kind of friendship where an egomaniac like Hugo would have been willing to pen such an inscription."

"What about the drawing?"

"He says it's total nonsense. Hugo never did that."

"Huh. So this all makes me wonder why the bad guys want it so badly," I said. "They must have the same information."

"You'd think."

"Another thing," I said. "Don't you think it's weird that Olga was there? And that she moved in the day after Oscar was kidnapped?"

"Very weird. Although it could be a coincidence."

"Wait," I said. "Wasn't she supposedly staying with her uncle, the general? Isn't that what they said on Christmas Eve?"

"Yes, I think they did say that."

"Robert, there are too many connections here for this all to be just happenstance. Oscar stays at a hotel next door to a bookstore where he tries to get the owner to help market the book. The mention of Olga's father makes Oscar turn white. Olga is now living at the bookstore, but doesn't get there until the day after Oscar was kidnapped. I wonder what the owner of the bookstore is hiding from us."

"I agree," he said. "But I don't know if we're going to learn more here. Let's go to Digne."

"When?"

"How about tomorrow. I'll get us some tickets, and I'll call you in the morning and let you know when we're leaving. Do you want to stay here tonight or come back to our place with me?"

"I'll stay here at the hotel. I mean, what could happen that hasn't already happened?"

"I don't know, Jenna. But I want you to promise me that you won't pick any more locks or do anything else you know to be illegal."

"I promise."

"And promise you won't go off on any more adventures by yourself."

"I promise that, too."

Of course, when I said that, I had my fingers crossed.

CHAPTER 24

Robert Tarza

By the time I got home, it was well past midnight. Tess was still up, sitting in the living room reading. I updated her on all that had happened, including Jenna's arrest and release.

"The general," she said, "is a good man."

"I agree he is a man."

"I do not understand what you mean with this."

"Never mind."

"Your friend Jenna, she is—I do not know the right word in English. She lacks the judgment."

"She is impulsive. That's the word. But, on the other hand, sometimes her aggressive approach to life gets her very far."

"Perhaps. But the speech that the general made to her is right. This is not her country, and . . ."

"If she's not careful, she'll get her ass in a sling."

"What is a 'sling'?"

I sighed. I was forever slipping up and using metaphors Tess was bound not to understand. "A sling is, in this case, a big bandage, like one you would use to support a broken arm."

"Eh, I do not understand this saying. I do not picture how an ass would be in a sling. This would not work. And even if in some way it will work, why is her ass in this sling a problem?"

"Let's skip the metaphor and just say she can get in trouble."

"Yes, in very big trouble. Our laws are harsh. And we do not like the foreigners to break our laws."

"She has promised me not to break any more laws."

"Good."

We sat in silence for a while. Tess went back to reading her book, and I picked up that day's *Le Monde*, which was lying on a coffee table. After a while, I said, "Tess, have you ever been to Digne?"

"No. I have only heard the stories passed from my *arrière grand-mère*."

"Your great-grandmother."

"Yes."

"Who was there almost a hundred years ago."

"Yes."

"Screwing the priest."

"That is a harsh way to say about it, Robert. But why are you asking me about Digne?"

"Jenna and I are going there because we found a receipt for a train ticket to Digne in Oscar's room. We have a hunch that many answers are there."

"What is this 'hunch'?"

"In French, *un pressentiment*."

"Ah, I see. Have you given this ticket to the police?"

"No."

"This is not smart. They can help you."

"Jenna doesn't trust them. She thinks they don't really care about rescuing Oscar."

"And you? Do you trust the police, Robert?"

"After what happened to me in Los Angeles six years ago, I have trouble trusting police anywhere. You know they tried to get me sent to San Quentin for murder."

"In truth, I do not know much of this. You were there, and I was here and you were not talking to me then."

"If you'd been there, you would understand."

"This is *ridicule*. The police here are not the police in Los Angeles. And the general, he rescued Jenna's liberty for her, did he not?"

"Yes, but for all I know it was so that he could follow her and learn what she knows. And anyway, he is in the army, not the police."

"I think you and Jenna are both children."

"Thanks."

"I am trying to help and to warn."

"What is there to warn about?"

"I wish us to be married. Then I would be able to tell you much."

"Tell me anyway."

She got up and began pacing about the room. Then she left the room and was gone for five or ten minutes. Meanwhile, I sat and continued to read *Le Monde*. Finally, she returned.

"I have received permission to tell you two things," she said.

"It bothers me that you have to get permission to talk to your future husband—from a person whose name I don't even know. But go ahead."

She glared at me. "I will not respond to this. Here are the two things. First, they know now that the finger is not the finger of Oscar."

"How do they know that?"

"In your state, when you become a lawyer, you must give your fingerprints. They have checked with your state the records of Oscar, and they find that the prints do not correspond."

"So the finger was sent by the kidnappers to frighten us."

"Yes."

"And the general and his friends were going to keep from us that the finger was not Oscar's. In order to leave us still frightened, right?"

"I do not know why they did not tell you."

"Fine. What is the second thing you got permission to tell me?"

"They have traced the signal that sent the text to Jenna. This one the general showed her at the café."

"Where did it come from?"

"From somewhere near Digne. They cannot say for sure exactly where."

"That's great. It means we're more likely to find Oscar by going to Digne."

"It means you are more likely to be killed in Digne. I pray you not to go."

"I promise to be careful. But we are going."

CHAPTER 25

I called Jenna first thing in the morning and suggested we take the train that left at 11:05 a.m., from Gare de Lyon to Aix-en-Provence, with a change there to the line to Digne-les-Bain. But Jenna protested that she had some errands to run first, so we ended up taking the 4:05 p.m. instead, which wouldn't get us there 'til very late.

The first leg of our trip, from Paris to Aix, took about four hours on the high-speed TGV. Surrounded by four other passengers in our compartment, we didn't talk to each other very much, just read and looked out the window as the scenery zipped by. After we switched trains in Aix, we were seated in a compartment that had four seats and was entered via a sliding glass door. Two of the seats were empty and remained that way, even as I heard the whistle indicating that the train was about to depart.

At the last second the sliding door opened and in stepped a priest, dressed in an old-fashioned long black cassock with buttons up the front from bottom to top and a white clerical collar. A large gold crucifix hung around his neck. He looked to be in his eighties, if not older, with a big potbelly nicely covered by the robelike cassock. He introduced himself as Monseigneur Jean-Claude Pardet from Digne-les-Bain.

It was soon clear that he did not speak English—which pushed Jenna back into her book—but I decided to press on in French and see what I could learn about Digne.

"Have you lived in Digne for a long time?" I asked.

"Yes. I have lived there all my life."

"So you have seen many people come and go."

He gave me a quizzical look, as if it was an odd question, which I suppose it was. "Well, yes," he said. "I suppose you could say that. I have seen them born, seen them married, seen them have children, and seen them die." He paused a moment. "And I have seen them lured away by the demon places."

"The demon places?"

"Why yes. Like the big cities, where iniquity and sin await them."

"But isn't Digne a tourist town, known for its hot pools? I would think sin and iniquity could easily take root there. You know, in the *les bain* part of it."

He stared at me again. "I think, monsieur, that you are making fun of me. But perhaps I am making fun of you, eh?"

I didn't know quite how to respond, and finally said something I hoped was very neutral. "I am simply trying to understand your world view."

"Eh, I see. And may I ask, what is bringing you to Digne-les-Bains?"

It ran through my head to say that we were going there for a little hiking in the mountains and relaxation and maybe a dip in the hot pools, but then I thought better of it and decided to just go for it.

"Well, Monsignor, a friend of ours purchased some anti-quarian books in Digne, and he thinks he was cheated—that he was sold a counterfeit book."

He laughed uproariously, causing his substantial belly to shake beneath his cassock. "Ah, non. Not another one."

"Another what?"

"Another fool."

"Why a fool?"

"He has fallen victim to an old tale—that in the early nine-teenth century, there was a priest in Digne who collected old books, books that were not so very old at the time, but are now, with the passage of time, very old."

"Is this legend not true?"

"Not so far as I can tell."

"You have investigated this?"

"Yes. You see, I preside over the very church in which this mysterious priest was supposed to have lived."

"You aren't retired?"

"Eh, yes, formally. But I still live on the grounds while some young squirt of a priest runs the church."

"What did you discover?"

"This priest's name was supposedly Père Gaudet."

"I thought he was a monsignor."

"Sometimes in the legend he is a humble *prêtre*—a village priest. Sometimes he is a *monseigneur*, and there is even one in which he is an *évêque*—a bishop. Imagine that!"

"What makes you think, by whatever title the priest is called, that he did not exist?"

"Because there is no record in the church of such a priest. Indeed, there is nothing in the records of the town or the depart-ment that a person named Gaudet ever lived in Digne."

"Does the church building perhaps have some secret room in which the books were kept?"

"The church does not even have a basement, Monsieur. And if there were a secret room, I would have found it."

At that point, Jenna looked up from her book and asked, "What is he saying?"

"He says that the story that a priest in Digne collected old books is just a tall tale."

"Try asking him if he's ever seen old books for sale in Digne," she said.

I turned back to the priest. "Monsignor," I said, "have you ever seen rare books for sale in Digne?"

"Eh, yes, of course. Almost every town in France has a store that sells anciens livres. The French are besotted with books. They will buy almost any old book, especially if it is said to be *very* old. They will even buy it if the cover is rotting away, which for most true collectors would make it of small value."

"What is the name of the store in Digne?"

"Bibelots et Livres."

"So it's a store that sells both trinkets and books?"

"Yes. And if you want to hear the legend spun in all its glory, go see the proprietor, who is an expert spinner." He smiled. "If you wish, he will even sell you one of Père Gaudet's famous books, and give you a special price because you are an American." He winked at me.

"Where does he get them?" I asked.

"I think he goes to the great city of iniquity and buys them from the booksellers along its river."

"Paris."

"Yes."

"Thank you for this information," I said.

"You are welcome. Now if you will excuse me, I have some reading I must catch up on."

"Of course."

I then brought Jenna up-to-date on all he had related to me.

"You know, that's very interesting," she said. "But our friend Oscar doesn't strike me as a gullible person. And didn't he say he paid fifty thousand euros for the book?"

"I think so."

"I'd expect him to have investigated the whole thing before plunking down that kind of money. Oscar is not the type of person to rush out and buy something on a whim."

"Don't you remember? He said he had found what he called an 'authenticator' that swept away all doubt. I think those were his exact words."

"I'd forgotten that. I wonder what it is."

We both went back to reading. At one point, I cast a glance over at the priest to see what he was reading. It was *L'Amant de Lady Chatterly*, which I assumed was a translation into French of *Lady Chatterley's Lover*. So much for avoiding iniquity.

We disembarked in Digne-les-Bains in late evening. The train station was nothing fancy—just a small two-story concrete building with a red tile roof. We walked quickly through the waiting room and out to the street, where there was only one taxi lined up. To my surprise, the priest was getting into it. And for the first time I noticed his footwear—blood-red tennis shoes.

He turned, saw us, and said, "Where are you heading?"

"To the Hôtel Central."

"That is on the way to my church. We can share this cab, and you can save some money." He smiled. "You will have more to spend on rare books."

"We're not planning on buying any, but we'll share the cab since there are no others. And thank you very much."

We all clambered in, Jenna in the passenger seat, and the priest and me in back. I couldn't help saying to him, "I see you wear red tennis shoes. I'm surprised a priest would do such an iniquitous thing."

"Eh bien, have you seen the red slippers the old Pope wore, the one who retired?"

"Yes."

"If the Pope can wear red slippers, an eighty-five-year-old monsignor can surely wear red tennis shoes, eh?"

The hotel was only a few blocks from the station, and not long after that exchange the cab pulled up in front. I thanked the monsignor for letting us share his cab, offered him ten euros to cover it—which he declined—and heard him offer to buy us an aperitif the next evening if we were still in town. He handed me his card.

"I will call you," I said. "We will perhaps still be here."

The hotel, when we entered it, was old, but clean, and charming.

"I'm surprised at your choice of hotel," Jenna said. "Usually, you want to stay at the nearest thing to a five-star hotel you can find, wherever you go."

"This was close to the center of town. It's just a guess, but who and what we want to find are probably near here some-where, and not in the burbs."

Once we had checked in and gotten our keys, I said, "Do you want to grab a drink?"

"It's late, Robert. I just want to go to bed."

"Alright, I'll see you in the morning. Our rooms are next to one another, so if there are any problems, just bang on the wall."

"What kinds of problems could there be?"

"I don't know, but you never know. Maybe you'll be arrested for shoplifting or something."

"Very funny, Robert. Sleep well."

After I had undressed, brushed my teeth and gotten into bed, I called Tess. There was no answer on the landline phone, so I called her cell, which she picked up after only one ring. After the usual how-are-you pleasantries, I said, "Tess, do you know the name of the priest in Digne who fathered your grandmother? When you told us that story, you never mentioned his name."

"Oui, his last name was Gaudet."

"Do you have a picture of him?"

"Non. I have only the letter he mailed to the father of my great-grandmother."

"What letter?"

"That one in which he says he is désolé for that which he has done and offers to pay for the child."

"Did they let him?"

"I do not think so. The histoire is that they never answered his letter."

"Okay, I will see you soon," I said.

"Are you at least staying in a nice place?" she asked.

"Yes, at the Hôtel Central. Old but clean."

"Good."

She paused, then said, "Je t'aime, Robert. Be careful what you do in Digne."

"I love you, too, Tess. And I will be careful."

"Good."

"Good night my love, sleep tight."

"What does this mean?"

"Never mind. *Dors bien*. Sleep well."

CHAPTER 26

I was awakened by a banging on the wall. At first, it was part of a dream in which a car I was riding in was backfiring. When the fact that the noise was real penetrated my consciousness, I sat up. It took me a few seconds to remember that I had told Jenna to bang on the wall if there was a problem. The banging grew louder. I jumped out of bed, threw on my robe and opened my door. A policeman was banging on Jenna's door and saying in French, "Police. Open the door please. Now." Another officer, with his weapon drawn, was standing to the side and slightly behind him. French police don't usually carry guns, and he looked nervous holding it, which made me nervous.

"Officer," I said in French. "What's going on? It's five in the morning!"

"I am the chief of police in Digne-les-Bains, and I have a warrant for the arrest of the woman who is staying, according to the hotel, in this room. Please step back and do not interfere."

"She is my colleague. I will ask her to come out if you will tell me what this is about."

"She is accused of theft in Paris."

"That charge was dismissed."

"This warrant says that it is a new charge, issued just yesterday. As the local police chief, I am obligated to find her and detain her until she can be returned to Paris."

"Alright. Let me phone her and explain." I stepped back into my room, grabbed my cell and called. She answered on the first ring.

"What? There's some jerk banging on my door."

"Jenna, that jerk is a police officer. He has some kind of warrant for your arrest on a theft charge in Paris. I'm sure it's just a mistake of some kind, but you'd better come out."

"I'm not coming out so these assholes can hassle me again."

"You have to or they will come in and get you."

"Alright, I suppose I don't have much choice. I'll come out."

I rushed back outside and waited for the door to open. It did, revealing Jenna still in a bathrobe. As soon as she emerged, the police chief thrust a piece of paper at her. After she'd glanced at it for only a few seconds, he told her, in French, to put her hands behind her back. She didn't comply, of course, because she didn't understand.

"Monsieur," I said. "She does not speak French. Let me translate, please." And without waiting for a response, I said, "They want to handcuff you. Please place your hands behind your back."

"This is outrageous. I don't even know what that piece of paper says. What kind of country arrests people while telling them why in a language they can't understand?"

"Jenna, please just comply so we can straighten this out. You and I both know that in the United States, if you continued not to cooperate, you would be charged with resisting arrest. So whatever the underlying charge here, you don't want to add to it one for resisting lawful authority."

She grudgingly put her hands behind her back, and I watched as the police chief cuffed her and started to read her the rather limited set of rights that are available in France—in French, of course.

"He's telling you that you have a right to a lawyer and the right to remain silent."

"Great. Please find me a lawyer."

"I'll call Tess and see if she can help."

A door down the hall opened, and Tess herself appeared. I was stunned. "Tess, what the hell are you doing here?"

"I thought you two would get in trouble, so I took my plane to Grenoble last night—the airport that is close to here had much mountain fog—and rented a car and drove here in the night. I drove three hours."

The police chief looked at her and said, in French, "I must ask you both to stop speaking in English since I do not understand it, and I do not want you plotting the escape of my prisoner."

Tess walked up to the policeman, removed a placard of some sort from her back pants pocket and flashed it at him. She shoved it back in the pocket so quickly that I couldn't see exactly what it was except that it had some kind of embossed red seal on it. The police chief reacted to it as if he'd seen a snake. He actually shrank back.

"Chief, please walk down the hall with me for a moment," Tess said.

The two of them walked down the hall, and engaged in quiet conversation. When they returned, the police chief unlocked Jenna's handcuffs. Then he said to her, still in French, "You must take yourself to Paris within forty-eight hours to present yourself to the *juge d'instruction* named in the summons for investigation. And you must now surrender your passport to me."

I translated what he had said.

"I don't want to give up my passport."

"This is only going to get worse if you don't," I said.

"Alright. I will go and get it. It's in my purse."

I explained to the chief where it was. He told me that the other officer would need to go with Jenna into the room. I translated that for her, too.

When she emerged with the passport and handed it to the chief, I looked at Tess and said, in French, "What, exactly, is this all about?"

"Jenna is charged with theft for when she went into Oscar's room at the hotel in Paris."

"That charge was dismissed."

"Yes, it was. But the charge, it has been put back by the *partie civile*."

"The what?" I said.

"In France, Robert, if the public prosecutor dismisses a charge, the civil party who claims to have been injured can start the process all over again. And the public prosecutor, he cannot stop it. It is given to a *juge d'instruction*—what you would call an 'investigating judge'—to look into the allegation in detail and to tell the trial court if the allegation is good or bad, worth pursuing or not."

"Who is the civil party here?" I asked.

"The owner of the hotel. He claims something was stolen by Jenna from the room of Oscar."

"What does it say she stole?" I asked.

"An antique pen of great value, and she also damaged a lock by picking it. Beyond that, it says nothing. It does not need to say in great detail right now."

"A pen? You've got to be kidding."

"That is what it says."

"That's ridiculous. Why would Jenna steal a pen?"

She shrugged. "Again, this is what it says."

"So this is like a summons to appear?" I asked.

"Yes. But because Jenna is a foreigner, they have ordered her arrest to be sure she does not flee. I pledged on my personal word that she would appear at the chambers of the judge within forty-eight hours and they have, as a result, released her to my custody."

"Tess, are you some kind of high-level spy with super-powers?"

"No. Like I have told you before, I am just a citizen of France who sometimes helps my government."

She turned and said something more to the police chief in a voice so low I couldn't make it out. He handed the summons to Jenna, and he and the other policeman left, apparently satisfied.

"I am going back to bed, Robert," Tess said. "You should, too. Do you want to come to my room?"

"I don't think so right now. I need to sit up and think about this whole development."

"Alright. At nine we will all three meet for breakfast down-stairs, yes?"

"Yes."

Tess went back into her room. Jenna just stood there, hug-ging herself as if she needed to keep warm, waiting for me to explain to her everything that had just gone on. I realized, to my embarrassment, that Tess and I had been speaking French the whole time, leaving Jenna out in the linguistic cold. I switched to English and explained it all to her.

"Fuck!" she said, and went back in her room, slamming the door so hard the entire corridor shook.

CHAPTER 27

We ate breakfast the next morning in the semi-rustic hotel café, which was furnished with ladder-back wooden chairs with cane seats on wood-plank floors. The meal was tense. Jenna was sullen and said hardly anything except to complain about the unavailability of American breakfast food. Tess was in lecture mode.

"I think the two of you must return to Paris," she said. "It is for you dangerous here. And for you, Jenna, you must prepare for this *reunion*—I mean this meeting—with the juge d'instruction."

"Don't you think that to prepare I will need a lawyer?" Jenna asked.

"Yes, and I will arrange this for you. I know several who work in this area of money washing and terrorism."

"Now they think I'm a terrorist?"

"*Pas du tout.* Not at all."

I had noticed that of late Tess had begun to say something in French and then repeat it in English. Which would have been annoying, except that I often did the same thing. Mixing the two languages in that way was not unusual among long-time expats.

"Well, if this is *pas du tout* about terrorism"—Jenna's mimicry of the French words flattened the vowels in a way that was jarring even to my ears—"then why are you thinking of getting me a lawyer who is expert in that? Don't I need someone expert in the law of theft, since that is apparently the stupid charge against me?"

"It is stupid. I agree with this," Tess said. "But it is for some reason on terrorism that the police wish to concentrate themselves here. They want to think somehow this concerns the washing of money. But a lawyer who knows about this will also know about the law of *vol*, of theft."

"Do you know the name of this judge?" I asked.

"Yes. The *chef de police* told me his name," Tess said.

"Which is?"

"Roland de Fournis."

"Tess, that name is very familiar to me, but I can't quite place it. Do you by any chance know him?" I asked.

"Yes. He is well known for pursuing corrupt officials and terrorists."

"Oh, now I remember. I read about him in *Le Monde*. What have you heard about him beyond that?"

"That he is very strict, but very fair. Which should be good for Jenna. Because the charge to be investigated for Jenna is not a *crime*, which here in France means what you call a 'felony.' Her alleged infraction is a mere *délit*, which I think you call only a 'misdemeanor.' In fact, it is strange that he is to investigate such a minor thing."

"Oh, so the maximum is only a year in jail and/or a fine?" Jenna said. "How comforting."

"Ah, non. A délit, this can be ten years in jail and a fine that is very big," Tess said. "I have not looked to see exactly the penalty for un vol."

"I'm so heartened that this is *only* a misdemeanor," Jenna said. "Where I can spend *only* ten years behind bars."

Tess pursed her lips. "I think that the most that will happen to you, Jenna, if this judge's reputation for fairness is a true one, is that you will have a fine and expulsion from France."

"After a long investigation in which my name is dragged through the mud and probably ends up on Page One of the *Los Angeles Times*—"Prominent Law Professor Jailed in France for Money Laundering." Do you know what that will do to my career?"

"I am sorry for all this, Jenna. I will try to make it okay. But this is why I think you should go home to Paris and stay in my apartment and not go outside."

"Tess, we don't know each other very well, but that is not me, and that's not what I'm going to do. The way I figure it, I can spend all day here trying to figure out where Oscar is, or at least where the book is, and still make it back to Paris in time to meet with this judge tomorrow."

Jenna's mind was clearly made up, so there was no point, I had long ago learned, in discussing it further, and I was hungry. "Let's order," I said.

After we ate, Tess announced that she was sorry, but she had to get back to Paris because someone from her "other life" had called an emergency meeting. She declined to say what the meeting was about. She again urged Jenna to come back with her, which Jenna again declined. She got Jenna to pledge once again that she would be in Paris in time to meet with the judge, after reminding her that she had given her personal word of honor that Jenna would show up. Then she got up and left.

"Well," Jenna said. "What now?"

"I guess we see if we can find the cab driver who gave Oscar the receipt when he was here."

"Let's go do it."

* * *

It proved not to be difficult. Digne-les-Bains is a small town, and there are not very many cabs. We did not have the cabbie's name, but we had the cab number, and after about an hour's search, we found a cab matching the number on Oscar's receipt idling not far from the railroad station.

I opened the back door and we got in. The cabbie was some-what disheveled looking, and he had a black pipe clenched in his teeth, apparently unlit. He took the pipe out of his mouth and asked, in unaccented English, "Where to, my friends?"

"How did you know we speak English?" I said.

"Your shoes, man."

"I see. Well, you speak quite good English, apparently."

"Yah. Lots of tourists come here from the UK, and a lot of Germans and Swiss come here, *après ski*, as they say, and a lot of them speak English, but I don't speak German or whatever they speak in the non-French parts of Switzerland. So I focus on getting my English right. Gets me bigger tips." He grinned.

"You studied English on your own?"

"Not much. But it helped that that I was born in and grew up in Manhattan and went to NYU."

"Oh," I said. "How did you end up here?"

"It's a long story, too long for now. I just need to know where you want to go so I can turn the meter on."

"Well," I said, "we're not going anywhere in particular. We're looking for the cab driver who picked up this fare and took him somewhere about ten days ago." I handed him the receipt, and he studied it.

"Ah," he said. "I see that this receipt has the same number as this cab, but I don't always drive this cab, and I think I was off duty that day."

"Would you be able to find out who was driving that day?" Jenna asked.

"Madame, I think that would be very hard."

"Why?"

"The cab company doesn't like one driver to know the affairs of another—or how much money he makes on a particular shift—so they keep the records under lock and key. I can't think of a good excuse to ask to look at them."

"If we give you a description of the fare who took the cab and give you his picture, too, could you ask around?" she asked.

"Maybe, although this time of year there are lots of fares—people coming to ski up in the mountains and all that."

"Let me give it a try with the photos," she said. "Maybe they will jog your memory." She found some pictures of Oscar from our Christmas Eve dinner and held her cell phone up where the cabbie could see them.

"Here are some of him that I took at a recent dinner party," she said.

The guy looked at the pictures, pursed his lips, shook his head in the negative and said, "Sorry, they don't ring a bell."

As he and Jenna were conversing, I was looking around the cab. I noticed that there was a pipe rack bolted to the dashboard in front of the passenger seat, and a picture of a woman and child—presumably his wife and kid—taped to the dashboard. It seemed unlikely to me that anyone else drove that cab. In my long career as a lawyer, I had met witnesses like the driver before. I thought I smelled what this was really all about.

"You know, sir, I realize that asking around among the other drivers could end up taking a lot of your time and divert you from making money as a cabbie," I said. "We're more than willing to compensate you for your time." I reached across and dropped a five-hundred-euro note on the front passenger seat.

He looked over at it as I continued: "And if there's money left over after you conduct your search—charging us a reasonable hourly rate of course—you can just drop it off at our hotel. We're staying at the Hôtel Central."

After a minute or two, as we all sat in silence, he picked up the five-hundred-euro note and said, "You know, now that I think about it, I do remember the dude you're talking about."

"Do you have a record of where you took him?"

"I don't need a record, man, because he wanted to go somewhere from the railroad station that no one else ever requested to go, at least directly from the station."

"Where was that?"

"It's only a few blocks from here. Why don't I just take you there?"

"Sure."

Jenna gave me a look, as if to say, *Are you crazy? This guy could be taking us off to be killed.*

I just shrugged.

A few minutes later, after turning a corner or two, but still in the heart of town, the cab came to a stop in front of a store with a big plate glass window. The sign overhead said "*Chapeaux et Foulards.*"

I gaped at it. "You took him to a hat and scarf store?"

"Yes. He even had the exact address with him."

"Are you sure you didn't take him to Bibelots et Livres?"

"Yes, I'm absolutely sure. I brought him here."

"Did you actually watch him go in?"

"No, why would I? I mean, if he wanted to go to a hat store, that was his business. Maybe the owner was a friend. Who knows?"

"I just thought maybe it was unusual enough that . . ."

"Listen, I pick fares up and I drop 'em off. Unless it's a child or a little old lady, I don't pay close attention to what happens after they pay me and close the door behind them. I'm just going to be looking for my next fare."

"Well, that makes sense, I suppose. Did you ever see him again?"

"No. Now do you want to be dropped here, or did you just want to learn where he went and then have me take you somewhere else today?"

Jenna was already starting to get out of the cab. "I guess we're getting out," I said.

"Do you want anything back from that five hundred?"

"No, you keep it."

"Thanks, man. I'm gonna take the rest of the day off and take my wife and kid out to dinner." He leaned back and handed me a business card. "If you need to go anywhere else in town while you're here, call me. It will be on me."

"I'll keep that in mind." I got out and watched as he drove away, thinking that I would one day get the money back from Oscar.

"Wasn't five hundred at least five times too much?" Jenna asked.

"Well, you know, it was a bribe. And you have to remember what an old mafioso once said about that."

"Which was?"

"If you're going to bribe someone, you can never pay too much. If you offer too little, the guy may just be insulted and turn you in. Make it large enough to change his life. He's more likely to take it, and will ever after be in your debt because you can turn *him* in."

"Well, okay, but I think two hundred, or even one hundred, would easily have changed *his* life." With that, she opened the door to the store and stepped inside. A bell made a little jingling sound. I followed.

CHAPTER 28

The store was filled with men's and women's hats of all kinds, including fedoras, berets, broad-brimmed women's hats and a single pith helmet. Some were black, others colorful, some unadorned, some with feathers, all displayed on plastic heads supported by thin metal poles set into holes in the floor. A few heads grew out of beige plastic shoulders with scarves wrapped around them. The heads were all eerily faceless and swayed slightly from the breeze that came in through the open door.

As we entered, an impeccably dressed man who looked to be in his early fifties was coming from the back to greet us, presumably alerted by the tingling of the bell. He was wearing a long winter overcoat, a black homburg and kid gloves, as if he was about to leave.

"Bonjour, Monsieur," I said. And in the microsecond between that greeting and trying to decide what, if anything, I wanted to say next, I decided to just go for it. *"Nous sommes venus pour vous parler d'un ami qui a visité ici il y a une semaine ou deux."*

"Bonjour, Madame et Monsieur," he said, and then, in English, "So you have come to inquire about a friend who visited here in the last week or two?"

"Yes, that's what I said. But how did you know we are English speakers?"

"Your accent, Monsieur. If you will pardon me, you are obviously an American. Your French is quite good, but your accent is not, shall we say, perfect. And I speak English well, as my mother was British. But if you would prefer to speak in French, that is fine, too."

"No, my friend here does not speak French, so using English is great."

"Wow," Jenna said, "two in a row."

"Two what in a row, Madame?"

"Two French people in a row who speak English."

He raised his eyebrows. "Madame, this town may be small, but it is not a village in the *Massif Central*. It is a sophisticated place for tourists from around the world."

"I'm sorry," Jenna said, "I did not mean to insult your town."

"Eh, no offense taken. I am Tomas Condelet, the owner of this shop. And who might you two be?"

"I'm Robert Tarza and this is my colleague Professor Jenna James."

"I am pleased to meet you. As you can see, I was about to go out, but I am certainly happy to delay if I might be of service to you. Who is this friend you are seeking to know about?"

"We are looking for a friend named Oscar Quesana," I said. "We think he came here a couple of weeks ago, perhaps to buy a book."

"What kind of book?"

"A first edition in English of *Les Misérables*."

His eyes twinkled. "Why would someone come to a hat store to buy a book?"

"I don't know that he did buy it here. All I know is that he came here and sometime after that, bought the book."

"Did you inquire at our local antiquarian bookstore, Bibelots et Livres?"

"Not yet."

"That might be a better place to ask about this."

Jenna interrupted and said, "Well, before we do that, do you recall such a gentleman?"

"Yes, actually, I do."

"Did he buy a book here?"

"Yes, he did."

Clearly, Jenna had remembered what I had taught her as a lawyer years before, but had forgotten: Make the witness answer *your* question, not the question the witness wants to answer. I probably would have taken his suggestion that we start at the bookstore to mean that Monsieur Condelet, by his sneaky answer, was denying that Oscar had been to his store or bought a book there.

"What did he buy?" I asked.

"He bought a first edition in English of *Les Misérables*. As I'm sure you must know if you figured out that he came here. And I am impressed at your detective work. There is a special word in English for that, but I have forgotten it."

"Sleuthing."

"Yes, 'sleuthing.' I am impressed at your sleuthing."

"Why does a hat store sell rare books?" Jenna asked.

"Ah, this is a very good question. It has to do with history."

"What history?"

"The history of a small Catholic church in this city. Not the big one that everyone goes to. But the small one, tucked away, that has almost no congregation left."

"Let me guess," I said. "This is a church where a wayward priest once upon a time collected first editions of the works of Victor Hugo."

"Yes, exactly."

"Exactly what?"

"Many years ago, my father acquired these books, and my family has been selling them off one by one over the years, as a kind of income-generating asset. Would you like to see those that remain?"

"Perhaps." I looked at Jenna, who shook her head in the negative. "I guess not right now."

"May I try on a hat?" Jenna asked.

"Of course. This is a hat store."

Jenna walked over and picked a black bowler from one of the heads and put it on her head at a jaunty angle. "How does this look?"

"Well," he said, "it is a man's hat, but it looks not bad."

"Is there a mirror I can use?"

"Yes, of course. It is toward the back and around that little corner there."

"I will be right back."

While we waited for Jenna to admire herself in some distant mirror, we continued talking.

"This woman you are with is a bit strange, is she not?"

"At times, yes."

Jenna returned and said, "When we are done I think I will buy the hat. It becomes me. But in the meantime, I have another question about these rare books you sell."

"Yes?"

"How did your father acquire them?"

"Well, by the same means that many great fortunes are initially acquired. He stole them."

"Won't someone want them back if they find out?"

"I don't know who would have a claim on them, frankly. The priest who collected them is dead almost a hundred years, and I have made sure that there is no record of him left in the church archives."

"Wait," I said. "Did you know that the edition our friend bought has a personal inscription from Victor Hugo to Charles Dickens?"

"Yes, of course I know that. An inscription that is almost certainly a forgery. As is the little sketch that purports to be a self-portrait of Hugo, although when they were forged is unclear to me."

"You have no idea?"

"The most intriguing theory is that it was forged by Victor Hugo's son, who was a great French translator. Perhaps as a joke, or perhaps to sell to some gullible British person to make money. There is no way to know."

"So Oscar was aware that you thought it was fake?"

"Oh yes. But for some reason he wanted it anyway and was willing to pay more than I think it is truly worth."

"And you sold it to him at that price despite your view that it contains a forged inscription and drawing?"

"Of course. If a man wants to pay you the price of a diamond for a potato, why would you not accept?"

"Are you aware that Monsieur Quesana has been kidnapped?"

He shrank back. "No. Is this true?"

"Yes, I'm afraid so, and it seems to have to do with this book he bought from you."

"I am truly shocked at this. Truly shocked. And I now fear I may have had something to do with it."

"Explain, please."

"After your friend bought the book and took it away, a few days later another man appeared—a Russian—and he, too, wanted to buy this book. I told him I had already sold it."

"And?"

"And he insisted that I tell him the name of the buyer."

"Did you?"

"Well, to do so would have been unethical. In the book trade, one cannot do such a thing unless one has the permission of the buyer. Some people like to keep the nature of their collections private."

"But you did anyway, didn't you?"

"The Russian gentleman made it difficult to refuse."

"With money?"

"No, with an assistant who sported a pair of brass knuckles."

He rubbed his chin. I didn't know if that meant that he'd been hit, and that it was still healing, or if it meant that even now he felt the threat.

He raised his left hand as if he were being sworn in, left-handed, on a witness stand. "But I had no idea, I swear, that this Russian would turn to illegal means to acquire the book. Oscar had said to me he planned to sell it, and so I thought perhaps the Russian would be a buyer from him."

"Did you give him Oscar's address?"

"Yes, I gave him Monsieur Quesana's business card. I assumed he would make Monsieur Quesana an offer to purchase it from him. I assumed that Monsieur Quesana would at that point be pleased to rid himself of what he had presumably concluded by then was a fake."

"That was very generous of you," I said. "By the way, did you pay the government the value added tax on that transaction?"

"I have not yet filed my tax returns for that sales period."

"I see."

There seemed something wrong with the story, but I couldn't put my finger on it. "What did the Russian guy look like?"

"He was short and fat and almost bald."

"Like Khrushchev?"

"I am too young to remember Khrushchev."

"Ah, no doubt true. I always forget how much of history has gone away."

"Well, if you have no further business with me, I need to get going. And you may consider the hat to be a gift, Madame."

"Why, thank you."

"Are you sure you don't want to see the collection?"

"No," I said. "I think we have learned what we came to learn, and we thank you for your candor."

He backed up a few steps, pulled a gun from his left pocket and pointed it at us. "I'm afraid I have to insist that you inspect the collection. Move toward the back of the store now, slowly."

I looked at him carefully, trying to decide if we could take him without being shot. I concluded that the answer was no. Plus his hand was shaking. That suggested he didn't normally use a gun, and people with no experience with firearms are even more likely to shoot you. My hand was shaking, too, which showed that beneath what I hoped was a calm exterior, I was scared out of my mind.

Jenna was already moving toward the back, and I followed.

"Stop there."

We did. He moved to one side of us, still pointing the gun, and, with his right hand, which was also shaking, reached down and pulled aside a throw rug. Beneath it was a metal ring set into the floor. He reached down and pulled up on it, although he seemed to wince as he did so. A trapdoor opened, and a spring-loaded, segmented wooden ladder, attached to the trapdoor by some kind of trip cord, unfolded downward, its bottom hitting on the floor below with a bang.

"Take your cell phones out of your pockets and place them on the floor."

We did as he asked.

"Now, Madame, please take off that hat and lay it on the floor next to the trapdoor. There's no point in losing a good hat."

Jenna complied.

"Now climb down the ladder. If either one of you tries to run or does anything funny, I will shoot both of you."

We climbed down the rickety ladder into a dimly lit basement, whose walls were lined from floor to ceiling with books.

"I hope you will enjoy the collection while you are down there. You will not be there long, though. There are some people who I suspect want to talk to you. And I apologize, but the light switch is up here. I think it better that you stay in the dark."

He closed the trapdoor, which blotted out almost all light. I heard rather than saw the ladder snap upward, and then the snick of a lock of some kind being closed. A few minutes later, I heard the very faint jingle of the bell on the front door as he left.

"Well, Jenna, good thing he doesn't know you can pick locks. I'm sure that, even in the dark, you can have us out of here in no time." It was a statement of hope more than logic, used to stave off my growing fear that we weren't going to get out of this alive.

"Robert, that was the sound of a long metal bolt being slid through a u-shaped piece of metal on the other side of the trap-door. In locksmith jargon, the u-shaped piece is called a staple. It's a primitive from of deadbolt. I saw one on the outside of the trapdoor when he opened it. It can't be picked from the dead side, which is where we are."

I was silent. Finally, I said, "Why did you try on the hat?"

"A crazy person just locked us in a basement and you're asking about the hat?"

"I'm trying to keep my fear at bay by engaging in small talk."

"I used the time when I was out of sight at the mirror to send a short text to Tess telling her I thought we might be in trouble. I told her if she did not hear from us in an hour, to come to this address and bring the police and a dog that could find us. The clothes that are left in our room should have our scent on them."

"You put all of that in a short text?"

"You don't text much, do you?"

"No."

"Trust me, it was short."

"Well, in any case, it's very good you did tell her to come look for us."

"Yes, but we may not have an hour. We may be dead in less than that."

"Why were you suspicious? He seemed kind of nutty but harmless."

"Because he used his left hand to do things, and he seemed awkward at it, as if he were actually right-handed but for some reason couldn't use his right hand. And then I looked carefully at his right hand and saw that the ring finger of his glove was flopping loose. There was clearly no finger inside it."

"So?"

"There was also what looked to me like dried blood that had soaked through the base of the glove's ring finger."

"How do you know what dried blood looks like?"

"I worked in a hospital OR one summer during college. And I was a little kid once, weren't you?"

"I guess. But with the blood, you think . . ."

"That the finger we received in the box was his."

"We need to get out of here."

"No kidding."

CHAPTER 29

After a few minutes, Jenna said, "I don't think we're going to have a problem. I just remembered that I have a second cell phone. It's in my purse. It's the one I carry in the US. When I got to France, I rented a local one at the airport so I wouldn't have to pay the outrageous roaming charges."

"Great!"

"Yeah. If that guy had been a pro he would have searched my purse, but he didn't."

I watched as she rummaged in her purse, found the cell, turned it on and waited for it to power up.

"Shit. The battery's dead."

"Try shaking it. Sometimes that works."

She shook it, hard.

"Didn't work."

"Try taking the battery out and putting it back in."

She tried that, too.

"Still dead. I guess we have to try Plan B."

"Which is?"

"I wish I knew."

By that time, my eyes had fully adapted to the dark. I could see a bit better by the small beam of light that leaked through the crack between the ceiling and the trapdoor. What I saw didn't help much. Just books and more books. Nothing with which we could try to ram the trapdoor and break the hardware that held the deadbolt in place.

"We need to look around," I said.

The basement was in an "L" shape. We could see a bit in the part we were standing in. When we rounded the corner into the other section, it was pitch black. We felt our way around the walls and found nothing but books. Finally, though, I did come to a closet of some sort. It was unlocked and I opened it. I couldn't see anything inside.

"I don't want to go in," I said. "There could be a pit or something, and it smells bad."

"I could go," Jenna said.

"I don't think you should. We can't afford for either of us to be injured."

"Okay." We returned to the area under the trapdoor, sat down on the concrete floor and talked through various means of escape, rejecting one after the other as impractical. Every time there was a small noise, we both jumped, thinking it was the owner coming back with his gun. At least an hour went by with no solution found. I started to sweat and began to understand what the smell of fear meant.

Periods of talking through solutions—and one discussion of how to disarm the store owner if he came back alone—began to be replaced with periods of resigned silence. My sweat had begun to turn cold, and I was starting to shiver. Suddenly, Jenna said, "I have an idea that might work."

"Which is?"

"Give me one of your shoe laces."

"What are you going to do with it?"

"Just give it to me."

I bent down, unlaced my right shoe, pulled out the shoelace and handed it to her.

"Oh, good, it's one of those flat, unpolished stiff ones from your lawyer shoes. I knew you male lawyers wore those ugly shoes for some good reason."

"I'll ask again. What are you going to do with it?"

"Here's my idea. If I can get up to the bottom of the trapdoor, I think I'll be able to see a little piece of the long bolt that runs across the crack that the light's coming through. Then I can wrap the shoelace around the bolt and rotate it by pulling the ends of the shoelace back and forth, like we used to do in camp when we were twisting a stick back and forth between our palms to try to make a fire."

"Won't that just leave it in place?"

"Maybe, but if I lean and pull in one direction while I rotate it, maybe it will eventually slide in that direction, away from the U-bolt that's holding it down. I only got a quick glance at it, but it looks as if it's the simplest kind—a straight rod with a right-angled handle that just pushes the rod into a U-bolt. Usually, the right-angled handle would be locked down in some way on one end, but I think the piece that locks it down must have broken off because I didn't see it."

"Maybe he doesn't have frequent occasion to lock people in his basement."

She laughed. "Yeah. Or maybe he does, considering that the ladder won't come down when you're down here and the trapdoor is closed."

I heard a sudden scraping noise somewhere behind me. It snapped my head around. Jenna must have heard it, too, because she, too, turned her head abruptly. We both stood stock-still and listened. It didn't recur.

"Probably a rat in the wall," I said.

"Yeah, probably."

"Back to your idea. It's clever, Jenna. It might work."

"The only problem is that I have to get up to the ceiling."

"It's a really low ceiling," I said. I stood up, raised up on my toes and stretched my hands over my head as far as they would go. "I can almost touch it."

"Maybe I can stand on a pile of books," she said. "Or maybe you could, since you're taller."

We both turned and began to pull books off the shelves. "Let's try to find the thick ones," I said.

After a couple of minutes, we had created two piles of thick books, set up side-by-side so there'd be more area to stand on. We placed them right beneath the trapdoor. Jenna climbed on top and reached up. "I can just barely touch my fingers to the bottom of the trapdoor, but I'm not close enough to thread the shoelace around the bolt."

"Can you reach the ladder and somehow unsnap it so it folds down again?"

"No."

"Maybe I can reach either it or the bolt," I said.

She jumped down, handed me the shoelace, and we switched places. I was at least six inches taller than Jenna, and once on top of the books, I was easily able to touch the ceiling, although I couldn't unlatch the ladder, which was secured in a clever way that defeated all of my attempts to lower it.

I focused instead on the bolt, which I could see clearly through the crack. After a couple of tries, I was able to thread the shoelace through the crack and around the bolt, then wrap it around a second time so that when I pulled it tight, it had captured the shaft in its grip. I began to saw it back and forth, using both hands to rotate it, while leaning slightly to the right so that as the shaft rotated it would pull itself away from the U-bolt that was holding it in place. Which is when I fell.

Jenna managed to break my fall, and although I banged my elbow on the floor, I didn't seem otherwise hurt.

"This isn't working," Jenna said. "The book stack is too unstable. And we can't afford for you to fall again."

"Obviously."

"How strong are you?"

I shrugged. "I don't know. I go to the gym three times a week and lift weights. Plus I work out on a spinner bike."

"Maybe I can sit on your shoulders and reach the trapdoor that way."

"How much do you weigh?"

"About one-twenty."

"I'd have to, in effect, press your weight from a squat."

"Not fully. I can climb onto your shoulders from a tall stack of books. So I could get on without your being at a full squat."

"I'm willing to give it a try."

We piled a few more books onto the stack and Jenna climbed from the top of the stack onto my shoulders, which I had bent forward. I managed, just, after she got on, to straighten up.

"Where is the shoelace?" she asked.

"It's still wound around the shaft up there."

"I've got it. Now let's see if this will work."

She sawed away at it for at least two minutes. My legs were beginning to ache and to vibrate a bit. I decided to make light of it to take my mind off of them. "Jenna, do you think your law school would approve of your doing this with a student?"

"Shut up, Robert."

Just then she said, "Got it. The bolt's retracted."

"Be careful, Jenna. When you push the trapdoor up, it may automatically release the ladder and knock both of us to the floor when it comes down. I'll have to move quickly to get out of the way. That might bring you crashing down."

"I think right after I flip the trapdoor up, I can grab on to the edge and hoist myself up. You'll be able to see the ladder coming at you and jump aside just as I hoist myself up."

"Can you chin yourself? Because that's what you'll be doing."

"I don't know. But I'm gonna try."

"Say when."

"Okay. I'm going to try to flip the trapdoor up on the count of three. One . . . two . . . three."

I heard more than saw the door flip up and the ladder unfold and hurtle down at me. I jumped aside, and it missed me, just. I looked up and saw Jenna hanging onto the ledge, obviously unable to chin herself up to the floor above, and too far from the ladder to scramble onto it. I started for the ladder, hoping she'd be able to hang on long enough for me to climb up, reach out, grab her under the arms and hoist her to the floor.

Which is when she fell. I caught her as best I could and we both crumpled to a heap on the floor.

"Are you okay, Robert?"

"Yeah, sort of. I don't think anything is broken. Are you?"

"Yeah. Let's get out of here."

We got up and started up the ladder one at a time, Jenna first. When she had cleared the top, I put my foot on the bottom rung and heard running behind me. What? How could we have been down there so long and not have known someone else was down there, too? I spun around, intending to try to take out or at a minimum delay whoever was running toward me. At least Jenna would get away.

It was Olga, still in a slinky dress, but tattered and dirty. "I come," she said. My reaction to seeing her was somewhere between pole-axed that she was there and happy to have another friendly body if we needed to fight our way out. Or would she be an enemy?

Jenna looked back down through the hole. "Where are you? Oh, shit."

I stepped aside and motioned Olga up the ladder. That way, if she was an enemy, she was in front of me, and somehow I felt safer. When the three of us were at the top, she said something to Jenna in Russian, and Jenna responded.

"What did she say?"

"That 'that guy' threw her in the basement."

"Ask her what she was doing here."

"Later. We need to get out of here."

Our cell phones were sitting on a table next to the trapdoor. So was a purse. We grabbed the phones and headed for the front. Olga grabbed the purse and stayed close to us. Jenna stopped abruptly, went back and scooped up the discarded hat. "Souvenir," she said.

Once outside, we looked around to see if anyone was watching us. We didn't see anybody and started walking away from the store, fast. Or as fast as I could go with my laceless shoe flopping on and off of my foot.

"We need to get out of Dodge," I said.

"Not to mention Digne," Jenna said.

We rejected going to the train station or a car rental place because that's where they'd likely be looking for us.

"What about calling the police?" Jenna asked.

I thought about it for a second. "Who knows whose side they're on down here?"

"I know," she said. "Our friend the cab driver."

Before she'd finished speaking, I had picked up my cell, dug his card out of my pocket and punched in the number. He picked up almost immediately.

"Hi," I said, "this is the guy who left you the five hundred euro tip. We need to get back to Paris right away. Can you take us? There's another five hundred euros in it for you, plus we'll pay for the gas."

"No problemo," he said. "Shall I pick you up in an hour at your hotel?"

"No, we need to go right now." I looked around at the street signs and gave him a pickup point about two blocks from where we were at that moment.

"Okay, I'll see you there in five."

"I hope that we can really trust him," Jenna said.

"I don't think we have much choice."

CHAPTER 30

We walked to the pickup point, found a doorway nearby and huddled in it, trying to look inconspicuous.

Olga said something to Jenna again in Russian.

"What'd she say?"

"She wants to come with us."

"Tell her okay, but also ask her what she's doing here."

I listened to the Russian flow back and forth for a few seconds.

"She says she is too upset to talk right now."

"Okay. We'll try again later."

The cabbie arrived as promised, and we piled into the back, with Olga between us. I'd never been so relieved to get into a car.

"No luggage?" he asked.

"No."

"What's that all about?"

"Do you recall that you told us that how you got to Digne was a long story?" I said.

"Yes."

"This is, too. Just get going, please."

"Who's the chick?"

"Also a long story. We *really* need to go."

When we were about five minutes outside of town, Jenna began talking rapidly to Olga. Olga handed over her purse, and I watched Jenna go through it. "No cell phone so we're okay there," she said. "Her father won't be tracking us."

"What about elsewhere on her?"

"That dress doesn't have any pockets, so I think we're safe."

"You know, you better text Tess and tell her not to come find us in the hat store."

"Right. Shall I tell her everything that's happened?"

"Yes, and after that, I think we should call the general and tell him what's gone down. We're clearly out of our depth."

"You're right, but—" She pointed at the cab driver.

"Hey guys," he said, "I saw her gesture in the mirror. Really, I don't know what you're up to, but I'm good. I don't tell anyone what my fares say when they're in my back seat. Cab driver privilege, you know? But if you want me to pull over somewhere so you can get out and talk in private—or want me to get out— that's cool."

What went through my mind was that Tess had turned out to be a spook, the hat guy had turned out to be a killer, and the general had turned out to be allied with some elite police force instead of being in retirement from the army. Who knew who the cab driver would really turn out to be? But I decided that we might as well go for it. If we stopped, we wouldn't be putting distance between ourselves and Digne. And if we didn't call, we'd give the hat guy more time to get away or cover things up.

Jenna called Tess while I called the general.

We told them everything. Or at least, as it turned out later, I did.

At the next substantial town, which took us about an hour to reach, we were joined by two unmarked police cars, which began to trail us at a discreet distance. I didn't know if Tess had arranged it or if the general had. Either way, it was comforting.

After we had been underway with our escort for a little while, Jenna had fallen asleep and I was just about to doze off when the cab driver said, "That's a very interesting story you guys are involved in."

"I thought you didn't listen," I said.

"I didn't say I didn't listen. I said I kept what I heard to myself. Anyway, there are a few small parts of the story you're missing that might be of interest to you."

"Which are?"

"Well, for one thing, that guy you met on the train? The priest?"

"Yes?"

"He's the father of the hat store owner."

"I thought the guy we met on the train was a priest."

"He is. He had a kid before he became a priest, and the hat store guy is that kid. They're really tight."

"So when the hat store guy said his father acquired the books, he must have acquired them—stolen them—directly from the church."

"That's the rumor, although it was a long time ago, and they claim they bought the collection."

"What else is there to know?" Jenna asked.

"I thought you were asleep, Jenna."

"I sleep with one ear open."

"Well," the cab driver said, "first of all, it's not a secret in town that those guys have all those books in their basement. Once in a while they even donate one to some good cause, like a church auction."

"That's kind of them," Jenna said.

"Yeah, well, the story they tell is that they have a 'special room' where the really valuable books are kept. The ones with inscriptions by famous people. They've never donated any of those."

He stopped talking after that. We eventually stopped for a meal at a small roadside café. Our protectors stopped with us but sat at two separate tables, one on each side of us. I noticed Jenna go and buy three more throw-away cell phones.

When she came back, I said, "Jenna, do you think those guys are our protectors, or are we their prisoners?"

"Prisoners probably. As you know, I'm a wanted felon."

"Wow. What's that about?" our cab driver friend asked.

We told him. Then we moved on to something I really wanted to know. "What else can you tell us about the hat seller-book dealer?" I asked.

"There has long been a rumor about a scam they run," he said.

"Which is?"

"They apparently have some book that has an inscription in it from a famous person. But it's only valuable if the inscription is real. They think it's not real. So they offer it for sale and actually tell people they think it's a forgery. But people buy it anyway."

"Why?"

"Because our guys drop hints that it just *might* be real."

"Let me guess," I said. "The sucker persuades himself that it is real."

"Yeah, and these guys offer the sucker a great deal. They sell it to him for more than it's actually worth if there were no inscription but less than it would be worth if the inscription were real. A big bargain."

"Then what happens?"

"The sucker takes it to antique book dealers in Paris and gets laughed at."

"And then tries to return it?"

"Yeah. And our guys tell him, 'Hey, we told you it was a fake. Why should we buy it back?'"

I could see it coming. "And then they split the difference with the guy and give him only half his money back?"

"Right, and then they sell it again to the next sucker."

"Wait," Jenna said. "This doesn't sound like something a cab driver finds out about. Where did you hear this?"

"From the wife, who works for the police chief."

"Do you always call her 'the wife'?" Jenna asked.

"Sure, is there a problem with that?"

"Does she call you 'the husband'?"

"No. She doesn't speak English."

"Leave it, Jenna," I said. "We've got a long drive still back to Paris. I'm going to try to sleep some."

It took us another seven hours to get there. Our cab driver seemed not to want to exceed the speed limit with the cops trailing us.

About two hours outside of Paris, Jenna's cell buzzed. She looked down at a text message.

"Shit. It's from the kidnappers."

"What does it say?"

"It says, '*We know you have book now. Confirm and we arrange pickup. DO NOT TELL POLICE.*'"

Jenna bent over her cell and tapped out a reply.

"What did you say?"

"I said, '*we don't have book. you have Oscar. we have Olga. will trade you.*'"

"You think Olga's father, Igor, is on the other end of all this?"

"Yes."

Her cell buzzed again.

"What's it say this time?"

"It says, *'who is Olga?'* But I think that's bullshit. They know damn well who she is. And I think she knows where the book is. And maybe where Oscar is, too. I'm not gonna bother to respond."

"Speaking of who is Olga, you should try again to find out more from her," I said. "Start with who she is and what she's doing here. She should be recovered by now from the shock of being locked in that basement."

Jenna gave it a try, and I listened for a while as they conversed in Russian. Eventually, I dozed off. Later, Jenna poked me in the shoulder, and I woke up with a start.

"Wake up! I learned some things."

"What things?"

"She says her father brought her here to follow Oscar. That he knew Oscar had bought the book, but her father wanted to buy it from Oscar. But he wouldn't sell for a price her father wanted to pay."

"I'm suspicious. Why is she telling you anything?"

"She's scared and thinks she's in over her head. She just wants to forget the whole thing and go to college."

"I don't know if I'm buying it, but what else did she say?"

"That she followed Oscar to Digne during the week after Christmas and watched him go in carrying a big box. She says he came out without the box. She figured that he had left the signed copy of *Les Misérables* at the hat store, and she went back after the store closed yesterday to try to find it. She got caught and put in the basement."

"Did she say who told her to look for it there?" I asked.

"She said it was her own idea, that her father didn't know about her plans. That she wanted to impress him by showing him she wasn't just a young nobody."

"Typical of young adults these days, I guess. Did you learn anything else, Jenna?"

"No, and when I began to press her for more details, especially about her father, she clammed up."

"Do you believe her? About what she said?"

"Not really, Robert. I feel like she's leaving something out."

"Maybe she was looking for the authenticator that Oscar said he found."

"That would make sense in a way, but I wasn't going to ask her about it directly since she might not yet know about it."

The rest of the way to Paris, we all mostly dozed. Once in Paris, we stopped at Jenna's hotel, and one of the plainclothes officers who had been trailing us accompanied her inside to collect her belongings. As we left, I saw the owner standing in the doorway glaring at us. Then we went to Tess's.

We paid the cab driver and bid him goodbye. "Hey," he said, "thanks so much. I'm going to bring the wife and kid up here for a few days of a little unexpected vacation. They've never been to Paris. So if you need anything, give me a holler." He waved and drove off.

When we walked into the building, the concierge seemed to have acquired a new friend in the form of a uniformed cop, who was standing post by the elevator. In the apartment, Tess greeted each of us with a hug and a kiss on both cheeks—including Olga—gave us some hot chocolate and put us to bed. I tried to tell her the story the cab driver had told us, but she said, "*Demain.* Tomorrow. You both need to sleep well. Jenna has a big day. She will see the magistrate at ten in the morning. At nine, she will meet with my lawyer, Maître Bertrand. He is very,

very good. And he speaks excellent English. Better than mine." She turned and smiled at me.

Olga went to bed first, on the pull-out couch in my study. After her door was closed, Jenna said, "Tess, do you have some twine and a scissors?"

"Yes. I will obtain them." She went into the kitchen, and I heard a drawer open. She came back a minute later and handed Jenna a ball of white twine and a small scissors. "What will you do with them?"

"I don't want Olga to escape during the night."

"Are you going to tie her up? She is not a prisoner," Tess said.

"No. But if she gets up and goes somewhere tonight, I'm going to follow her."

Jenna took the ball of twine, wrapped several loops around the doorknob on my study door, then unwound the string as she walked into the guest room, where she was sleeping. She cut the string and tied the loose end to a small alarm clock that was sitting on a night table.

"If she opens the door, this will wake me up, and I'll see what she's up to."

"Who teaches you this?" Tess asked.

"My Uncle Freddie. He called it a 'poor man's door alarm.'"

After that, we all went to bed.

* * *

The next morning, Tess, Jenna and I were all seated at the breakfast table sipping coffee and munching on pastries, which Tess had gone out to fetch. Olga was apparently still asleep.

"Well, Jenna, did Olga get up during the night?" I asked.

"Yes."

"Where did she go? To find her father?"

"She went to get a glass of milk out of the fridge."

I smiled, and I could tell that Tess was suppressing a laugh.

"It's not funny. If she had gone somewhere during the night, I would have been able to follow her and perhaps unravel the mystery."

Jenna is a great lawyer, but she doesn't have much of a sense of humor.

Not long after that, the lawyer that Tess had arranged for Jenna, Maître Bertrand, arrived. He was wearing a blue pin-stripe suit and a red tie. He looked like Jack Kennedy. I could tell that Jenna was immediately smitten. Or at least initially.

We all retreated to the living room, where Jenna told Maître Bertrand everything she knew about the kidnapping, our trip to Digne and the events at the hotel the night she picked the lock. He made careful notes on a yellow legal pad. When Jenna was done, he asked a few questions, noted the answers, and looked up from his pad. "It is unusual for me to give advice to a client with others around." He glanced at Tess and me.

"Why don't you make an exception in this case?" I said. "I don't know what the privilege rules are here, but in our country, although having all of us hear your advice to Jenna might blow the privilege, it's unlikely anyone would ask Tess or me what we had heard."

"You don't know this judge," he said. "De Fournis can be very thorough. But I will leave the decision to Jenna, who is my client."

"Let them stay," Jenna said.

"Alright," he said. "First, let me tell you, briefly, about the powers of a *juge d'instruction*, what you in America would call an 'investigating judge.' This kind of judge is among the most powerful in France. Once he has jurisdiction over a case, he can investigate *anything* related to the case. He can question anyone he wants under oath or subpoena any documents he wants. He can order wiretaps. He can direct the police to undertake raids to search for evidence. He can even go on the raids himself if he wishes. And he can ask another judge to put you back in jail. This particular judge, de Fournis, is famous for stretching his powers."

"Well, the jail part isn't good, obviously," Jenna said. "But this investigating judge sounds like he has the power to get to the bottom of the whole kidnapping. And maybe, unlike the police, he will be truly interested in finding Oscar."

"That depends, Jenna, on how long you want to stay in France."

"What do you mean?"

"An investigation into the kidnapping could take months. And the judge will not let you leave until he has finished."

"Well, I do need to get back for the start of the semester, which is not too far away."

"Then I suggest you tell the judge only about picking the lock, and pass it off as a joke you were playing on Oscar."

"That will leave Oscar to his fate."

"I think you underestimate the police. They may have focused on money laundering, but they will ultimately find him if he can be found."

"What do you mean by 'if he can be found'?"

"Hasn't it occurred to you that he may already be dead?"

A long and sandy silence invaded the room. The idea that Oscar might be dead had, of course, occurred to each of us. But it had never been spoken aloud. It was almost like uttering "Voldemort" in a Harry Potter book.

Finally, Jenna said, "Of course it's occurred to me. But until someone tells me he is, and I see his body, I'm going to go on trying to find him."

"Well, it is up to you what you want to tell the judge. I have given you my advice. We will see when you meet with him this afternoon what you do. The choice is yours."

"I will need to think about it."

I spoke up. "Isn't it unethical for you to suggest to Jenna that she lie?"

"Perhaps, but it was, in a way, a prank. It was just not a prank done to make anyone laugh. And so I have advised her to speak, not a lie, but something short of the whole truth. Surely you lawyers in American do the same thing?"

I had to admit that we sometimes did. I didn't want to say that out loud, though, so I just kind of grunted.

Before he left, Bertrand gave Jenna instructions on how to get to the Palais de Justice, where the judge had his chambers, and told her that if she had occasion to address the judge, the French equivalent of "Your Honor" is "Monsieur le juge" and the proper honorific for lawyers is "Maître."

"And dress professionally," he added.

"I'm not an idiot."

I was no longer so sure that the two of them were going to get along well.

CHAPTER 31

Judge Roland de Fournis

I, Roland de Fournis, investigating judge of the Fourteenth Panel of the Chamber of Investigating Judges of Paris, was not having a good day. Not only did I have a bad cold, but the trip to my small place in Provence—where the temperature was a great deal warmer than it was in Paris—had been delayed by a small and insignificant case that the presiding judge had *insisted* I must take up immediately. A predecessor had started the investigation the day before by issuing a summons to some woman in Digne-les-Bains, then departed on vacation and left me with the file. I would have assumed, now that I had finished off the investigation into the cabinet financial scandal, that I was due some time off. But apparently not quite yet.

In front of me on my desk, placed there by my investigator, lay the case dossier with its red cover. The paperwork within described not a major crime, but a minor and simple *délit*—the picking of a lock on a hotel room door by an American tourist and the alleged theft by her of an antique pen said to be worth two hundred euros.

Just then, my court clerk—my *greffier*—who doubled as the court stenographer, came in.

"Bonjour, Marie."

"Bonjour, Monsieur le juge."

"The trip to Provence is off. At least for now. Instead I have a new matter."

She shrugged and asked the question she had asked on arrival each day for the more than twenty years we had worked together: "Who's on the griddle today, then?"

"A rather small fish," I said. "We should be able to fry her up quickly—the accused is a woman, by the way—and get out of here before it gets any colder. I have requested that she appear first today. If she admits the crime, we can work out some sort of plea with the public prosecutor and be done with it."

There was a knock on the door and an attractive, professionally dressed woman who looked to be in her thirties entered along with her lawyer, Maître Bertrand. He was in his usual court garb—black robe and white cravat. My office was, after all, a court, even if it was just a box of a room with two desks and a few chairs, and even if I was wearing a suit rather than a robe, which was the tradition of simplicity in our chambers.

I was pleased to see Bertrand. He had appeared before me many times, and had always been candid. And best of all, quick.

"Please sit down," I said.

"If I may, Monsieur le juge," he said, still standing, "before we begin, I would like to tell you a bit about this case."

"Of course. Please proceed."

"First, my client, Professor James, does not speak French. So we will need a translator."

"Why did no one tell me of this?"

"I do not know."

I was annoyed. Getting a translator was going to take at least several hours, and unless some miracle occurred, I wasn't going to be leaving for Provence any time soon.

"But," Bertrand said, "with my client's permission, I can tell you about the case in a way that I think will be helpful to a quick disposition—even though she will not be able to understand what I say."

"I speak a little English, Maître Bertrand. Let me try to make sure this is okay with your client."

I addressed Professor James in English. "Professor James, it will work with you if your lawyer talks to me in French for a little, but you cannot understand?"

"Yes, Monsieur le juge."

I smiled at her use of the honorific in French. We would perhaps get along.

"Okay," I said to her. "We will do this."

Then I turned to Maître Bertrand. "Maître, you may proceed in French."

My greffier interrupted, "Monsieur le juge, do you want me to transcribe this session or leave it unofficial?"

"I see no harm in your transcribing it."

"Okay." She popped open her notebook computer—the device she used to transcribe testimony—and we were ready to begin.

"So, Maître Bertrand, what do you want to tell the court?"

"It is this, Monsieur le juge. The public prosecutor dismissed this case after the accused had been held in garde à vue for only a few hours—because it is a nothing case and there is no proof."

"Maître Bertrand, doesn't your client admit she picked the lock on the hotel room door of another guest?"

"Yes."

"How can you then say it is a nothing case?"

"It was a joke, Monsieur le juge, played on someone she knows."

"Really. What kind of law professor picks locks as a joke? Is that something common among the Anglo-Saxons?"

"No, Monsieur le juge, it is not. It is like a party trick."

"They must have very different kinds of parties in America, eh?"

"It is no doubt very different there and, if I might say, since my client cannot understand what I am saying, more barbaric."

"Yes. I visited there once. It is a country without a deep culture. But why has this case not been disposed of? Normally, the public prosecutor would take this simple délit directly to the criminal court."

"In this case, Monsieur le juge, the public prosecutor saw no value in the case, dismissed it and released Professor James from garde à vue. He no doubt assumed it would continue as a civil matter between the parties, focused on damages. But then the hotel owner insisted, as is his right as the partie civile, that it continue as a criminal matter. And here we are."

"*Merde.*" I looked over at my greffier. "Please take that word out of the transcript. Substitute *zut alors.*"

"Of course, Monsieur le juge."

I sat and thought about it for a moment. There was a way to end this quickly. I had the power to bring the suspect and the hotel owner together in front of me for an *interrogatoire simultané*—a face-to-face confrontation. Perhaps that way I could coerce the suspect into giving the hotel owner what he no doubt really wanted—money—and then finally get on my way to Provence, even if a little later than planned. I needed to know a little bit more, though.

"Maître Bertrand, have the judicial police investigated this? I do not see anything in the case file except the barest mention of an investigation."

"Yes, the, uh, regular Parisian police."

I caught his hesitation and assumed there was more he was not saying. "By anyone else?"

"Eh, yes. By the Brigade Criminelle."

"For a stolen pen? They investigate terrorism!"

"Yes, yes they do."

The case before me had suddenly become, at the same time, more interesting and, for me personally, threatening. After eleven three-year terms as an investigating judge, I intended to make the corrupt cabinet investigation—which had included no end of political abuse being heaped upon me—my swan song, and I had only a year to go on what was to be my last term before retirement. At age sixty, I had gone on working much longer than most of those with whom I'd entered the judiciary. Almost all had retired long ago. I wanted my final year to be without complication and without the necessity of facing the inevitable demand—if the case weren't finished within a year—to stay on.

So it seemed that Maître Bertrand and I had a mutual interest in not delving too deeply into why the Brigade Criminelle had taken an interest in the case.

"Eh," I said, "I suppose I will let sleeping terrorists rest for now. That will shorten what we have to do here."

"I agree," Maître Bertrand said.

"Good. Then let us go to lunch and reconvene at two. By then a translator will have been found and we can proceed."

Maître Bertrand thanked me, and they all left my court.

As I considered where to lunch, it occurred to me that I could just adjourn my court ten minutes after everyone returned. That way, I would have started the case that very day, just as the presiding judge had demanded. Then, when I got back from Provence, I could make this odd law professor who picks locks and the hotel owner confront one another, face-to-face. And get the matter hammered out in one hour. I had done it at least a hundred times before.

I ate lunch at a café that I favored near the courthouse, then took a long walk in the neighborhood. When I got back to my office, I found the professor and Maître Bertrand waiting for me on the long bench that faced the offices of the juges d'instruction, which are all lined up in a row along a narrow corridor. Beside them was a woman I assumed to be the translator.

We all went in. My greffier was already there and ready.

After we were settled, I asked the professor to take the chair in front of my desk and said to the greffier, "Please administer the oath to the witness. Be sure to wait for the translator to catch up before you say anything that follows on the oath."

She waited for the translator to translate what I had just said, then asked, "Do you, Professor, swear to speak without hatred and without fear, to tell the whole truth and nothing but the truth?"

"I do," the professor said.

After that the translation ran smoothly, almost as if the translator were not there.

"Professor," I asked, "are you aware that you have the right to remain silent? Has Maître Bertrand told you this?"

"Yes, he has."

"And you wish to waive the right to remain silent and testify?"

"Yes, I do."

"Very good. And has he explained to you the nature of these proceedings, that even though I am not in a robe, I am a judge, and that I am charged with investigating the crimes with which you are allegedly involved, picking a lock and stealing a pen, which are violations of the Penal Code? And that if I find the evidence is sufficient to think that you have committed these crimes, I will pass my dossier on to the appropriate criminal court with a recommendation that you be prosecuted?"

"Yes, he has explained all of that."

"Did he explain that the possible punishment for these crimes, if you are convicted, is up to ten years in jail and a fine of up to five thousand euros?"

"Yes."

"Very good. Let me ask you first, then, did you pick the lock of your hotel neighbor"—I had to look at the file because I had forgotten his name—"Monsieur Oscar Quesana?"

"Yes, I did."

"How did you do that?"

"With a nail file and a bobby pin."

"It says here in the dossier that the hotel owner asserts that the lock was damaged. Was it?"

"No. It's a very simple lock. A child could probably open it, and there is nothing to damage. I just suppressed the tumblers, retracted the bolt and turned the handle."

I was curious where the professor had learned to pick locks, even though it wasn't especially relevant. One of the joys of being a judge is that you can satisfy your curiosity. "Professor, where did you learn to pick locks?"

"From my uncle, when I was in high school."

"Was he a professional thief?"

"No, he was a private detective."

"Ah, I see. Once inside, did you take an antique pen, as it says here in the dossier, again as charged by the hotel owner?"

"No."

"Did you see an antique pen in the room?"

"With the door closed behind me, the room was dark. All I had for light was a tiny flashlight. I had left my cell, with its flashlight app, in my room. The only thing I managed to search before I was caught was the closet, and I hadn't even finished searching it. I'd hardly even had a chance to look around the rest of the room."

"So you deny taking the pen?"

"I didn't even see a pen."

"Why did you break into the room?"

"It was to play a trick on a colleague."

"What kind of trick?"

"Uh, I hadn't quite figured that out yet. Something to tell him I'd been there."

"Why did you expect him to find that funny?"

"He's an odd kind of guy."

"Wouldn't most people find it offensive that someone had broken into their private quarters, even if it was to play some kind of joke?"

"Well, Oscar might not find it offensive."

"I see."

Bertrand interrupted. "Monsieur le juge, if you please, since my client has admitted she broke into the room, is it necessary to explore all of this in detail?"

"I think it is. It may shed light on whether she took the pen."

"Okay."

Over my many years as a judge, I had developed a sixth sense as to whether witnesses were telling the truth. I did not think this one was—and the attempt of her counsel to divert the questioning strengthened my feeling about it. But what did she have to hide? Sometimes, a direct approach worked best.

"Professor, I can't say exactly why, but I have the sense you are not telling me the full story."

"I think I am."

"You are not only a professor in your country but a lawyer, is that correct?"

"Yes."

"You practiced law at one point?"

"Yes."

"And did trials?"

"Yes."

"Criminal trials?"

"Some."

"So in your country do you, as a lawyer, owe an obligation of truthfulness to a court?"

"Yes, of course."

"Do you think that just because you are in a foreign country and are not a member of our bar, that you do not owe this court the same duty?"

"I don't know, that's a tricky question."

"I did not mean it to be tricky."

"I know."

"Why did you really go into the room, Professor?"

"I thought there might be a clue there as to why Oscar had been kidnapped."

"Kidnapped?"

"Yes."

"Maître Bertrand, are you aware of this?"

"Yes, your honor, but I thought it was not really related to the matter before the court."

"Really. I think it might well be very related. Professor, are the police looking into this matter?"

"They are looking into whether money laundering was involved. I don't think they're really looking for Oscar, unless they just happen to stumble on him while doing the rest of the investigation."

"When was he kidnapped?"

"New Year's Eve. Near the Odéon Theater."

"If you know, what is the name of the policeman who is in charge of the investigation?"

"Well, there is Captain Bonpere, who began the investigation. But then it was taken over by General Follet. But I don't think he's in the police."

"Maître Bertrand, you have appeared in my court many times. Did you not think it appropriate to let me know what this case was really about?"

"I apologize, Monsieur le juge. I did not think you would want to know about these, uh, complications to a rather simple case of breaking and entering."

"I see. Well, when this is over, we will have to discuss your candor. Or lack of it. For now, I will take a brief recess so that I can call the general."

"You know him?"

"Oh yes. Over many years."

"Okay. How long will the recess be?"

"I think if you and the professor and the translator just wait on the bench outside, that should be fine."

They left the room and I called General Follet, who had once upon a time been my regular tennis partner, until a broken elbow had sidelined me. How long had it been since I'd seen him? Five years, maybe? Surely he would welcome coming to my office for a cup of coffee and a renewal of our acquaintance.

CHAPTER 32

When I reached the general I was surprised to learn that he had emerged from retirement and was doing something—he avoided saying exactly what—with the police at 36 quai des Orfèvres. Which was unusual. The military does not usually play well with the police.

He was at first reluctant to accept my offer of coffee, despite the fact that my office at the Palais de Justice was, with short-cuts, at most a two-minute walk from where he was. I threw in an offer of almond croissants, which I recalled he loved. He relented and said he'd be at my office in thirty minutes. I did not tell him what I wanted to discuss.

I asked my greffier if she would go out and buy four of them, including one for herself. She had overheard the call and readily assented to go. "Anything else?" she asked.

"No. I think our espresso machine is working well, is it not?"

"Yes."

"Then that should suffice." I had long ago put in a coffee machine so that my guests would feel at home while they spoke to me, even if they might later find themselves on the way to jail due to my professional ministrations.

"What about Maître Bertrand, the witness and the translator, whom you have left sitting out on that narrow and uncomfortable bench?"

"Please send them home, but ask them to be prepared to come back tomorrow. I will let them know what time."

"Okay."

The general arrived on time and we exchanged the various greetings expected of old friends who have not seen each other in a long time, including the fatuous promise not to let so long go by until the next time. Then we sipped coffee and munched on croissants and finally, when we had each eaten about half a croissant, we got down to business.

"Mon général, old friend," I said, "I have today taken jurisdiction over a strange case."

"What case is that, my friend?—A friend who ought, by the way, to be retiring. You are too old for this game, as am I."

"Eh, retirement is coming soon. The case is one in which an American professor, a tourist, is accused of picking the lock of a hotel room door and stealing an antique pen."

"What idiot assigned such a petty case to you?"

"The presiding judge of our panel."

"You are much too senior for this. You deal with terrorism and important matters."

"That is just the thing. The professor, whom I began questioning this morning, has mentioned that she broke into the hotel room in order to find clues that might lead to the recovery of a friend of hers who has been kidnapped."

He took a sip of his coffee and another bite of the croissant and chewed for a few seconds, as if gaining time for a response.

"That is quite extraordinary."

"Yes, and what is most extraordinary is that she mentioned that she had spoken with you about it."

"In what regard?"

"She asserted, mon général, that you are running the investigation into the kidnapping."

"I see."

"Eh, see or do not see, or whether you are or you are not, I am going to look into this kidnapping and I thought as a courtesy between old friends I should let you know."

"You do not have the jurisdiction to look into it."

I was truly shocked at his statement. I had genuinely thought that that he would welcome my help, but since he did not, I took another tack. "General, has another magistrate been asked to take jurisdiction of this matter?"

"I do not know."

"Well, I know. I have looked at the list of pending matters. There is no other judicial inquiry at the moment concerning the kidnapping. So I am seizing jurisdiction."

"You can only do that if the public prosecutor asks you to."

"In normal circumstances, you are right. But here—and perhaps you do not know this—the public prosecutor dismissed the case, and the partie civile resuscitated it." I handed him the dossier. "Look for yourself." He took it, looked at it briefly, and handed it back to me.

"So," I said, "you can see that for the moment the public prosecutor has no role. The case is mine, and I will investigate what I must to achieve the goal I always try to achieve to the best of my limited abilities."

"Which is what, to satisfy your personal curiosity?"

"No, to do justice."

He sighed deeply. "Monsieur le juge—and I use your formal title intentionally—justice is a slippery thing. If you interfere here, I fear you may do a small justice and sacrifice a much larger one."

"Will you answer a few questions about your knowledge of this thing? Perhaps you can persuade me to back off."

"Is this a formal hearing?"

"No, it is a conversation between friends."

"I will respectfully decline to answer then."

"I can always send you a summons and make you come here to answer under oath."

"You will find I have immunity from a civilian court proceeding."

"Since you are retired, I don't think you do. But we can test that very soon." I grabbed a blank summons form from my desk drawer, filled it in and handed it to him. "Your hearing is tomorrow at fifteen hundred hours. You can contend that it's not timely, if you want, I suppose, or that you are immune from service. In either case you can appeal the order, and this matter will become more public, which will be fine with me."

He glanced at it and smiled. "Tomorrow is my birthday. Surely you would not . . ."

"Give it back, then."

He handed it to me. I modified it and returned it to him. "Now it is the day after tomorrow, same time."

"If I choose to come, I assume I can bring a lawyer with me."

"Oh, by all means. Try to bring someone who plays tennis. Maybe we can find a fourth for the late afternoon and put together a couple sets of doubles when we are done. My elbow seems healed now."

He didn't commit to tennis, but he did leave.

I turned to my greffier. "Did you take all of that down, even though it was not official?"

"Of course, Monsieur le juge."

"You are the best."

Before I left for the day, I put in a call to Captain Bonpere, whom I had met a few times, but didn't know well. She was out. I left a message to please call me.

I also called my caretaker in Provence and told him I would not be coming after all. At least not for a while.

* * *

The next morning there was a message on my phone from Captain Bonpere. I called her back and she agreed, without hesitation, to come to my office.

I offered her a croissant, and apologized that they were yesterday's and perhaps a bit stale. She seemed not to care, but declined coffee. Which was good, because my greffier had not yet come in and I was terrible at making coffee.

"So," I said, "we have met a few times at conferences, I believe."

"Yes, we have. What can I do for you, Monsieur le juge?"

"I now have jurisdiction over a case involving a professor from America who is accused of breaking into a hotel room and stealing a pen."

"Ah, yes. I know the case. My unit started to investigate it, but it was taken away from us by General Follet. He says he is working on it with the Brigade Criminelle."

"Do you doubt he is?"

"I have not seen anyone from there, but on the other hand, they have no reason to pay attention to me. I am a mere police captain in charge of a squad."

"But you have met and interviewed the professor?"

"Yes. I believe she is honest in saying she broke into the room because she was trying to solve the kidnapping of her friend Oscar Quesana."

"Are the kidnappers demanding a ransom?"

"Yes, but in the form of a rare antiquarian book that they believe the kidnapped man has hidden somewhere."

"That is a new one."

"Indeed."

"Is anyone else involved?"

"The man the professor was with the night of the kidnapping is also trying to find Monsieur Quesana."

This was new. "Who is he?"

"Ah, his name is Robert Tarza. He is also an American, and a former colleague in a large law practice with the professor. He is older and now retired."

"A romance?"

"No, no. He has lived here in Paris for many years now with Madame Tess Devrais."

"I have heard that name somewhere. Who is she?"

She looked around the room, as if checking to see if anyone was listening. "Um, do you have a security clearance, Monsieur le juge?"

"Yes, of course, or I could not have worked on certain terrorism cases."

"Is it still current?"

"Yes."

"May I see it?"

I actually have a certificate. I got it out of my desk drawer and handed it to her. She looked at it with great care and then handed it back.

"Madame Devrais," she said, "is a consultant to the highest levels of the government on national security–related electronic infrastructure."

"How do you know this?"

"I worked with her several years ago on an investigation involving an electronic penetration of an ultra-secure facility."

"What was that about?"

"Despite your security clearance, Monsieur le juge, I do not think you have a need to know, so, with all due respect, I would prefer not to discuss it."

"May I ask how Madame Devrais came to be in this position? It is unusual for a woman."

"Yes, I think I can tell you that, to the extent I know it."

"Go on then."

"Madame Devrais founded her own software company when she was only twenty-five. She sold it several years later for several hundred million euros."

"I do not recall that. You'd think I would. It is the kind of thing that would have been in the newspapers."

"She sold it to the government in a closed and secret sale. Kept very quiet somehow. And much of the information about the company was wiped off the Internet, which was very young then. It was much easier to do that at the time."

"And then?"

"She gave up operational control of the company but continued to consult on special projects."

"I see."

"She also did something very clever."

"Which was?"

"When she became a consultant, apparently certain figures in the military and police treated her badly."

"In other words, they treated her like a young woman who did not matter."

"Yes, but she did something about it."

"What?"

"She insisted that if she were to continue consulting, she must be given a civilian rank equivalent to a divisional general—which is a rank with three stars."

"Ah, so then she outranked most of the assholes."

"Yes."

"Is she trying to help find the kidnapped man?"

"She was trying to help us before the matter was taken away from us. She has to be careful because she has no operational role in the security services. She is only a consultant. But I suspect she is trying hard to find out what is going on."

"Thank you for your candor, Capitaine. Let us stay in touch. And please call me right away if you learn anything new in this strange tale."

"I will do that, Monsieur le juge."

She had not been gone long when my phone rang. It was Maître Bertrand. "The professor has received a new text from the kidnappers," he said.

"I wasn't aware that she had ever received any texts from the kidnappers."

"Ah, yes, I apologize. I forgot that we had not gotten into the details of all of this before, Monsieur le juge. You left us to sit on the bench for a while."

"What are those details?"

He then summarized—quickly—the story as he knew it, including the text messages that had been exchanged and the bizarre goings-on in Digne-les-Bains. When he had finished, I said, "Well, that is quite an histoire. What did this newest text from the kidnappers say?"

"It said that the victim had relented and told them where the book is hidden. They have given instructions for its delivery to them once the professor retrieves it from its hiding place."

"By 'the book,' you mean the one the kidnappers are demanding as ransom?"

"Yes, that one."

"And where is this book supposed to be now?"

"In a secret compartment in the hotel room that my client broke into. It's apparently well hidden."

"And you are telling me this why?"

"My client believes that the general reads the texts she sends and receives. She also thinks that he has tapped her cell phone. Therefore, she has no doubt that the general has already read this new text and will try to get there first and retrieve the book himself."

"What is the basis of her belief?"

"There is a phrase in English she uses. I am almost embarrassed to tell it to you. She says her 'suspicion-o-meter' tells her this."

I raised my eyebrows. "What does that mean?"

"It is difficult to translate into French, Monsieur le juge. Perhaps 'pifometre'—it is as if something does not smell correct. But I think it means that she trusts her intuition about people, and her intuition about the general is not good."

"The professor was a trial lawyer for many years in Los Angeles?"

"Yes, and apparently a very good one."

"Eh bien, trial lawyers often have superior intuitions. But even if she is right, won't the general just use the book to free the kidnapped victim?"

"She fears not. She thinks he might do something else with it, because she thinks he doesn't care about the victim."

Before my strange meeting with the general, I would have found the idea that he would use the book for anything other than a legitimate purpose preposterous. Now I was not so sure.

"What exactly do you want from me, Maître Bertrand?"

"I respectfully request that you issue a search warrant for the book at the hotel and have the police carry it out. As soon as possible."

"You believe I have the authority to do that?"

"Monsieur le juge, you have opened a judicial inquiry into the allegation that my client broke into the hotel, and so . . ."

"And so you think exploring this kidnapping that led to that break-in is within my jurisdiction."

"Yes."

"I have concluded the very same thing. So I will do it."

"How long will it take to carry out a search?"

"If the police will treat it as an urgent matter, we should be at the hotel in an hour."

"You're coming, too?"

"Yes."

"May I bring my client?"

"Yes, as long as she doesn't interfere."

"I will ensure that she will be on good behavior."

CHAPTER 33

The judicial police usually carried out the searches I ordered. But the Paris Police would do it, too, if I so requested. So I called Captain Bonpere, told her of the situation and requested assistance. She enthusiastically agreed to help and mentioned that she had an officer who spoke good English, and that she would send him to pick me up and take me to the hotel.

After I hung up, I prepared the search warrant. I initially considered writing it out narrowly, to focus on a search for a specific book in a particular hotel room. Then, after thinking about it, I instead prepared one that called for a search of the entire hotel to look for the book or anything related to it or the kidnapping.

The police car picked me up thirty minutes later. This would, I remarked to myself, be the first search in many years where I'd accompanied the police myself. The young policeman who spoke English—a Lieutenant Joly—was the driver, and two more cops, both armed with handguns, rode in the back seat. I assumed that force would not be necessary, but you never knew.

Some people tended to have a seriously adverse reaction to police going through their personal stuff.

We were at the hotel within an hour of my call to Captain Bonpere.

I was only mildly surprised, when we arrived, to find the general and an aide standing in the lobby, talking to a man I assumed to be the hotel owner. As Professor James had predicted, the general had gotten there first.

The hotel owner had a narrow, pinched face, a turned-down mouth, protruding ears, and fingernails that needed cutting. I had tried to train myself, as a judge, not to let appearances prejudice my attitudes toward people, but human nature dies hard. I had the feeling, even before the guy opened his mouth, that I was not going to like him.

I was not disappointed. He looked at me and said, "Who the devil are you?"

"I'm Investigating Judge Roland de Fournis. We're here to serve a search warrant." I nodded to Lieutenant Joly, who handed the man the warrant. The owner looked at it, shoved it back at Joly and said, "I need my lawyer to look at this before I agree."

I stepped forward, got up in his face and said, "Unfortunately, Monsieur . . . I don't think I have learned your name. What is it?"

"Crépin."

"Alors, Monsieur Crépin, this is not a situation in which you get to wait for your lawyer while we delay the search. You can call your lawyer, and if he gets here while the search is going on, fine. And if he doesn't, that is also fine. Now we are going to begin with room 406. May I have the key, please?"

"I don't want to give you the key."

"If you don't, Lieutenant Joly can go back to his squad car, get a crowbar and break in the door. Your choice."

He went behind the desk and handed me the key.

"Monsieur Crépin," I asked, "is there any guest staying in that room at the moment?"

"No."

"Good, we will go up."

The general said, "I will go, too."

"I'm sorry, mon général, but this is a search by the court and police assisting the court, and you are neither."

"That is outrageous."

"If you ask politely, Jean, perhaps I will permit you to accompany us." I had intentionally dropped his title and called him by his first name in front of strangers—an unforgiveable insult, which is what I intended.

I waited a moment to see what he would do.

"Alright," he said. "May I accompany your search?"

"Certainly."

At that very moment, Professor James and her attorney, Maître Bertrand, rushed into the lobby.

"I am so sorry we are late," Maître Bertrand said in French. "We were delayed by traffic. Are you doing a search here?"

"Yes."

"May we accompany you? I think my client might be able to be of use."

"Why not? We will make this a search party."

In the end, all of us—the professor, her lawyer, the general, the three policemen and the hotel owner—went up to the 4e étage, some via the elevator, some by the stairs. I put the key in the lock and opened the door to room 406. Lieutenant Joly and I went in. I asked the others to wait in the hall. We looked around but could see no obvious safe or place that a safe might be hidden. I asked the lieutenant to ask the professor and her lawyer to come into the room. I didn't ask for the general. I was enjoying letting him stand in the hallway.

"Will you translate, Lieutenant Joly?"

"Of course."

"So, Professor," I said, "when you searched in here, did you see anything that looked like a hiding place for a safe?"

I waited for her answer to be translated back to me.

"No, but it was dark and, as I said before, all I really had time to search was the closet. There might have been something in there that could be a safe. May I look again now to be sure?"

"Certainly. But let me look inside first." I stuck my head in. The only thing I saw was a man's suit hanging on a hanger. "Go ahead," I said.

She went into the closet while her attorney and I continued to inspect the room. Lieutenant Joly got down on his knees and looked carefully at the floorboards. "I think that it's very cleverly disguised," he said, "but it looks like there is a crack here that might be the edge of a trapdoor."

I got down on my knees—which creaked as I bent down—and examined the crack. "Get the hotel owner in here."

Lieutenant Joly went into the hallway and fetched the owner.

"Monsieur," I said, when he arrived, "do you know if there is a disguised trapdoor here in the floor?"

"I don't know."

"Eh bien, if that's the case, we'll just take the crowbar to that thin, strange crack on the floor to see if we can rip it open, because it certainly looks like a door. And if it's damaged, I'm sure the French State in all its majesty will compensate you. Eventually."

"Alright, alright," he said. "It is a trapdoor. The ring pulls to lift it up are under the two thin floor boards at right-angles to each end of the crack. If you pry the floorboards up with your fingernails, you'll see."

Lieutenant Joly did as he suggested and, sure enough, two ring pulls appeared. Joly grabbed them with both hands and tugged. A door came away, revealing a square hole in the floor that was perhaps half a meter deep and half a meter across. At the bottom were five books, stacked one on top of the other, each covered in a transparent plastic protector.

While we were working on the trapdoor, Professor James had walked up to look over our shoulders. When Joly opened it, she looked in and shouted something.

"She is saying that those volumes are the victim's copy of the book," Joly said.

"Ah, bon. Lieutenant, did you bring plastic gloves and evidence bags?" I asked.

"Yes."

"Please pick those five volumes up and put each one inside an evidence bag" I said. "We'll have to take them to the crime lab for both fingerprint and DNA analysis."

"I will do it," Joly said.

The professor peered into the hole. "Lieutenant, do you see that small triangular piece of plastic there, just a few centimeters on a side?" she asked. "It's probably just a tiny piece of plastic book cover that has flaked off and is of no significance. But could you be sure to bag it, too? And before you put it in the bag, I'd like to look at it."

"The professor would also like to look at that small piece of plastic," Joly said, pointing to it.

"I have no problem with that," I said.

Joly took the plastic gloves from his front pocket, skinned them on, and took a bunch of folded-up plastic evidence bags out of his back pocket. He reached into the hole and deftly lifted up the small piece of plastic between thumb and forefinger. He held it up for me to look at first, and then showed the professor. She shrugged, and he dropped it into one of the Ziploc bags. Next he lifted up the top volume and was about to put it in an evidence bag when the professor said something to him.

"Now, Monsieur le juge, she wants to check out the inscription on the first volume," Joly said.

"I would not mind seeing it myself. They told me that it is on the title page."

Joly opened the first volume, flipped to the title page and held it up. There was no inscription.

I spun around and looked at the professor, who was talking excitedly.

"She says," Joly interpreted, "that if Oscar left the original here, someone must have swapped it for this one. She says the general is her number-one suspect."

That seemed far-fetched to me, and I would need to question her about why she thought so. But since the general was standing out in the hallway, I thought I'd ask him a key question along those same lines before he got away.

I walked outside and said, "General, were you here the night that the professor broke into this hotel room?"

"No."

"Were any of your people—whoever they are—here?"

"No. What did you find?"

"Some books. But not *the* books, apparently."

I noticed that the weasel-faced owner of the hotel had just emerged from the room and come out into the hallway. "Could you remind me of your name again, Monsieur?" I said. "I'm embarrassed to say I have forgotten it."

"Crépin."

"Ah, yes, Monsieur Crépin. I think I have something for you."

I had, as a precaution, brought with me several summonses, which were folded up in my back pocket. I had filled each of them in with everything except the name of the witness and the date of the appearance. I withdrew a summons from my pocket and asked the general if he had a pen, since I'd forgotten mine.

"Of course," he said, and handed me his.

"May I borrow your back for a moment, General? I need something to write on."

He looked nonplussed, but turned around anyway. I filled in Monsieur Crépin's name on the summons, together with the next day's date and an appointment for ten thirty in the morning. I handed it to Monsieur Crépin, who took his reading glasses out of his pocket and read it.

"Tomorrow? Isn't that too soon? Am I not permitted more time to find and consult a lawyer?"

"Under normal circumstances, yes, but I have declared this a situation of urgency since someone's life and safety is at stake. So you must comply, I'm afraid. You have plenty of time to find a lawyer and, in any case, they are all over the courthouse. I will see you tomorrow."

Everyone had by then emerged from the room, and Lieutenant Joly was holding the evidence bag with the book's five volumes in it.

"Lieutenant," I said, "I am declaring this room a crime scene and would appreciate it if you would tape it off and post a guard. I am afraid, as a result, that the rest of you must now leave. Except for you and your client, Maître Bertrand. I would like a word with you."

After the others had grudgingly left, I said, "Maître Bertrand, I would like to save the extra time it takes for a translation. Can you just ask your client why she suspects the general of having swapped out the book?"

He spoke to the professor for a moment and said, "She says the general collects rare books himself, that he has been tapping her phone, that he hurried to get here before her and that he came alone. She thinks that if you had not showed up, he would have found the book himself and taken it without telling anyone."

"Could not the same thing be said of her?"

He translated, and I saw her face harden.

"She says that the difference is that it is her friend who was kidnapped and will be released in exchange for the book."

She had a point.

"Maître Bertrand, I have a question for you," I said.

"Yes?"

"When you told me this long histoire of what has happened here, you said your client was surprised by the police in the hotel room she had broken into."

"That is my understanding."

"How did the hotel owner know that she had broken into the room?"

"I don't know."

"Does she know?"

"I'll ask her." He turned to her, then turned back to me. "She has no idea, but she says the hotel owner told her after she was arrested that 'he knew she was up to no good.'"

"Where was her room that night?"

"It was two doors down." He pointed to room 404.

"This is all very interesting. Could you and your client return to my court tomorrow at 10:45?"

"Yes, but isn't that the same time you asked Monsieur Crépin to appear?"

"No, he is coming fifteen minutes earlier. I am thinking it might be useful after he has been there a little while to have a face-to-face between Monsieur Crépin and the professor, where I can question them jointly, under oath, and find out what really happened the night she was arrested. It could be very informative." Not to mention entertaining.

As Maître Bertrand and his client were leaving, I added, out of earshot of the hotel owner, "By the way, please don't come early. And when you get there, I'd appreciate your just sitting on the bench outside my office without announcing yourselves."

Face-offs were even more entertaining if they were a surprise to at least one of the parties.

CHAPTER 34

I was in my office bright and early the next morning. I spent an hour doing a little Internet research. It's amazing what you can learn in a short time. Not long after I finished my research, my greffier came in.

"Bonjour, Marie," I said.

"Bonjour, Monsieur le juge. You look quite happy this morning. Even if you did not get to go to Provence."

"Yes. I am planning a face-to-face."

"Ah, you love those. I do not if they become heated. They are hard to transcribe."

"I will try to keep this one not so hot. By the way, I'd appreciate it if you could call the translator and ask her to stand by since I'm going to be taking testimony again today from the professor. Please tell her just to wait on the bench outside with the witness."

"Of course."

Monsieur Crépin arrived a few minutes before his ten thirty appointment. I was pleased that he had not brought a lawyer. All the better to make him feel at home, comfortable and, if things went well, off his guard. I offered him coffee, which he accepted. The greffier administered the oath, and we began.

My first questions were, as usual, easy ones, designed to put him at ease—name, age, occupation, a bit about the hotel and how he came to own it. Then I started to get into it with him.

"Monsieur Crépin, which room was Professor James in?"

"She was in 404."

"And Oscar Quesana was in 406, correct?"

"Yes."

"Is there a room between them?"

"Yes. Number 405."

"Who was staying, if anyone was, in 405?"

"I do not recall."

"Do you recall if there was a guest in that room at all?"

"I do not. Sorry."

"No need to be sorry as long as you are testifying honestly."

Usually when I said that, witnesses went out of their way to assure me of their honesty. I noted that Monsieur Crépin did not.

"So it might have been empty or it might have been in use?"

"Yes."

"Do you have records that would show who was in the room that night?"

"Yes."

"If I lent you my computer, would you be able to access them?"

"I am not very computer literate, so probably not."

"You do not have a smart phone or a tablet or anything like that?"

"No, just one of those old flip phones that makes phone calls. That's about it."

"Monsieur Crépin, is it correct that the police caught the professor in Monsieur Quesana's room?"

"Yes."

"How did they know she was in there?"

"I called them and told them she was."

"That was quite late at night, wasn't it?"

"I suppose."

"How did you know she had entered Monsieur Quesana's room?"

"I was just suspicious of her, so I went up to the fourth floor to look."

"To look at what?"

"To guard the room."

"You had a premonition she would enter that room?"

"Yes."

"Based on what?"

"I looked her up on the Internet after she checked in, and I saw that on her law school profile, where it said 'fun facts about Professor James,' it said that she knew how to pick locks."

"I thought you were not good at the Internet or computers."

He had begun to look uncomfortable, and I noticed that he was licking his lips. I asked him if he needed a glass of water. It was an old technique of mine. Witnesses who accepted often had trouble holding the glass without their hand shaking, especially if they were lying. Those who didn't accept seemed to be made nervous by the request itself, as if I was asking because I could actually see that their mouth had gone dry with fear.

He declined the water, then said, "Eh, I can, Monsieur le juge, do some things on the computer."

"Do you research all of your hotel guests?"

"Yes. It is a good idea. You never know who is going to show up."

"When you saw that she knew how to pick locks, what made you think she was likely to pick a lock in *your* hotel?"

"Just a suspicion."

"When you went up to guard the room, as you put it, did you hide someplace so you could watch the room?"

"No, I just more or less patrolled the hotel, making sure to go by that floor frequently to be sure she wasn't doing something bad. The hotel is my only asset, and so I cannot be too careful."

"Were you there when she actually picked the lock?"

"I was just down the hall, in a dark area. I could see what she was doing."

"So it was just happenstance that you were there watching the moment she entered Monsieur Quesana's room?"

"Yes."

"And you called the police?"

"Yes."

The man was obviously lying about something. There was also the odd coincidence that the room used by the accused was only two doors down from the room of Monsieur Quesana.

"Monsieur, how many rooms are in your hotel?"

"Twenty-two."

"How did you happen to assign the professor to a room only two doors down from the room she wanted to enter?"

"It was happenstance. When the hotel doesn't have a large census, which it didn't that night, I try to concentrate guests on one or two floors. It makes it easier for the maids."

"I see. Are you sure you still do not recall who was staying in room 405?"

"No."

I decided to take a shot in the dark, based on my growing suspicions. "Monsieur, is it possible that General Follet was staying in that room?"

"I don't recall that."

He had, in effect, denied it, but his eyes had widened when I asked the question. Before I became a judge, I would have doubted that eye-widening could be used as an indicator of unwelcome surprise, but over the years I had learned that it is an involuntary reaction for some people.

"Let me turn my attention now to Monsieur Oscar Quesana. When did he check in?"

"Several days before Christmas. I'd have to check the log to be sure of the exact date."

"Was he there the day his room was broken into?"

"No. He had not been there in several days."

"Were you worried about a hotel guest who had not been there in several days?"

"No, he had paid in advance. Through today, actually."

I had to suppress a laugh. "Monsieur Crépin, putting aside whether the bill was paid, did you have any worry about the safety of your guest? That something might have happened to him?"

"No. People are free to come and go as they please. I do not concern myself with their personal business unless they ask me to."

"Is it unusual for a hotel guest to be gone for several days?"

"No."

"Can you remember the last time that happened?"

"Not immediately, just that it happens from time to time. And frankly, Monsieur le juge, I think you misunderstand the role of a hotelier in this day and age. If I worried about the personal behavior of my guests—of the man with a wedding ring who welcomes a woman to his room late at night or the salesman from another country who claims not to speak French but sits in the lobby and reads *Le Monde* from cover to cover—I would not have time to run my hotel. Not at all."

Monsieur Crépin had at that point entered into what I often referred to as the "be truculent and try to change the subject" mode. Some witnesses did that when, sensing that their testimony was not going well, they hoped to divert me from my line of questioning. The truth was, though, that I was mostly done with that topic. I had saved the best part for last.

"Monsieur, you were there yesterday, were you not, when we opened the trapdoor in the floor of room 406?"

"Yes."

"Are there trapdoors like that in other rooms in the hotel?"

"No. It is the only one."

"Did Monsieur Quesana request a room with some kind of hiding place?"

"No."

"Did you at any point tell him about the hiding place?"

"No."

"Assuming for the moment that he put the books we saw yesterday in the hiding place, do you know how he found out the trapdoor was there?"

"No."

"He just happened to discover and pry up the floorboards himself?"

"I suppose so."

"Just another happenstance?"

"Yes."

"Is it not the case that, after the professor was arrested, that you went in there, found the books and hid them under the trapdoor, planning to get them out later, when things calmed down?"

"That is not true."

"I remind you, Monsieur, that you are under oath."

"I am telling the truth."

"You were planning to sell them, right?"

"No."

"But you would have had a means of doing that through the antiquarian bookstore in which you are a part owner, wouldn't you?"

"Perhaps, but I did not do this."

"Are you an expert on antiquarian books?"

"I know something about them, but I am hardly an expert."

"Did you get a look at the books we removed from the secret compartment yesterday?"

"Yes."

"Do you think they are valuable?"

"I don't know."

It was time to make him sweat a bit.

"Monsieur Crépin, I have another witness I want to interview. But I want to return to you. Could you please go out and sit on the bench outside? I will come and get you when I need you. I don't expect it will be too long. Oh, and could you ask the witness who is there to come in?"

"Of course, Monsieur le juge."

I knew, of course, that he would come upon the professor and be startled. And then he would sit out there while I questioned her and wonder which of his lies she was exposing. Or so I hoped, since I didn't really know which things he had said were lies or half-truths, just that some of them had to be.

The professor, her lawyer and the translator came in. I offered them coffee, but they declined. I then took a moment to look something up on my computer about which I'd become curious. When I had finished, we got started.

"Professor, you recall you are still under oath?"

"Yes."

"And you recall you should wait for the translator to translate your answers into French before you add anything to your statement?"

"Yes."

"Then let us get started. Tell me, please, if you know, how did the police know you had broken into the hotel room?"

"I don't know."

"You have no idea?"

"No."

"Did you notice anyone in the hallway before you picked the lock?"

She stopped and thought a moment. "At one point, I thought I detected some motion at one end of the hall, but I figured it was just headlights reflecting on the window at the end of the hall."

"Do you now think it was not headlights?"

"I don't know."

"Monsieur Crépin has testified that he was watching you."

"That could be, but I just have no knowledge of it one way or the other."

"Thank you. When you went into the room, what did you see?"

"Almost nothing. It was very dark and all I had was the light from a tiny flashlight. I started searching the closet, but the police came very soon after I began, so I didn't see much of anything beyond the closet."

"Did the police turn on the lights in the room?"

She thought a moment. "Yes. That's what alerted me that they were there. The lights went on."

"When that happened, did you see anything unusual in the room?"

She paused again. "No, or not that I noticed. I was too focused on being arrested."

"Did you notice an antique pen in either your room or Monsieur Quesana's room?"

"No. Well, I couldn't see anything in his room. My room was very plain. It didn't even have a desk, let alone a pen."

"Okay. Now I am going to bring Monsieur Crépin back in and I am going to question you together, in what we call a face-to-face."

"We don't do that in our system."

"You should perhaps try it. It can be very effective to help a judge get at the truth."

"I would have to move a thousand years of history."

"Yes, I have heard that the Anglo-Saxons are resistant to change. In any case, we need to get started."

CHAPTER 35

My greffier, having heard me say we needed to get started, went to the door and invited Monsieur Crépin to come in. I noticed that when he saw the professor sitting in the witness chair, he stiffened slightly. I guess he thought that since he was coming back, she would be leaving.

"Have a seat, Monsieur," I said, as my greffier produced an extra chair for him. After he took his seat, he and the professor were seated side by side, facing me across the desk. Which was exactly the way I wanted it.

"Monsieur Crépin, I remind you that you are still under oath."

"Yes, I remember."

"And please wait for the translation to finish before responding to my questions. We need to give Professor James the opportunity to understand the question before you answer."

"I'll try to do that."

"Monsieur, you contend that Professor James, who is seated next to you, stole an antique pen from room 406 of your hotel, is that correct?"

"Yes."

"Where was the pen located in the room?"

"On top of the bureau that is in the room."

"Professor, did you see such a pen when you entered room 406 the night you picked the lock?"

"It was very dark, so not only did I not see it, but I could not have seen it even if it was there."

"What about after the police turned the lights on?"

"I was not looking at the decorations in the room at that point, so I didn't see it then, either. If it was there."

"Did you take it or anything else from the room?"

"No."

"Monsieur Crépin, do you have any pictures of this supposedly purloined pen that we might show the professor?"

"I don't think so."

"When you say it was an antique, what do you mean by that?"

"I mean it was over one hundred years old."

"Where did you buy it?"

"At the flea market near Clignancourt."

"That is to say, at the Marché aux Puces de Saint-Ouen?"

"Yes."

"Why were you buying things for the hotel there?"

"When I inherited the hotel, the rooms were bare of decoration, and so I went to the flea market and bought many decorative items for the rooms."

"How much did you pay for the pen?"

"I don't recall exactly. Maybe two hundred euros."

"That's a lot at a flea market."

"The prices there run the gamut."

"Isn't it a little odd to pay that much for a decorative item for a hotel room, especially for the kind of thing a guest might walk off with?"

"At the time I didn't know a lot about running a hotel."

"Do you have a receipt for it?"

"I don't recall. I'd have to look, but maybe not."

"How do you know it wasn't taken by an earlier guest, or even someone who works at the hotel?"

"I'm sure it was there when Monsieur Quesana moved in."

"How can you be so sure?"

"I just am."

"How do you know Monsieur Quesana didn't borrow it and not return it?"

"It is eighteen inches long with feathers on the end. Too awkward for someone to carry around."

"Do you recall doing an inventory of the room before he moved in?"

"I don't recall whether I did or not. I'm just sure that, had it been missing, I would have noticed that."

"Did you survey all of the rooms every day?"

"No."

"Do you recall surveying room 406 in the days before Monsieur Quesana moved into it?"

"I don't really recall. I might have."

"Do you have any additional evidence, other than your own testimony, that the pen was stolen by the professor?"

He thought for a moment. "No."

"Could any of your hotel employees testify that it was there one day and gone the next?"

"I don't think they pay much attention to that kind of thing."

"Has anyone, to your knowledge, seen the professor with this antique pen in her possession?"

"Not that I know of."

"Alright, let's talk then about the supposedly damaged lock. How was it damaged, Monsieur Crépin?"

"It didn't work properly after she picked it. It sticks when you turn the knob, but it didn't before."

I noticed that he didn't look at the professor as he made his allegation. Usually, in my experience with face-offs, when one person accused the other, they looked at them or pointed at them. Here, Monsieur Crépin was entirely avoiding eye contact.

"Monsieur, I couldn't help noticing when we entered the room yesterday that I had no problem with the lock. The key turned smoothly when I put it in the lock, and the doorknob turned without a problem."

"It only sticks sometimes."

"Have you made any effort to have it repaired?"

"No, because I thought it should be left as evidence. If I'd had it repaired, the damage to it would no longer be evident."

He had a point, although it was, so far, the only point he'd made that helped his case.

"Professor," I said, "do you believe that you damaged the lock in picking it?"

"No. It's a very simple lock, and all I did was push the tumblers back, one at a time, with a bobby pin so that the cylinder would turn smoothly when something was inserted into the keyhole—in this case I used a nail file—even though I didn't have a key."

"I don't have any experience with picking locks," I said. "How did you get the bobby pin between the lock cylinder and the outside of the lock? Couldn't that have damaged the lock?"

"It was easy because there is a large gap between the cylinder and the outside of the lock. Probably because the lock is very, very old, or perhaps because it was poorly made in the first place. And so the bobby pin did no damage. In fact, it slipped into the lock without making a scratching sound, which meant that it was hardly touching the lock cylinder."

"Did you have trouble opening it?"

"More than I anticipated because my hands were shaking and I was sweating, but not technically."

I put my hands behind my head—an old and possibly not very judicial habit that I engage in when I am about to make a decision—and said, "Monsieur Crépin, the principal reason that we permit the civil party to continue a criminal case when the public prosecutor has decided not to pursue it is to allow the civil party to recover money damages for harm allegedly done in the course of the crime. The civil party has no real interest in pursuing a criminal penalty. That is the business of the State."

"Yes," he said, "I understand. But I was damaged."

I nodded at him as if to acknowledge his point and continued. "Based on the evidence adduced here, I find you have not proved your damages with a sufficient amount of evidence. You do not have any proof that the pen was in the room at the time the professor entered, and you do not have any proof that she currently has it or that anyone has seen her with it. And even if you had those pieces of evidence, you have no proof of its value, since you have no receipt or photo. We have only your word for it as evidence and, beyond that, only the black abyss."

"Can I appeal?"

"Yes. But wait, because you will have more to appeal. I am also likely to find that you have no evidence to show that the lock was damaged. I suppose I could permit you to hire an expert to examine it, but my own opening of the lock yesterday is persuasive evidence that there is nothing wrong with it."

"Are you saying that I'm going to lose?"

"I'm saying that you are very likely to lose, and in that case I will issue a *non-lieu* and that will be the end of it."

The translator spoke up. "Monsieur le juge, I am not sure of the exact translation into English of *non-lieu*."

"Just say that I am probably going to dismiss the entire case."

"Can I appeal?" Monsieur Crépin asked again.

"As I said before, Monsieur, certainly. Our system is replete with appeals and do-overs. So if you want to pay the lawyers, you may appeal."

"What about the fact that she picked the lock? Isn't that at least a délit in which the State is interested?"

"Not very interested. The public prosecutor chose not to pursue it, and although I might pursue it and pass it on to the criminal trial court, I will probably not do so, because it seems to me a minor crime given the professor's reason for doing it. She was trying to find a friend who has been kidnapped."

"That is outrageous."

"I think not. But in any case, this matter is not over, because, until some higher authority tells me that I must step aside, I am going to continue to investigate this kidnapping, which is an offense against the State far more serious than the picking of an old lock."

I looked at the professor and saw, as the translation was completed, that she was beaming.

"Are we done then, Monsieur le juge?" Monsieur Crépin asked. He started to get up.

"Not quite. Please sit back down. I also want to investigate whether you have committed perjury in the course of these proceedings, although ultimately I may need to pass that inquiry to another judge."

He turned pale. "What perjury?"

There was no reason to tell him, of course, what every lawyer knew about our peculiar legal system: in a preliminary inquiry, unless you lied about facts related to a crime and were later convicted of that very crime, you would not normally be prosecuted for perjury.

"The possible perjury I refer to, Monsieur Crépin, is that you told me that you were suspicious of Professor James because on her UCLA page it said, under Fun Facts, that she knows how to pick locks."

"It does."

"Well, I looked myself and could not find it. Professor, is there any such mention of that on your Fun Facts page?"

"No. The only 'fun fact' listed is that I spent one summer on a treasurer salver ship helping to look for sunken Spanish treasure."

I smiled. "Did you find any?"

"No."

"How do you explain that, Monsieur Crépin?"

"That she didn't find any treasure?"

"No, that there is no 'fun fact' on the UCLA website stating that the professor picks locks."

"It was there and was taken down no doubt. You can do that easily."

"Eh, I am going to hire an expert who can look at the historic web—I'm told we can do that easily—to advise me if the page you say you saw was *ever* there. And if it was not, I intend to find out who told you that the professor could pick locks. Or whatever it was that they told you so that you'd keep watch on her."

"No one told me anything."

"Monsieur Crépin, this is now a situation in which you should get a lawyer, so I won't ask you any more about that topic for now. But this investigation is far from over."

"What else is there to investigate if you're dismissing my claim?"

"Other than your possible perjury, there is the kidnapping. And that reminds me, Monsieur, you said earlier that you didn't know who was staying in room 405. I will look much more kindly on you if you go back to your hotel, look at the guest register and tell me who was staying in room 405 the night that Professor James picked the lock on 406."

"I will do that right away."

"By checking the records?"

"Yes."

"Be sure to read them accurately, because I'm going to ask to look at those records myself."

"I will do it carefully."

"Good. The hearing is adjourned for now. Professor, please continue to hold yourself available for a resumption of this hearing."

Everyone thanked me, and we adjourned. I could hardly wait to learn who had been staying in room 405.

CHAPTER 36

I didn't have to wait long. Early in the afternoon, after I had returned to the office from a leisurely stroll along the banks of the Seine—the steep concrete stairway that led down to the river was only a block from my office in the Palais de Justice—my greffier told me that there was a call from Monsieur Crépin.

"Bonjour, Monsieur," I said.

"I have the information for you as to who stayed in that room."

"Ah, good. I am going to put you on the speakerphone so my greffier can transcribe the conversation, okay?"

"Of course."

After I had done that, I said, "Okay, you're on the speaker-phone now. Monsieur Crépin, can you confirm that you're on the other end of the phone?"

"Yes, this is Philippe Crépin."

"Please recall that you are still under oath."

"I understand."

"Now, Monsieur Crépin, who stayed in room 405 in your hotel the night that Professor James was arrested?" I then revised the question to add the specific date.

"Olga Bukova."

"Who is she?"

"A young Russian woman—or at least she had a Russian passport."

"How young?"

"I didn't check her birthdate, but I'd guess twenty or twenty-one. Something like that."

"When did she check in and out?"

"She checked in on December 26 at four in the afternoon, and checked out very early on the morning after the professor was arrested. At eight."

"Did you speak with her while she was a guest at your hotel?"

"No, because she did not speak French. Nor English, which I speak a little. We communicated in sign language, so to speak. But it was just checking in and checking out, really."

"Did you notice if she mostly stayed in her room or went in and out?"

"To the extent I observed her, she was like any other guest. Mostly gone during the day, often there in the evening."

"Do you have a record of the credit card she used?"

"Yes. The room was charged to Igor Bukov, on American Express. Do you want the number of the card?"

"Yes."

He gave me the number along with the code.

"Did you notice anything at all unusual about her activities while she was there?"

"No."

"The evening that the professor was arrested, do you know if she was in her room at the time?"

"I don't recall."

"This time, Monsieur Crépin, I actually believe that you don't recall."

"I was being honest the times I said I did not recall, Monsieur le juge."

"So you say. Monsieur, does your hotel have a security camera by the front door?"

"Yes."

"How long do you keep the recording?"

"Only forty-eight hours. It recycles after that."

"Are there any other security cameras in the hotel?"

"Yes. There is one by the front desk. It also cycles after forty-eight hours."

"Any others?"

"No."

"The registration record that you mentioned, could you make me a copy of that?"

"Yes, I can print it out from the computer."

"Good. Please do that and fax it to me. My greffier will give you the number after I get off the line."

"Okay."

"Thank you, Monsieur Crépin, for your help. I don't have anything more today, but please hold yourself available for further questioning."

"Have I cooperated enough that you are going to put aside your thoughts about perjury?"

"Not yet. Au revoir, Monsieur."

I was, I have to admit, disappointed. I had expected him to tell me that General Follet had been staying in room 405. The name Olga Bukova was somehow familiar to me, but I couldn't place it. Finally, I asked my greffier, "Was an Olga Bukova mentioned somehow during these proceedings?"

She paged through the transcript on her computer. "Here it is, Monsieur le juge. She was mentioned by Maître Bertrand, when he was telling you the complicated histoire of this entire matter."

"Mentioned how?"

"As the woman who was trapped in the basement of the hat shop along with the professor and her friend. She returned with them to Paris. She is currently staying with Madame Devrais."

"Eh, that's interesting. Would you please call Maître Bertrand and tell him about her residence at the hotel, along with the dates she was at the hotel? In fact, please just read him Monsieur Crépin's testimony of today."

"I will do that right away."

"Thank you."

"Anyone else you wish to reach, Monsieur le juge?" my greffier asked.

"Yes. The police chief in Digne-les-Bains. I want to find out if he has the bookstore owner in custody yet."

CHAPTER 37

My greffier quickly reached the police chief in Digne. After the appropriate greetings, we got started.

"Capitaine, I have jurisdiction of the case of Professor Jenna James here in Paris. You were kind enough the other day to serve a summons on her issued by my immediate predecessor on this case. For which I thank you."

"Eh, Monsieur le juge, that is so. Did this professor respond to the summons in a timely manner?"

"Yes, she did."

"Alors, what can I help you with today?"

"Professor James has told me that the morning after you served the summons on her, she and two others were forced into a basement at gunpoint and held there by a hat store owner in Digne. A serious crime."

"Yes, I am aware of it. A Madame Devrais reported it to our local police chief. We have the hat store owner, a Monsieur Tomas Condelet, in custody. He is in garde à vue in my jail while we investigate. But he is on suicide watch."

"Why does he want to kill himself?"

"He says that if he goes to jail, his family will be impoverished. If he kills himself, he has much insurance that will pay."

"A very practical reason for suicide, I suppose. Rather stripped of emotion."

"Yes. We don't think he is very serious about it, though."

"I trust it is an effective watch, and, just in case he is serious about it, he will not be able to kill himself."

"We have never lost anyone on that watch."

"Good. After the forty-eight hours expire, will he be held in preventive detention?"

"Whether to apply for that is, of course, up to the investigating magistrate who will be in charge of this matter."

"Has someone already been appointed?"

"Yes, one of our best, Judge Caroline Denam."

It would have been better if no judge had yet been appointed, because then I could have questioned the witness directly without the need for another judge's permission, and perhaps brought the entire case within my own jurisdiction. Now it was not exactly permission I needed, but I felt obligated to extend the courtesy of informing the other judge involved in an overlapping investigation.

"Well, I will need to talk to her then because I want to question Monsieur Condelet. I believe he has information important to my investigation of a different matter here in Paris."

"Of course. I know you have the judicial directory, but for your convenience, here is her number."

"Merci."

I could have asked my greffier to make the call, but I decided to place it personally. Caroline Denam and I had gone to judge's school together—the École Nationale de la Magistrature in Bordeaux. We weren't close back then, but we did know each other, and it would have seemed pompous to her for me to have had someone else place the call, especially since we were of equal rank.

She answered the phone herself, and I said, "It is Roland de Fournis."

"Oh! Quelle surprise! It has been many years. How are you, Monsieur le juge?"

"I am fine. And you, Madame la juge?"

"I am good, too."

And then we both laughed at the absurdity of addressing each other by our honorifics, so far removed from the time we and others had planned and carried out moving the arrogant school director's car up onto concrete blocks, all without being caught.

"Alors, Roland, what can I do for you?"

I explained the situation and the need to question Condelet.

"Yes, of course, you need to do that," she said.

"I can come to Digne tomorrow. Does he have a lawyer yet?"

"He has been offered a lawyer and declined. We will need to offer again before you begin to question him."

"Yes, I understand. When is the forty-eight-hour hold up?"

"Unfortunately, it will expire tomorrow afternoon."

"I will need to get there quickly then. Are you going to try to have him held in preventive detention?"

"You know the problem with that these days."

She was referring, of course, to the fact that not very long ago, investigating magistrates could, on their own motion, have an accused held in preventive detention to stop them from escaping or harming the public. But not anymore.

"Yes, I know it well, Caroline. One of us will have to apply to a JLD to hold him." All because the soft hearts on the European Commission on Human Rights had pressured our government into changing the law. Now to keep someone in jail we had to apply to the ludicrously named Judge of Liberties and Detention.

She sighed. "In this case they will probably say no, since it does not obviously involve terrorism, and no one was actually harmed."

"Agreed. But you will apply anyway?"

"Yes, or I can ask the public prosecutor to apply. But if you can leave tonight and get here tomorrow morning, and assuming he doesn't hire a lawyer, you can question him before he gets out of garde à vue."

"Good. I have an appointment this afternoon, but I can take the night train and be there in the morning. It will be good to see you again after all these years."

"Yes."

"One more thing before you go?"

"What?"

"I am nervous about his being on suicide watch. And there is one thing I want to know above all others."

"What is it?"

"Who ordered him to put the foreigners in the basement? Please go and ask him. And if he tells you, try to get a name."

"I already asked him and he refused to say. Do you want me to try again?"

"Yes. I think the answer may be the key to all of this."

"I will go to the jail again as soon as I can get away from here."

"Thank you. See you tomorrow morning. Oh, and where are you located?"

"I'm usually in the same building as the Prefecture. You'll easily recognize it. It looks like a concrete tissue box with windows."

"I will see you in Digne."

Just then there was a knock on the door and an elegantly and expensively dressed woman entered and said to my greffier, "Bonjour, Madame, I am Tess Devrais. I have an appointment with the judge."

My greffier looked surprised. "I do not have you on the schedule—"

I interrupted. "It is okay. I made the call myself to ask Madame to come in."

My greffier shot me an annoyed look, which I ignored.

"Bonjour, Madame Devrais," I said. "Please sit down." I gestured to one of the chairs.

"Merci, Monsieur le juge," she said.

My greffier, without needing to be asked, sensed that Madame Devrais might be more comfortable talking to me without anyone else present. She got up, saying she had an errand to run and would be back later. She closed the door quietly behind her, although I had the feeling that she had wanted to slam it.

"Alors, Madame Devrais, may I offer you some coffee?"

"No, I have had enough coffee today. You said on the phone you wanted to discuss the kidnapping of Monsieur Quesana. So let us discuss it. What do you want to know?"

"Eh, first, I understand from Captain Bonpere that you have a, ah, special position with our government."

"Are there any recording devices going here?"

"No."

"Yes, I do. I sometimes, as Captain Bonpere probably told you, aid our government when it has need of my services."

"This is official?"

"Yes." She took a placard from her purse and handed it to me.

I examined it and its red seal and handed it back. "I am impressed, Madame. It is personally signed by the President of the Republic."

"I believe it is actually signed by an automatic pen, but, still, it is his signature."

"You must be very proud of that."

"I will be prouder when it is the signature of a woman. But that is another conversation. Monsieur le juge, what is it you want to know?"

"Is this kidnapping in any way an operation of the security services?"

"What do you mean?"

"Has our own government arranged this kidnapping or in some way prevented its solution?"

"Not so far as I know. I have made inquiries, and the answers—I have asked several highly placed people—have been 'definitely, absolutely not. The government has had nothing to do with it.'"

"Would they lie to you?"

"I do not think they would."

"Why, then, Madame, if you know, is the general involved? He seems somehow to reek of clandestine operations."

"I do not know. I have made some inquiries there, too, but have come up with nothing. I did ask the chief of the Brigade Criminelle about it, because the general told me he was working with them to solve the kidnapping. Which he believes involves money laundering."

"What did the chief say?"

"That it was true. That the general was working with them on the case."

"I made the same inquiry and got the same answer."

"Eh, but do you know the head of the Brigade?"

"Yes."

"Then you know he is a man far out of his depth. The general could just as easily be using the people from the Brigade to tend to his garden and mix his drinks at night. He could be working on this kidnapping on his own, and the chief would not be wise to it."

"Madame, how well do you know the general?"

"Very well. Or so I thought."

"How long have you known him?"

After questioning thousands of witnesses, I had developed the ability to detect very small changes in body language that indicated discomfort. I thought Madame Devrais had just displayed a flash of anxiety. But without visibly pausing at all, she said, "A very long time. Since we were very young."

I decided not to pursue it further. We agreed to keep in touch, and she left. My greffier, who had apparently decided simply to wait on the bench in the hallway, returned a few seconds later. "Marie, can you make me a reservation on the next train to Digne-les-Bains?"

"Of course."

After a few minutes work she said, "With a change in Aix-en-Provence you'll be there by midnight. And I've booked you into the Hôtel Central. Not fancy, but near the courthouse and the jail."

"Perfect. I have an important interview with Monsieur Condelet in the morning. If he is willing to talk and be candid, I think it could solve the case."

CHAPTER 38

My trip to Digne was not easy. My train from Paris was late getting into Aix, and I missed the connection to Digne. It was the last train out that night, and the one the next morning wasn't going to get me to Digne until noon. I wanted to be there earlier, so there was little choice but to rent a car. The car's GPS said it was a four-and-a-half-hour drive. It was only six o'clock, so I assumed that, even with a stop for dinner, I could make it by midnight.

By the time I'd driven less than half the distance, I felt my eyes begin to close on two different occasions. I didn't relish the thought of having my obituary on the front page of a local paper beneath the headline, "Paris Judge Hits Tree and Dies." I stopped for the night in Montpellier, got up very early the next morning and was in Digne by nine.

I checked into the hotel, apologized for having missed my reservation the night before—I'd be charged for it anyway, of course—and walked to the courthouse. Caroline's description of the courthouse was not far off, and I found both the tissue box building and her chambers easily. We greeted each other

as long-lost friends, she offered me a chair and some coffee—
which I declined—and I plunged right in.

"Did you manage to see Monsieur Condelet?" I asked.

"You didn't get my message?"

It was then I realized that I had muted my phone when I
boarded the train in Paris, because I had been in the quiet car. I
had forgotten to reset it when I got off.

"My God, I forgot to turn the ringer on my phone back on.
Has something happened?"

"I texted you about it. Monsieur Condelet tried to kill
himself."

"How?"

"Hanging. Last night. He put a stack of books on top of his
bed, climbed on top of them and tied a sheet to a pipe on the
ceiling."

I got up and began to pace about the room. "Is he dead?"

"No. Unconscious. It is not clear if he will make it."

"Did you get to talk to him before he tried to kill himself?"

"Just after he tried. They let me know as soon as he was discovered, and I rushed to the jail. They were just putting him in
the ambulance as I got there. I leaned over the gurney and asked
him again your key question—who told him to put the foreigners in the basement."

"Did he answer?"

"He just said 'Russian,' and even that was kind of slurred.
Then they slid the gurney into the ambulance. I actually got in
with him, but on the way there they had an oxygen mask over
his mouth and I couldn't get anything more out of him."

I thought about it for a moment. "It could mean almost anything. I mean, Olga's father is Russian, but why would he put his
own daughter in the basement?"

"You're right. It could even mean that he was confused and was just trying to tell me who was in the basement, referring to Olga."

"Right. So as evidence it's useless, and it's not much help as a clue either. Can we go see him?"

"I think so."

We got in her car and drove to the hospital. On the way, I said, "I thought he was on suicide watch."

"So did I."

"Who gave him the books?"

"According to the police chief, he asked one of the jailers for some books to read. He told the man he was a book dealer and that he liked the classics. The jail only had mysteries, romance and sci-fi. So they went to the local library and got him *The Count of Monte Cristo*, *The Three Musketeers* and things like that."

"All big books."

"Right, the better to stand on."

"Only in France would jailers think that a request to read the classics wasn't odd."

We got to the hospital and went up to Condelet's room. A police guard was posted outside. As soon as I saw Condelet, I knew that we weren't going to get anything useful out of him. He was intubated, with tubes in both his nose and his mouth, and he was breathing with the aid of a machine on his chest.

We introduced ourselves to the doctor standing next to the bed, and I asked, "Is he likely to make it, doctor?"

"Monsieur le juge, I doubt it. He was apparently hanging up there for quite a long time. While it is possible—miracles do happen—it is very unlikely."

Caroline asked, "If he does make it, will he be brain damaged?"

He shrugged. "Hard to say, Madame la juge. As I said, we don't know exactly how long he was deprived of oxygen before someone cut him down."

Bottom line, I thought to myself, we weren't going to be able to talk to him very soon, if ever. We left instructions that if he were to awaken, we should be contacted immediately, although the doctor reminded us that Condelet would be unable to talk because he'd still be intubated. Caroline pointed out that he might be able to write.

On the way back to Caroline's office, I asked her, "Is the police chief corrupt?"

"How do you mean?"

"If someone offered him money to help a prisoner kill himself, would he take it?"

She pursed her lips. "Eh, there has never been any allegation against him of anything even approaching that. I talked with a couple of the jailers. I think this was a case where they thought that he wasn't that serious about killing himself, and that if they just took his belt and shoelaces and kept him away from knives and sharp objects, it would be enough."

"This isn't Paris, I guess."

"No, it's not."

"Why are you even here, Caroline, so far from, well, anything?"

"I like to ski?"

"Is that the only reason?"

"Probably not, but I have given up being introspective."

We left it at that.

I caught the next train back to Aix, and this time I made the connection and was in Paris by late afternoon.

On the train, I had time to think, to try to put the pieces together in various ways. But try as I might, they just did not come together into a sensible whole. The general had been my prime suspect, but the chief of the Brigade Criminelle had vouched for his conducting a genuine inquiry. And even if Tess Devrais was correct that the chief was an idiot, that didn't change the legitimacy of what the general was doing. Although I still had my suspicions. Just nothing to base them on.

What about Madame Devrais herself? That made no sense, either. She was as rich as Croesus, so she'd have no need to make money from the sale of the book. Besides that, the victim was a friend of her fiancé. She was not, so far as I knew, a book collector herself.

Then there was the hotel owner, but he seemed like too much of a lightweight to have put together a kidnapping. He did have a motive in that he owned a part of the antiquarian bookstore next door. But they'd have trouble marketing such a potentially famous book. Or would they? Maybe it could be sold in a careful private sale.

Finally, there were the mysterious Russians, Igor Bukov the father and Olga Bukova the daughter. I had not interviewed either as yet, but it seemed the time had come to do so. I texted my greffier and asked her to prepare a subpoena for Olga to testify under oath. I also reminded her of the need for a Russian translator. As for the father, since he was still in Russia, I'd have to see if I could find him and try to persuade him to talk with me on the phone. Either way, neither one of them seemed much of a suspect unless I believed that a father would order his own daughter held in a basement. Which I didn't.

Somewhere, there was a key piece of information I did not have, or there was something I thought I understood that I in fact did not. If I could find what it was that I was getting wrong, the pieces of the puzzle would fall into place.

I decided to drop by the courthouse, even though it was past six. I had no plans for the evening and perhaps in the judicial ambience I could generate some additional helpful thoughts. My greffier was surprised to see me, although I was equally surprised to see her there so late.

"Bonsoir, Monsieur le juge. I had not expected you back until tomorrow. And I don't ever recall your coming back to the courthouse so late."

"Eh, late or early, it is good you are here. I want to issue more subpoenas and set up more meetings."

She handed me a set of papers. "I have already prepared the subpoena for the first new one on the griddle, Olga Bukova, as you requested. But I do not know where to find her."

"I will ask the professor. I have a feeling she will know where to locate her. In the meantime, I have some other things I want."

"Which are?"

"I want to issue a subpoena to the French army for the personnel records of the general. And to the civil service for the personnel records of Madame Devrais."

She raised her eyebrows, and I could tell that she was struggling with whether to make a comment about my request—something she almost never did.

"Monsieur le juge, if I may, this seems to me dangerous. The general is a powerful man, and he is far removed from this affair of the hotel room."

"In my imagination, he is at the heart of it. And if it is dangerous, well, it is dangerous."

"Do you recall what you told me when I came to work with you, many years ago?"

"That one of your most important duties was to bring in pastries in the mornings, but that I would reimburse you?"

"No, not that." She smiled. "You told me that you endeavored always to remember that you were investigating only the case in front of you and not the entire French Republic, which would be the job of several lifetimes."

"I did say that. But this is different. A man's life is at stake. This is above and beyond a hotel break-in."

She seemed to accept that we were going forward with the request. "Okay. But we've never served a subpoena for military records before. I will have to research where to start."

I wrote out a name on a piece of paper and handed it to her. "I think you should start with this man. I am sure his phone number will not be hard to find."

"Who is he?"

"Many years ago, before you came to work with me, I was a judge in the juvenile court. This man, who is now high in the administrative function of the military, had a sixteen-year-old daughter who did something stupid."

"Something serious?"

"Yes. She could even have been tried as an adult, and the public prosecutor for juveniles wanted to do that. I talked her out of it, and it was arranged that the girl's sentence would instead involve education and community service."

She looked at the name on the paper I had handed her again. "His name is familiar, but I cannot quite place it."

"He is one of those men who has quietly occupied many positions of importance in the military while avoiding serious public attention."

"And he is grateful to you for what you did for his daughter."

"Very."

"And you are about to—"

"Cash in the gratefulness chit. I think it is still good. Call him and arrange for me to see the general's records, even if it needs to be informal while they consider the formal demand."

"And Madame Devrais?"

"For her, we should limit our request to her civil service records before she reached the age of twenty-five. That is, I think, when she went to work for the security services in some capacity. There is something about her relationship with the general, based on her body language when I asked her how long they'd known each other, that I don't quite understand. Sometimes the very old histoire can explain the newer histoire."

"When do you want these records for the general and Madame Devrais?"

"By two o'clock on the day after tomorrow, which is when the general is coming back to be questioned."

"This will take time to arrange. You will have to get your own pastries tomorrow morning and the morning after that as well."

"I will survive."

CHAPTER 39

Robert Tarza

It had been five days since Jenna and I had returned from Digne-les-Bains. So far, we had accomplished nothing. Each day we'd had a report from the general telling us that they were making progress in finding Oscar and developing plans to rescue him. But he refused to supply any details. Captain Bonpere had called, too. She was sympathetic to our plight, but had nothing much to add because the general had cut her out of the loop.

The lack of information was agonizing. For all I knew, Oscar was being tortured, and we were sitting on our butts in Paris, doing nothing. I spent much of the day stewing about it. Finally, in late afternoon, I asked Jenna to walk down to the Casimodo with me. It's a restaurant on the quai, right across the river from Notre Dame and only a couple of blocks from Tess's apartment.

The weather was, if not exactly warm, at least not bitter cold, and we sat at an outdoor table, where we could take in the view.

Jenna had just polished off an apple tart, and I was nursing the last of my café Americano.

"You know," Jenna said, "the punny name of this place is too much."

"Really? I think it's great. The name is so bad it's good. It's one of my favorites near Tess's apartment, and it has a great view of the cathedral."

"Maybe so. Anyway, we should go soon. In not too long it will be dark, and when the sun goes down, it's going to start getting cold."

"Before we go, Jenna, I want to talk about trying harder to find Oscar, because we are exactly nowhere in that effort. The general is doing whatever he's doing, and I guess that the judge is investigating something, but we are doing zero. But I'm at a loss for next steps. Do you have any ideas?"

"I do."

"What are they?"

"Do you remember that on the day we went to Digne, I told you I had some errands to run in the morning before we could leave?"

"I vaguely recall that."

"Well, one of my errands was some research in an Internet café."

"Into what?"

"Into Oscar's parents, the Brioches."

"And what did you find?"

"I think they are buried in the Père Lachaise cemetery."

"I have a feeling this is going to be a long story, Jenna. So why don't we walk back to the apartment, and you can tell me why this even possibly matters."

As we walked along, Jenna picked up the topic again, as if there'd been no interruption.

"The reason it matters is this." She held up a tiny, very rusty key.

"What is that?"

"When the judge let me go back into the closet in Oscar's hotel room, when he was looking for the book under the trap-door, I searched again through the pockets of Oscar's suit that was hanging in the closet. One of the pockets had a small hole in the bottom, and this key had fallen into the lining. I fished it out."

I shrugged my shoulders and raised my eyebrows in what I hoped was a very French manner. "Alors? So?"

"So I'm betting this is a key to the tomb where Oscar's parents are buried and that he left something important in there."

"How on earth did you put that unlikely story together?"

"You found that torn-up map to the Père Lachaise cemetery in his wastebasket, plus a bus ticket that had '69' written on the back. That's the bus route that goes from near where he was staying to the cemetery."

"It's a big stretch. I mean even if he did go there, it was probably just to memorialize his parents."

"Maybe, but I'm betting the key fits the gate on the Brioche tomb."

"How do you know that?"

"Two days ago I went to the cemetery and took one of the tours that are led by private guides. When the tour was over, I located the grave."

"How did you find it? There are thousands, maybe tens of thousands, of graves there, and miles of internal streets."

"With my iPhone. The cemetery has an interactive website where you can look up the location of gravesites by name. It shows you the section the grave is in, and after that, it doesn't take all that long to find it if you're willing to walk up and down the lanes for a while."

"And?"

"I'm sure this key fits the lock on the gate to the Brioche family tomb. It looks like it will fit."

"What do you mean it looks like it will fit? That makes no sense."

"When you've spent time around keys and locks you can sometimes look at a key and just visually see if it's likely to fit into a particular lock. This one looks like a fit."

"Did you try it?"

"I was about to when a guard came by. He kept staring at me and wouldn't go away, so eventually I left."

We had by then reached the apartment building. Jenna waited politely as Monsieur Martin—my newfound buddy— and I exchanged oh-so-polite greetings just this edge of enthusiasm. In the elevator, I said, "So you failed to open the gate to the tomb. What are you going to do now? Register as a fake relative or something to gain legitimate access?"

"No, I'm going to go back there tonight and try the key."

"All Paris cemeteries close when it gets dark. In the winter, closing is five thirty, I think. How are you going to get in?"

"I haven't solved that problem yet."

"Well, when I took a tour of Père Lachaise a few years ago, the guide pointed out that the whole thing is surrounded by high walls topped with barbed wire and mean-looking, downward-facing curved spikes."

"Yeah, I saw those. Serious protection. But the guide claimed that all kinds of odd things go on inside at night. Drugs, devil worship, sex. If that's true, those people are getting into the cemetery somehow."

"Maybe they boil up from hell."

"Very funny, Robert."

"So your crazy plan is to take the 69 bus there and figure out how to get in when you get there?"

"No. I'm going to have our favorite cab driver take me. I already talked to him about it. And he said he'd ask around with cab driver friends and find out how you get in. I'm sure he'll come up with something."

"Uh-huh. Sounds like a plan to get arrested again."

"Not if you help me."

I was immediately on guard. "Like how?"

"All I want you to do is be my spotter. To stand outside the part of the wall where I get in and text me if someone seems to be investigating."

"They probably have detection equipment inside, not outside."

"Are you coming or not?"

I thought about it. If I said no, it would mean I wasn't serious about renewing our push to find Oscar.

"Okay, I'm in, but only if you tell Tess about your plan so she can try to talk you out of it."

"I'll tell Tess if she keeps it to herself."

We were by then inside the apartment. After we'd hung up our coats, Tess emerged from her study and asked, "What is up?"

I refrained from telling her that no one said it that way, and tried to imagine Bugs Bunny saying "What is up, doc?"

"What's up, my dear Tess, is that Jenna here thinks the key to finding the book and Oscar is in the Brioche family tomb in Père Lachaise."

Tess was not immediately dismissive of the idea, which surprised me. "Why, Jenna, do you think you will find something there?" she asked.

"I will tell you if you will promise to keep my plans secret."

More easily than I expected, Tess said, "Okay, I agree."

Jenna explained her theory. Tess looked thoughtful. "It is not a crazy idea," she said. "But it is filled with risk. If you are caught you will go to jail, and I will not be able to help you this time."

"You didn't really help me last time."

"I did, but in ways you do not see."

"Well, whatever. I for one care about Oscar, who is probably about to be killed by his captors. And so I'm willing to risk it. You and Robert can just sit here on your butts and spin theories if you want, but I'm going to do something."

"I will not go," Tess said, "but there is a thing I can do to aid you. One moment." She went to her study and came back a few minutes later holding a small black address book, the old-fashioned kind that has little alphabet tabs.

"I will give you a name of someone to call. But I do not know if he can help you tonight," she said.

She took a pen, consulted the address book, wrote something on a small piece of paper and handed it to Jenna.

"Guido daNucci," Jenna read aloud. "Who is he?"

Tess looked slightly uncomfortable and was quiet for a few seconds. Then she said, "Once upon a time, well, it was not really so long ago, but before I met Robert, I had *ennui*—'boredom' is your word, I think—and I sought adventure. And this man, Guido, arranges adventures, often at night. He calls himself 'le Guide Nocturne.'"

"He does cemetery tours at night?" Jenna asked.

"I have never been on a tour of a cemetery with him, but I think, yes. If he still works. I have not talked with him in a few years."

"Does he speak English?"

"Yes, some of those who went on our adventures were rich people from England who had ennui. One was a lord of some kind. He was ridiculous."

"So I can use your name when I call him?" Jenna asked.

"Please, no. Just say . . . I do not know. You will think of something."

"How, when you went on these, uh, adventures, did you protect your reputation as a spy?" I asked.

"Merde. This tires me. Again, I am not a spy. But I went with false identification that daNucci furnished and, sometimes, in a kind of disguise. I took a big risk."

"And you'll tell me all about it when we're married?"

She smiled a very broad smile. "If you wish."

"I'm going to go call him," Jenna said.

"Jenna," Tess said, "Robert has told me you bought throw-away cell phones, yes?"

"Yes."

"Use one of those to call. You do not want the general or anyone else who may listen to know where you go tonight."

Jenna left the room and came back a few minutes later. "He is available tonight. For a price."

"Which is?" I asked.

"One thousand euros. Which I don't really have to spare."

"Even though you stayed at the George V."

"Which is why I don't have the funds to spare."

"I do," I said. "I'll supply the money and come along and wait outside. What time will we be going?"

"Not until after midnight tonight—two in the morning. He says we have to wait until midnight has passed because the 'midnight-crazies' will be there before that doing their thing."

"They fade back into the drainpipes after midnight?"

"Whatever."

"Where are we meeting him?"

"He gave me an address along one of the streets that borders the cemetery. Our cabbie friend can take us there. Oh, and he said to wear old clothes."

"So I can get some sleep in before that."

"Yes. We both can."

As I drifted off to sleep, I realized that I didn't know where Olga had been during our long conversation. But I was so tired that I put it out of my mind.

CHAPTER 40

I slept fairly soundly, and then, with the help of the alarm, got up and got dressed in blue jeans and an old sweatshirt. Tess hardly stirred. I walked into the living room just before one thirty in the morning. Jenna was already there. I grabbed an old overcoat from the closet. Jenna was wearing a blue parka.

When we opened the door to leave, I was surprised to see Tess come into the room, belted into her floor-length, white terry cloth robe. "Bonne chance," she said. "Good luck."

The concierge was, of course, asleep. I wondered, as we crept through the lobby, if he had finally gotten the surveillance camera running, or if he had some kind of alarm to tell him if people came or went late at night. If so, he gave no sign.

Jenna had asked the cab driver to wait for us a couple of blocks away so that we wouldn't be seen being picked up in front of Tess's building. We walked to the rendezvous spot quickly, and there he was.

We got in, and he said, "I'll take you guys where you want to go, but, hey, really sorry, none of my cab driver buddies up here have any ideas about how to get in."

"That's okay," Jenna said. "We've arranged some help in that department."

"Okay. I hope you'll be alright. A few people told me it's really dangerous in there at night. Not to mention scary."

"I don't believe in ghosts," I said.

"Oh me neither. Me neither! But still, you can't be too careful around the dead. Because you never know."

"So you do believe in ghosts?"

"Well, not exactly. I'd just say when you've got thousands of bodies lying around underground something has to be weird. Especially at night."

"Yes," I said. "There are a lot of superstitions about that."

Jenna had remained silent throughout the ride and didn't say whether or not she believed in ghosts. I decided not to inquire.

The cab dropped us at the appointed place, on a narrow road that runs to one side of the cemetery. We asked him to come back for us in thirty minutes and told him if we weren't there, to come back every fifteen minutes until we showed up. When we got out, I looked up at a high wall topped with thick ivy. But when I looked more carefully, I could see that the ivy obscured barbed wire and spikes. It would be hard to climb over the wall without tearing yourself to shreds. I wondered what tricks the guide had up his sleeve to get us in.

We waited a few minutes on the road, standing in a thin, cold mist. It was that time of night when even the insects and birds are asleep, and the silence enveloped us. It was also pitch black. There were no lights on in the houses behind us, and there was no moon. I felt myself shiver slightly, even though I didn't believe in ghosts.

"Bonjour."

The voice came from behind me and made me jump. Jenna startled, too. I had not heard anyone coming and, clearly, neither had she.

I turned to greet the voice, who I assumed was the Guide Nocturne. It was a little hard to see him in the dark, but, despite that, the man's appearance was a surprise to me. I'm not quite sure what I was expecting—a big, burly guy, perhaps, able to scale high walls? This guy was instead short, almost bald, and dressed in a three-piece suit. He reminded me of a dandier version of that guy with the unpronounceable, all-consonant name who is Superman's mortal enemy. He was also carrying a wicker picnic basket.

Meanwhile, as I looked him over, he looked us up and down. Eventually, he said, "And who might the two of you be?"

"Robert Tarza and Jenna James," I said.

"Ah, good. May I see your IDs, please?"

I thought it an odd request, but we both complied. He looked at our passports and seemed satisfied.

"Why did you want to see our IDs?" I asked.

"To be certain you are not *les flics*, as we call the cops here. And I am satisfied that you are not. It would be too much trouble for the police to falsify two American passports just to catch someone entering a cemetery at night."

"I see. And you are Monsieur daNucci?"

"For these assignments, I am le Guide Nocturne. Without name otherwise. I'm sure you understand."

"I guess so."

"May I also have my fee, please?"

"I'd prefer to wait to pay you until you get us in and out."

"Ah, Monsieur, as I told Madame James on the phone, I have only agreed to get you in and to show you how to get back out.

So, assuming things go well, I will be long gone when you come out."

I looked at Jenna, who was nodding her head in the affirmative. Not that she had told me any of that. I grudgingly removed ten one-hundred-euro notes from my pocket and handed the bills to the guide.

"Merci, Monsieur. Please follow me."

We walked down the road perhaps fifty yards, where there was a depression in the soil. Our guide pointed to the depression. "If you brush away the ivy there, there is a culvert that goes under the wall, and since neither of you is fat, you will be able to crawl through with minimum damage to your clothes."

"You've got to be kidding."

He smiled. "Actually, I am, in part. The way in is different." He took out his cell phone and tapped a few keys. A minute or two later, a small gate in the wall opened. There was a man on the other side who looked like a cemetery worker—French workingman's brimmed cap, a light blue jacket and work boots. The jacket was unzipped enough to show the Père Lachaise logo on the shirt beneath.

"Entrez, s'il vous plaît," he said, and stood aside to give us room to move through the gate.

"So you were only kidding about crawling through the culvert," I said to the guide.

"For getting in, yes. This is so much easier."

I was about to ask him how he had persuaded the guard to let us in when I saw him slip a wad of bills into the man's hands.

"Now," the guide said, "listen carefully, both of you. This gentleman will take you to the gravesite. I have given him the grave location and family name which you gave to me. He will not note what you do there, except you may not take anything away with you."

"We understand," Jenna said.

"Also, when you get to the grave and again when you leave the cemetery, you should tip him. A tip, not a bribe. I have already bribed him. Four or five euros each time will do."

"What is the picnic basket for?" I asked.

He handed it to me. "It has the usual picnic materials in it—a baguette, jam, cheese, a half-bottle of wine with a corkscrew, and so forth. Also a tablecloth and napkins. When you get to the gravesite, put down the tablecloth and set out the food. If you are accosted by anyone—there are many guards, not just this one—you are to say you are part of a religious group which believes in dining with your ancestors, and it must be at night so they will not be afraid to come up from below."

"You're serious?"

"Yes, very. Here, I have written it out in French, what you are to say."

"Won't they be suspicious?"

"Perhaps. But if you make sure they know you are Americans, it will be more believable."

"Why?"

"Most French people think Americans are uncultured, and this is exactly the kind of thing that someone from a barbarian civilization would do."

"I see, I guess."

"And the advantage will be that if they think you are simply nuts, they will simply kick you out. If they think you are up to no good, they will have you arrested."

"Okay," I said.

"One more thing. Do you have a flashlight with you?"

"Yes, we do," Jenna said.

"Do not use it. There is just enough light to follow this man without it if you stay very close. If you turn the light on it will attract attention from . . . other guards. Good luck."

"Wait," Jenna said.

"What, Madame?"

"How do we get out?"

"If all goes well, this gentleman will escort you back to the gate and open it for you."

"And if it doesn't go well?"

"You will crawl out through the culvert. Its opening on the inside of the wall is right there." He pointed to a large pipe. "And with that, I will just say bonne chance, good luck."

"Why do all French people always say good luck to us in both French and English?" I asked.

"They do not think saying good luck in an inferior language is effective in bringing luck," the guide said.

He turned and walked away, leaving us with the inside guy, who took us, without speaking a word, to the Brioche grave site. On the way, we passed by dozens of mausoleums, many with elaborate doors, grillwork, and statuary, some with inscriptions, most built of concrete, a few rendered as horizontal slabs in marble or onyx, all crowded together in a formation just shy of a jumble. Fortunately, it was only a five- or six-minute walk from where we entered to our destination. I looked over my shoulder several times as we walked and thought we'd be able to find our way back to the gate on our own if we absolutely had to.

The Brioche family tomb itself was modest compared to many of the others. It was unadorned concrete, perhaps eight feet high, with double doors and plain grillwork on the top half of the doors. There was no inscription on the tomb save the name "Famille Brioche."

We spread the picnic cloth on the ground, as instructed, with all the food laid out. I broke off a piece of the baguette and took a bite, just to show that we really were there to eat. I tipped our guard five euros, after which he moved back a fair distance and began to study something on his cell phone, never looking up.

Jenna went up to the tomb doors, pushed the key into the small lock and turned it. It made a faint scratching sound of metal on metal. To my relief, it opened easily, and she walked inside. After she was in, she gestured to me, and I walked forward into the tomb.

Inside it was even darker. Despite the instructions not to use a light, Jenna had taken her flashlight out of her pocket and was shining it around. Dust motes kicked up by our shoes shone in the air, and cobwebs hung between the roof and the floor. Along one wall, five small urns sat on a stone shelf. One of the five was much smaller than the others. I assumed it held the remains of a child. Each urn bore a name. The names of Oscar's parents adorned two of them.

"I don't see anything that looks like Oscar might have left it," Jenna said, shining the light around again.

"I don't either. Or anything else of interest, for that matter."

A scurrying noise caused us both to jump.

"Probably a mouse," I said.

"Yeah. And this looks like it was a total waste of time," she replied. "There's nothing other than what you'd expect in a tomb."

"There is something, Jenna. Do you see the little grilled gate beneath the urns?"

"Yes."

"There's something bright white inside it."

She tugged on the gate, which opened with a squeak. Inside there was a sealed plastic bag that had a white business-size envelope inside. She pulled it out.

"Should we open it?" I asked.

"No, we should just take it and get out of here. This place gives me the creeps."

"What about the rule that we shouldn't take anything?"

"Who will know? It's not like we're taking an urn or someone's ashes." She picked up the envelope and shoved it in her purse.

We walked out of the tomb and looked around for our guard. He was nowhere to be seen.

"Maybe," Jenna said, "we should wait a few minutes and see if he comes back."

"Okay." We sat down on the blanket. I was suddenly hungry, so I broke off another piece of bread and spread some soft cheese on it. "You want some, Jenna?"

"No. You know, we should have gotten his cell number."

"Yeah. We forgot."

After ten minutes had passed, I was beginning to get nervous that our guard was not coming back. "What do you think?" I asked. "Should we wait longer or get out of here?"

"The longer we wait, the more chance some different guard will find us, and I don't know if the picnicking with the dead excuse is going to fly."

"Alright, let's go," I said. "I think we can find our way back to the gate we came in. Maybe he's waiting for us there."

I packed up the picnic basket. My initial inclination was to leave it, but then I thought that if we were accosted by someone, it was at least some kind of excuse. So I took it along.

It proved not all that easy to find our way back. Most of the tombs looked more or less alike, and we took several wrong turns. After ten minutes or so, it was clear that we were lost.

"Try your GPS," Jenna said.

"Yeah. I should have thought of that to start with." I popped up the GPS app.

"Can you tell where we are?"

"Not really. It doesn't map true in here. The glowing dot shows us about ten feet to our left, in the middle of those tombs."

While we were talking, the mist had begun to close in. I looked down and realized I could hardly see my feet. As for the GPS, I was stymied by not knowing exactly where we had come in and the fact that the map showed several paths that led to the area where I thought we'd entered. I had to admit that it was also getting kind of scary. The tombs seemed to be closing in around us. Maybe I did believe in ghosts. I tried to cover up my anxiety with a joke. "I guess we should have left some glowing bread crumbs."

Jenna ignored me. "If that map isn't doing us any good, you should shut it down. The glow in the mist is marking us as intruders."

"Okay. I closed it. But I can't see a thing now. Can you?"

"Shh. I just heard something that sounded like footsteps."

We both stood stock-still and listened. I heard faint sounds that might have been muffled steps, but then they stopped. I could feel my heart pounding in my chest. Jenna brought her mouth up to my ear and whispered. "We came uphill on our way in. Let's go downhill. We'll hit the outer wall. Then we can follow it around—we want to go left I think—until we get to the gate."

"Okay," I whispered back.

Just then a voice—not too far away, although it was hard to tell because of the way the mist distorted the sound—called out, *"Allo? Qui est là?"*

I had no intention of answering his query and telling him who we were. We started to move downhill, following the road we were on. I thought I heard footsteps close behind us again. I put my hand on Jenna's shoulder to stop her from walking and felt her trembling. We both stood and listened. I heard nothing. Maybe it had been my imagination.

We finally reached the wall, went left and eventually stumbled upon the gate, which was locked with a chain and a padlock.

"What do you think?" I asked. "Do we crawl through the culvert?"

"I don't know of any other way out," she said. "The gate is locked with this padlock"—she tried opening it but it wouldn't budge—"and we know there's barbed wire on top of the wall. If you have a better idea, Robert, tell me."

"I don't."

I dropped the picnic basket and crawled into the pipe. It was dirty, wet and cold. The only way I could move was by squirming forward on my knees and elbows. One of my gloves fell off, and my hand touched soft, cold muck. After not too far, I ran into a mesh screen that was clearly designed to keep intruders out. Or maybe spirits in.

I felt Jenna bump into my feet. "What's the problem?"

"There's a screen in the way. I don't have any way to cut through it."

"Try pushing on it. Maybe it's old and rusty."

I pushed but nothing happened. I pushed harder, and it still didn't yield. I heard a voice behind us again, echoing inside the pipe, *"Qui est là?"* Finally, I put my head down, curled it into my shoulder and shoved with all my might. I heard a scraping sound as the screen gave way. I crawled over it, ripping my pants and my sweatshirt. A minute later I reached the other side, crawled out through the vegetation and stood up. Jenna emerged a few seconds after that, looking as dirty and ragged as I felt.

I heard the guard making noises on the other side of the metal gate. I couldn't see him through the thick mist, but I assumed he was peering out, looking for us, but unable see us. I heard him fiddling with the padlock on the gate.

Just then, our cab drove up and slowed to a halt in front of us. We clambered into the back seat. The cabbie turned and looked at us. "You guys are filthy. You'll get the back of my cab dirty. Please get out and clean yourselves off first."

"Forget about that," I said. "We need to get the hell out of here! Now! Go!"

He stepped on the accelerator and we took off down the road, slipping slightly on the wet pavement.

Jenna looked at me. "That night guy guide has never been through that pipe," she said. "We ought to demand our money back. If that screen hadn't been rusted out, we'd still be in there and probably getting arrested."

"You're right. But we got out."

The cabbie turned his head around. "You guys are really ruining my back seat."

"Look," I said. "We've already paid you a thousand euros."

"For services already rendered."

I ignored the point. "Just use a little of that money to get your back seat cleaned off."

"Okay, but try not to move around too much. Really, it's hard to get that seat clean when it gets dirty."

"Do you know the British phrase 'sod off'?" I asked.

"Yeah."

"Well sod off and take us back to where you picked us up."

He was none too happy about it, but he did it.

By unspoken agreement, Jenna and I avoided mentioning the purloined envelope while we were in the cab. We'd let the driver listen to a lot of stuff on our way to Paris from Digne, but this seemed like something we should keep to ourselves. As soon as we got out, Jenna said, "Do you think we need plastic gloves or something when we open the envelope?"

"We can try to wipe our prints off later if we need to. And anyway, your prints are already on the plastic bag. Let's find a place to open it."

CHAPTER 41

We were about two blocks from Tess's apartment. There were no open cafés nearby, so we walked up a side street and sat down on the curb. Jenna opened the bag and then the envelope, which wasn't sealed, and took out a single sheet of folded paper. She took out her flashlight, scanned it and handed the document to me. "It's in French. You read it."

It was handwritten, and it took me a minute to decipher. I read it through twice, to be sure it really said what I thought it said.

"What does it say, Robert? Come on. Tell me."

"It's a letter from François-Victor Hugo, who I think was one of Victor Hugo's children, to someone named Charles Hugo."

"And?"

"It says that he has finally persuaded 'their' father—so Charles Hugo must have been François-Victor's brother—to inscribe a copy of an English-language edition of *Les Misérables* to Charles Dickens, with a personal and flattering message. And that when he is in London next month, he thinks he will be able to use it to arrange a dinner with Dickens for himself."

"Oh my God. That would authenticate the inscription in the book that Oscar bought, wouldn't it?"

"It would seem to. If it's real it gets rid of all the arguments about how the inscription on the book must be fake because Hugo and Dickens didn't know one another, met only once, that Hugo didn't speak English well, et cetera."

"But how do we know it's not itself a fake?" Jenna asked.

"Exactly," I said. "It might be part of a fake set, where each seems to authenticate the other."

"If it's real, what do you think it does to the book's value?" she asked.

"Probably makes it even more valuable than if Hugo had signed it because he knew Dickens personally," I said. "It gives the book a great backstory."

"So if the letter is real it works as an authenticator of the book," Jenna said. "The son wanted his father, one of the most famous French authors, to inscribe one of his novels to make it easier for the son to gain an audience with the best-known English author of his time."

"Precisely," I said. "*If* it's real."

"Is the letter dated?" Jenna asked

I looked at the letter again. "Yes. June 1, 1870."

I could see Jenna was excited. I was, too.

"I want to learn more about François-Victor Hugo before we jump to conclusions about the letter's authenticity," I said. "I mean, it makes sense on one level that the inscription he came up with for his father to sign would mention Shakespeare. He was the main translator of Shakespeare into French at the time. On another level, the whole thing seems too good to be true."

"That antiquarian bookstore owner told you about the Shakespeare connection, right?"

"Yes. But here's a puzzling question. If François-Victor Hugo gave the book with the inscription to Dickens, what's it doing in France?"

We hurried back to the apartment. When we got there, we discussed whether we dared look up what we wanted to know, or whether we should use an Internet café. In the end, we decided that even if our computers were being hacked, the hackers wouldn't learn much just from seeing that we were researching Dickens, Hugo and Hugo's children.

I hadn't spent more than a few minutes at the task when it became apparent why the book, if the inscription was real, had ended up in France.

"It was bad timing," I said. "Charles Dickens died on June 9, 1870. If François-Victor Hugo was writing to his brother Charles on June 1 of 1870 that he was going to England 'next month,' that would have put his trip in July. Dickens would already have been dead a month."

"Maybe François-Victor Hugo kept the book, and somehow, after he died, it was eventually acquired by the lecherous priest in Digne."

"We'll probably never know how it got to Digne, Jenna."

Tess came into the room, dressed, as she had been when we left, in her bathrobe. "You two," she said. "What have you found? What is this letter you are holding?"

We explained the whole thing to her. She examined the letter and said, "It seems very old, the paper. An expert must examine it and the ink to be certain. And we must learn where Oscar is. But if we assume it is real . . ."

"Yes," I said, "if the letter is real, we have begun to solve the problem of the book's authenticity."

"Except you have not solved much," Tess said. "You still do not know where Oscar is, and you do not know where the book is. If the kidnappers kill Oscar, this letter is not of importance."

"I agree," I said. "The question is whether there's any way to use the letter to find both Oscar and the book."

Jenna looked thoughtful. "I have an idea."

"The last one ended up with me crawling through a drain."

"You got out, didn't you?"

"Yes. So, okay, what's the idea?"

"Do you know the old saying about how to catch a mouse?" she asked.

"Put out the cheese?" I shrugged. "I'm afraid I find that not very helpful. Please explain."

"My thinking goes like this. The book alone, if all it has is the inscription, is worth something, but not much because everyone will say it's a fake."

"Which is what they are in fact saying," I said.

"Right, but Oscar told us he had an offer to buy the book for a lot. So he must have told the potential buyer about this letter—the authenticator he mentioned. And the kidnappers must know about it, too. Otherwise, there would have been no reason to go through this whole exercise."

"But the kidnappers have not said a thing about the letter," I said.

"True," Jenna said. "But if we let all the people we suspect know that the letter is here, whoever is behind the kidnapping will come and try to get it, whether they knew about it beforehand or not. It's the cheese, and when they come we will catch the mouse."

"Let it be known how?" I asked.

"We'll send the info out on our cell phones so the general and the police can read it, and we'll send a text to the kidnappers telling them somehow. I haven't figured out the details yet."

"How will we know when they come to get it?"

"Tess, do you have access to people who can put a camera in your study?" Jenna asked. "One we can watch from somewhere else?"

"I think I can do this."

I had been mulling over the cheese ploy. There was something that troubled me. "Jenna, what if no one at all comes?"

"If no one comes, I will agree that we should just turn this whole thing over to the police and go home—that we will have done all we can for Oscar, and that anything else we might do will be futile."

"Well, one other thing, speaking of mice," I said. "Where is Olga?"

"She went out early yesterday morning," Tess said. "She said she will not come back until tomorrow after noon."

"How did you manage to speak to her?" Jenna asked.

"Eh, we have been using Google translate, on the computer. She types a thing in Russian, and it translates to French. I read it and type in what I want to say back in French. And so the program translates it the other way, to Russian."

"That's clever."

"Perhaps. But I think it is truly not necessary. Olga speaks French. I am certain of this."

"How do you know, Tess?" I asked.

"Because I said in French, while I stood in front of her, 'There is a spider in my hair,' and began to touch my hair wildly to find it. I saw when I said this Olga started to find her own hair, then stopped. I think she remembered she pretends not to speak French."

"That's a hard thing to pull off, pretending not to understand what people are saying all around you," Jenna said.

"Perhaps not for this girl. She told me she studies how to act in Moscow."

"Studies how to behave?"

"No, no. How to be an actor."

With that information in mind, we spent the next half hour kicking around some ideas about how to implement our plan. Then we all went back to bed and slept late.

Around ten the next morning, Tess, Jenna and I gathered at the breakfast table to plan the caper.

"Let's plan out Operation Cheese, as I now call it, in detail," I said.

"Okay. How do you want to go about that?" Jenna asked.

"Since it was your idea, you should lead."

"Alright, we need to let each mouse know that we have the letter from Hugo's son, what it says and where it is. That way, whoever now has the book will come looking for the letter so they can have the proof that the inscription on the book is real."

"Where are you going to leave it?"

She looked at Tess. "In Tess's study, if that's okay with her."

Tess nodded her head. "Yes, certainly."

"How are you going to let them know about it?" I asked.

"In the case of the hotel owner, I will simply go to the hotel and tell him about it and let slip where it is," Jenna said. "In other words, I'll play the dumb American who can't keep her mouth shut."

"And what about the general?" I asked.

"I will send you an email about it, Robert. And in that email, I'll say how glad I am that we've finally encrypted our phones. The general will be able to read the email, think that we didn't manage to encrypt it—that we screwed up—and he'll have the information."

"In other words, once again, that you're a stupid American."

"Yes."

"And Olga?"

"Why don't we have Tess just speak about it on the phone—in French—while talking to you? That way, if Olga really does understand French, she'll get the information but assume we don't know she has it. So she'll just assume that you didn't mean to spill the beans."

"Why do I want to spill beans?" Tess asked.

I broke in. "It's a metaphor. It means to give information away by accident or on purpose."

"Ah, we would say *vendre la mèche*."

"Doesn't that mean 'sell the wick'?" I asked.

"No, no, here it will mean the same as *spill the beans*. I will explain to you later how these words mean that."

"Well, wick or beans, I think it will work. But, Tess, what else are you going to do for the project?"

"I will contact some people now to set up the cameras and alarms. You will see tomorrow."

* * *

The first workmen arrived the next morning at seven. They installed ten tiny camera lenses, each no bigger than a button. One held the entry door to the apartment in its gaze. The second through fourth focused on the walls of Tess's study. Still others went into the living room, the dining room, my study and the guest room, along with motion detectors and microphones in each room. The only rooms they skipped were the bathrooms and the kitchen. They also installed an invisible-beam electric eye across the thresholds of both the front door and the study.

When I went out to pick up some food for breakfast, I saw men working in the elevator and the building lobby, installing still more equipment. I nodded to Monsieur Martin as I passed him, and he nodded back. He appeared mesmerized by all of the activity. I wondered if he'd actually installed the new, automatically-recording camera he had told me about or if it was still in its box.

I brought the food back and set it all down on the dining room table. Tess and Jenna were already there, observing the activity.

"This is all very cool," Jenna said. "But where is the feed going from all of these cameras?"

"There is a vacant apartment on the floor above this one," Tess said. "Yesterday afternoon, I rented it for one month. We will arrange to be out every evening and then stay in it and watch the screens."

"And when we see somebody come into the study and grab the envelope, what exactly are we supposed to do about it?" Jenna asked.

"We will alert the police to our plan. They will be nearby and will arrest this person. They will have evidence from these videos. I have arranged with them how this will work. How they will capture the criminals."

"I don't know if we can trust the police," I said. "Whom did you speak to?"

"Captain Bonpere. I think we can trust her. Do you not agree?"

"I guess so. What do you think, Jenna?"

"Works for me."

The men finished their work at around two thirty.

After that, we inspected the "safe room," as Tess had inaptly labeled it, in the rented apartment. It had a bank of monitors in the living room, each one labeled in both French and English to match the room, wall or door the camera was watching. There were also monitors for the motion detectors and two small lightbulbs, one red, one green, each set to flash in the safe room if someone crossed the threshold of, respectively, the front door or the door to the study.

"How does the feed get here?" I asked. "I didn't see any wires."

"It is all via encrypted radio," Tess said.

We tried out the system. Jenna went downstairs and intentionally triggered the red and green lights. She stood and waved in front of each camera, and I could see her easily. The motion detectors worked, too.

"Tess, will they work if it's dark in there at night?"

"We will let the lights stay on, but if they are extinguished, each camera also has an infrared ability. Donc, we will see in the dark."

At that moment, Tess's cell phone rang. She answered it, and I heard her say in French, after listening for a moment, "Yes, I can come there if it will not take long." And then, shortly after that, "Now? If it will help find Monsieur Quesana, why not?"

"Who was that?" I asked.

"It was the judge. He says he has some small questions to ask me, to fill in some things."

"Now?"

"Yes. I told him 'why not?' I will not be gone long. You can begin to get ready for the mouse while I am away."

"We will wait for you to return," Jenna said. "We need to be sure we are fully coordinated among us. But hey, tell the judge I said hello."

"I think I will not do this," Tess said, and left.

CHAPTER 42

Judge Roland de Fournis

I had enjoyed my full day off. It had been a long time since I'd taken such a day for myself. The next morning, still enjoying my leisure time, I did not rush into work as I usually did, but instead puttered around my apartment. After lunch, I finally headed for the courthouse, but dawdled along the way. I looked in shop windows and watched old women feed the pigeons in the plaza in front of Notre Dame. I even thought of going into the cathedral and lighting a candle for my parents, but decided to save it for another day.

When I finally got to the courthouse, went into my courtroom and sat down at my desk, I saw, lying on top of the red dossier I had been compiling, two manila folders. My greffier, who was already there, smiled at me, as if to say, "I can still do the impossible."

I lifted up the first folder and read through the contents. Ten pages gave me a detailed history of what the general had been up to since he was a cadet at Saint-Cyr, the military academy that has, for the last couple of centuries, graduated most officers of the French Army.

The second folder contained the civil service employment history of Madame Devrais. It was only half a page long and ended when she was about twenty-five, as I had requested. Nothing about the file suggested that she had been involved in any way in spying or national security matters. Indeed, in her early twenties, she had been a mere clerk in the Foreign Ministry, although the dates and location of one part of her assignment there were very interesting indeed.

Not long after I finished reading the material, the general arrived for his appointment. It got off to a bit of a bumpy start. He sat down, waved the summons at me and said, "I have been talking to lawyers since I last saw you, and I think I can make out a good case that this summons is illegal."

"Why?"

"For one thing, you're beyond your proper jurisdiction. You were assigned a simple theft case. For another, you did not give me enough notice for this appearance. And for a third, as I told you before, I believe my current position gives me immunity."

"Whatever your current position is, which you've still not made clear."

"I can do that."

"I'll tell you what, Jean. All I want is some information. If you are willing to give it to me, we can do this informally today without your taking an oath."

"And if you want it to be sworn testimony?"

"After hearing you out, if I need it under oath, I can call you back and we can find out before the court of appeal whether I have the authority to summon you."

"Alright, let's give it a try."

"I apologize for not having any almond croissant for you today."

"It's not a problem. What do you want to know?"

I smiled. "Since this is an informal session, I'll ask you an informal question: What the hell is going on?"

"I'm trying to find this guy who was kidnapped."

"You're not making much progress so far as I can see."

"I am. I have found the source of the money with which this American bought the book."

"Which was?"

"He borrowed one hundred thousand dollars from Bank of America."

"Is that suspicious?"

"It could be. He has no history of borrowing money, and he didn't specify in the loan what the money was for."

"So?"

"It's unusual. I'm sure the bank has done nothing wrong, but we now suspect that this is some kind of money laundering, possibly done for a gang in Russia that uses the purchase and sale of rare books as a way to move money around the world without suspicion."

"I thought people like that were interested in washing millions."

"This may be a starter effort—to see if he's reliable."

"Do you at least know where he is?"

"We do."

"Where?"

"As I told you once before when you asked me this, I'm hesitant to give you any information along those lines for fear you'll interfere."

"I'll not press it for the moment. But how did you figure it out?"

"The kidnappers have been clever, using throw-away phones and moving around a lot. But they recently slipped up by using one of those phones twice in a thirty-minute period from the same location: the first time to send a message to the professor and the second time to send one to someone else. We were lucky and able to triangulate more closely, using a drone nearby."

"Well, I will ask again, where are they?"

"Do you promise on your oath as a judge not to interfere?"

"I promise."

"And do you promise not to tell the busybody professor and her friends?"

"I promise that, too."

I looked over at my greffier to be sure she was quietly transcribing the conversation. I had promised not to take the general's testimony under oath. I hadn't promised not to make a record of it. One of the great things about the notebook computer the greffiers use is that you can't tell if they're transcribing or just working on something else.

"They are in a small town near Digne-les-Bains in a converted barn," he said.

"How near to Digne?"

"I'm going to leave that unsaid."

"Are you going to try to rescue him?"

"Soon."

"How soon?"

"Not today, not tomorrow, not the day after that, but soon."

"How will you do it?"

"We will use the GIGN."

Those initials stood for the *Groupe d'Intervention de la Gendarmerie Nationale*, a military unit known for its special tactics, body armor and aggression. It was a highly professional and meticulously trained group that had rescued lots of people.

But there was always the risk that this time it would fail and the hostage would die.

"Jean, that group would not have been my first choice in what seems to be a pretty run-of-the mill kidnapping, not a terrorist plot."

"We've been monitoring their activity and we think it's appropriate."

"Who is 'we'?"

"I've told you before, I'm working with the Brigade Criminelle."

"Ah yes, you did mention that."

He started to get up. "I hope you've appreciated my candor. Now I have some things to attend to."

"I have a couple more quick things. First, do you know where the book is?"

"No. I wish I did. I could exchange it for the hostage."

"There's also something that puzzles me about this whole thing."

"Which is?"

"It seems, from what I've been told, that this inscription in the book is almost certainly a fake. So why does anyone want it?"

He shrugged and threw up his hands. "I don't know. Some people are crazy and hope against hope that it is not fake? I really have no idea."

"I see."

He started to get up again. "Are we done now?"

"Just one more. Do you know a young woman named Olga Bukova?"

He sat back down. "Yes, of course."

"Why 'of course'?"

"She's my niece. My brother's daughter."

I was stunned. After a few seconds of silence, in which I wasn't able to speak, I asked, "What is she doing involved in all of this?"

He sighed deeply. "I have been trying not to get involved with her and her project, but I suppose this was inevitable."

"Do tell."

"My brother, Igor, wanted to buy the same book that, apparently, Oscar Quesana bought. But Oscar got there first. So my brother wants to buy it from Oscar at a good profit for Oscar. Oscar refuses to sell."

"And so your brother kidnapped him?"

"No, no, not at all. My brother, you see, is stuck in Russia for the moment. Some kind of trouble with the government. So he sent his daughter, Olga, to find Monsieur Quesana and up the offer to three times what Oscar paid for the book."

"Is that why she was at the hotel?"

"Apparently."

"I've been told that the hotel he was staying at was secret. Did you tell her where to find him?"

"No, and I didn't initially know where he was staying. As you probably know by now if you've been told the whole story, Tess Devrais had a Christmas Eve dinner party. The book was apparently there, and Olga saw it somehow. She told me that she put a very tiny GPS tracking button on it, and later followed Quesana to his hotel. And then to Digne."

"So you had nothing to do with it?"

"Nothing. I wish she'd go home to Russia. I'm going to make her do that as soon as I find her. I don't know where she is at the moment."

I thought about telling him that I knew where she was, but then thought better of it. After all, he was the witness, not me. I also decided not to mention that I'd just been told that she did not speak French or English, which raised the question of how she was going to negotiate with Monsieur Quesana.

"One more question."

"Yes?"

"If she's your brother's daughter, why do the two of you have different last names?"

"My parents divorced when I was four. My brother and father stayed in Moscow. My mother and I moved here and she changed our last name to be less Russian. At the time, being Russian was not a plus."

"So you are not Olga's father."

"Whatever would make you think I am?"

From the expression on his face, I had just proposed to him something totally false, idiotic even.

"Your presence in Moscow around the time she was born," I said.

"I don't know how you have found that out, but whatever inferences you have drawn from it are totally false. She is my brother's daughter."

He got up and left without even saying *au revoir.* After he had departed, I asked my greffier, "What do you think?"

"I think he's telling the truth but not the whole truth."

"I agree. The question is, which part of the truth did he leave out? That is what I have to figure out."

"How are you going to do that?"

"I'm not sure. But to start with, I happen to know the chief of the Brigade Criminelle. His number is in the computer. Could you get him on the phone?"

"Of course, Monsieur le juge."

He picked up the phone immediately—most people do when they hear a judge is calling—and disappointed me. He said that General Follet was indeed working on a special investigation of a kidnapping. He didn't know the details, but assured me that all the proper protocols were being followed.

His call showed me, once again, that not all hunches pan out.

Next, I picked up the phone, called Madame Devrais and asked, if she were not too busy, if she might drop by sometime in the next hour. I told her that there were a few details of the case I needed to wrap up, and she might just have the answers. I added that it might help find Monsieur Quesana. She didn't ask what details, and said that, certainly, if it would help to find Monsieur Quesana, she would be happy to come. I could tell from her tone of voice, though, that she was wary.

For the next little while, I busied myself with some administrative matters. Then there came a knock on the door, and Madame Devrais entered. Without waiting for an invitation, she sat down in the witness chair.

"Bonjour, Monsieur le juge, what can I do for you?"

"I have been reading your civil service personnel file."

"I am surprised they gave it to you."

"Only the part before you turned twenty-five."

"Ah, that perhaps makes sense. Did you find it interesting reading?"

"Only in part."

"Which part?"

"The part that says you were a file clerk in the Foreign Ministry posted for two years to our embassy in Moscow."

"And?"

"In itself, that is not so interesting, although I do assume, given what came later for you, that you were actually doing something besides filing."

"That could be. Are you interested in what I filed?"

"No, but I am curious if you speak Russian."

"I can do 'entrance' and 'exit,' and 'hello' and 'goodbye,' but beyond that very little. My 'filing,' if we call it that, was electronic in nature, and I was discouraged from mixing with the locals. I rarely left the compound except for some special missions."

"I see."

"So what are you interested in, Monsieur le juge?"

"What I am interested in is a coincidence because I have also been reading General Follet's file."

As I said that, I watched her closely to see if she had any reaction to it. There was none. Apparently, my inquiry during out last conversation about how long she had known the general had steeled her, should the topic come up again, against displaying even the flash of emotion she had let slip the last time.

"What coincidence?"

"You and he were posted to Moscow, at the embassy, at exactly the same time. He was a military attaché; you were a clerk. You were each there for almost two years. And you both left on, it would appear, the same day, twenty-one years ago next month."

"I don't truly recall that we arrived at the same time. We did leave at the same time."

"And why was that?"

"We were both about to be expelled from the country for various actions of which we were suspected by the Russian security services. We preferred to remove ourselves from Russia before that could happen. He had full diplomatic immunity; mine was more limited in scope."

"Were you lovers?"

"I have an inclination to tell you that it is none of your business and far beyond the scope of your inquiry."

"I can understand that inclination. But it is not mere voyeurism that inclines me to ask. If I were to tell you that your answer would not be recorded and not go in this dossier"—I held the red folder up for her to see—"would you be more inclined to answer?"

She sat for a moment, clearly thinking about it. "Are you promising on your oath as a judge that your greffier will not transcribe what I say and that you will not put it in the dossier and will not speak of it to anyone else?"

"Yes."

"What about Madame?" She gestured toward my greffier.

"I will not transcribe it, and I will also keep your secrets," Marie said.

"Alright then, I will tell you, since it seems important to you. Yes, we were lovers. Although it was not a complete secret. It was known to a few others at the embassy at the time."

"Others also in a certain type of employment?"

"Yes."

"Thank you for your candor."

She started to get up, assuming we were done. "I don't know why this is so important, Monsieur le juge, but if you have nothing further, I need to go now."

"I do have one more question."

"Yes?"

"Are you Olga's mother?"

She was still standing up, but betrayed no bodily surprise at my question. "That is a crazy idea."

"Yes, but is it true, Madame?"

"No. Whatever made you even suspect it?"

"I obtained her birth certificate from the Russian consulate—they were happy to oblige—and I noted when I read your file earlier today that Olga was born two weeks before you and the general left Moscow."

"And you think I agreed to put my own child up for adoption?"

"It was a possibility."

"It is nonsense. I had never met Olga—or even heard of her—before the general brought her to Christmas dinner at my apartment. And I would *never* put a child of mine up for adoption."

"Eh bien, I apologize then for bringing this up. But tell me, do you know who Olga's mother is?"

"No."

"Do you know who her father is?"

"I assume it is this man Igor Bukov. Do you have reason to think it is not?"

"It is only a suspicion raised by the fact that the general has a different last name from his supposed brother, Bukov, even though the general has a handy explanation for that."

"I see. Eh, I wish I could help you, but I have no reason to doubt what the general says about who Olga's father is. I have never met Igor, by the way, even though he is said to be the general's brother. And please remember that we were in Moscow just after Boris Yeltsin finished being president of Russia, and relations between us and them were thawing. The general was sent there precisely because his brother was in the Russian military. It was thought to be a good connection for us."

"Thank you for that explanation, and I take you at your word about the other things. Thank you for stopping by."

She left, and I watched her go, again looking to see if she would betray by some gesture that she had been lying—a shaking hand on the doorknob, a twitch in her neck, anything—but there was nothing. She was probably telling the truth. And so there was another theory gone.

Just then the phone rang and my greffier answered it.

"Monsieur le juge, it is again the chief of the Brigade Criminelle."

"Ah, perhaps he has more to report," I said, and picked up the phone.

"Rebonjour, Monsieur le juge," he said. "I was embarrassed when we spoke that I knew so little about this affair of the kidnapping. So I have inquired further."

I felt my heart speed up. Perhaps he was about to tell me that this kidnapping was indeed something the general had planned and executed.

"And?" I said.

"I have read all of the reports of the general and discovered that all is as it should be. He is even now working with the chief negotiator of our group to put a detailed plan in place so that when the kidnappers are confronted with armed force, the hostage will be kept absolutely safe."

"Who is the chief negotiator?"

"Anton Morel. GIGN's very best."

"I see," I said. "Thank you for taking the time to look into it. It is much appreciated."

"You are welcome, Monsieur le juge. Bonne journée."

So it was not the general who had conspired to kidnap Monsieur Oscar Quesana. But who was it then? That was something I would need to turn over to my successor when I returned from a few days in Provence, and, after a chat with the presiding judge, passed this matter on to a new judge.

Or did I really intend to pass it on? I then had the same conversation with myself I always had when I pushed my jurisdiction beyond the original assignment: *Why am I doing this?* And I got back the answer I always get: *out-of-control curiosity.* It had been a curse since childhood. And then there was the other thing. Someone was lying to me in this matter. I loathed being lied to. I wanted to find out who it was.

"Marie?"

"Oui, Monsieur le juge?"

"I must once again put off going to Provence. Instead, I would like you to find out the cell phone number of the chief hostage negotiator employed by the Brigade Criminelle. His name is Anton Morel."

"Do you want me to obtain it directly from the Brigade?"

"If you can find it out without contacting them, it would be preferable. Someone in this vast courthouse must know it."

"And then?"

"I want to call him."

Not two hours later, she handed me a slip of paper. "Here is Monsieur Morel's cell phone number."

"He is a civilian?" I asked.

"Yes."

I called him and he answered on the first ring. I explained who I was and what I was investigating and told him I wanted to meet with him as soon as possible. He initially demurred, saying he couldn't imagine what information he had that would be useful, but eventually agreed to meet with me if I were willing to meet late in the evening near where he lived, since he was in intense preparation for an operation and did not have time to come to the courthouse.

"Is the operation you're preparing for one that involves Oscar Quesana's kidnapping?" I asked.

"No, I am aware of that situation, but this involves an entirely different matter."

"So you are not involved in any operation tonight involving Monsieur Quesana?"

"No."

We agreed to meet at eleven that evening at Casimodo, which was convenient for him, but also for me since it is only a few blocks from where I live. I could walk there and walk home.

The fact that he was not involved in a Quesana operation that evening heartened me. It meant that the general had told the truth when he said the rescue operation would not be that night. Thus, there was still time to try to ensure Monsieur Quesana's safety, and talking directly to the negotiator seemed a very good way to start.

I would reflect later that I had not asked Monsieur Morel quite the right question.

CHAPTER 43

Jenna James

Tess returned from her visit to the judge in late afternoon.

"It was nothing," she said, addressing both me and Robert. "A few details he forgot to ask of me this last time I saw him."

She then looked directly at Robert and said, "The judge did say about something private that we need to discuss later." She turned to me. "It does not concern Oscar's kidnapping or the book."

I figured it had to do with what she was allowed to tell Robert about her activities as a spy, and I decided not to push it.

Next, the three of us prepared to trap the first mouse.

As planned, Robert texted me that he had encrypted his cell phone, and I texted back that I had encrypted mine, too. I added that, finally, we could communicate without fear of being overheard by the general or anyone else.

It wasn't true, of course, but at least it would explain to those intercepting our messages why we were about to start speaking so openly about things.

At five o'clock, we put a copy of the François-Victor Hugo letter in an envelope in the safe in Tess's study. We "accidentally" left the door ajar, in case someone showed up to grab it who didn't have the combination. To make the letter look authentic, we had used special copy paper—the crinkly old-looking stuff on which they print tourist copies of the Declaration of Independence. Earlier in the day, I had managed to find a blank ream of that type of paper in a stationery store.

At six, we put out the cheese for the general and whoever else might be listening. I texted Robert:

> As agreed, François-Victor Hugo ltr to brother in Tess study safe.
> Combo 3-30-12 if need access. Will take to bank deposit box in am.

"Tess, you have the first shift," I said. "Robert and I are off to see the hotel owner. We told him I wanted to come over and apologize and also pay for the lost pen even though I didn't take it. We'll be sure to tell him the exciting news about the letter and where it is."

"What will be your excuse for talking about it front of him?" Tess asked.

"We are going to offer to let the bookstore—the one in which he owns an interest—market the letter."

As Robert and I were about to leave, Olga came flying into the apartment from wherever she had been, plopped herself down on the couch in the living room and started to read a book. Because she was lying down, the book covered her face. It was clever. If she did indeed understand French or English, we wouldn't be able to read her facial expressions as a clue. Despite that, Tess and Robert put the plan into effect by talking to each other at length about the letter. Robert even had Tess remind him about the combination to the safe, on the excuse that he was forgetful and needed to write it down.

Olga, still reading her book, didn't even twitch.

Robert and I again started to leave to visit the hotel owner when my cell buzzed. I looked down at it and gestured toward the kitchen. We all moved there, out of Olga's earshot, just in case she actually spoke English.

"It's a message from the general," I said. "It says that they have intelligence that the kidnappers have given up finding the book and are about to kill Oscar. He wants to know where we are so he can come and meet with us about their plan to prevent that."

We looked at one another, and the question we all had in our minds was clear: should we ask the general to come to Tess's apartment or meet him elsewhere?

"Agree that he comes here," Tess said. "One of us will go up to the apartment and watch. It will be a test of the system."

"I'll go up," I said. "I'll text him back and tell him to come here right away to meet with you and Robert, and say that I'm out but will be back later."

I took some snacks out of the refrigerator and left for the hideaway. Twenty minutes later, I watched on one of the monitors as the general arrived. When he came in, Tess, ever polite, offered him coffee, which he declined. The three of them sat at the big table in the dining room and talked. The monitor showed Olga in the living room, too far away to overhear.

"We have been watching the barn Oscar is being held in and now we are worried," the general said.

Robert's face turned purple. "When did you discover exactly where the barn was? You told us you only knew that it was somewhere near Digne, but not its exact location. You lied to us."

"It was true at the time I told it to you. Later, we put a drone in the area and got a better triangulation on their phone messages."

"Why the hell didn't you tell us as soon as you found out?" Robert asked.

The general's eyes twinkled. "To prevent you from trying to rescue him yourselves."

Sitting at the monitor, I had to admit he had a point. That's exactly what we would have done.

"Alright, General, why are you now so worried?" Robert asked.

"We have managed to get some listening devices onto the roof of the barn—without being detected—and they are talking about killing Oscar."

"Why now?" he asked.

"They have not said so directly, but we think it is because, somehow, they have gotten their hands on the book with the inscription and no longer need Oscar."

"Well, mon général, that must mean whoever removed the book from the hotel room has given it to them, or they know where it is and think they can get it without Oscar."

"Precisely," the general said.

"Why do they wish to kill him? Is it not more sensible to permit him to go?" Tess asked.

"We do not know, Tess. Perhaps it is because he knows too much or can identify them."

"Do you know where in the building he's being held?" Robert asked.

"Unfortunately, we do not."

Robert and Tess glanced at one another, and it was clear they were both having the same thought I was having: if the general and his pals didn't know where Oscar was in the building, and they were going to attack anyway, it was much more likely he'd be killed instead of rescued.

"Mon général, what is your plan?" Tess asked.

"We are going to use the GIGN to rescue him."

"Does this not risk that he will be killed?"

"Yes, there is a risk, but it is very small. The GIGN is known around the world as very skilled at hostage rescue. And if we do not act, the kidnappers will kill him in any case."

I glanced at the monitor for the dining room and noticed that Olga had moved from the couch to a big chair, where she was much closer to the dining room and could probably hear what Robert, Tess and the general were saying. Maybe she really *did* also speak English.

"Is the GIGN like SWAT teams in the United States?" Robert asked.

"Yes, Robert, but with more skill and more firepower."

"How much firepower do you need to kill a few kidnappers?"

"We believe these people are terrorists and money launderers, and that they may have heavy weapons themselves."

"General, there is something you don't know," Robert said.

"What is that?"

"There is a letter from Victor Hugo's son, François-Victor, to his brother, which authenticates the inscription on the book."

If the general already knew about it from reading our texts, he covered it up well. His face showed no surprise, just curiosity.

"Please tell me more about this."

Robert did, and when he had finished, the general asked, "Where is it now?"

"In the safe in Tess's study."

"It is a very hard safe," Tess added. "No one will steal it from there."

"That's good, that's good," the general said. "But wouldn't it be better to entrust it to us? We have even better safes, and we have people to guard the safes. Here, your safe may be good, but this apartment has no security."

"I wish to keep it here," Tess said.

"Alright. I have no right to make you give it to us. But I still think you are taking a large risk."

"Wouldn't it make sense to let the kidnappers know about the letter?" Robert said. "They will want that, too, and perhaps they will put off their plan to kill Oscar until they get it."

The general put his first finger to his bottom lip, as if giving my suggestion serious thought. Finally, he said, "No. This would not make sense. I think it will put Oscar in even more danger."

"General, will you be leading the GIGN unit in the rescue mission?" Robert asked.

"No, I am not a member of the Gendarmerie. It is true they are part of the military, but they are attached to the Department of the Interior. It would not be appropriate for an army general to lead that group. It is not in my chain of command. And besides, I am retired."

"Retired. Of course. I had almost forgotten," Tess said. "Who then will lead this rescue mission?"

"General Lemoins will lead it. He has my entire confidence."

"When will it take place?" Tess asked.

"It will begin at midnight. They post only one night guard, and we can hear him snoring, so we think he sleeps rather than guards. I will be in direct touch with General Lemoins during the operation, which we have named *Opération de sauvetage américain*—in English, 'Operation American Rescue.'"

I looked down at my watch. It was already six o'clock. That meant we had only six hours to catch the mouse and then find some way to call off the so-called rescue, which I was sure was going to kill Oscar. The name they'd given it—so on the nose as to be ridiculous—made me even more certain the rescue wasn't being taken seriously.

"Will you keep us posted, General?" Robert asked.

"Yes, of course."

As the general got up to leave, I scanned the monitors for the other rooms in the apartment and saw something in Tess's study that astounded me. As soon as the general closed the door behind him, I rushed down to the apartment.

"Let's go back to Tess's study," I said to Robert and Tess, as quietly as I could. I gestured toward the book-hidden lump on the nearby chair in a way that I hoped communicated, *I don't want her to hear us.*

When we got there, I shut the door.

"Did the system work?" Robert asked.

"Like a charm," I said. "I could see and hear everything clearly, and the general tripped the alarm when he went through the front door. But now there's something I need to show the two of you." I pointed toward Tess's copy of *Les Misérables*, all five volumes of which were sitting on the bottom shelf of the tall bookcase, which was to the left of the safe. "Look carefully at the first volume of *Les Misérables*."

Robert looked and said he saw nothing he hadn't seen before.

Tess looked at it, too and said, "I see no thing that is new."

"Look carefully at the cover of the first volume," I said. "Do you see a little triangular piece of plastic that has crumbled off the dust protector?"

"I see it," Robert said. "And so?"

"So do you remember, Robert, when Tess showed us her copy of *Les Misérables* the first time? Back when she told us the story of her great-grandmother's affair in Digne?"

"Sure, Jenna."

"At that point, I'm sure that the plastic cover on the first volume of Tess's copy was unblemished. There was no missing piece."

Tess walked over to the bookshelf, bent down slightly, and examined the cover more carefully. "I do not remember if it had a missing piece."

"Watch this," I said. I pulled the book off the shelf. "I'm willing to bet this volume has the inscription to Charles Dickens." I opened it to the title page and held it up for all to see. And there it was, the inscription itself.

Tess was the first to react. "That cannot be."

"It is," I said. "Here, look for yourself."

Tess took the book from me and looked hard at the inscription. "How do we know this is not a copy?"

"We know because when they pulled the books from the hiding place in Oscar's hotel room, a very small triangular piece of plastic cover had fallen off one of the volumes. That piece was exactly the same shape as the small piece that's missing from this cover."

"Where's the piece now?"

"The police took it as evidence. It will match, I'm sure."

Robert took the book from Tess, closed it and examined the cover again. "Jenna, are you referring to the little piece that's missing from the upper-right corner of the spine?"

"Yes. And that's what tipped me off. The camera in this room is pointed directly at the safe, and I was just upstairs looking at the image of the safe and the bookcase next to it and noticed the missing piece on the cover."

"Jenna, are you sure about the match?"

"Absolutely sure. And therefore certain this is no copy, but the very book that was stolen from Oscar's hotel room. I don't know if the other four volumes were switched, too, but this one was for sure."

Tess collapsed into the big easy chair in the corner of the room and continued to repeat, "This cannot be."

I retrieved the book from Robert and reshelved it. "It can be, and the question is, who put it here, to hide it in plain sight?"

"I suppose you suspect me, do you not?" Tess asked.

"You're the logical person, the one who's had the best opportunity to put it on the shelf," I said.

"How do you imagine I removed it from the hotel room of Oscar, Jenna?"

"I don't know that yet. Maybe someone else got it out of there and gave it to you to hide, and you picked this perfect place."

"Who?"

"How about Olga?" I said.

Tess just stared at me. "What is my motive?"

"To replace your copy of the first volume of *Les Misérables* with one that is much more interesting. Not for the money—you have plenty of that—but just to keep yourself amused. So you will not have ennui."

Robert just stood there, clearly caught between my logic and his loyalty to Tess.

"Jenna, I can't believe Tess would do this," he said. "The logical explanation is that Olga took the book when she was staying at the hotel and then managed to stash it here somehow when she arrived here as a guest."

"Which means she was lying to us about what she was looking for at the bookstore in Digne," I said. "She was actually after the authenticator."

"That sounds right to me."

"But going back to the book, why would she bother to hide it here, in a place she might lose access to?" I asked.

Robert shrugged. "How about as a temporary storage place while she and whoever she's conspiring with figure out what to do with it? They probably think no one will bother to open Tess's copy of the book. And, Jenna, if you hadn't noticed the missing piece, they'd be right."

"Why do you think Olga conspires with anyone?" Tess asked.

"Good point," Robert said. "I don't know. Maybe it's because she's young, so I underestimate her."

"Maybe we should go out there and ask her. In whatever language she speaks," I said.

"You go," Robert said. "You can speak Russian to her. And report back to us."

I looked at Tess, who was still collapsed in the chair, and thought to myself that I had left poor Robert the unenviable task of asking his fiancée some very hard questions. I felt bad I'd had to bring it up. But I had not seen any alternative. Perhaps some time alone would help, and in any case I had another mission to carry out.

CHAPTER 44

I marched out into the living room to confront Olga, who had returned to lying on the couch, her face again covered by a book.

Without further ado, I said, in Russian, "Пожалуйста,брось книгу подальше."

She lowered the book and said, in flawless English, "You know, your Russian sucks. You meant to say, I think, to please put your book away, but you ended up saying 'please throw your book away.' Happy to help you out." She overhanded the book across the room, where it landed with a bang in the corner.

I was simultaneously glad to have Tess's suspicion that Olga spoke English confirmed, while at the same time enraged at Olga for deceiving us and angry at myself for having been stupid enough to talk about sensitive things in front of her as if she were deaf. I was also on some level amused as I recognized in her the same kind of easy insouciance that I had beamed out to the world when I was her age.

"Whether it sucks or doesn't suck, please sit up so we can have a decent conversation."

To my surprise, she complied.

"How many languages do you speak, Olga?"

"Three well—Russian, French and English. And a little German, too. Enough to get along there."

"Where did you learn them?"

"I went to an international school in Moscow, where all the instruction was in English. I spoke Russian at home, and I took French lessons. German I picked up watching German TV. Does that answer your nosy questions?"

"Why did you hide that you spoke other languages?"

"I learned a lot that way, don't you think? And I'm studying to be an actor. This was a great part. It's actually hard to pretend not to understand what people are saying all around you."

"Maybe you'll get an Academy Award."

"More likely you and your friends will share the dummkopf award."

I was fast leaving being amused behind and entering into total anger. "How old are you, Olga?"

"Twenty. I'll be twenty-one next month. Old enough to go to your country and get merked every night."

"'Merked'?"

"Drunk, whatever."

"I doubt very much my country will let you in. At least not if I have anything to say about it."

"Too late. I finished acting school in Moscow, and I've been admitted to college in the United States. I already have my visa."

"Good for you."

"Jenna, why did you bother to walk out here to talk to me? Aren't your best buds back there in the study with the fake letter from François-Victor Hugo?"

"So you overheard that. What makes you think it's fake?"

"It's too convenient. Just one more person trying a clever way to pump up the price of that book with the fake inscription on it. All of the letters of Victor Hugo and his family have been pored over for more than a hundred years. How come someone just found that one?"

Olga was, of course, expressing the same doubts I'd been harboring since we first saw the letter. But there was no strategic advantage in letting her know that. "Other than that logic, what makes you think the letter's a fake?"

"Just is, and I'm already totally tired of this whole conversation."

I considered just walking away, but then thought better of it. Maybe if I asked her directly what I wanted to know, I'd get some answers.

"Olga, did you take the book with the inscription out of Oscar's hotel room?"

"No."

"You answered 'no' rather quickly. How did you even know what I was talking about?"

"I keep up. As you know, my father was very interested in this book."

"Was?"

"Yes. He thinks now that both the book and letter are fakes, so he's no longer interested in them. You can keep the letter and the book, too, if you find it. Two fakes aren't any more valuable than one fake."

I heard a noise behind me and turned my head. Robert and Tess had entered the room and were standing in the doorway.

"How do we know you tell the truth?" Tess asked.

"The truth about what?"

"That you did not take this book from Oscar's hotel room. The judge who has this case told me you had the room next to Oscar."

"You should believe me because I have no reason to lie about any of this. If I did, I'd still be acting my part, pretending not to speak English or French, you know? That way I could go on hiding in plain sight like before and spy on all you dumbos some more."

"This argument does not prove you tell the truth, Olga," Tess said.

"Whatever. I'm going out now. I'm getting together with my mains." She got up from the couch and headed for the door.

I grabbed her arm. "You're not going anywhere, Olga."

"Let me go!"

"No. I think you should stick around until this is all resolved."

"Under French law, to prevent someone from leaving is kidnapping."

"I'll risk it," I said. "Just think of yourself as our guest. And by the way, you should be careful whom you accuse of a crime."

"Why should I? You're nobody."

"Well, some of *my* mains are at the American consulate here in Paris—drinking buddies, I'd call them. If I let them know a US visa holder is a suspected antiquities thief, you can kiss your sweet visa goodbye—ya know? But don't worry, I bet you can still get into some acting school in Vladivostok or somewhere like that."

She looked momentarily perplexed. Like I'd actually painted a picture of a future that she actively worried about.

"Why would I go to Vladivostok?"

"'Cause I'm guessing you were kicked out of your acting school in Moscow. Why else would you be here acting a part, as you put it, on this small stage? You're not exactly performing a lead in *Romeo and Juliet*."

As I was finishing my brief tirade, Tess came over and whispered in my ear, "Let her go. She is one of the mice we must permit to smell the cheese."

I thought about what she said for a few seconds. She was right. There was no point in screwing up the experiment. I released my grip on Olga's arm. "Olga, go where you want. But don't come back."

"Coming back to this shithole is of no interest to me."

"So pack up your stuff and go."

"Don't have any stuff, remember? It's all still in Digne."

"Then go without stuff."

She walked to the door, opened it, and, just before slamming it hard behind her, gave us all the finger, complete with upward thrust.

"Well," Robert said, "it would seem her school in Moscow teaches even the small details of American cultural expression."

Tess laughed. "In this you are right, Robert. Certainly, her hands do not speak French. We have different motions for this."

"So," I said. "Assuming her hearing is as acute as most people her age, she probably at some point overheard one of our discussions about this. Which means we have inadvertently notified one mouse that the letter is in the study."

Shortly thereafter, Robert and I left to see the hotel owner. We agreed that Tess would stay in the apartment until early evening. Then, as the evening wore on, we would let all of the mice know, by one means or another, that we had all gone to dinner and a late movie. At which point we would repair to the rented apartment.

CHAPTER 45

Robert and I returned to Tess's apartment at about nine in the evening. Things had gone well with the hotel owner, Monsieur Crépin. We had exchanged apologies and then dined together in the hotel restaurant. There had been many toasts to future *amitié* and other things I couldn't remember. By the time it was all over—at which point we told him we were meeting our friend Tess to go to a late movie—I had consumed more wine than I was used to, and I was feeling slightly buzzed. Or maybe more than slightly.

"So," I said to Robert and Tess, "shall we trip off to the spy nest?"

Tess just looked at me like I was drunk, which perhaps I was. And the kidnappers must have thought so, too, when they received my next text message, which said that I was tired of talking to them that day and was going out to dinner and a late movie, and I hoped they'd do the same and enjoy their evening, and that I'd talk to them tomorrow. I sent it on my own cell-phone so the general would be sure to see it, too.

Not long after, Tess and Robert actually went to the nearest movie theater—just in case anyone was tracking their location, too—and sent me a text message urging me to hurry up and join them. I sent them a message back saying I was on my way. Then they returned to Tess's apartment via a circuitous route, taking, they later told me, three different cabs in a row and hoping that doing so made them hard to follow.

After their return we all took the elevator to the floor above and went into the spy nest to await a mouse. It was tedious work, in part because there were a lot of screens to monitor. And although Tess had a motion detector installed in each major room, we had to listen for the sound of those alerts, too.

We worked in thirty-minute shifts, which seemed about the limit of our attention spans for scanning the screens and listening for the hoped-for buzz of the motion alerts. For a long time, there was nothing. We had already rotated through several shifts when I took over again at eleven. A few minutes later, I heard a buzz. The blinking icon told me the alert was coming from the study, but as I swept my eyes across the screens, I couldn't see anyone in any of the rooms.

Both Tess and Robert had dropped what they were doing, and were now standing behind me, looking at the displays.

"I see it now," Robert said. "There's an infrared image of someone crawling along the floor of Tess's study. It's hard to tell who it is, though, because they've turned off the lights."

He was right. The blurry infrared image made it hard to be sure about the intruder's gender, let alone his or her identity.

"I think it's Olga," I said. "Just from the size of the person."

"Look," Robert said. "She's reaching up to the safe and pulling it open, and now she's taking out the envelope with the fake letter."

As I watched, she crawled toward the bookshelf that was just to the left of the safe, reached up and grabbed the volume of *Les Misérables* that had the inscription. Then she took a backpack off her shoulders and put both the book and the letter in it, turned around and crawled toward the study door. The alert from the study blinked again, telling us she had left the room.

"So she did know the book was there," I said. "She lied to me. Again."

"Not exactly shocking," Robert said. "But how did she get in? The alarm on the front door wasn't triggered, and she wasn't detected in the living room by either the motion detector or the camera."

"Merde," Tess said. "She has come in by the back door in the kitchen. I forgot this. I took the garbage out and forgot to reset the alarm."

Tess put her fist to her forehead, in what I assumed was the equivalent gesture to hitting your forehead with your open palm in the United States—*how stupid am I.*

"What door in the kitchen?" I asked.

Robert answered. "There's a door in the kitchen that leads to a servants' stairway. It goes all the way down to the trash room in the back of the building, and there's a door from there to the outside."

"Like the one I used to escape from the general's wife's apartment."

"Yes," Robert said. "And the very one through which the caterers covertly brought in Christmas dinner."

"I forgot," Tess said. "I forgot to reset."

"Guys, let's not dwell on it," I said. "The question is, what are we going to do about it?"

"I will call Captain Bonpere for the arrest when Olga leaves the building," Tess said. "The captain can send her men to the back door and find her there. This entry into my study is recorded and will be proof of a crime."

"I don't agree," Robert said. "If we have her arrested, we won't find out who's really behind this. She must be like a drug mule—just the low-level person they sent to take the risk while the real perps hang back."

"I think Robert's right," I said. "The kidnappers still have Oscar, and if we have Olga arrested, she won't be able to call them or whatever she was planning to do to let them know she grabbed the book and the envelope and so they can let him go. We should have her followed instead."

At that moment, there was a knock on the door. We all looked at each other.

"*Qui est là?*" Tess asked.

A female voice answered in English tinted with a French accent. "It is Captain Bonpere. We have seized someone at the back door."

Tess opened the door, and Olga forced her way into the room, brandishing a short-barreled shotgun, which she pointed directly at Tess.

"All of you get against that wall over there, with your hands on the tops of your heads. Now."

I moved there. So did Tess and Robert.

"Alright. Now take your cell phones out, put them on the floor and kick them toward me."

We complied.

"This is not smart, Olga," I said.

"Shut up."

"I'm not going to shut up. I don't know what your exact plans are, but whatever, you're going to end up in jail. And your father, too. The fact that he's in Russia isn't going to save him."

She just stared at me, then reached into the pocket of her jacket and pulled out three pairs of plastic handcuffs. She slid them toward us along the floor. "One by one, pick up the hand-cuffs and cuff yourself to the radiator behind you."

I looked behind me and saw that the radiator had a long pipe along the top, separated from the radiator body by about six inches.

My heart was beating fast, and I felt every part of me move to high alert as adrenaline flooded my body. I hoped Olga couldn't sense it because, somehow, I was going to try to take her out.

"And if I don't cuff myself?" I asked.

"I'll shoot you, and then we will see if the others would like to comply." From the look on her face, I thought she'd probably do it, but I thought it was still worth trying to talk her out of it.

"Olga, it will make it a lot easier for you to escape responsi-bility for this if you just let us go," I said.

"Yeah, sure, it'll be messy, but you know, at least I won't have to listen to your big mouth anymore—in any language. Particularly when you butcher Russian."

"I think your plan has a big problem," Robert said.

"Yeah? I don't think so. But if you three don't cuff yourselves now, you will not get to tell me about this problem."

Both Robert and Tess cuffed themselves to the radiator. I listened as they did it. When they thrust the hasp into the cuff, it made only a single click instead of the sound of a ratchet clos-ing, as it would in a professional pair. So they were cheap mod-els, probably kids' cuffs she'd bought in a toy store.

"You, too, Jenna," she said. "Hurry up."

I put the cuffs on and looped one around the radiator pipe.

"Okay, Robert, what is this big problem with my plan?" Olga asked.

"The book you have in your backpack isn't the one with the inscription in it," he said.

"Bullshit. The plastic protector has the same little triangular piece out of it as it did when I put it on the shelf," Olga said. "So it's the right one."

"Oh it's the right plastic cover alright. But after we discovered your little swap, I found Tess's original under the bed in the guest room, where I assume you dumped it when you made the switch. So I put Tess's original in the plastic cover with the piece missing and put that one back on the shelf. And then I took the one with the inscription and hid it where you're not going to find it if you kill us."

I saw Olga's eyes widen as she realized that she had just grabbed the book from the shelf without checking the title page to see if the inscription was there.

"I think you're lying," she said. She crouched down, shotgun still pointed at us, and, using one hand, swung the backpack onto the floor in front of her. She reached in, pulled out the book, laid it flat on the floor and thumbed to the title page. "Shit. This isn't even a copy of *Les Misérables*. It's *The Three Musketeers*."

"I thought it was kind of appropriate," Robert said, grinning.

"That doesn't change anything," Olga said. "I'll just go back downstairs and find the right one."

"Good luck with that," Robert said. "I doubt you'll ever find it."

"You're going to come with me and show me where it is. If you don't, I'm going to kill your girlfriend and Jenna, too. Right now."

"Since your plan is apparently for all of us to die, why should I bother to come with you?" Robert asked. "Let's talk this through instead. I mean, why are you even doing this? You're young and have everything to live for. This will ruin your life."

"My father can't afford for me to go to college in America. He used to be rich, but now he is broke. I have found a buyer in Japan who will take the book for a lot of money. If it is together with the letter, he will pay even more. I will be rich for the rest of my life, and I won't have to go back to fucking Russia."

"What makes you think you won't get caught?"

"Everyone with evidence to convict me will soon be dead. The bookstore owner in Digne is already dead."

"You are making that up," I said.

"He committed suicide, and although he lingered awhile, he is now very dead. I know this."

"How do you know?" I asked.

"I have my sources."

"Who?"

"This is not your business, and anyway, you and Robert will soon be dead, and so will Oscar. The GIGN is on its way to him, and he will be killed, along with the kidnappers."

"Do you know the kidnappers, Olga?"

"They are high school classmates who are in med school here. They are too stupid to understand what a GIGN siege is like. They are expendable."

Tess had been utterly quiet, but suddenly said, "Olga, I have much experience in these things. Something will not be right and you will be caught."

I was developing a plan, but I wanted to keep her talking for the moment.

"You know, there's a judicial investigation going on down there, and it will lead to you," I said.

"Maybe, but it won't result in anything. I followed Oscar to the railroad station the day that he went to Digne. I loitered nearby and heard him buy the ticket. When you found me there, I had gone by myself to see if the letter from François-Victor

Hugo was hidden in the store. I never talked to the owner about why I was there. And since he is dead now, it doesn't matter what he knew."

"Not so fast," Robert said. "The authorities in Digne are no doubt looking into exactly what went down with the bookstore owner. Sooner or later, they will come looking for you, too."

"I'll just have to deal with it."

"The hotel owner will rat you out," I said.

"I am paying the hotel owner one-third. He will keep his mouth shut, and his bookstore will get a percentage for the actual sale, off the top."

"How much will you obtain, Olga?" Tess asked.

"I am also taking one-third."

"And the final third?"

I would have loved to have known the answer to Tess's question, but the time had come. Olga had her eyes on Tess, and she seemed increasingly anxious. If I waited much longer, she might just go ahead and kill us. I didn't know if it was going to work, but I thought it worth the try.

I lunged at her and heard the hasp of the toy handcuff break away from the pipe behind me, even as my wrist screamed in pain. She pulled the trigger. There was a tremendous blast as heavy shot from the gun blew by me and shattered the window.

Olga had been holding the shotgun out in front of her, without cradling it against her shoulder—she had probably seen too many movies where people held shotguns that way. The recoil from the blast spun her around, toppled her over and knocked the gun out of her hand. Her head hit the floor with a distinct thunk, and then I was on top of her, hands gripping both sides of her head, pounding it into the floor as hard as I could. I heard her skull crack and watched as her eyes rolled back. I don't know why, because she couldn't possibly have grabbed the gun, but I kicked it away. I was appalled at what I had done to her head, but at the same time I wanted to go on pounding it until it turned to mush.

"Jenna, can you get the key out of her pocket and let us out of these cuffs?" Robert asked.

"Just pull hard on the cuff, Robert. They're kids' toys, and they will come apart with just a little effort. You can probably thank whatever the French equivalent is of the Consumer Product Safety Commission for our survival. I guess they don't let kids' handcuffs really work here."

"You're right. It just comes apart. Well, I guess we'll never find out who was getting the other third, but thank God you did that, Jenna."

A voice behind me said, "I was going to get the other third."

I turned and saw the general standing in the open doorway, holding a large black handgun. He looked down at Olga. "Is she alive?"

"I don't know," I said.

"She's my only child." He bent down, still keeping the handgun trained on us, and put two fingers against her neck to take her pulse. He looked up. "She's dead."

I should have been taken aback at having killed someone or been worried that the general would now kill me. Instead I felt an intense desire to pound Olga's head into the floor five or six more times, just to be sure. And at that point I didn't care whose daughter she was.

"You are her father?" Tess asked.

"Yes."

"Who is the mother?"

"Do you recall the cute little blonde barista who worked in the embassy coffee bar?"

"While you were going out with me?"

"Of course. I am French."

Out of the corner of my eye, I saw Robert react to that. If we all survived this, Tess would have some explaining to do. It seemed unlikely we were going to survive, though.

"And you put her up for adoption?" Tess said.

"No. She has been raised by my brother in Russia. But we have kept in touch as father and child. In close touch."

"And her barista mother?"

He shrugged. "Disappeared. Somehow."

"What are you going to do now, Jean?" Tess asked.

"I am going to kill all of you, then take the book and the letter. And then do what Olga and I started out to do."

"What about Oscar?"

"He will likely die in the GIGN attack, which is due to start"—he glanced at his watch—"in about ten minutes."

"Unfortunately for you, General, the real book isn't in the backpack," Robert said. "Nor the real letter."

The general shrugged. "I will find them, presumably in Tess's apartment. But if not, not. And you will all die no matter what, and pay for the death of my daughter. Tess first." He gripped the gun with both hands and aimed at Tess.

I tried desperately to think how to save us. But my brain wasn't really working anymore, and neither was my body. I was beginning to shake badly, and my limbs felt like rubber.

Out of nowhere, a man appeared behind the general in the doorway and clubbed him sideways across the head with a large object. The general fell to the ground. I stumbled forward and pried his gun out of his hand. Tess, who had released herself from the handcuffs, snatched up the shotgun.

The man who had clubbed the general was none other than Pierre Martin, the concierge. He had used the building's new surveillance camera—a self-recording one, not yet installed—as his weapon.

He and Tess exchanged several sentences of rapid French.

"Robert, what did they just say?" I asked.

"Pierre said that Olga offered him a cup of coffee and left to come up the elevator, but he didn't drink it because it smelled weird. And then the general came running through carrying a gun and Pierre saw him holding a gun on us."

"How did he see us?"

"When Tess's people were here installing the equipment, he asked them to install a camera in the hallway on each floor with the screens in his office, so he was able to look through the open door into this apartment. When he saw the general holding a gun on us, he decided to do something about it."

I suddenly remembered what the general had said just before he was clubbed with the camera. "Oh my God," I said. "We need to stop the GIGN." I knelt down beside the general's body and fished his cell phone out of his pocket.

I asked of the room, "What was the name of the man he said was in charge of the GIGN unit?"

"I think it was General Lemoins," Tess said.

I searched the directory on the phone for the name and found it. I handed the phone to Tess, "Please call him off."

"I can do that," a voice said. It was Captain Bonpere, standing there in the doorway. It seemed like that door had become a new exit from Alice's rabbit hole.

"What are you doing here?" I asked.

"We were waiting outside on the street," she said. "The general called and told us to go home, that the action was over tonight. But when we drove by, we heard the gunshot and saw the window blow out and came to investigate."

She looked at Tess. "Please give me the phone. I will talk to General Lemoins and call off the attack."

Bonpere spoke on the phone for a few minutes, at one point raising her voice to a shout, then said to us, "Lemoins refuses to call off the assault on the barn on my word alone. He says I am not a member of the Gendarmerie, and he will take orders only from the proper constituted authority. He will not say who that is. We do not have much time left. I need to call someone higher up."

Suddenly, another voice spoke in rapid French. It was Judge de Fournis, a new apparition in the doorway. Bonpere said something in French and handed him the phone. He put it to his ear, spoke briefly and listened for a few seconds. Then the pitch of his voice deepened, and even I could tell that he was issuing a stern order.

He handed the phone back to Bonpere.

"Robert, what just happened?" I asked.

"He threatened to have General Lemoins investigated for murder if he did not call off the assault and any harm came to anyone."

"Did it work?"

"Apparently."

"But why did the judge even come here?" Tess asked.

"I will ask him," Bonpere said.

After a moment of conversation in French, Bonpere said, "It is complicated for me to explain this in English."

"I'll translate," Robert said. "The judge said that moments ago, he met at a restaurant near here—the Casimodo—with the GIGN's chief negotiator. The general had informed him that this negotiator was the point person in negotiating Oscar's rescue. But at Casimodo, the negotiator told him the true story. The negotiator's superiors at the GIGN told him there was no need for his services in Oscar's case because they were planning a straight assault on a group of terrorists. No negotiation."

"Oh my God," I said. "They weren't planning to rescue him at all. They were going to kill him. But, Robert, how did the judge know to come here?"

"He says he was passing by, on his way home from his meeting with the negotiator, thinking about what he'd just been told. And trying to put it together with what he'd learned in the hearings. Something that you said, Jenna, was the key for him."

"What was it?" I asked.

Robert laughed. "He says it was your suspicion-o-meter, which your lawyer told him about. He was impressed when your meter correctly predicted that the general would try to get to the hotel before you. He said that after he met with the negotiator he decided to follow your lead and treat every single thing the general had said as false. Doing that told him Oscar was in great danger from the GIGN."

"Okay, but how did he get here?"

"It was pure serendipity. He was walking by, having just left the Casimodo, trying to figure out what to do next, when he saw Captain Bonpere rush into this building. He knew it was Tess's building because he'd seen her address in his case dossier. He figured something bad was going on and followed the captain up here. Except she took the stairs, and he took the elevator. That's why he was slightly behind her. He said he should have taken the steps himself—he was once a paratrooper—but he is out of shape."

"You know, I don't know if I buy all of that," I said. "It's just too convenient. Call me suspicious." To myself I thought, *that's true only if pigs can fly.* It didn't, however, seem like the right time to say so out loud.

I looked over at Tess, who had been listening to both the judge's explanation in French and Robert's translation, and saw her smiling. Maybe after she and Robert got married she'd tell Robert how the judge really came to be there, and he'd tell me.

After that, more police came, along with the emergency people, and I watched as they handcuffed and tried to revive the general—who looked to me to be dead—and worked on Olga, who seemed to be breathing. The general had apparently been wrong when he said she was dead, which was too bad.

I caught the judge's eye. He smiled, gave me a thumbs-up, turned and disappeared back through the doorway through which he had come.

While we stood there, Bonpere interviewed us briefly about what had gone down before she arrived, and then, not long after, Robert and I found ourselves once again in the back of a police van headed for 36 quai des Orfèvres. I was still shaking badly. I looked over at Robert, and he was, too. Our trip to Number 36 this time was to be debriefed further. Tess went too, but she got to ride in Captain Bonpere's squad car and was brought up to date in a separate room.

CHAPTER 46

It took two days of negotiation by Anton Morel, but Oscar was finally released unharmed. He had all of his fingers. The kidnappers eventually surrendered.

We had to wait two days after Oscar's release to actually see him. They wouldn't even let us talk to him on the phone before that. Captain Bonpere said they were still interviewing him and tending to his physical needs. We decided to take her at her word.

When he finally walked—well, shuffled—through Tess's door, I was shocked. His face was gaunt and his clothes hung loosely from his skeletal frame. Where was the always-dapper Oscar?

I rushed up and gave him a hug, but gently, as you might embrace an elderly relative. I could feel his ribs through his sweater.

"Welcome back, Oscar," I said. "We were so, so worried about you."

"Thank you. It is very good to be back."

As we ended the hug, I thought I saw a tear trickle down his face, and I had trouble holding my own tears back. And then I thought to myself, just like the old song, why can't I cry if I want to? And I did.

Robert and Tess came up and hugged him next. I noticed that Tess didn't give him the two-cheek French kiss, but just hugged him tightly. Maybe too tightly. He winced a bit. By the time they were done, we were all crying.

Captain Bonpere had come through the door right behind Oscar, and she, too, looked close to tears.

"My friends," Oscar said, "I need to sit down." He headed for the big wing chair in the corner and sank into it with a distinct exhale of breath.

"Do you wish something to drink or eat?" Tess asked.

"Yes, yes. That would be good, Tess, thank you. They didn't feed me much, and the doctors have told me that I must go easy for a few days. I would love a cup of coffee with a little milk or cream and something like a small sweet roll."

We had, of course, in preparation for his coming, bought a party's worth of pastries, four bottles of fine wine and a case of beer. A few minutes later, Tess returned with the coffee and a small Danish.

Captain Bonpere had warned us in advance that Oscar was suffering from at least a mild form of post-traumatic stress disorder, and that, although she understood we were all very anxious to know what had happened, we shouldn't push him if he didn't want to talk about it.

We said that, of course, we wouldn't push him.

She also reminded us that the police, under the guidance of the public prosecutor and a soon-to-be-appointed investigating judge, had begun an inquiry into the whole thing. Because we would be witnesses ourselves, and could testify best if our memories were not clouded by others' accounts, we might want to avoid discussing certain topics. Plus, the story had become known to the press, and she would just as soon we not know certain things so we would not be tempted to tell them too much.

We said that we understood.

For a while, there was just chit-chat about not very much. Finally, I decided to ask Oscar what everyone wanted to know. If he didn't want to talk about it, he could always decline to answer. He'd never been a shy, retiring flower.

"So what was it like, Oscar? What happened?" I asked. "If you don't want to talk about it, we'll understand."

"No, that's okay. The psychologist I met with told me it's good to talk about it."

"Okay, but if we press you in a way that makes you uncomfortable, just say so."

"Well, you saw the kidnapping, or you and Robert did anyway. Right after they shoved me into the car, the two thugs in the back seat blindfolded me. And they shoved a gun in my neck and told me they would use it if I resisted."

"Did they speak English?"

"Yeah, but they had what I thought were Russian accents. Not long after that—maybe ten or fifteen minutes—they pulled into a garage and put me in the trunk."

"Did they tie you up?"

"No."

I looked around and realized that everyone was held rapt by what he was saying. On some level, I felt like a voyeur. I mean, really, it didn't matter to us exactly what had happened. Or at least it didn't matter a lot. But those thoughts didn't keep me from continuing.

"What happened then?"

"I don't know exactly where we went because I was either blindfolded or in the trunk. We ended up that first night and for a night or two more in a house somewhere near Paris. I know it was nearby because we drove for only about an hour after they put me in the trunk. They didn't take my watch." He grinned. "It really was amateur hour."

Robert broke in. "Did they say why they had kidnapped you?"

"Oh yeah. Right away. Even before they put me in the trunk, they said 'If you tell us where the book is, we'll let you go right now.'"

"Why didn't you?"

"One reason was that they had just stuck a gun in my neck and for all I knew they would kill me right after I told them where it was. So it seemed as if not revealing the location of the book might be the key to staying alive."

"That makes sense," Robert said.

"Yeah. And after that, I refused to tell them because I'm stubborn."

"That's certainly true," I said. "Stubborn as a mule sometimes."

"After a while," he continued, "I got the idea that if I told them where it was, they would probably let me go. Not kill me. But I've been having a lot of financial problems lately—I've hidden that from you guys, I know—and I had a prospective buyer who'd offered five hundred thousand dollars for the book. And I thought there might be other buyers who'd offer more. That kind of money would solve all of my problems and then some."

There was a silence in the room. Finally, Tess said, "Oscar, I can lend you money you need, or just give it to you."

"Tess, that is very generous, but I don't like to take charity."

Tess didn't respond. In truth, there wasn't a lot you could say in response to what Oscar had said, except to repeat your offer and say it's no problem, and it's not charity. But she chose to remain silent.

"There is something I want from you, though, Tess," Oscar said.

"What?"

"Another of these pastries."

That broke the tension. Tess went to get the pastry, and we all talked again for a moment about nothing at all. Finally, when the pastry had been delivered, we got back to it.

Robert took up the questioning. "But, Oscar, you did eventually tell them where it was."

"Yeah, but first I tried to bargain with them, and offered them a one-third share of the profits. That would still have left me with enough money to get out of difficulty."

"Didn't work?" Robert asked.

"No. They responded to that by letting me watch them take target practice with the gun, with me standing to the side of the target."

"That wasn't smart if they wanted to keep you alive."

"Like I said, it was total amateur hour, which is probably the thing that scared me the most."

"Because they weren't professional kidnappers?" Robert asked.

"Because they seemed to have no plan. Finally, after they put me back in the dark room, I was getting really cold and really hungry, and I just wanted to get it over with, whether they'd let me go or would kill me. Or as you'd say, Jenna"—he looked over at me—"whatever. So I told them where I'd hidden the book. But not where the authenticator was, or even that it existed."

"Where did you find the authenticating letter and how do you know it's real?" Robert asked.

"First I found the book in Digne and bought it. Then I went looking for something to authenticate it. I originally found the letter in a private archive on the Island of Guernsey, where Victor Hugo and most of his family went into exile after Napoleon III became emperor. I bought it from the owner. As for its legitimacy, there was no reason for anyone to have faked that letter—it has very little value on its own—and I have had the handwriting confirmed and the ink and the paper authenticated as to age. Once I'd done all that, I began to talk it up enough to establish a market for the book and the letter as a pair."

"Talk it up to whom?" Robert asked.

"To rich people in China, Japan, Brazil and Russia."

"Not England?"

"There aren't all that many truly rich people left in England, Robert, and most of them have no interest in French authors. But to change the topic, Captain Bonpere tells me you and Jenna found the authenticator. How the hell did you find it? I thought it was unfindable where I hid it."

"After Jenna was arrested for breaking into your room, I went in there and looked in the wastebasket," Robert said. "I found your torn-up map of Père Lachaise and a metrobus ticket with '69' written on the back."

"And from that you deduced that there was something at Père Lachaise? Really?"

"Jenna is the one who actually figured it out," Robert said. "And we had something of an adventure there. She also figured out your real name, Monsieur Brioche. But, Oscar, what I really want to ask you about is what you learned when you were in the barn about who all Olga worked with to put this plot together.

And was it really all just for college money? I mean, I know college is expensive, but—"

Captain Bonpere, who had been silent until then, interrupted. "I would really rather you did not ask him any more about that right now. What happened in the barn will be an important part of the criminal prosecution. The things they did and said there will make this more than just a mere kidnapping. It will enhance the charges. But I'm afraid you will have to wait to find out the details."

"May I tell them about the funny medical thing?" Oscar asked.

"Certainly."

"They were medical students and every day they came into my dark room and took my vital signs—blood pressure, pulse, temperature, and listened to my heart with a stethoscope. It was almost like they were doing a study on an old person who is being starved."

"That does sound odd," Robert said. "Why do you think they were starving you?"

"I think they had assumed it would all be over in a day or two and didn't bring enough food. Then they were afraid to go out to buy more for fear of being caught. But that's just a guess."

"May I ask him about Digne?" Robert said, looking at Captain Bonpere.

"Yes, some," Bonpere said. "But only because the hat store owner has died, so we don't need to prosecute him."

"Okay," Robert said, "we know you bought the book from the guy in Digne. Did you go back after that?"

"Yeah. He called me a couple days before Christmas and asked me to come back. He said he had a buyer who wanted to buy it from me for a lot of money, and he'd be the middleman. He wanted to do the meet in person."

"That's not the way he told the story to us," Robert said.

"Well, that's the way it happened. Anyway I went back to Digne, but without the book because I didn't think it was smart to take it. Even then the whole thing sounded weird."

"You hid it in your hotel room?"

"Yes."

"Did he really have a buyer?" Robert asked.

"Yeah. It was this Russian guy, Igor Bukov. We had a conference call with Igor, made from the back room of a café, using someone else's phone."

"Did Igor make an offer?"

"Yeah, not for much at first—he was still treating it as an interesting fake—but after I told him I had an authenticator and described it, he said if he could validate that, he'd pay two hundred fifty thousand."

"And then?"

"I told him I already had an offer for five hundred from a man in China, and he said that was too rich for him."

"In those words?" Robert asked.

Oscar laughed. "Yeah, but after that he said, 'Russian billionaires are not what they used to be. Or at least this one is not.'"

"But," Robert said, "you seemed afraid of him on Christmas Eve, when you were here."

"Indeed I was. Because it just seemed like too much of a coincidence that his daughter—as she was said to be then—would show up here when the box with the book was in the back room. I assumed he had not been honest in saying he was dropping out, and that I was about to be strong-armed in some fashion."

"You now think he really did drop out?" I asked. "You don't think Igor was behind the kidnapping at all?"

Captain Bonpere spoke up again. "I would prefer he not answer that. I will tell you that we believe that Olga learned from Igor about the book and its value and that after he dropped out of the bidding, she organized the kidnapping herself, to make money for herself. And got her father, the general, to help her out for a cut."

"I think we already know most of that," Robert said. "But how did Olga arrange to be with us for Christmas dinner?"

"It was luck," Captain Bonpere said. "She was by then following Oscar, and she saw him come here with the big box. And when she told her father the address, he by chance knew Madame Devrais and invited himself and Olga to dinner."

I had, at that point, just been following along, but finally I asked something that I'd been wondering about for days. "So," I said, "Olga really did go back and look at the book when she was supposedly using the bathroom?"

"That is our guess," Captain Bonpere said, "and we are told she put a tiny GPS tracker on the book. We also think she was probably the 'young man' that Monsieur Quesana said tried to mug him in front of your building. To confirm this we will have to interview her when she regains consciousness. If she ever does."

"There's something that doesn't make sense, though," Robert said, looking at Oscar. "Oscar, Olga was at the hat store *after* New Year's, when we found her there, and you just told us you went there to buy the book *before* Christmas and then went back, again *before* Christmas."

"Yeah, but I went to Digne a third time, too, toward the end of the week after Christmas, a couple days before I was kidnapped. The hat store owner had called to say he had a second signed Victor Hugo book that might interest me. One that others had rejected as fake. So I went back to look at it."

"You didn't buy it?"

"No, when I got there I looked in through the window and saw that Olga was there—which was a big surprise—and the two of them were clearly having a huge fight about something, yelling at each other and waving their hands around. I saw that and decided not to go in. I turned around and went back to Paris. Looking back on it, they may have been planning to kidnap me right then."

"Well," Robert said, "sounds as if Olga developed some continuing relationship with the hat store guy. But they must have had a falling out that eventually caused him to stick her in the basement."

"So it seems the pieces came together a bit differently than we thought," I said.

"Actually, I have one more question," Robert said.

"What is it, my friend?" Oscar said.

"Do you recall folding your umbrella when you were shoved into the car by the kidnappers?"

"Ah, that," he said. "I have been shown that video by Captain Bonpere. There is a simple explanation. That umbrella, you see, which was very expensive, has a button that not only opens the umbrella but, when pressed, pushes it closed, too, with a snap. The action of opening it loads the spring to close it. So I must have bumped that button accidentally. I certainly didn't do it on purpose."

"I see," I said. Although I really didn't. I'd never seen such an umbrella.

"I am sure you all have many more questions, my friends, but I am very tired."

"We should go then," Bonpere said.

"You are most welcome to stay here," Tess said.

Bonpere replied that that was very kind, but that Oscar was staying at a nice guest house owned by the judicial police, and that they needed to debrief him for another day and get him further checked out medically. Then he could return to Tess's.

Oscar struggled to his feet and said, "Tess, if you have some glasses and an alcoholic beverage, I'd like to propose a toast."

Tess went into the kitchen and came back with five glasses. "Instead of wine, let's use this wonderful bottle of cassis that I just got," she said, casting a sly glance at me.

After the glasses were filled, Oscar raised his and said, "My friends, I do not know how to thank you for all you have done— and all the risks you took—to rescue me. But I am working on it. And"—he turned to Captain Bonpere—"I must also especially thank you, *ma capitaine*, for your role in securing my release, and how kind you have been to me since. *A votre santé!*"

We raised our glasses, voiced *santé!* with a mutual shout, and clinked all around.

At that point, there was a knock on the door. Tess opened it. It was Marie, the judge's greffier. She commenced to hand each of us a sheet of paper with an official-looking seal on it and said, as she handed them out: *"Bonsoir, Mesdames et Messieurs. J'ai ici pour Monsieur Tarza, Madame Devrais, le Professeur James et Monsieur Quesana une convocation à comparaître devant le Juge d'Instruction Roland de Fournis. Le Procureur de la République poursuit en justice les personnes qui ont enlevé Monsieur Quesana, et le Juge d'Instruction Roland de Fournis a été désigné pour instruire ce dossier. La date et l'heure de vos convocations à comparaître sont indiquées sur la convocation elle-même que je vous remets."*

"What did she say, Robert?" I asked. "What is this?"

"She said the judge has been appointed to investigate possible charges against the men who kidnapped Oscar, and we are invited to testify under oath."

"Invited?"

"Well, compelled."

"When?"

He looked over the paper that had been handed to me.

"Two weeks from today."

"I have to get back to UCLA to teach my classes before then."

"Maybe," Robert said, "you can work something out. But there are lots of things to see in Paris while you're here. Have you seen the Père Lachaise cemetery?"

"Very funny, Robert."

EPILOGUE

In the end, I was able to testify two days after the summons was served, so I didn't have to miss the start of classes at UCLA.

I had begun to find the French criminal justice system fascinating, and I resolved to talk to the dean about teaching a course on international criminal law. It would give me the chance to explore something new. Not to mention the opportunity to go to a lot of cool conferences in other countries.

It turned out that the general was indeed very dead, but that his daughter, Olga, was not. She recovered fully after many weeks in the hospital and, for reasons that are obscure to me but have something to do with her father's long, meritorious service to the French state, she was permitted to serve her prison term in Russia. But a few days after she arrived in Russia, she was released under mysterious circumstances.

She was, of course, no longer welcome in France or the United States and was unable to obtain a visa to attend university in any other member country of the European Union. She is now continuing her acting studies at a small school in a suburb of Perm, Russia, which is near the Ural Mountains.

The medical students who kidnapped Oscar were sentenced to fifteen years in prison, and the hotel owner was given a reduced sentence of two years in exchange for his testimony against the others.

Igor Bukov, Olga's uncle, had in fact been interested in purchasing the book from Oscar, but lost interest because the price was too high. It turned out, upon investigation by the judge, that Igor had been totally ignorant of the general and Olga's attempts to acquire it on their own after he dropped out of the bidding.

Judge Roland de Fournis married his greffier, Marie, and they now visit Provence more regularly. Tess and Robert were guests at their wedding. I was also invited, but was unable to attend. I sent them, as a wedding gift, two UCLA hoodies. The French are nuts about that Bruin stuff.

Pierre Martin was given a small raise by the building owners' council, effective July 1, in recognition of his meritorious service to the building. He was also given a minor medal for courage by the Mayor of Paris, which was delivered to him by mail. Tess tells me that he has still not installed the automatically-recording front door security camera. He claims it was damaged when he hit the general with it.

I'm planning to go back to Paris in April. Tess and Robert are getting married. The fact that Tess had a long-ago affair with the general but failed to mention it to Robert has apparently not gotten in the way.

I still think Tess is a spy.

ACKNOWLEDGMENTS

I am once again indebted to my agent, Erica Silverman, this time for solving a puzzle. Early in the process, I mentioned to Erica that in this novel I wanted to have Victor Hugo inscribe a copy of *Les Misérables* to someone famous, but I hadn't yet come up with who that famous person should be. Without hesitating, she said, "Well, Charles Dickens, of course!" As I explored that idea, it turned out to be perfect.

I also want to thank my editors at Thomas & Mercer, Alan Turkus and Kjersti Egerdahl, for encouraging me to write a third novel following on the adventures of Robert, Jenna and Oscar in *Death on a High Floor* and *Long Knives*, and thank the rest of the crew at Thomas & Mercer, especially Jacque Ben-Zekry, Gracie Doyle, Tiffany Pokorny, Anh Schleup and Alison Dasho for making the publishing experience such fun.

And once again, I want to express my deep appreciation to my great developmental editor, Charlotte Herscher, who not only spots flaws in a manuscript that others may have missed but quickly—and gently—suggests excellent ways to fix them.

And my deep appreciation as well, to the copy editor, Dara Kaye, who did a terrific job of smoothing and improving prose, nailing inconsistencies, wrestling the manuscript into compliance with the various style conventions and, among many other things, made sense of and implemented the conventions in the style manuals concerning when and where italics are to be used for foreign words—something that drove me crazy before she took it over and mastered it. And my profound thanks to Julianne Molinari, the proof reader, who did an excellent and meticulous job of ferreting out all the myriad small errors that can creep into a long manuscript, not to mention nailing a few large ones that, left unfixed, would have been distracting to readers.

I also want to acknowledge and thank the many friends who provided encouragement, who read the manuscript in its various stages and drafts and then gave me such helpful, candid notes, as well as those friends, old and new, who were kind enough to share their expertise with me, from rare books to French legal procedure, as well as those who were just generally supportive. The entire list is long, but it includes especially Roger Chittum, Brinton Rowdybush, Linda and John Brown, Melanie Chancellor, Amy Huggins, Annye Camara, Marty Beech, Andy Schepard, Deanna Wilcox, Cynthia Cohen, Richard Schepard and Michele Schubert-Schepard, Jean-Baptiste Parlos, Céline Garçon, Claude Bendel, Hugues Calvet, Eric Dezeuze, Sylvie Morabia, Bob Rawson, Jack Walker, Phil Pirages, Elaine Katz, Eric Grangeon, Nicole Kaneza, Christine Anderson, Jessica Kaye and Richard Brewer, Julie Rutiz, Bob Stock, Wendy Perkins, Michael Haines, Françoise Queval, Nadine Eisenkolb, Maxine Nunes, Prucia Buscell, Dale Franklin, Deborah Dowling, Tom and Juanita Ringer, Marie Francoise and Pierre Levaillant, and Aisha Asanova.

And with thanks, too, to my son, Joe, for his terrific notes on the early drafts, and, as always, to my wife, Sally Anne, for her patient and perceptive editorial comments on this, my third novel. No husband could ask for more.

ABOUT THE AUTHOR

Charles Rosenberg is the author of the bestselling legal thriller *Death on a High Floor* and its sequel, *Long Knives*, as well as the 1994 viewer's guide to watching a criminal trial, *The Trial of O. J.: How to Watch the Trial and Understand What's Really Going On*. He was one of two on-air legal analysts for E! Television's live coverage of the O. J. Simpson criminal and civil trials. Rosenberg has also been credited as the legal script consultant for the television shows *Boston Legal*, *L.A. Law*, *The Practice* and *The Paper Chase*.

During college, Rosenberg spent a year in France, where he had many adventures. He traveled around the country in a VW Bus with some young Belgians he met while admiring the Bayeux Tapestry in Normandy, attended a French-language "boot camp" in Besançon, worked for two months on an apple farm in a small village near Dijon and studied French history for two semesters at a university in Southern France. He has returned to France many times since, most recently to interview lawyers, judges, law students and law professors as part of his research for *Paris Ransom*.

Since graduating from Antioch College and Harvard Law School, where he was an editor of the law review, Rosenberg has had a long career as a partner in large law firms and as an adjunct law professor at several prominent law schools, including Loyola, UCLA and Pepperdine. He is currently a partner in a three-lawyer firm in the Los Angeles area, where he lives with his wife.

Made in the USA
San Bernardino, CA
27 May 2015